Cypress Nights

STELLA CAMERON

Cypress Nights

MIRA®

MIRA

ISBN-13: 978-0-7783-2540-6
ISBN-10: 0-7783-2540-7

CYPRESS NIGHTS

www.MIRABooks.com

Printed in U.S.A.

For Jerry

Chapter
1

Toussaint, Louisiana
Early evening

He was a worthy man, a brilliant, necessary man. His decisions benefited everyone in Toussaint. They would never recognize the good he did. Just as well. Their ignorance kept him free. Foolish interference with his plans would not be tolerated. Could not be tolerated.

Justice, that was his rightful name.

The final caress of warmth had seeped from the old, stone church. This wasn't the place he would have chosen to deal with a threat to his plans, but he had no choice. Where else could he be certain of finding Jim Zachary alone tonight?

Jim must be stopped before he could do what he planned to do in an hour or so. He had forced Justice's hand.

St. Cecil's and the holier-than-thou hypocrites who minced through its doors represented the enemy. The people who loved to simper and whisper in the pews, to frown while they condemned the innocent for their supposed sins, and to utter pious words of forgiveness they didn't mean, enraged him.

Judgment. He had been judged and punished. Now it was his turn to judge. And punish—and to take his reparation.

Fresh flowers spread their fickle scents, but the stench of old, rotted stems in unwashed vases ensured that no one forgot that this was a place where memories of the dead lingered. They had come here as innocent children with sweet flowers in their hands, then as adults with roses in their hair and in their buttonholes and, when it was their turn, they came with lilies on their coffins.

From behind the bronze screen that hid tables loaded with hymnals, bulletins, donation envelopes and baskets where the hopeful left prayers written on scraps of paper, he watched the side door that Jim Zachary used when he arrived for solitary evening prayer.

The knife felt slippery. Sweat wouldn't be allowed to make the death noisy or less swift.

Zachary was late.

Around the walls of St. Cecil's, sconces flickered on. Rather than make one lone visitor more conspicuous, the small lights reduced the interior to a wash of shadows in shades of brown.

An outer door creaked, groaned on its great hinges, and metal-capped heels clattered on stone flags.

The inner door squealed open... Voices marred the silence.

Justice half knelt to watch. His heart squeezed and thudded when scrawny little Jim Zachary entered the nave with Father Cyrus Payne behind him. The tall, well-built priest accentuated the other man's almost childlike stature.

Weak and helpless in the strong hands of Justice.

But not with the priest around.

Father Cyrus's laugh echoed between the walls and the pillars. He picked up a clipboard from a table near the door and said, "See you at the meeting later?"

"I'll be there," Zachary said.

Father Cyrus gave Zachary a wave and left.

Justice's breathing returned to normal and the iciness in his legs thawed. *You will not be at that meeting, Jim Zachary. I know what you plan to say there. I will not let you do that. Come to me. You have brought this on yourself with your bleeding-heart charity obsession. Walk this way. You know where you sit—just a few feet from where I stand. You always sit there. Did you ever think that a habit could be dangerous? It is a great help when certain plans must be made.*

From a distance, Zachary's face couldn't be seen. He held his head slightly turned and bowed—always—in a sign of humility. Or perhaps of subservience and insecurity.

Closer and closer Jim Zachary drew, his steps small, his gray hair falling over his tilted brow in a thick, straight wad.

Into the pew, put down the kneeler, bury your head in your hands, abject in the knowledge that you are not worthy.

Justice slowly produced the Italian switchblade he treasured, fired its silken smooth action open with the slightest audible *snick* and wiped its grip. He held ten inches of unforgiving stainless-steel blade. The tight gloves he had pulled on had thin leather stitched to the palms and fingertips; they would serve him well since the knife handle had dried. His own hand was strong, and now it was cool.

On the balls of his feet, and rapidly, he left the cover of the screen, crossed the aisle to stand near a pillar and allowed a few seconds to pass before he got behind Zachary and slammed his left hand over the small man's face.

At first Zachary didn't move. He allowed himself to be pulled to his feet and yanked backward over the seat. With Zachary's head crammed against his chest, Justice raised the knife.

Zachary flung out his arms and tried to twist free. He braced his feet on the back of the pew in front of him and pushed hard, but his opponent was like an iron jaw closed on a feeble catch. Gurgles burbled from Zachary's throat, and then a quavering scream.

He bowed his body into an arch and jerked from side to side repeatedly.

"You wouldn't listen," Justice said against the other's ear. "Even when you knew your plans were wrong, you would not back down. This will make Toussaint and this parish stronger. It is for them." And the good of *Justice*.

With one deft thrust, he sunk his long blade into the man's neck and all the way through. Shoved him, headfirst, to the seat and skewered him against the wood. He jerked, thrashed. So much blood, pumping out a man's life. Why couldn't Zachary have stayed away from church politics? Killing him now, before Justice was completely ready, was a difficult inconvenience.

Gradually, the violent movements weakened, then faded. A rolled pamphlet was ready in Justice's other pocket. He removed this and left it, just as he had planned.

In minutes, the great gush of blood from the artery in Zachary's neck ebbed to a trickle and stopped.

Dead men didn't bleed.

Chapter
2

Later the same evening

"Why are you here?" Bleu Laveau said. She knew Roche Savage had come to the parish hall meeting, because she was the one giving the presentation. He couldn't have any interest in plans to build a new school.

He had come for her.

A tall, rangy man, with curly, almost black hair and the bluest eyes she had ever seen, he was in the business of fixing minds. And from his reputation, he was very successful. She wondered if he could somehow have found out her secret and if she was a challenge to him now.

Only one person in Toussaint was aware of the life she had been trying to outrun, and her cousin, Madge Pollard, wasn't the gossiping type. That didn't mean Roche couldn't track her down some other way.

Why didn't he say something? Dressed in jeans and an open-necked shirt with its sleeves rolled back over his forearms, he looked casual but Bleu felt his tension. She edged away from him.

His relaxed stance didn't match the way he stared at her. As if he was planning his next move.

Roche weighed what he should do. Bleu's behavior had caught him off guard. The woman trying to put distance between them, as if he might pounce on her, wasn't the one he'd first met a couple of weeks ago over a cup of coffee. Something had happened to make her afraid of him, and he wished he didn't feel so certain about what that was.

Bleu was still moving. With her hair streaming in the wind, she took sideways steps up the slope from the parish hall to the spot where she had parked her Honda in the lane above.

Roche didn't follow her. "Just talk to me," he said. "That's all I want. Tell me what's wrong and I'll try to make it right."

She had been the last to leave a packed meeting about plans to build a new school where the old one had burned down years ago on existing church property. Everyone else had already driven off.

And the instant she saw him, she had just about run away. He didn't get it.

Bleu's head pounded. "Please excuse me, " she said. "I have to get home. Tomorrow's a full day."

What she wouldn't ask him was if he knew about her marriage, about the horrible, personal things she'd been forced to discuss with strangers. If he did know, he could also be aware of the way her former husband had turned sex into something horrifying and that she had been left with a fear of intimacy.

Yesterday, the potential truth about Roche's interest in her suddenly became clear. She had been looking forward to having dinner with him when she figured it out: She wasn't his type. He had another reason for wanting to spend time with her—to see if she would make an interesting case study, maybe?

Roche felt furious that he'd missed some signal she must have given him. He picked up some of the documents and files she'd dropped when she saw him waiting for her. "You'll need these," he said.

Last night, she stood him up for dinner, but he had put it down to her preoccupation with getting ready for tonight's meeting. Obviously he had been wrong; she'd ducked out of the date to avoid him.

Damn. He was a healer, a seasoned psychiatrist who had only ever wanted to help people, not a man who terrified women in the dark.

When he looked up again, she stood like a stone, utterly still. He saw her honey-blond hair glint in the moonlight, saw the glitter in her eyes. In the daylight, they were bright green—always questioning, always vulnerable.

She took the paperwork from him. "Thank you." Her soft words were difficult to hear in the wind.

Bleu Laveau, with her unassuming air and the way she listened closely when he talked, and her passion for the job she'd come to Toussaint to do, had captured him. His fascination with her, the urge to protect—and possess—almost disoriented Roche.

Disorientation was dangerous. He had to be in control of himself at all times.

She must not get any idea of his single-minded focus on her—not unless he could be sure she wanted it.

"I heard your presentation," he told her. *And afterward, I stood in the shadow of a wall out here, waiting for you. You and I were meant to be together, Bleu. If someone's told you I like adventure with my sex—the wilder, the better—they're more or less right, damn them, but I can be whatever you want me to be. I'm the one in control, not my sex drive. You'll never be afraid with me.*

She looked from him to her car, probably figuring out how fast she could get away from him and what the chances were that he wouldn't catch up.

About zero, lady.

Bleu felt foolish. She took another small step. He must be adding up symptoms to analyze later. He would be thinking she seemed nervous, and she was.

The only way out of this was to change the subject and calm down. "It will be a fight to rebuild a school here," she said. "So many people are against it." Holding her ground wasn't easy.

"If anyone can do it, you can," he said. Bleu had come to Toussaint to do a study on the feasibility of building a new school on St. Cecil's property. The church, the parish hall and the portion where the school had originally stood came close to filling the available space, and it had been made clear that buying additional land wasn't financially feasible.

The rectory had been built next to St. Cecil's but was separated from it by small Bonanza Alley. That was the full extent of their holdings.

"A lot of people are angry," she continued, her voice tight. "The money hasn't even been raised yet, but they're talking about using it for a multipurpose center instead."

Now she was babbling. One more symptom for his list.

"Yeah," he said. "Some of them. Not all."

Roche finished gathering her papers from the ground and walked toward her. The pale moon did nothing more than suggest a light all but snuffed out, and his eyes looked black, fathomless.

"Some of them made it clear they wish I'd go away," Bleu said.

Roche would have expected her to be tougher. He knew she had been through the same type of process a number of times before. "They'll come around," he said. "There are a lot more children in need of a good education than there are folks who play bingo. They've got the parish hall for that. Anyway, who could resist you for long?"

That had been the wrong thing to say. She turned away at once. Her breath came in loud, rough gasps.

"Bleu! Damn it, why are you afraid of me?"

She had made a pact with herself that no one would frighten her again. Now the pact was broken.

"I'm not afraid of you," she lied. "I've got to go."

"Fine. Here, take these and I'll wish you goodnight."

"You don't understand," she told him.

"No, I don't. What is it about me that's suddenly disgusting to you? We've had coffee together, and—"

"All Tarted Up was packed that morning," she shot back. "The only empty seat in the whole café was at my table. You asked if you could sit there."

He held out the folders. "We enjoyed talking. Can you say that's a lie?"

"It's—not a lie." She inched forward to take her files, then held the whole pile of documents against her chest. "Thank you for picking all these up. I'm... I got rattled in there tonight. That's all."

Her excuse didn't cut it with Roche. "That afternoon when I ran in to you by the bayou, you seemed glad to walk with me. We talked about a lot of things. You're great to talk to." *But you're damaged, even if you do try to put up a good front.*

"I was interested in the clinic, and your brother Max and the plastic surgery he does. And in your work out there. That's all. You're making too much of it."

The cut didn't bother him. What he wanted was to figure out the reason for her change in attitude.

"You had lunch with me at Pappy's Dancehall. I invited you, and you accepted. You seemed comfortable. You met Annie, and if you didn't like her, you put on a good act."

Annie was Max's wife and she managed Pappy's.

"She's nice," Bleu said. "Thank you for introducing us."

"Last night, you were supposed to have dinner with me. You

didn't call. You just let me show up at your place and find out you weren't there. You didn't forget, did you?"

"I'm sorry." The thin skirt of her dress blew back, gripping her thighs.

Roche felt the swell of anger. "You don't have to be." She was small, but her shape was sweet, curvy, all woman. What the wind did with her dress against her legs also did things to him.

"Good night, then," she said.

The old wildness attacked him. Bleu hadn't gone two steps before he reached her and settled a hand on her shoulder. "Look at me." Her pause let him know this could go either way, but then she turned toward him. Roche stepped up beside her. "I'm not a threat to you," he said.

Bleu couldn't hide her spasms of shivering. "Roche," she whispered. "I don't know you. You don't know me."

He knew himself. This was a test and it wasn't going well. He had decided to prove he could be alone with a woman he wanted desperately and not make the kind of move that might turn her off.

"It's time we did know each other," he said. He didn't give her a chance to argue.

He kissed her, and her body tensed.

It had been so long since she had felt like this—invaded. Yet Roche didn't intend to violate her. Her eyes closed and she tried to relax. With the tip of his tongue he made soft, sleek and persuasive passes until her lips parted. Where they touched, she tingled. Her muscles softened and she leaned closer.

Finally, it had happened. The cold place she had lived with for so long was thawing. She wanted intimacy. The excitement she'd dreamed of but been denied hammered at her. And it was this man who had stirred the feelings she thought she'd never have.

Tightening low in her belly stole her breath and her attention.

Downward between her legs it went, sharper and sharper. Then she felt wet.

"Women are weak, they need saving from themselves."

That voice she thought she had forgotten, the one from her wasted years, sounded so clear that she braced for the shove, the fall to the bed and the punishing pressure of a big man's body on top of her.

"No." Bleu jerked her head sideways. "I don't want this."

Roche held her firmly, wrapped his arms around her and pressed her face into his shoulder. "Hush," he said, wishing her damn paperwork wasn't between them like a shield. For a little while, she had started to respond to him, but she was rigid now.

Careful. Don't push too far.

He used his thumbs to raise her chin, and he brought his mouth to hers again. Holding her against him with pressure on the back of her head, he emptied her hands and leaned them both sideways to put the pile on the ground.

She kissed him in return, but not like a woman who had done a lot of kissing. With his mouth and tongue, turning her head with his fingers, delving deep, he showed her that this wasn't about putting one mouth to another. It was a connection, and could be a prelude, a small, erotic promise of a closer joining.

A promise wasn't enough.

Already hard, he strained against his jeans.

"You're okay with me," he whispered, leaning away.

No, she wasn't entirely, but he had a logical mind and he worked to make it heed him in situations like this one, where lust had taken him over the edge in the past.

His heart thudded. Slowly, gently, he put his hands beneath her arms. Her body was warm, the bodice of her dress made of a silky stuff.

His palms settled on the sides of her breasts.

Again, she stiffened in his arms.

He rested his forehead in the curve of Bleu's neck. Tonight, he felt leaden, but even that didn't dampen his need to make love to her. Nothing had ever dampened that need, only kept it in check.

"You feel so good," he whispered, his lips against the soft skin of Bleu's neck.

"I don't... I'm not ..."

"I know," he murmured. "You're not casual. I like the way you are." Moving carefully, he nipped her ear then kissed her shoulder—and wasn't quick enough to avoid the slap that landed on his face.

He flinched and gave a surprised laugh. Her next swipe cut off the laughter.

"You've made your point," he said, ducking number three.

She dropped her arms to her sides. He could hear her hard breathing and see the glimmer of tears on her cheeks. "You're going too fast for me," she said. "But I shouldn't have hit you." She sounded upset, but not sorry.

"I'll live," he said. "I deserved what I got."

Bleu looked at the sky and felt a stillness capture both of them. "Why would you deserve it? You couldn't know I'm not ready...for anything, really. Maybe one day I'll tell you why. Not now."

If she could think of the right words, she'd tell him he had already changed her and she was grateful. That would have to wait, at least long enough to find out if she continued to feel grateful.

He moved as if he would touch her, but pulled back. "Okay. I'll ask you to do that, but I'll give you some time. You need to go home. But I warn you, I'll be calling you again and inviting you out."

"I feel like an idiot." She arrived at her car with Roche right behind her. "Don't waste time on me. I'm too much of a liability emotionally. Move on, Roche."

His heart turned, and he realized the sensation was new. "Don't sell yourself short." She might not know exactly what he meant. He dealt with the kind of "liabilities" she talked about every day. It could be that they had a chance to heal each other—or create a kind of hell for themselves. Whatever the risks, Roche felt like taking them.

He heard the sound of a door slamming, a muffled sound.

"Where was that?" Bleu said. "The church?"

The church was the closest building to the parish hall.

"I don't think so. Farther away and not so heavy. The rectory. There's Cyrus, I think. He's across the alley."

The window of Bleu's car was open, and she threw everything but her purse inside.

Together they hurried downhill again and past the church. They met Cyrus just inside the gate to Bonanza Alley. "What are you two doing here?" he said, not sounding like himself. "I thought you'd gone home, Bleu."

"I had to finish up," she said. "Roche was seeing me to my car. It's pretty dark to be on your own out here. Is Madge still at the rectory?" Her cousin, Madge Pollard, was Cyrus's assistant.

"She left with that... Sam Bush drove her home. He's our accountant, Roche." Cyrus stared at Bleu for a moment. "I shouldn't have left you. I wasn't thinking."

Cyrus, Roche thought, often seemed to have a great deal on his mind these days. If he didn't, he wouldn't have forgotten that Roche already knew Sam Bush and got along with him well. Cyrus might not be so keen on Sam, since the man openly showed his attraction to Madge. Cyrus and Madge were a complicated story, seemingly without hope of a happy ending.

"Did you see Jim Zachary at the meeting, Bleu? I saw him earlier.

He always spends a little time in the church. He said he'd be at the meeting, and now I can't remember if he was."

"I don't know him," Roche said.

Bleu thought about it. "He wasn't there," she said slowly. "No, I'm sure he wasn't. He would have spoken up if he had been. I don't know why I didn't miss him at the time."

"He could have changed his mind," Roche pointed out.

"No," Cyrus said, "he couldn't. Jim does what he says he'll do. He's a bachelor, and he and the widow who lives next door keep an eye out for each other. She just called me, because he told her he'd be home around ten and it's almost eleven."

"Maybe he went out for dinner. Or for drinks with friends," Bleu said.

"He's not the kind to go out to dinner. And he doesn't drink. He'd tell you himself that he's a recovering alcoholic." Cyrus sounded distracted. Abruptly, he let out a breath. "Is his car still here? Maybe he got hung up somewhere. Jim's always doing things for people. That's what's happened."

"What does he drive?" Roche asked.

Cyrus considered, then said, "A Camry. Black. Fairly old, but they don't seem to wear out, do they?"

"No," Roche agreed. "There was a black Camry behind my car when I parked in front. See. I'm facing this way."

Bleu turned to see. The cream-colored BMW showed up clearly—so did the Camry once all three of them got closer.

"Was he upset about something?" Roche said, visualizing the dark, sluggish bayou beyond the church grounds. How easily a man could slip into those waters.

"I don't think so," Cyrus said. "No, he was his usual cheerful self. Mrs. Harper said she tried to call him but he didn't answer on his cell phone."

"Would he have his phone on in the church?" Bleu said.

Cyrus shook his head. He pulled a phone from his belt, peered at a piece of paper and pressed numbers. Roche could hear the faint ringing from Cyrus's phone.

"Nothing," he said.

"He's a nice man," Bleu said. "He's really behind building a school."

Roche nodded. "A lot of people will be." He looked at Cyrus who frowned absently.

"I'd better check inside the church," the priest said, and started walking toward the vestibule door. "He could have collapsed in there." He broke into a run.

Roche and Bleu ran with him and they filed inside the gloomy building. This was Roche's first visit, and he wrinkled his nose at pungent scents he didn't recognize.

"I don't see him," Cyrus said. He went rapidly to the top of the center aisle and scanned from side to side, carefully.

"He always sits in the same place," Bleu said. "I've noticed."

"Does he?" Cyrus seemed surprised; Roche figured the priest got too involved in what he was doing to see who sat where during services.

"Over there," Bleu said, pointing fairly far back. "He sits on or near the aisle. And he usually ushers, so he's on his feet quite a bit."

They all stood with their hands on their hips. "Does he have any relatives at all?" Bleu asked.

"Not that I know of." Cyrus turned away.

"Did you hear that?" Bleu said, raising her chin and listening.

Roche had. "Sounded like a little drill."

"Or a phone set to vibrate," Bleu said.

Cyrus looked at each of them, then covered distance in a hurry. He crossed to the side aisle and started toward the back of the church.

"Wait here," Roche said and went after him. He expected to

hear Bleu's sandals following on the stone flags, and she didn't disappoint him.

Cyrus skidded to a halt beside a pew. Even at a distance, Roche saw how the other man blanched. "Stay where you are, Bleu," Cyrus snapped out.

Roche caught up with him. "Bastards," he muttered.

Sideways on the bench, his legs sprawled, one on and one off the seat, his arms twisted above his head, lay an elderly man. His eyes were open—and empty. Clots of congealed blood matted his thick gray hair, spattered his face, the pew and the floor. His lips were drawn back in a grimace, and a rolled piece of paper stuck out of his mouth.

"Jim," Cyrus said softly. He flipped open his phone and called 911.

Bleu's long, uneven breath meant she had seen the dead man. "He must have been stabbed so violently." She shuddered but didn't glance away. "Whatever it was went right through his neck. It cut his jugular."

Looking at the body from all angles, Roche went behind the pew and bent over to examine the obvious knife wound in the corpse's neck.

He was too slow to stop Bleu from pulling the yellow flyer from Jim Zachary's mouth. "Don't touch," he said to her. "They'll want to dust for fingerprints."

She puffed up her cheeks and backed away, holding the paper by one top and one bottom corner and unrolling it.

"Bleu," Roche said. "Don't."

"I already have and I'm glad." She stared at him. "Do you think he brought this with him?"

"He could have. But why would the killer stuff it in his mouth?"

"To make a point," Bleu said. "This is one of those flyers that got spread all over—the one telling people not to vote for the school."

Chapter 3

Early the following morning

Roche felt Bleu watching him in his rearview mirror. He liked the sensation.

At around one in the morning, with Cyrus as well as Bleu in his car, they had finally left the church and he'd driven to the police station. Sheriff Spike Devol had kept his questions coming for hours.

"I'm not going to park right in front of All Tarted Up," Roche said, as he drove the three of them to breakfast. "Better not give the regulars more to wonder about than they'll already have."

Bleu was glad Cyrus sat beside Roche. That allowed her to be in back with a good view of Roche's profile. He had gotten her all stirred up and confused, when she was supposed to be concentrating on the job she was here to do.

"What could they make out of us being in the same car?" she said.

Roche laughed. "You can bet someone will ask where we've been so early. This way, we can say we just bumped in to each other on the way to breakfast."

Cyrus didn't comment, but then, he didn't voice a lot of what he might think.

Tilting his head to one side, stretching tensed muscles in his neck, Roche sensed that Bleu was still staring at him. When he glanced in his rearview mirror, he saw that he wasn't imagining a thing.

He smiled, just a little, and decided he wouldn't look over his shoulder and let her know he'd noticed.

Main Street was coming up. Roche picked out a convenient parking spot a block away from the café, pulled toward the curb— and turned to meet Bleu's eyes.

She looked away at once.

Good. He liked it that she was paying him plenty of attention.

Roche parked the car beneath the branches of a sycamore tree, one of many planted at intervals along most of the town's larger streets. If it made sense to call any of the streets in Toussaint large.

Once out of the car, they were greeted by the telltale signs that this would be a super-humid day. Already, any chill had left the air, and the wind, although it had dropped, was warm.

"It's going to be a hot one," Cyrus said. He looked as tired as Roche felt. "I'm going to give away one of my secrets. I make a point of stopping by All Tarted Up after there's been a disaster in town. News travels very fast here, and if anyone's going to be discussing recent events anywhere, it'll be there—or at Hungry Eyes." Hungry Eyes was a book shop and café at the far end of Main Street. Elie and Joe Gable owned the place.

All Tarted Up belonged to Jilly Gautreaux. Roche had his own memories of encounters at the town's favorite eatery. His brother had gotten into a fight there once, something Max liked to pretend never happened.

"I think I'll skip breakfast and walk down to St. Cecil's for my car,"

Bleu said. She stepped onto the sidewalk, but didn't join Cyrus and Roche. "I should get home and finish up some work before I go in today."

Some said Roche was too silent, but this morning he was grateful for his habit of thinking before he spoke. He felt watchful—and edgy. There were too many potential hazards to negotiate with this woman, especially when he had his own demons to control.

"You've been up all night," Cyrus said to Bleu. "The church is too far for you to walk when you're tired, and you need a good meal. Jilly will fix you up."

Bleu still seemed uncertain, but after a huge sigh, she said, "Okay. I'll get my car afterward if you don't mind taking me back, Roche." She moved purposefully in their direction and they all set off for the café.

He couldn't, Roche thought, have done as good a job of persuasion as Cyrus had managed.

Flanked by the men, Bleu straightened her back and ran her fingers through her hair. She should feel good being escorted by two such impressive specimens who gave her obvious attention. Well, she supposed she shouldn't think of Father Cyrus that way. She looked up at him. Darn it, what a shame for a man like him to be wasted.

Her face turned hot. It was so wrong to suggest he was wasted as a priest. You weren't supposed to contemplate things like that.

Once around the corner and on Main Street, Bleu walked behind the priest and immediately stepped off the curb.

A hand caught her arm with a painful grip and yanked her back onto the sidewalk. "You really aren't doing very well," Roche said, while a car passed at a good clip. "You do need to eat. Then go home and sleep. I'll drop you off and arrange for your car to be brought over for you."

Bleu didn't say a word. This was not a good time to lead with her irritation. "Thanks," she said, making sure the street was clear, and setting off ahead of the other two.

The bright pink door at All Tarted Up had received a fresh coat of paint and it shone. Bleu's feet moved slower. Inside the shop, at a window table, she saw faces turned in her direction and recognized Lil Dupre, who was Cyrus's housekeeper, and Doll Hibbs, proprietor with her husband of the only hotel in town, the Majestic.

Doll was the town bullhorn, or so Bleu had been told. Lil was the woman's good friend but Bleu had heard, more than once, that Doll was a bad influence on Lil.

"For crying out loud," Roche said, taking her by the elbow and marching her to the opposite sidewalk. "Have you got a death wish?"

There wasn't time for her to feel fragile, but tears pricked in Bleu's scratchy eyes just the same. "What's the matter with you?" she asked. His fingers dug into her flesh. Not a vehicle was in sight.

He looked into her face. "You stopped in the middle of the street," he told her.

He loomed. Her stomach flipped, when she looked up at him and sensed his anger.

Feeling foolish, she twisted free of him and dodged around one of several large wooden containers filled with tall, slender bamboo and coral honeysuckle that climbed the living canes.

"Are you crying?" Father Cyrus said suddenly, mortifying her. "Bleu, look at me. You've had a terrible shock. That's what's upsetting you."

"We all had a shock," she said. "I'm as capable of dealing with it as either of you."

Only she wasn't, Roche decided. He shouldn't be harsh with her, but he didn't feel so hot himself and he hadn't been thinking when he snapped at her. "Of course you are," he said, and to Cyrus, "How was that woman who lives next door…lived next door to Jim Zachary? Mrs. Harper." Cyrus had insisted on going to the woman's house with the deputy who'd been charged with breaking the bad news.

"Really broken up," Cyrus said. "I think she already knew something awful had happened to Jim, because he didn't normally alter his routine. Day by day, always the same. They may have been closer than I'd thought. She made dinner for the two of them every night and had done so for years."

"Poor woman," Bleu muttered, her attention on the windows ahead and the not-very-casual way people turned their heads to watch her approach with Cyrus and Roche.

Roche. He was the most unexpected thing to happen to her—in her whole life. Complex, certainly not a talker most of the time. When she was with him she didn't breathe quite normally and her skin became supersensitive. She didn't imagine that he felt vaguely dangerous to be with. These were not signs that brought her any peace. They thrilled her, though. Quiet he might be, but he had a big personality, and when it touched her, she wanted more of him— even if the reaction tensed her muscles until they ached.

In the darkness last night, he almost paralyzed me. I never knew that sensation before. He can't know what an enigma he is, can he?

When he looks at me now, by daylight, my breath rushes away. For moments, I forget who and what I am. All I can think about is sex—what it would be like with him.

I feel this even in the forbidden daylight and it is strange, foreign, to a woman who was taught that she should hate the realities of intimacy. Michael only approached me at night, in the dark.

Since he died, when the shadows gather, what should be quiet hours teem with distorted pictures, spin into a black miasma that is a mirror image of my marriage. Again, I'm huddled up in long, ugly nightgowns until my husband comes to rip at my clothes as if he was raping me. He assaults my body, pounds out his disgust with every stroke.

Then, when he is satisfied, he leaves me on my own.

What do I want? To see Roche by day when lust wakes up? Or to venture to him by night when terror could either hold me back from him, or crack open and send me to swarm over him until I've sucked him dry?

Bleu felt wild, shocked. She stared ahead, but saw nothing clearly. *I want him. I want to feel again, and hope to be alive inside.*

"You're hovering," Roche said.

She started, and everything came back into focus.

"Are you okay, Bleu?"

"Of course. I was just waiting for us all to catch up," Bleu said, avoiding looking at him, and pushing open the pink door.

A wave of warm, fragrant air met them. Bleu smelled freshly fried beignets and the subtle sweetness of the powdered sugar they were dredged in, and realized just how hungry she was. She walked inside on unsteady legs, still reeling from thoughts and images that she could not have imagined before she met Roche.

She felt him close behind her. He might as well be touching her with his body—stroking every nerve ending.

"Hi, Miz Laveau."

Bleu collected herself and looked at a familiar face from last night. The woman had sat in the front row at the parish hall. "Hi, there," Bleu said.

"I'm Jan Pierce," the woman said. "I work for the paper. I've got two kids and we really want that school."

"Thank you for telling me," Bleu said, and moved on.

Looking around at other friendly faces, she returned smiles and waves. Her heart lifted. There were a lot of good people in Toussaint.

"Hey, you three," Jilly Gautreaux said loudly from behind the bakery cases, grinning at them as if they came in together daily. As always, there was a line waiting to buy pastries and coffee to take away.

Roche said, "Hi." He liked Jilly because she was real. Most people wore armor of various kinds; Jilly faced the world as she was—soft spots, prickly spots and all—and so did her husband, Guy.

Guy Gautreaux, a former New Orleans police detective, ran his P.I. business from the flat above All Tarted Up. His oversized black dog, usually flaked out at the open front door beside the shop, was the signal that Guy was up there and available.

"You here for breakfast?" Jilly said with her strong Cajun lilt. When they all nodded, she pointed to an available table close to the front of the shop. "Best table in the house. Saving it for you." She winked. "Sidney, she'll be right over."

Roche put a hand on Bleu's shoulder and guided her around the line for counter service. A faint tremor passed beneath his fingers, and she moved a little closer to him. Surprised was a weak word for the effect the little move had on him, as was pleasure. He felt almost lightheaded. She had come near to draw strength from him; he was certain of it.

To feed on his strength.

Arousal brought with it the inner flush, this time with even more force than he expected. He hardened. And he clamped his teeth together.

Staying away from her could be the kindest thing. That would keep her safe from him.

But need would bring him back to her again and again. He must fight his instincts to pursue until he captured.

Bleu sat down by the wall, facing the windows, and he sat beside her. Cyrus took a chair opposite.

"They're talking about us now," Bleu said, so quietly that Roche had to bring his ear almost to her mouth to hear. "They're making something out of nothing."

"What do you mean?" he asked, although he was aware of surreptitious glances quickly averted.

"I don't know. They watched us outside when we were coming here. Then I thought everything was fine—until we came inside. Now, they're pretending not to look at us and talk, but it's obvious they are. What can they be saying? Do you think they've heard about Jim Zachary yet?"

"I doubt it," Cyrus said. "Lil won't have been at the rectory yet. Everything was done so quietly last night and there was no one around but us, then Spike and his guys. It'll all come out soon enough. Everyone will be questioned."

"Yep," Roche said, catching a pair of interested eyes that looked away at once. "You're right though, Bleu. We're the entertainment around here this morning—at least for some."

Cyrus cleared his throat and bent forward over the table. "Don't put too much emphasis on that. Not at all," he said. "Small towns have their own habits. The folks are interested in everything. Yes, they surely are. You haven't been here long, Bleu, so you're the latest unknown quantity. They're still sizin' you up all right. I don't know why they'd look at Roche and they surely wouldn't bother with me. They're so used to me, I'm pretty much invisible."

Bleu let out a short laugh. How could a man be so oblivious of his presence. "Father Cyrus, you couldn't be invisible if you tried. And every woman who sees Roche just about drools."

Her hand, audibly slapped over her mouth, made Roche smile, and he didn't miss the way Cyrus tried to squelch a grin.

Embarrassed, Bleu said, "I just meant you're easy on the eye. Well, nice to look at, anyway. So people are bound to watch you."

Bleu glanced at Cyrus, who raised his eyebrows and gave her a great big smile.

"I guess I'm just a smooth talker," she said, chagrined at her own clumsy efforts. "I've led a pretty sheltered life, so you'll have to make allowances for me."

Sidney, her dark eyes clear and cheerful, arrived with a bunch of coffee cups strung on her fingers. Deftly, she swung off three and set one in front of each of them. " Coffee?" she said. "Leaded or unleaded?"

She wriggled menus from the pocket of her apron and passed them around. Sidney had worked with Jilly for several years and took pride in the café.

"Leaded with cream," Bleu said.

"Leaded, black," Cyrus said, and Roche asked for the same.

"You havin' cooked breakfasts?" Sidney asked, pouring coffee from a carafe. Her shiny brown hair hung in a single braid down her back.

"Oh, an omelette," Bleu told her, pretending to faint against the wall.

The others laughed. "Bowl of grits, and the morning man-blast," Cyrus said. "Two sausages, two pieces of bacon, two eggs, hush puppies, corn bread, honey—and whatever else you can get on the plate."

"Make that two of those," Roche said, feeling better already, even if he was having a testosterone rush. Or maybe that was making it a perfect morning.

Bleu's gaze met Roche's and she made him feel suspended in time until she looked away.

He had a bad case; in fact he had the worst case he could recall. He had always been a hotblooded boy who knew trouble was his middle name when it came to women.

Cyrus said Sidney's name softly and she went to bend down beside him. The little smile on her lips suggested that she'd expected him to approach her for something. She nodded, and deep dimples popped into her cheeks before she sped away.

"What was that about, Cyrus?" Roche asked, and got himself a puckish grin as an answer.

"Sidney and I have our own secret," Cyrus said. "I'm very good at keeping secrets."

"Hey, Bleu," Jilly called over the din. "Great presentation on the school last night. One of these days, Guy and I will be wanting our kids to go there."

A hoot swelled among the customers and Jilly glared at them. "When we're expecting, you folks will be among the last to know," she said in a neutral tone of voice. Her meaning sank in and boos replaced hoots.

When the noise died down, Bleu said, "Thanks, Jilly. We've got a long way to go yet."

It would be hard to miss the rumble of low voices that followed.

"Here you go, Father," Sidney said, her face pink from the warm kitchen. On the plate she put in front of Cyrus were two large, golden-brown tarts.

"I'm a happy man," Cyrus said. He closed his ever-changing blue-green eyes and breathed deeply. Then he picked up a tart and sank in his teeth, closing his eyes again as he chewed the first bite. After that, all restraint disappeared and he chomped through both pastries until nothing but crumbs remained on the plate.

"Oh-oh, I'm gonna get to heaven," Sidney sang, "on a marzipan tart." She left humming her ditty amid laughter on all sides.

Bleu peered at Cyrus's plate and said, "It's all right, Father Cyrus, I didn't really want a bite of one of your tarts."

"Good," he said.

More coffees arrived, soon followed by their meals.

Before they could do more than take a few bites, the door opened hard and Ozaire Dupre, Lil's husband and the caretaker at St. Cecil's, made a wild-eyed entrance. His bald head shone when he turned from side to side. He raised his thick arms like wings, obviously searching for someone.

Lil said, "There's a chair for you here, Ozaire," and pulled one out.

He ignored her, but his round chin jutted when he saw Cyrus, and he pushed his way past complaining people to reach the table.

"Good morning, Ozaire," Roche said, but the man focused only on the priest.

"Father," he said, panting for breath. "You can't have heard. Lordy, lordy, we've got the devil unleashed on us."

"Sit down," Cyrus told him.

Already an intense silence had blanketed the place.

Ozaire remained standing. He pulled a handkerchief from a pocket in his denim overalls and swabbed his face and scalp, the back of his neck.

"Have a seat," Roche said. "I know you'd rather have a quiet chat about what's on your mind."

"Jim Zachary's dead," Ozaire all but shouted. "Stabbed through his neck, all the way through. In the church. And that pamphlet we all got about not wanting the new school—stuck in his mouth."

Roche actually saw Cyrus give up on the situation.

Shocked exclamations burst out, and people stood up.

"It'll be okay," Bleu said loudly. She sensed the glances coming her way. "Spike and his department are already on it."

"There's no mystery to be solved?" Ozaire said. "This ain't nothin' to do with more buildin' at St. Cecil's. That's just a red herring. We all know Kate Harper is the one who'd want Jim dead."

Chapter
4

Later the same morning

A priest must expect to be tested. Cyrus didn't smile at his own small sarcasm. Priest-testing had been getting heavy around here.

After he got to St. Cecil's, he went into the rectory by the kitchen door at the back of the house. He had hoped to get inside without talking to anyone, but Lil, who must have rushed to get back from town before him, stood at one of the old-fashioned marble counters, punching down bread dough.

As soon as she saw him, she picked up a dish towel and came toward him, rubbing her flour-covered hands and arms. "Don't be angry with him, Father," she said. "Him, he was upset about Jim Zachary and he didn't think what he was sayin'."

"Yes," was all Cyrus could think of to say.

"Ozaire and me, we value working here."

It wasn't always quite true but Cyrus said, "I value both of you."

Lil's shoulders dropped a couple of inches and she smiled tentatively. Her new "do," a reddish-brown dye job on short hair combed upward all around, reminded Cyrus of Peter Pan. Even the top of the hair stood up.

"This couldn't have happened to Jim because of the school," Lil said. "Some people really don't want it, but I can't think of a one who'd do something like this to Jim."

"Neither can I."

"There's a lot of older folk who resent the school idea. They want a big activity center that's mainly for them. They've wanted it for years."

And so had Lil and Ozaire, but Cyrus didn't mention the obvious. Ozaire in particular had wanted the site of the old schoolhouse, burned out many years before Cyrus arrived in Toussaint, replaced by a multipurpose building where he could open a gym—paying rent to the church, of course.

"Lil," Cyrus said quietly, "Bleu is the person to talk to about space and cost. She's already mentioned the possibility of both a school and another facility. We all know the parish hall is too small."

"Too small for anything," Lil muttered. "Not even big enough for a good bingo game."

"I think it manages the bingo games just fine," he said, so tired that he longed to put his head down.

"What will they do to Kate Harper then? Put her in jail, I suppose." Lil didn't look pleased at the thought. Kate was one who always showed for bingo.

"The less said on that subject, the better," Cyrus said incredulously. "I can't imagine where Ozaire got such a wild notion. And I don't expect you to mention it again, Lil. This is a police matter, of course. They're the ones who'll find the murderer."

"Plenty of folks know Kate Harper took advantage of Jim," Lil said, the color in her face rising. "He paid for everything—"

"You don't know that," Cyrus said.

"Everyone does. They all know Jim paid off Kate's mortgage. Her husband didn't have anything to leave her. Jim did."

He wanted to walk away and not hear what Lil was going to suggest next. "Okay, what are you saying?" Best get this over with.

Shrugging, with tears suddenly spilling over, she said, "I don't want to talk bad about anyone, but sometimes Kate said things about Jim. She'd call him 'set in his ways.' He was in a rut, and she couldn't make him get out of it. She... Kate wanted to go dancing and have some fun—that's what she told me. I used to tell her she should be past that." She paused, cleared her throat. "Kate said she had plenty of dancin' time left and she might just have to find herself a younger man to be her partner."

He waited.

Lil wiped at her tears with the back of one arm, and left patches of white flour on her cheeks. "Now I've started, I better finish. Jim had plenty. No family, everything come to him after his mother died, and a good job in the surveyor's office all those years. And he left everything to Kate."

And so he had the story according to Toussaint's amateur sleuths. "How did Kate kill Jim?"

A fresh torrent of tears made Lil's words unintelligible. With her apron held over her face, she wept.

As much as he wanted to, Cyrus didn't comfort Lil.

She blotted her cheeks and looked at him with red and swollen eyes. "I don't know," she said in a tiny voice.

"You do know how he died?"

"He was stabbed," she said.

"Where? The details?"

Lil shook her head. "In his back, I suppose. Oh, I don't know where."

"No," Cyrus said. "You don't. But Kate Harper couldn't have done it. I saw what had happened, and it would have taken a lot of strength. Kate is a small woman—and not strong."

"Ozaire said either she did it herself, or she could have paid someone else to do it."

Patience, already stretched thin, snapped for Cyrus. This enraged him. A crazy man, someone very powerful, had driven the knife through Jim's neck and left a hole in the pew where the blade had been hacked downward with such force.

"Father?" Lil said tentatively.

He looked through the windows toward the white church. Official vehicles clogged the driveway normally used only for funeral cars or utility vehicles. The ends of the yellow crime-scene tape that stretched across the entrances to the church, fluttered like ribbons. The day was becoming cloudless—perfect, even if there was thick moisture in the air—yet a sickening and heavy pall dulled the scene before his eyes.

"Don't you worry, Father." Lil's hand on his arm surprised him. "The truth will come out. The good Lord will help us get through." She sighed. "Poor Jim Zachary. Just yesterday I talked to him."

"This is difficult for all of us," Cyrus said. "Take some time off today if you need to, Lil. But don't get drawn into any speculation about Kate Harper. I thought she was a friend of yours."

"She is." Repeated sniffs made Cyrus feel very sorry for Lil. "Ozaire said it was—"

"It's all right," he said, rubbing her left arm. "We've all got to do anything we can to make sure the murderer is brought to justice. We won't help if we point fingers and confuse everything."

"Yes, Father," she said.

Cyrus smiled at her, but felt uneasy. He'd hear more of Ozaire's theory about Kate Harper.

He continued through the kitchen and into the corridor. The dark wainscot that reached halfway up the walls was as old as the house, and it shone from regular polishing.

Cyrus loved this rectory.

But he detested the confused, angry, vengeful thoughts that gripped his mind like the rapid run of waves on the shore. The moment he thought they had gone away, back they rushed to swamp him again.

There was no peace left for him in Toussaint, and his difficulties only increased. He couldn't quit when the need for him here was so great, but he had been tempted to ask for reassignment.

If he did that, what would he gain? The only answer that came to him was, regret.

Halfway along the corridor, he heard voices. A man *and Madge*. Cyrus paused. He crossed his arms and looked at his shoes.

Nothing they said was clear. He was grateful for that. How had he sunk to listening to his assistant's conversations—or trying to? Cyrus knew the answer. Madge had given him too many good years of her life, and recently, when he'd been deeply shaken by the strength of their friendship, he had pushed her to start dating. Now, each time he saw her with a man, even a man who was a stranger, he could barely restrain himself from whisking her away.

He leaned against the wall and tipped his face up to the ceiling. Tears? Tears stung his eyes as if he was some moonstruck kid who didn't get the girl. When had he started allowing himself to question his calling?

No, he didn't question that, but he would be a liar if he didn't admit that he was a man with two passions, each of which deserved all of him: the Church, and Madge Pollard.

A door opened and a man said, "I don't want you getting upset, Madge. I'll take you back to Rosebank tonight, and we'll have dinner. This is all too much for you."

Cyrus shrugged away from the wall. His throat felt closed and he heard the pounding of his blood in his ears. Forcing himself to move, he carried on toward his office. Madge's was next door and Sam Bush, the parish accountant, stood partly out of her room, but with his head inside. Above-average height and well-built, his relaxed posture and easy manner underscored his self-confidence.

Cyrus hesitated again. He couldn't just go into his office and shut the door without saying a word to Sam or Madge.

Sam Bush wasn't Cyrus's choice for Madge, not that the choice would ever be his. The man's wife, Betty, had left him without any sign that she was unhappy, or so Sam insisted. He'd been alone for a year and recently he leased a long-stay apartment at Rosebank, the resort where Sheriff Spike Devol and his wife ran a destination resort and rented suites of rooms. Madge had rooms in the same building, and until Sam moved in, Cyrus had felt good about her being there.

Recently, there had been talk about Sam looking into a way to be officially single again. Joe Gable, Jilly Gautreaux's brother and the town's lawyer, knew what was going on, but Joe would never reveal even a hint of a client's business.

Sig Smith was the man Cyrus was encouraging for Madge. A psychologist, he was a thoughtful, intellectual type who worked for Roche Savage and seemed as if he could be right for Madge.

"Okay," Sam said into Madge's office. "So Vivian Devol would come and pick you up in your car if it's fixed today. It probably won't be. I'll check in with you later anyway. It would be easier for me to give you a lift. We're going to the same place. Either way, we'll have dinner."

Cyrus didn't hear Madge say anything to that.

Sam hadn't taken long to get over the loss of his wife and start looking elsewhere. Cyrus remembered Betty Bush, a vivacious and pretty woman. Why would she disappear like that when she seemed happy in her marriage? What made Sam think he could have her declared dead so soon—if that's what he was trying to do—unless he knew something he wasn't talking about?

Grim, annoyed with his runaway speculation, Cyrus approached Madge's office. "Hey there, Sam," he said, moving briskly. "Have you finished with us for today?"

"Hey, Father," Sam said, straightening up and turning serious gray eyes on Cyrus. "Yes, all finished. I've got plenty waiting for me at the office, though."

Cyrus indicated that he was going into Madge's room and Sam released the door.

"Is Madge's car playing up?" Cyrus asked Sam, passing him. "Don't worry about it. I'll make sure she gets back if necessary."

He nodded at the man, and smiled until Sam shrugged and walked away without a word of argument. He headed toward the kitchens and eventually left the house by the back door. It slammed, and Cyrus was left to think about what he would say to Madge.

"Good accountant, Sam Bush," he said, turning to look at her. "Are you still pleased with him?"

She sat behind her desk, elbows resting on the shiny top. Her hands propped her chin, but her dark eyes stared into his. There was no need for words; she understood him and saw through any clever maneuver he tried to pull off.

He shut the door and sat down carefully in Madge's favorite striped easy chair. Immediately, Millie, Madge's black-and-white papillon, ran from beneath the desk and leaped onto his knees. He stroked her absently. Often the tiny dog and her silky fur could relax him, but not today.

Seconds passed, and he couldn't look away from Madge. "What are you thinking?" he finally asked.

When she was happy, her eyes were warm and bright. When she was sad, they still shone, but the light turned distant—it was distant now.

"Madge? Say something, please."

"Sam's just a friend."

He felt embarrassed by his own behavior. "I know that. Would he like to be more, do you think?"

"Would you approve of that?"

She was backing him into the kind of corner he was trying so hard to avoid. "If he's what you want, of course I do. You wouldn't pick him if he wasn't a good man," Cyrus said.

"I would always try to choose good people as friends. Sam's a decent man. He would like to be more than a friend to me."

Cyrus shifted. He breathed harder. Millie got up, made a perilously fast turn on his thighs, and plopped down again.

Madge smiled. "She doesn't appreciate tension, that girl. You're tense."

"And you're not?" he snapped back and wished he hadn't. "Forget it. I don't have any right to ask that. And I shouldn't be interfering in your private life."

She rubbed her brow. "What's happened to us?" she said. "Every time we're together and we're not working on something, we start digging at each other."

"No," he said and laughed. "We're just having a bad day and there will be more of the same. Until they catch whoever killed Jim, there won't be any peace for anyone in Toussaint."

"No—he—I can't believe it. He loved this church. He must have gone there for a few quiet minutes, same as he always does—did."

"Yes." Cyrus thought of walking up the path toward one of the side doors into the building with Jim at his side. "I went into the church with him yesterday. I'd left my clipboard there. The last thing he said was that he'd be at the meeting Bleu was holding."

Madge's mouth trembled and she pressed her lips tight together.

"I know, I know," he said, trying to comfort her as best he could from where he was. Getting too close to Madge was dangerous. They both knew it.

She covered her face with her hands. "Me, I don't know how we carry on after something like this." Her voice came to him, muffled by her hands. "We do it over and over when the hurt comes. Each time we console each other and we think evil things won't happen around us again. But they do. It's no good thinking you've had your share of unhappiness. It feels like too much already, but more comes along soon enough. Why is that, Cyrus?"

Her hands rested on the desk now, and her tragic, puzzled face turned toward him. She wasn't asking a rhetorical question. Madge wanted him to explain why his God, and hers, let these things happen.

"You know it doesn't work that way," he said. "What happened to Jim is man's making. Don't try to find another reason."

When Madge's tears came, they broke in sobs and she swung her chair around, away from him, so he couldn't see her cry. He stood up, holding the dog under one arm.

"Forgive me," she said. "Just let me calm down. I'll be fine."

She would be fine. Would she? Would either of them ever be fine?

Swiftly, he put the dog down and moved behind her chair. Awkwardly, he patted her back, then stood beside her and rubbed the nape of her neck.

Madge got up. She turned to him, her eyes awash and shimmering. A pretty, dark-haired woman with a big heart. And he had failed her completely.

She walked straight into him and rested her face and fists against his chest. He felt her tears dampen his black shirt.

He felt as if she tried to burrow inside him, to hide and be kept safe.

A useless man wasn't a man at all.

Putting his arms around her was what any friend would do for her, and he did. Sometimes he forgot how small she was. The top of her head didn't reach his chin. With hands that betrayed him by their jerky efforts, he smoothed her back through her cotton blouse. She moved her arms at once and put them around him. She held on tightly.

Cyrus bowed his head. With one hand, he stroked her hair. "Be quiet, Madge. Inside, be very quiet. Make your heart calm."

When she nodded, her nose pressed into his chest even harder.

"I'd like a promise if you can spare me one," he told her.

Once more, she nodded.

"Be very careful, my friend. Don't be alone after dark in any of the buildings here. Think before you go wandering. Just ask me, and I'll go with you as soon as I can. Rosebank is a big, secluded place, too. Once you're in your rooms for the night, stay there. And always, at any time, call me if you're worried about something." After a pause, he finished, "Call me, even if you just need a friend to talk to."

So, he had taken several steps backward from the distance he'd promised to put between them. He was only human.

Madge kept her face close to his chest, but looked upward at him.

She held her heart in her eyes, and there was longing, but also acceptance in the gentle way she remained close.

There was no decision; he kissed her forehead lightly, softly, asking nothing of her, but desperate to give her some peace.

Her eyes closed.

Millie barked sharply.

Cyrus and Madge sprang apart.

The dog barked louder. She jumped and turned circles at the same time. And she quivered before she ran to hide in an open cupboard.

Madge gave a weak smile. "That's our big, bad watchdog. Someone must be coming to the door."

Before she'd even finished, the front doorbell rang.

Running her fingers through her short curls, Madge visibly pulled herself together. She took a tissue and blotted her eyes. A final sniff and she stood very upright. Cyrus admired her strength. He had no tears to wipe away, but he hurt where no one could see.

Dodging around him, Madge left the office and went to open the door. In moments, she was back, a beautifully wrapped package in her hands. "It's for you, darn it. Must be from one of your legion of admirers."

He smiled at the expression on her face. "Women like presents, don't they?" he said.

"Yes, of course they do. We're shallow things."

"You'd do me a big favor if you'd open that for me. I always make a horrible mess with the paper and ribbons."

"You're sure?"

"Yes."

She put the box on the desk and undid a scarlet ribbon with a bow so large and intricate it covered the top. After this, she lifted away pieces of tape without tearing the shiny white paper scattered with red roses.

"Hmm." She looked at him and her lips were pursed. "It's from an admirer all right. Look at the way it's wrapped."

He sighed and did his best to look abashed.

The lid on the box inside had also been taped shut. Madge used her fingernails, ran them under the box rim to free the lid.

Holding the box aloft, she removed the lid with a flourish.

A cloud of dust rose from inside. It billowed. Madge coughed and Cyrus's eyes stung.

"Drop it and get back," he shouted. Madge dropped it on the floor between them. He grabbed her and pushed her behind him.

Small pieces of burned paper floated up from the box. Black, oily-looking, they drifted down to settle everywhere, including on Cyrus and Madge.

"A silly joke," Madge said, picking bits out of her hair.

Cyrus took up the phone, called Spike but got his second-in-command, Marty Brock. "If you think we need the fire department, call 'em," Cyrus explained to him, after giving him the general rundown on what had happened. "I don't smell anything much except old smoke."

"Spike's tied up, but Marty's on his way over," Cyrus told Madge. "Stay where you are."

He made his way around the perimeter of the room until he had a clear view of the open box. Dust was settling. Dust and ash. He wrinkled his nose at the acrid scent. Slowly, he went closer. "Someone stuffed the box with burned books," he told Madge, getting even closer. "That's all it is—old burned books."

A piece of lined paper, folded once, lay on the old carpet. Cyrus picked it up, and by the time he read it, Madge was beside him.

And the new schoolhouse went away
all burned up.
Suffer the little children
suffer and die.

Chapter
5

At the same time

Spike had never been inside Kate Harper's house before but nothing about it surprised him.

Every pale blue, flower-sprigged upholstered chair and couch stood on spindly gilded legs. So many roses in crystal bowls sat on shiny surfaces that he struggled not to wrinkle his nose at the overpowering scent.

"Do sit down, Sheriff," Kate Harper told him. "Choose just anywhere that pleases you. It's not often enough that I have the company of a handsome young man." She actually fluttered her long, dark lashes at him. Red hair, piled high on her head, spilled down into ringlets around her face.

He had dreaded coming here and didn't feel any better now he had arrived. "Thank you, Miz Harper."

She flapped a white hand. "Kate, Sheriff. Call me Kate like everyone does."

Damn, if she wasn't flirting with him, even if only a little. He sat on a chair and straightened his back. He needed to remember that Kate was a traditional Southern woman from a class taught to flatter men. "Kate," he said. "I didn't want to come by so soon, but one or two things have happened since Jim's death yesterday that I surely didn't expect. I want you in the picture, and I'm hoping you can give me some useful ideas."

Kate's age was a matter of local conjecture. Without staring too closely, he decided she must be in her fifties, which was younger than he'd expected. She had a regal carriage and almost floated across the polished wooden floor to take a place on the edge of a couch. She settled the skirts of a green, polished cotton dress carefully. Kate had a nice figure, a voluptuous figure.

She sat quite still with her hands folded in her lap and her eyes downcast.

"There's nothing I can say to make this any easier," Spike told her. "I can't even imagine the depth of your shock."

She made a little choking noise and nodded. When she looked at him, her eyes shone with moisture. "My Jim's—my Jim was the best man in the world. The kindest, gentlest man I ever met. You have to find his killer, Sheriff. Please find him and bring him to justice real soon."

"I intend to do my best," Spike said. The room felt expensive, but it was common knowledge that Jim had lavished gifts on Kate, his companion of a number of years. He had stepped in to comfort and help the woman when her husband died and apparently left her with very little.

"I know what they're sayin' about me," Kate said. A luminously pretty woman in that pale manner common in the Southern redhead who never forgot her hat or gloves.

Spike searched for the right thing to say.

"What's wrong with Sam Bush comin' by to see if I need anythin' extra now and then, that's what I want to know?" She raised her shoulders almost to her diamond drop earrings. "If Jim thought it was a good idea, then there's no one who should make anythin' of it."

"Of course not," Spike said cautiously. He had no idea who did or didn't pay attention to any visitors Kate had.

"Same with George Pinney. You know George, Sheriff?"

"I've never met him, but I know he and his wife look after Jim's place." Jim Zachary's house was the closest one to Kate's. In fact it was the only other house in this pretty little area just out of town.

"That's right," Kate said. "George runs little errands for me, too. These things don't mean I've got a mess of strings to my bow like the busybodies in this town are suggestin'. And why would they bring it all up now, anyway? You tell me that. If they think I could...do what they're suggestin', what would Sam or George have to do with it just because they're good to me?"

He had refused iced tea and now regretted not accepting a glass. Despite fans slowly turning overhead, the big room stifled him. "Beautiful roses," he said. He had to get past thinking Kate was too fragile to be questioned. He didn't have the luxury of waiting to work on this case.

"I pick them myself," Kate said. "I've got a beautiful rose garden. Jim made sure of that."

"When was the last time you actually saw Jim?" Spike said.

"Yesterday," Kate said, sniffing. "He stopped by at lunch, because I was worried about a mold George found on one of my trees. Jim knew all about those things."

"How did he seem?" Spike asked. "Anything unusual about his behavior?"

She shook her head. "He was his usual sweet self."

"He didn't mention any plans for later in the evening?"

Kate bristled. "What are you suggestin', Sheriff?"

He sighed. "These are routine questions. They don't mean anything but what they say."

"No, then. Jim always came home after he'd been at St. Cecil's." Kate raised her chin.

"So after he left you yesterday lunchtime, you never saw him again?"

Tears popped into Kate's eyes, and ran down her cheeks. "So cruel," she said. "So harsh. I don't need you to squeeze my heart for me."

She meant he was cruel and harsh?

Exasperated, Spike said, "Would you feel better if you had a friend with you, Kate? Someone you trust."

"I've lost the people I trust. Lil Dupre was a good friend but now I know she's as bad as the others and that husband of hers is nothin' less than evil."

Spike let those comments pass. "Do you think you can manage talking to me for a few minutes? We can always do this at the station if you'd feel better there. Neutral ground can be helpful."

Kate flashed her palms. "The idea. The *police station?* I will not go there, not under any circumstances. I can just hear the tongues waggin' over that. Only it's not goin' to happen, Sheriff."

Spike propped one booted foot on the opposite knee and put his hat on top. He settled back, deliberately making himself comfortable. "I don't blame you. I just wanted to make the offer. I came on my own, because I thought we could have a friendly little chat. Nothin' too official."

She opened a pink lace fan and fluttered it rapidly before her face. "Thank you. You're very kind."

"Would it be all right if I took a few notes?" Spike asked, trying not to tense visibly.

"I suppose so. If you want to."

He slipped his book from a breast pocket and slid out a pen. "Now. Jim was home for a bit yesterday, because you wanted him to check mold on one of your trees."

"He surely was. Just as well. George was goin' to spray the wrong stuff."

"Then, Jim left and you went about your business. Did you go out in the afternoon, Kate?"

"I never go out when it's so hot."

"So you were here all afternoon?"

"That's what I said. And all evenin', although there will be those who are disappointed by that."

He gave her a questioning stare. "Disappointed?"

"Don't ask me how they think I would do such a horrible thing, but—" she let out a shuddering sigh "—but you know it's been said I wanted Jim to die. Can you imagine that?" Her voice climbed the scale and shook. She cried without attempting to hide the tears.

Spike looked around for tissues, but Kate produced a white handkerchief with lace edging and dabbed her eyes.

"Why would anyone say such a thing?" he said.

"Because Jim insisted on leaving everything he had to me. I told him I didn't want that, but he wouldn't hear of anythin' else. He said that with him bein' so much older, he'd rest better when his time came if he could be sure I was taken care of."

"I see." What, Spike wondered, would a man see in a vapid, selfish woman like Kate Harper. "So you're going to inherit Jim's estate."

He thought her eyes hardened just a little. "Yes. Everything. And that Ozaire Dupre, nasty, avaricious man that he is, can't stand it. He spends his life lookin' for schemes to make money, and I just stay quiet and unassumin' and money comes to me. He's jealous, so he's suggestin' these vile things."

Spike looked at the top of his hat. He needed a new one but the old one was worn-in now. Kate couldn't have sent a knife through Zachary's neck. No way. But if he wanted to get cold about it, she did have a motive, the only logical motive he'd come up with so far.

"Well," he said. "We'll keep on doin' our job. We'll get the killer. Of course, if he doesn't kill again it'll make the case easier in a way, won't it?"

She pinched her lips together and narrowed her eyes. "How would that be, Sheriff?"

"We'll know this was all about getting rid of Jim, and we won't be lookin' for a serial killer. That'll narrow things down." He deliberately let his gaze slide away from hers.

"If that isn't the way things always go in this world," Kate said. She jumped up and stood with her hands on her hips. "It's a man's world, right, Sheriff? If you can make it look like I killed him for his money, you will. Anythin' rather than go after one of the *boys* you hang out with in town. Men stick together. Well, there isn't enough money in this world to make me want to be without my Jim. You just remember that."

Spike also stood and went closer. "It's not that way at all, Kate." He started to put a hand on her shoulder, but she turned away.

"You're missin' things right under your nose," she said, swaying, swinging her skirts back and forth. "I'm not goin' to be like some people, but I can tell you I'm not the one you should be lookin' at. Someone else in this town's got plenty of reason to make sure no one looks too close, but you haven't even thought about him."

Spike took a breath through his nose. "Who would that be?"

"That would be purely conjecture on my part, and I won't be party to spreading gossip. But you better think about why Jim died—and it wasn't because I wanted his money." She spat the last words out.

"It looks as if it's got something to do with the new school."

"There isn't a new school," she snapped back.

"The one they intend to built at St. Cecil's."

She didn't answer at once.

"I know what I'm pretty sure of," Kate said after a pause. "Someone's got a reason to want that school stopped, and it's nothin' to do with money. Think about that. Why wouldn't they want that school, hmm? Then think back to anythin' else unusual that's happened. Somethin' you never figured out, maybe."

"If you know something, it's your duty—"

"It's my duty not to say anythin' unless I'm sure. I'm not, but it makes sense. You go back over situations you never got to the bottom of, Sheriff. Could be you need to do some serious diggin'."

Chapter
6

Later still, the same morning

Finally Bleu was home—but not alone.

Roche jogged around his BMW and met her before she could climb out.

Her own car was in the carport, driven there by Madge with help from Sam Bush.

Roche bent down to look at Bleu.

She got the full effect of his vivid blue eyes.

"Are you sleeping?" he said.

Bleu let out a breath. "I was thinking," she said. "But I might be able to sleep with my eyes open. At least this morning."

"I'd better get you inside, and make sure you're okay."

She wasn't okay, not as long as he hovered over her, so close she wouldn't have to move to touch him. Another very deep breath didn't help much.

Now, she had to tell him he wouldn't be coming in or making sure she was okay. She still couldn't imagine why, out of all the women he must meet, he seemed determined to make her one of his conquests.

That was a mean thought. As soon as he'd shown interest, she had encouraged him, and he probably had no idea about the fears that never completely left her.

Roche held out a hand and said, "Hold on and I'll pull you up," which he did. "Holy... You don't need much of a pull."

"Wait till breakfast settles on my hips." She said the darndest things when she was rattled.

He gave her a quizzical stare and stepped back to look her up and down. "Okay, if you say so." The slight shake of his head wasn't subtle enough to be missed. "Do you want to get the stuff out of your car?"

She had forgotten all about the work she'd left there. "I'll do that," she said. "But you don't need to waste any more time with me. I'm great now."

He didn't move, while she went into the carport and pulled on the door handle of the Honda. It slipped painfully from her fingers, bent one of her nails back. She sucked in air and flapped her throbbing hand. Madge would never leave someone's car unlocked and she hadn't this time.

"You okay?" Roche said.

"Ow, ow, ow."

"You're not okay?"

"I'm stupid. I do everything in a rush and end up hurting myself." The darn nail felt awful. "I guess I earned my reputation for being a klutz."

She kept pressure on her nail bed and glanced at Roche. Now what had she said? His face was expressionless, but he studied her so closely she felt hot all over.

"Give me that," he said, taking her hand in his and pressing harder than she had. Roche wasn't holding her hand with a fraction of his strength. If he were angry, or frustrated, he could be formidable. He could crush her if he wanted to.

Irrational thoughts didn't strike Bleu often, but when they did, they troubled her deeply.

"Where are your keys?" He took the strap of her purse from her shoulder and opened the flap for her.

"Darn it! Last night when we heard Cyrus coming from the rectory, I threw all my things into the car. My keys were on top of the pile."

He frowned at her. "So Madge drove here, then what? She locked the car and took them back with her?"

"Don't worry about this. I'll figure out how to get inside the house. Please, I'd feel better if you got on with your day. You're a busy man."

"My assistant is covering for me today. You've met Sig Smith? He's the psychologist who works with me."

He's letting me know he's cleared his day. "I've met Sig," she said. "He's a really nice man. Go home and sleep now. Thank you for putting up with me."

The way he moved, or rather readjusted his stance, raised the tiny hairs at the back of Bleu's neck. A subtly wider planting of his feet, his weight shifting slightly onto one leg.

Her townhouse stood at the far end of Cypress Place and he had made himself more of a barrier between Bleu and the rest of the cul-de-sac. A visual exertion of power.

Or one more example of her insecurity around men. She was reading something into every move he made, and that wasn't fair—to either of them.

But there was a stillness about him, a watchful waiting. Her reaction to him, the intense awareness, gnawed at her.

"Who lives next door?" he asked, squinting into the sun.

"Nobody right now. It's kind of nice."

"Kind of remote, you mean." He glanced around. The townhouses were in a cul-de-sac, but nothing had been built on the access street. Looking at her again, he said, "You're all on your own out here. I don't like that."

He had no right to like or dislike anything she was or did, yet he gave his opinions as if they should carry weight with her. Did his assumption of power, of having the upper hand, make her feel important to him—or belittled? Her husband had put her down, devalued her—and punished her—all in the name of showing her how weak she was.

"Bleu?" Roche said. "What are you thinking?"

"Just that I'm not on my own out here. Reb Girard's clinic isn't far away."

Dr. Reb took care of general medicine in Toussaint.

"On Catfish Alley?" Roche said. "Unless you can jump the high fences behind this place, you'd have to run the equivalent of four blocks to get there."

Bleu wanted him to go, but wanted him to stay, both at the same time. Some quiet time on her own was essential. "I'm not expecting the enemy to charge in right now."

He didn't respond, just watched her face with those quiet eyes. He also continued to stand, unmoving, a solid flesh-and-blood barrier to her moving around as she pleased.

She was being fanciful, and she couldn't stand wimpy, fanciful women.

Her cell was in her bag and Bleu needed a diversion. She dialed the rectory and got Madge who asked Bleu to wait.

After a long pause when Bleu would have sworn Madge covered the mouthpiece at her end, she came back on and said, "Sorry about that. Just the things you'd expect after what's happened over here. Give me another second."

Another pause followed, while Bleu carefully avoided looking at Roche's face. Instead, she followed the long, muscular lines of his legs inside well-washed jeans, faded at the knee, the pockets and over the part that stretched tight enough to show his metal zipper. A damp rush heated her up all over.

"Bleu?" Madge said.

"Yes, here," Bleu said. "Before I come into the office, I want to go over the feedback forms I got last night. I could be pretty late, because I'm only just going to start."

"Sounds good. I'll tell Cyrus."

Bleu could hear voices in the background, but didn't mention the noise. "Thank you for driving my car back. All my papers are in it. Madge, where did you put the keys? My house key's on that ring, too."

Madge groaned. "I was going to hide them there, but they're in my bag. My car's in the shop. Sam followed me when I drove yours over, but he's gone now. It's okay. What am I thinking? Cyrus will let me use the Impala."

Bleu heard a male voice that didn't belong to Cyrus, and Madge said, "I won't be able to leave yet." More male rumble. "I don't know when I will be able to come."

"It's okay," Bleu said. "I've got plenty to do today. I'll work on some cost analyses. By this afternoon I'll be back to normal and I'll walk over there."

The jeans were loose at Roche's flat belly. They rode a couple of inches beneath his waist and humidity stuck his white shirt to his abs like paint applied on a corrugated metal.

Bleu moistened her lips.

Madge started to argue, but Bleu pulled her attention from Roche's body and cut her off. "Nope, I can get in. No problem. See you later."

Bleu put the phone back in her purse. "Thanks for waiting around," she said to Roche. "Go get some rest. You didn't sleep any more than I did last night."

"Anyone who was ever an intern is used to sleep deprivation. Slave labor and torture at the same time. It's all part of the initiation into medicine." He gave her one of his slight smiles and bowed his head. His thick, black curly hair had needed cutting for some time, but Bleu liked it just the way it was.

She also more than liked the dark shadow of beard on his face. *Sexy.* She couldn't look away, or grasp the feelings she was having. He made her want to be excited by him.

"How will you get inside?" he asked, sizing up her townhouse. "If you say you don't lock one of the doors, I may turn into a wild man."

Startled down to earth—almost—she turned up the corners of her mouth.

His hands, pushed into his pockets, tested the zipper cruelly.

"It's a secret," she told him, trying for lightness. "If I tell you about it, then I'll have to kill you."

Something like surprise entered his eyes. Did he think she was too serious to come up with a well-worn one-liner?

"You do have something unlocked, don't you?" he said. "Or something that's easy to undo. That won't cut it anymore. In future, this place has to be real tight."

"You're right," she told him. "I'll take care of it right away."

"I'll go get your keys," he said.

"No. Thank you anyway. I'll be ready for a good walk later."

He smiled slightly. "I liked kissing you last night."

His abrupt comment caught her off guard. Her stomach tightened. But she kept a smile on her face and gave him a little wave. "Thank you, Roche. You're good for my ego. I hope we'll see you at the building-fund party. Don't be surprised if someone suggests you'll be happier if you give a lot of money away."

He raised one eyebrow. "Sounds familiar. I'll be there. But I'm not leaving you here until I know you're safe."

She opened her mouth to argue, but he shook his head and said, "I mean it. This is as much for me as it is for you—almost. I wouldn't feel right if I drove away with you standing here."

As tired as she was, she could still think as fast as she needed to. "I understand. Once I'm in, I'll let you know." She hurried briskly toward the corner of the townhouse.

The building was on an uphill sloping lot. Although she had only been there a few weeks, on Bleu's side of a dividing fence there were already signs of new things growing, including some vivid bedding plants. Next door, the ground sprouted only patchy scrub grass.

She half ran up the slope beside the house and ducked under the gallery on the back of the house. The aluminum stepladder stored there was light and easy to drag out.

Sweat ran between her shoulder blades.

It wasn't so easy to haul the ladder up steps to the gallery and open it beside the door so she could climb up and reach the lintel. Dust fluttered down when she removed her hidden key. This was the first time she'd used it.

"I wouldn't need a ladder to get that," Roche said from behind her.

Bleu closed her eyes for an instant. "Lucky you. I'm not tall enough."

"Are you deliberately obtuse? Where do people usually hide spare door keys? Don't bother to tell me, I'll save you the trouble. *Over a door.* Anyone could get in with that."

She grimaced. "Lots of people put their spare key under a flowerpot."

"That's not so funny right now," he said.

"No one comes here."

"But they could."

He was getting angry. Anger was unbearable. "You're right," she said, climbing down to the wooden slats of the gallery floor again. "I'll find a good place for it. One of those magnetic key boxes would be a good idea. I'll get to it today."

Roche folded the stepladder. "Where does this go?"

"Under the gallery," she said.

"Uh-huh—really difficult to find, hmm?"

"Yes, but it's easier than having to carry it from the garage."

He whistled softly, wiped his free hand on his jeans. His big shoulders rose and stayed there. She felt a little sick. Roche thought she was idiotic. She *was* sometimes, but she didn't want him to think so.

What do I want from him?

"I'll put this back in the carport for now. An intruder might be afraid of making too much noise getting it off its hooks. There *are* hanging hooks?"

"Of course." She prayed there were.

"That's not a whole lot of reassurance, but it's some."

Carrying the ladder over his shoulder, he walked away.

Bleu opened the back door and all but fell through it, she was in such a hurry to be in her own place. She hurried through the kitchen and living room that covered most of the ground floor and, after a peek through lowered blinds, she opened her front door.

Roche was emerging from the carport, slapping dirt from his hands.

He looked up at her, smiled, and Bleu panicked.

"Thank you," she said, as loudly as she could. "See you later. Bye."

Standing inside the closed door, listening for the sound of Roche's engine, Bleu hated what she had become.

Chapter 7

Stay or leave? Roche took about sixty seconds to make up his mind.

He walked toward the steps and let out one of his best, piercing whistles. When he and Max had been kids, they'd worked hard on their whistles and the result was impressive.

"Bleu!" He shouted her name full force, which was also impressive. "The door blew shut!"

Frozen a few feet from the window where she could see Roche below, his thumbs in his pockets, Bleu couldn't believe what he was doing. Despite feeling a bit like a butterfly pinned to a board, she shivered with excitement at his audacity.

This man wasn't like any other she'd known. Her husband had ruled her with threats, pain and humiliation. He had used fear. Roche wanted his own way. He pushed ahead with wicked charm, when most people would back off. But she didn't want him to quit.

Suddenly he threw his arms wide and yelled, "Stellaaa!" and then looked around like a kid who just broke someone's window.

Bleu slapped a hand over her mouth. Either she was making the best decision she'd ever made, or she was about to do something she would forever regret.

She opened the door again.

"Hey, thanks," he said, and climbed steps toward her. "First, I need to wash my hands, then I'm going to proposition you." He grinned.

She had to smile back. And she relaxed. He was no threat.

She stood aside and he blew past into the hall where heat had already built up.

As soon as he was inside, he said, "You don't have air-conditioning?"

"Oh, yes, but it's not on unless I'm here."

He walked ahead toward the kitchen, turned on the faucets and lathered his hands. "You're here now. You shouldn't have to come into an overheated house when you're tired. I don't just mean now. Any day when you've finished work, heat like this will only stress you out."

She saw him as the man he was—privileged, or at least unfamiliar with the need to watch how much you spent. "I'm sure you're right," she said. "But it's wasteful to cool an empty house for hours. When I can get a dog, I'll have to use it then."

He held his hands out in front of him and looked around. A towel hung over the oven handle but apparently he didn't see it. He was used to other people anticipating his needs. Bleu had known another, if very different man, who expected the same service. She wouldn't go there again.

"Sorry," he said. "It's probably right in front of me, but could you tell me where the towel is?"

"It's over here," she told him, feeling small-minded.

He saw where she was heading and beat her to the oven. "Wow, that feels good," he said, chafing at his hands and arms. "It's probably more expensive to keep turning the air on and off than keeping it steady."

She felt as if Roche filled the kitchen, just as he seemed to fill every space where they encountered one another. Rather than look any closer at him, standing in sunlight through the window, she scooted to put the air-conditioning on. Fortunately, it responded quickly.

Roche felt cold air blast from a vent over his head and turned his face up to enjoy it. He was smooth, but not so smooth that Bleu wouldn't know he was going to pressure her to spend some time with him. Unsettling her was not fun, but this woman had issues and if he let her, she would slide into her cocoon again and any further attempts to reach her would only get more difficult. He intended to reach all of her.

"It cools down fast," she said, coming back to him. "I'm sorry it was uncomfortable."

"Why are you sorry?" he said automatically.

"Because you were uncomfortable." Her hands came together as they did so often and she laced her fingers hard enough to turn the knuckles white.

"You didn't want me in your home. I barged in. The only person who's comfort matters around here is yours."

He knew he should go, but he didn't want to.

Suddenly, she smiled. "You're welcome here." Her face brightened and her green eyes flashed. She tossed her hair back.

"That's a killer smile, Bleu." A catch in his throat surprised him.

"Is that a compliment?" she asked.

"I guess so. It means that your smile slays me, it's so beautiful. You look sad too often. You were meant to laugh a lot."

"Hah." She lifted her hair off her neck and pointed her chin at the cool air still pouring into the room. "I like the way you think. No one ever said that to me before."

"They should have." Watching her, the lines of her profile and neck, the tender underside of her uplifted arm—such a slender arm—

turned his skin cold, set his brain on fire. He'd like to see her dance, naked, without her knowing he was near. He could watch her endlessly.

What he really wanted was to have his hands on her, and his body. Painting her skin with something warm and wet, smoothing her breasts and belly, sweeping down between her legs, molding her with his fingers.... She would flush while he aroused her, and soon she'd be urging herself against him, asking for more.

He must go. Now.

"It's a beautiful day," she said, dropping her arms and putting her hands on her hips. She swayed a little, setting the hem of her dress flipping about her pretty legs.

No pat answer came to mind. The battle with his sex drive was on. He couldn't lose this time, or ever again.

"Thank you for staying with me this morning," she said. "I try to be tough, but I need people as much as anyone does. The least you deserve for putting up with me is some fresh coffee. You couldn't have had enough, of anything, not with all the interruptions at All Tarted Up. Sit at the table."

He sat where she said, at a round, light-wood table with matching chairs. It would be classified as 1950s retro. She must polish the table regularly. The furniture he could see was all older, but well-kept and from the same era. There was a large lime-green phone with a dial on the counter, and she had a corner booth that was classic Coca Cola diner. He made a guess at its purpose and decided she must use it as some sort of conversation nook.

Bleu couldn't have much money to play with. He'd never thought about that before, but on the kind of salary she would draw from a little parish like St. Cecil's, she would have to spend carefully— unless she had another source of income. He doubted she did.

"Orange juice?" she said, taking a jug from the refrigerator.

"Please," he said. Making sure she never had to worry about money again would bring him a lot of pleasure.

She put a glass in front of him and stood to drink from her own. With her head tilted back, her throat moved visibly. He wanted to touch her there so badly.

Go home, Roche, before you blow it.

Bleu finished her juice. She put the back of her hand to her mouth, then giggled at herself. "Sorry, I'm so used to being alone I forget my manners sometimes. The coffee won't be long. Do you take anything in it?"

His throat constricted. "Just black, thanks."

Mugs clattered on a tiled counter. She moved rapidly, no longer looking tired. In fact, she appeared luminous.

Deliberately, Roche looked away from her. He wasn't dealing with the two of them being alone together without experiencing physical reactions of the dangerous kind. Thank God she couldn't see inside his head, or rest her fingertips on his nerves.

His nerves must have the power to electrocute her.

"I don't have much furniture," she said. "But I like living here. It's kind of nice not to be dragging too much baggage around."

"Did you ever carry a lot more baggage around?" He kept the question light, but still wished he hadn't asked it.

"You might say that, I guess. Time passes, things change, and you learn what matters most to you."

Roche glanced at the Rolex watch he couldn't care less about. But could he say what mattered to him, really mattered—apart from his work?

Carrying two coffee mugs, Bleu approached. She set them down, returned to the kitchen and came back with a plate of pastries and a basket of apples and pears. She slid the food onto the table and whipped two plates from underneath at the same time. Napkins and silverware stuck out of the fruit basket.

"If I didn't know better, I'd think you'd been a waitress," he said.

"I have been. Several times." She sat opposite him.

She offered the pastries, and he took one.

"How could you be a waitress?" he said. "You're a teacher and you've got whatever qualifications you need to be a fund-raiser and planner."

"I worked to put myself through school. No big deal."

He knew it could be a big deal for some students, holding down a couple of jobs and trying to do well in school at the same time. "You said you were a waitress several times." He grinned and she narrowed her eyes. "Did you keep getting fired for puncturing the fruit with the silverware?"

"Nope. Never got fired—not as a waitress."

"So, why so many jobs? And what else were you fired from?"

"You're nosey, maybe even rude. In fact, yes, you are rude. One day I may answer all your inappropriate questions," she said.

She had a point. "You're right. It's an occupational hazard. I spend so much time asking personal questions, I sometimes forget it's not always appropriate."

"You're forgiven," she told him.

"I got fired from a job as a beach photographer," he said. "I chopped off heads, or feet. Couldn't manage to get the whole enchilada in at one time. It was the camera's fault. See—I'm not afraid to share my failures."

"Humility is always touching," she said. "Now eat."

He did, and he drank some of the best coffee he'd had in a long time—and said so. Waving a cheesecake-filled pastry, he indicated the Coca Cola tribute. "That's really something," he said. What were you supposed say about a set that belonged in an old diner?

Her smile was filled with pleasure. "Thank you! I'm into forties and fifties funk and retro. It makes me feel free. I'm on my own, and now I can have whatever I like around me. I'll gradually collect a few more pieces."

In other words, Bleu was newly independent, probably from a bad marriage.

"I like old jukeboxes," he said. "I've got a couple Max and Annie are storing for me. There isn't room at Rosebank." He told people he stayed at Rosebank because he hadn't settled on whether to buy an old house and renovate, or build a new one. What he should say was that he was too comfortable to move.

Bleu's silence stopped him from talking. He considered her wide-open eyes and parted lips. He shouldn't do that too often. "Did I say anything offensive?" he said.

"Oh." Bleu took a big swallow of her coffee. "No. It's just that one of my ambitions is to own a jukebox eventually. I collect pictures of them from auction offerings. I'll show them to you sometime.... Sorry, I'm sure you're not interested in pictures of old jukeboxes."

"Are you kidding me? I collect pictures myself, and I'm always on the hunt for a mint machine. Have you seen the one at Pappy's?" He blew out. "Wow, if you haven't we should take a close look. A Wurlitzer 1015. It's the real thing, not a copy."

"I haven't seen it," Bleu said. "I'll have to get over there again."

Roche couldn't believe she was actually interested. And she was. This was no act.

"I'll definitely show you what I've got at Max and Annie's. We'll have dinner with them sometime. If I volunteer to barbeque, they'll have us over anytime."

She still looked fresh, but the lightness and enthusiasm of a few moments ago had faded.

"Thank you," she said. "That would be fun. If you like, I'll have them back over here for—spaghetti, maybe? A simple Italian dinner."

She looked at her hands in her lap. Money was an issue for her, he was sure of it. Now she was ashamed of not being able to put on a big, fancy meal for Max and Annie.

"Italian will be great. And I've got another idea. Do you like to dance?" Damn, he was thinking about her dancing again.

"I really love it. Before I was married I used—" She closed her mouth.

"Good," he said quickly. Now he was certain she'd been married. Apparently she wasn't anymore. No ring and no signs of a man around the house. "Let's get up a party and go to Pappy's for an evening. We could dance and eat until we can't move. And we could ogle that Wurlitzer. How about that?"

The smile in her eyes was soft. "We'll see."

"Did something I say upset you?"

"No, no, Roche. Good heavens, no. I can't get Jim Zachary out of my head, is all. I keep seeing him there. So helpless and vulnerable. How can someone do that to another human being?"

"I've put in my time trying to figure that out," he said, thinking of the murderers he'd treated. "The reasons are different. They even change with the same killer. Mostly they like talking about themselves, and some of them only want to brag about what they've done. Victims mean nothing to them except as ways to get pleasure."

"Sick," Bleu said. "I'm worried about Kate Harper, too. I haven't even met her, but I can sympathize with a woman suddenly on her own. She's lost her friend—and now they're starting rumors about her. Jilly said Kate's a widow. She and Jim got together for supper each evening. It gave them something to look forward to. She cooked meals for him, and he kept her place in good repair. Seems like a perfect deal to me."

Roche sniffed his coffee before taking another swallow. "God, I hope Spike and his people find the killer quickly. We'd all be fools if we weren't waiting for another hit."

The murder hadn't left his mind, except, he'd have to admit, when Bleu had wiped his memory clean and left him only able to think about her. She was new, unaffected. The kind of rich, often spoiled females he worked with at the Green Veil clinic bored him—all but the patients he knew he was helping.

He saw his nonclinic patients at an office in Toussaint. There weren't many of them yet. These people he admired, not the least for their courage in bucking the trends in a town where old superstitions continued, like the respect for voodoun and the habit of carrying gris-gris, usually as charms or talismans in small cloth bags. Folks either believed in these collections, often of unspeakable things, or said they did out of fear that they should. Yet seeing a psychiatrist seemed to be a badge of shame, a sign of giving power over the mind, the property of practitioners of the old arts, to modern intruders.

Bleu gazed off, apparently not focusing on anything.

"Bleu, how much do you know about the woman, L'Oisseau de Nuit?" he asked. This person, a flamboyant woman, did her part to keep voodoo alive in these parts.

"Wazoo? I'm sure I don't know her anywhere near as well as you do, but I think she's terrific. She came here to visit and brought all kinds of goodies for me."

"What kind of goodies?" He frowned. "Nothing homemade?"

Bleu smothered a laugh. "Only the cookies and the cake. And the jam. She's a really good cook. And I think we could be friends."

He let out a long breath. "You and Annie. She thinks Wazoo walks on water. Not that I'd be surprised if that woman had figured out a way to make it seem that she does." There had been something close to proof that Wazoo was a "seer" as they called them, but Roche couldn't totally get past his skepticism.

Bleu frowned. "You think so. Well, in that case, I'm glad I didn't eat whatever it was she had in her little velvet bags. She said they're all wonderful and help keep you young."

"She did?" Roche slopped coffee on the table. "That's the sort of stuff they use to keep people in line, they—" He stopped.

Bleu giggled. She lowered her face and looked up at him. "Sorry, couldn't resist teasing you."

She was something else. He leaned a little forward on his chair and rolled his shoulders, but didn't feel a whole lot more relaxed.

"You don't like Wazoo? I guess that's to be expected."

"Why?" he said, propping his chin on the heel of a hand and watching her mouth.

Her smile was an impish one he didn't think he'd seen on her face before. "Because you're a medical doctor and medical doctors don't have any time to even think there might be effective alternative medicine. Wazoo's magic isn't black, not that I believe in all that."

"Alternative medicine?" He got up and stood over her. "Wazoo? Pet therapist, seer of the future and peddler of potions and super-stition? There's a name for all that, and it isn't the term you used."

"Ooh." She turned sideways in her chair and looked up at him, her eyes the green of new ferns, and so bright. "Science scoffs at the pos-sibility of arts as old as time. There aren't any scientific papers pub-lished about them. And the spells. Woohoo! Pure inventions of simple minds." She raised her hands and simulated spiders crawling in the air.

"You're laughing at me." Damn, even when she made fun of him, her smile made him amused by himself. What was he getting into?

Rushing into, even knowing as much as he did about people who were as wounded as he had decided Bleu was.

She nodded. "You're funny," she said. "What's the other name for what Wazoo does? Other than alternative medicine?"

"Mumbo jumbo," he said, anticipating the laughter to follow. "But I do kind of like her…sometimes. She may even be particularly perceptive…in a way."

Shaking her head, Bleu obliged him by laughing.

Roche stayed beside the table, watching while she laughed.

How could she make him feel like this—like a man shedding skins, a man finding the person he used to be before the cynicism of the life he'd chosen left him wrapped so tightly?

"Bleu," he said softly. He thought she might not hear, but she turned teary eyes up to his and caught her bottom lip in her teeth.

What a mouth.

Color rose in her cheeks. She couldn't quite control her mirth, but she was embarrassed in case she had offended him.

He held out a hand, palm up.

Bleu rested hers on top and he held her fingers, urged her to stand, and bent over her hand. He rested his lips lightly on the back, and ran the tip of his tongue over the delicate bones and tendons. And she shuddered.

Roche wanted her to shudder.

When he looked at her face, her eyes were closed and he allowed his own to shut.

Be careful.

He held their hands to his chest and kissed her eyelids. Giving in to the peace he felt was easy. Yes, he wanted to make love to her and to lie with her anywhere. To shed his clothes and get rid of hers. And then he wanted to stay here for hours, until she knew everything about him, and accepted him and he knew everything there was to know about her. He came close to smiling at his arrogance and hoped that once he knew her demons, he could help snuff them out.

She didn't make a move, but Roche was happy to have her near, even though the mixture of pleasure and pain on her features dug at him. Cautiously, he put an arm beneath her arm and around her slight body. Slight, but firm and curved, and the way he saw her in his mind was a dream.

He had to kiss her. Just as with the first time, he met resistance as she adjusted to the feel of his mouth. In her marriage, there couldn't have been long, erotic foreplay or wild, hot nights in secret places. He felt her inexperienced body hold back from him, felt it stiffen each time he bent with her a little. Who had her fool of a husband been? And hadn't there been boyfriends?

Bleu's mouth opened and he tugged gently at her bottom lip. Her head fell back and he heard her pant.

If you go too fast, you'll lose her. Take your time.

Barring some disaster, there would be time.

She pulled the hand he held away and rested her fists on his chest. Rising to her toes, she pressed her lips to his. At first the kiss was small and awkward, but he let her experiment until her mouth softened and she started to play, using the tip of her tongue against the end of his.

The shy lady was learning.

Rubbing her rib cage, he moved her closer, and moved his right leg, almost imperceptibly, so that it pressed between her thighs. He smiled when he realized she was too involved to notice.

Roche looked at her and smiled. Bleu smiled, too, but her gaze quickly shifted away. His thumbs fitted beneath her breasts so naturally. He nuzzled her ear, kissed her neck—and she grew very still. The wrong move and she would stop him completely.

Pounding, in his ears and spreading through his groin, was the price of restraint. Slowly, he rubbed her back and kissed her neck again and again, his mouth closed—small, firm kisses.

It was a weak excuse, but he was only a man. How often had he reminded himself of that recently? Her neckline, with it's simple ruffle, was too high for his taste. He shifted his face to her shoulder, closed his eyes and breathed her in.

She didn't attempt to touch him where he needed to be touched.

Try to make a date, then go home.

He said her name and she looked at him again. There was fear in her eyes, or anxiety, or uncertainty. He didn't know exactly what he saw, but she struggled—he saw that. She struggled against what she was feeling, and silently asked him for help.

Then he read that look. She was bewildered.

Red, swollen and very kissed, her mouth remained moist. Did he have to waste it if he wanted to have a chance with her in the future?

Unbelieving, he figured Bleu didn't know a lot about sex.

What she needed to learn was a little about what she'd been missing.

He leaned his thigh hard between her legs, spread a hand on her bottom and urged her higher on muscle that felt as if it had been turned to stone.

She made a sound.

What she was starting to feel would help him teach her the rest. Holding her against him, he unzipped the back of her dress, pulled the straps from her shoulders and bent to kiss the top of a pale breast.

She twisted. Pushing at him, she almost fell when she forced herself away from his leg, pulling her dress high onto her shoulders at the same time.

Bleu was too late to stop what he'd started. A convulsive shiver tore into her, he saw it, saw the shock, then the horrified embarrassment on her face. She caught at his arm for support and her knees started to buckle.

Roche knew panic when he saw it. He held her up. "Bleu—"

"It's okay," she said, backing away from him. "Really. Everything's fine. I—I get a bit claustrophobic sometimes." Her skin shone, and when he took firm hold of her wrist, it was clammy.

"Bleu."

"Wow, I need to get some sleep." She paused and her eyes closed. Another shudder slammed her. She made a sound like a deep sob and covered her face.

"Hey," he said and risked putting an arm around her shoulders. "You could be getting sick." He was making this up as he went along, but it was the best he could do to help both of them.

Years as a therapist had taught him that a woman like Bleu couldn't go too far, not so soon, or she would run from him because of some learned reaction to finding pleasure in sex. He hadn't learned his lessons so well. He'd gone much too far, much too fast, and now she was completely confused—and terrified of her own reactions.

"Let's forget this—you and me," she said. "I've disappointed you."

"No, you haven't. How could you? Tomorrow evening," he said, "do you think you could make that dance and dinner at Pappy's? It would be fun."

"Thank you." She chafed her crossed arms. "That sounds lovely. Is it all right if I wait until later to let you know for sure?"

He swallowed his disappointment. She wouldn't go. "Of course," he said. "Now I should leave and let you get some rest and do some work."

The look she gave him was long, questioning, then she said, "Thank you, Roche. You're very kind."

By the time he reached the front door, she'd turned away, but he didn't dare go back to her.

Bleu's climax had mortified her.

He knew she would cry and needed to make someone suffer for damaging her. And he intended to find out who that someone was.

Chapter
8

Early afternoon the same day

At the side entrance to the rectory, a young deputy faced off with Toussaint's most exotic citizen.

"Let me go through," she said. "The day when you make Wazoo stay out of any place she wants to go, is the day your teeny weeny gonna fall right off."

Madge arrived, panting, from the back of the rectory and skidded to a halt at a table where Wazoo had been stopped by one of Spike's young male officers. *Rose,* his name tag read, and Madge imagined he'd lived through plenty of grief because of that.

Wazoo, animal psychologist and practitioner of whatever opportunity arose, ruled Toussaint's information grid and used her contacts shamelessly, but once a friend, her loyalty stuck. People avoided turning her into an enemy by making her mad. She was really mad right now.

Deputy Rose and Wazoo dodged back and forth on their respective sides of the table. Rose sweated, trying to stop Wazoo from getting past.

"Him," Wazoo said when she saw Madge. "He about two days out of diapers and he tells me, *me,* I can't go see my good friends in the rectory. Do you believe it, Madge? Where's God Man? I wanna see him right now. He take care of this."

"Who's Godman?" Rose adjusted his creaky new gun belt.

Madge tried to signal for Wazoo to avoid the question.

Too late. "Father Cyrus Payne to you."

Cyrus detested Wazoo's pet name for him.

She looked marvelous in black lace with panels of red cotton swirling each time she moved inside her floor-length skirt. Her black hair sprang in long curls from a center part and almost reached her waist. Fine ringlets bobbed about her forehead and the sides of her face. Her eyes, too dark to fathom, glistened within heavy lashes. The makeup she used—clever, accomplished—heightened her mystery.

Years earlier, Wazoo had arrived in Toussaint to mourn an old friend. Then she had stayed. Her age was difficult to pinpoint, but most thought she must be in her thirties.

"Deputy Rose," Madge said, giving the slight young man a serious look. "Wazoo is a good friend of ours, and she worries about us. She wouldn't do anything to interfere with the investigation, would you, Wazoo?" She stared hard at her buddy.

Wazoo pursed her lips, wrinkled her nose and took entirely too long to say, "No."

"Miz Pollard," Rose said with a drawl that gave him away as a transplanted Texan. "The sheriff, he said nobody was allowed past the tapes if they weren't already on the other side. It's like this. We're checkin' for footprints, clues and the like, and if a lot of folks come messin' things up, we could lose—"

"*More insults*—you think I'm stupid, me?" Wazoo said, striking a pose. "I'm standin' here watchin' an army of people march all over where you don't want me to go. There's people everywhere. Outa my way."

"Stupid, Miz Wazoo?" Rose said, shaking his head. "Now you know I don't think that about you."

She straightened up, braced one hand on the table and the other on a hip. "Why?" she asked. "How come I didn't notice before?"

Rose glanced around. "Notice what?"

"How cute you are, of course. You got a girlfriend?"

He turned pink. "Not at the present."

"What's the matter with all the females in this town? You are one sexy, tingle-makin' hunk of male."

Rose twitched inside his uniform.

"Not two moments ago I was thinkin' someone ought to give you a good spankin' to make you wise up." She held the tip of her tongue between her teeth for a moment before adding, "Now I do believe I'll see about that spankin' myself. Oh, yes, that is one hard, high, spankable rump, and I'm the woman to make the most of it."

His face scarlet, Rose put more distance between them, but not before Wazoo leaned around to see his derriere. "Very nice," she murmured.

Madge closed her eyes. Wazoo could embarrass the pants off a bumblebee. No, no. Absolutely no pants were coming off around here.

Wazoo took off toward the back door with her hair flying and her skirts flapping.

"That one is something," Rose said. "I don't suppose there's any reason she can't go in this way, but I've gotta ask y'all to make sure she doesn't get near that front door. They're working around there."

"I'll do it," Madge said and hurried after Wazoo. "Hey. Wait for me. You are one bad girl sometimes. You go inside the kitchen and stay there. We're holed up there anyway. And you don't go near the front of the house. Got it, Wazoo?"

"Got it. I'm gonna call Nat. He'll get down here and fix these goons."

Nat Archer, New Orleans homicide detective and Guy Gautreaux's former partner, was tight with Wazoo, although no one could figure out what that meant in their case. Whatever it did mean, Nat was a big, impressive man and he didn't tolerate anyone treating Wazoo with less than respect.

"Have you taken a good look at that church of yours?" she asked. "You got enough uniforms over there to take on the streets of New Orleans. What they doin'? That's what I want to know. And cars and vans and trucks. Any minute, we gonna see the helicopters—maybe a couple of them things for on the water and on the land, too."

"Amphibious vehicles," Madge said automatically and looked at the sky. Why was she getting into this discussion?

"Like you just said," Wazoo said. "Them, too. We need Nat and Jilly's Guy on the job. They'll get things done."

"Please don't call Nat or get Guy riled up. Spike's already got enough on his hands without somebody else treating him like gum on their shoes."

"What did you just say, you?" Wazoo whirled to face Madge. "Gum on their shoes? I believe you must be keepin' questionable company and they teachin' you *bad* language. You goin' to the dogs."

"I didn't swear," Madge protested.

Wazoo laughed, showing off beautiful teeth and almost closing her big, black eyes. "You are way too serious, girl. I'm here because I figure I'm needed. We got trouble in this city again." She turned back and marched onward. "I need to talk to Spike—that boy is showin' more promise all the time. If I can teach him to accept that some of the things he can't see are more important than the stuff he can pick up and blow his nose in, he could go places."

"Yes," Madge said. She felt breathless. "You have a great sense of what's going on. We couldn't manage without you around here."

Wazoo stopped abruptly. She tossed her hair back and looked over her shoulder at Madge. "I was goin' to mention that. *'We?'* And, 'Wazoo is a good friend of ours and she worries about *us?'* Has this good friend, Wazoo, been kept in the dark about some big news?"

Madge frowned. The day only grew ever more humid, and she was already too hot. The tone of Wazoo's question, her sly sideways look, didn't ease the discomfort.

Wazoo moved in closer and spoke into Madge's ear. "I know nothin's changed. You got to teach that man you love to ride. Just one lesson and from then on, he be teachin' you. You'll have to hold on tight or be bucked right off. He is one sexy—"

"Stop! Please don't say any more. He's a priest."

"He's a priest and he loves you." Wazoo took Madge's face in her hands. "You are beautiful, you. And he's pretty darn beautiful, too. Mm—mm, yes, he is. You gonna be beautiful together. I can close my eyes and see the pictures. Moonlight on shiny skin, sweatin' skin...naked skin."

Madge swallowed air before she choked out, "That's not appropriate."

"I know," Wazoo said and chuckled. She took a couple of dancing steps and whirled on her toes. "I love not bein' appropriate. That's boring. I am never goin' to be boring. And I love you, Madge Pollard. I even love that scrawny little mutt of yours." She hugged Madge quickly and kept on laughing low in her throat.

"Thank you. I love you, too. Now get inside before someone else hears the kind of things you're sayin'."

Madge didn't know how much more tension she could take today. She hadn't needed Wazoo's outrageous suggestions. Madge had an imagination of her own. She held on to the memory of every touch and special word she got from Cyrus, and this morning, the way he'd held her, had been one of his most spontaneous reactions yet. He'd been a man who wanted to feel a woman in his arms, and she was that woman.

"Yes," Wazoo said. She frowned. She closed her eyes.

"What is it?" Madge whispered.

Wazoo shook her head. "Nothin'," she said, looking cross. "And there ought to be somethin' after what's gone on around here."

Cyrus came from the rectory without Wazoo noticing him. "Wazoo," he said quietly. "I'm sure you've come to help us all stay calm."

Holding back a smile, Madge listened to Cyrus's persuasive voice and watched Wazoo's reaction.

"Who would have thought you'd ever say you needed my help?" she asked. "In here," she poked at her chest, "I believe you and me have found a meetin' place, God Man. But in here," she poked her head, "I worry in case you're foolin' with me. I wouldn't like that, and I'm not sure what I'd decide to do about it."

"I don't lie," Cyrus said. "It's painful to me that you think I might."

"Then put aside your pain, God Man. I think you can still be saved and you're worth it." She looked toward the searing sky, then, gradually, lowered her gaze to the bayou. "I can smell the water. The fresh plants startin' to spread their vines on the surface and their leaves poppin'. See how the cypress trunks shine white…like dead men's bones."

"Wazoo?" Cyrus said, a warning in his tone, but she gave no sign of hearing him.

She shrugged. "Me, it's my job to listen for warnings." She turned her big, dark eyes fully on Cyrus, raised her nose and sniffed several times. "I think I smell blood."

"Why don't we go inside and have some coffee?" Cyrus said.

"I've got to be ready is all," Wazoo said.

"Ready for what?" Madge said.

Wazoo pursed her lips. She tapped a foot and looked even more annoyed. "Sometimes a woman's got to be patient and wait for instructions. I'm waitin', and I'm ready."

"Just don't talk," Cyrus told her. "You can frighten people who aren't used to you."

Wazoo waved a hand. "I didn't smell old blood," she said. "So far it's still runnin' in someone's veins. We better hope it stays there."

Madge tried not to stare at Cyrus, but failed, and he caught her eye. The sadness that welled into his expression squeezed her heart. The day after tomorrow she was supposed to go out with Sig Smith for the evening, and she didn't want to. But she would go and she would try to keep Cyrus's face from her mind.

The old tension was there between her and Cyrus. They both remembered Wazoo in time for Madge to see the woman's knowing stare. Cyrus had to see it, too. She climbed the back steps and pushed her way through the back door with Madge and Cyrus right behind her.

Madge was a part of his life and he didn't want to let her go. She had caught him staring at her again, but at least she couldn't know what he was thinking. He was trying to accept that she would learn to care for someone else. So far he hadn't started to make peace with the changes that had to come.

And he never would. He was going to hate any man she let into her life.

He shut the door, using the moment to calm down.

Just the three of them, and Bleu, were in the kitchen. Lil had taken Cyrus at his word and gone home for the rest of the day. Bleu usually worked in a small room on the second floor, but it was easier for her to be at the kitchen table as long as the sheriff's men were swarming over the front of the house.

As soon as Marty Brock stopped with his questions, Cyrus had driven over to Bleu's place with her car keys. She had followed him back, insisting she had to work—even though he had seen how her eyes drifted closed from time to time.

She wasn't anywhere close to nodding off now. Nobody slept with Wazoo around.

"Where's Spike? He over there?" Wazoo peered through a window over the sinks, toward the church.

"He didn't get here yet," Bleu told her.

Wazoo squinted at her. "There's somethin' goin' on here. No, I don't mean that you got a corpse in the church or wherever— somethin' else."

"Wazoo!" Bleu dropped her pen.

"Does that mean you've waited long enough for your woo-woo messages to start coming through again?" Madge said.

Cyrus appreciated her for taking the edge off Wazoo's comment.

Undaunted, Wazoo made a smug pout and said, "You keep on makin' fun, you. I don't say things I don't mean. And if I could see what I've been tryin' to see, I'd tell you about it. I'm thinkin' there's too much interference from you unbelievers for a hard-workin' seer to do her job."

Cyrus looked at Madge. She pulled a chair out from the big oak table in the window and sat down across from Bleu.

Wazoo didn't move, didn't speak again. She stared through the back window toward Bayou Teche.

Heavy footsteps sounded on the steps to the kitchen door, and Spike Devol let himself in. A circle from his hatband flattened a line in his dishwater-blond hair. "I got here as fast as I could," he said. "I was over at Kate Harper's. I need to talk to you. Are we still waiting for the box to be picked up by forensics? Is it in your office? Something's—" He stopped when he noticed Wazoo behind Cyrus.

"Wazoo just arrived," Cyrus said. "She's been having one of her feelings and—" He closed his mouth.

"Is that right?" Spike said sarcastically.

"The box is still in my office," Madge said. She got up and walked behind Cyrus. She rubbed his arm as she passed and he swallowed hard.

Spike had bright blue eyes that folks thought of as friendly. They weren't too friendly at the moment.

"That's right." Cyrus felt like a man up to his neck in water and trying to walk against a tide.

"Cyrus is right," Madge said. "Wazoo senses… She gets feelings."

"Have you forgotten I live around here, too?" Spike said. He propped his long, rangy body against a counter. "I do believe I've bumped into Wazoo's *feelings* before."

Spike's skepticism shone through and Cyrus figured there was almost no point in trying to change the sheriff's opinion of Wazoo. She'd been right about a number of things in the past, but that didn't seem to count for much.

"Annie Savage talked about you," Bleu said to Wazoo suddenly. "She told me you saved her life once. She wouldn't say how and neither would her husband. Roche isn't talking, either, but I could tell they were serious."

"What's the box you got here?" Wazoo asked. "What's in it?"

"Official business," Spike said. "Nothing to interest you."

"You one ungrateful, nasty man." She wagged a long finger at him. "I'll let myself out."

Instead of going toward the back door, she went to the corridor leading to the rest of the house.

"Quicker for you to go out this way," Spike said,

"I'm gonna do what I'm gonna do," Wazoo said. She walked straight at him without slowing down, and Spike jumped aside. "How come that lovely Vivian married you, I don't know. How come you got that sweet child, Wendy...well, now there's another mystery. And now you got another poor little victim. The longer David stays a baby, the better for him. And you don't respect that father of yours. Homer Devol is a saint."

Spike's dad could be crusty and difficult. A saint, he'd never be.

"Wazoo," Bleu said and laughed. "That is so unkind."

"I know," Wazoo said over her shoulder.

Cyrus went with Spike and followed Wazoo—straight into Madge's office.

The surface of the desk had been cleared and covered with white paper. An aura of fine dust hung over the box in its ripped cradle of fancy paper.

Wazoo stared. She walked a few steps to get a different angle into the box, then stayed where she was.

"Hey, guys," Roche Savage said, walking into the room. He saw Wazoo and the box of charred remnants and closed his mouth.

Cyrus nodded at him. Something about Wazoo convinced him not to say anything else.

"Was that left on the front step?" Wazoo said.

"Yes," Spike said. "We're trying to find out—"

"Who put it there?" Wazoo interrupted. "That would be a good idea. Nice thinkin', Sheriff."

She moved determinedly to the box and hauled out a handful of its contents.

"Don't do that," Spike said.

"I guess I already did. It's books."

"We know," Cyrus said, warily watching Spike's furious expression.

Wazoo calmly opened a little volume, knocking off charred edges as she did so. "School books," she said. "Little kids' readers. There's a picture of angels here. Must have come from the old school right here."

Cyrus's stomach turned.

Chapter 9

These were not happy people.

Roche wished he had arrived later, maybe much later. He had driven past Bleu's place and seen that her car was gone, then he'd dreamed up an excuse for coming to the rectory.

"That woman can be a pain in the ass," Spike said once Wazoo had made her exit. "She just mixes things up."

Roche crossed his arms and waited.

"I need to talk to you," Spike told Cyrus. He looked at Roche and frowned. "Where did you come from?"

"Good afternoon to you, too, Sheriff Devol," Roche said, with a big smile. "I've been looking at the Cashman property. Right next to the rectory and the rest of the church's property, it would get rid of the space problems for new building projects."

"Only it doesn't belong to the church and there's no money to buy it," Cyrus said.

He had chosen the wrong time to drop in. "Yes, well, I'll leave you two to talk," he said.

"You can stay," Cyrus said, a bit too enthusiastically. "Can't he, Spike? Unless there's something he can't hear, or—"

"He can stay," Spike said, his nostrils pinched. "We could use another brain around here. Make sure nothing you hear goes anywhere it shouldn't."

Roche smiled. "Things do seem to be going to hell in a handbasket."

"What do you mean by that?" Spike said. "D'you know something I don't know?"

"Not about the kind of work you do," Roche said hurriedly. "It just seems there's unrest hanging out around here."

"Fu—" Spike put a hand over his face, but it didn't cover enough of his skin to hide his blush.

Cyrus patted his shoulder. "This is tough," he said. "But it isn't the first time things have been tough in Toussaint." He raised his eyebrows. "Wazoo said she smelled something."

Spike gave a short laugh. "She's always smelling things. What else is new?"

"This time it was blood."

Roche figured his opinions wouldn't be welcome. He watched Spike's reaction and saw plenty.

"The hell it was," Spike said, his frown deep enough to rest his eyebrows in a straight line over his nose. "Why would she smell blood? What blood? Don't tell me she thought she could smell somethin' from the murder site in the church. If she did, that nose of hers will go to science."

"She said this was living blood," Cyrus said. "Belongs to someone who isn't dead yet."

This time Spike didn't have a quick answer.

Madge Pollard's little dog slunk from beneath the desk, then looked up at Roche with her shiny black eyes. "Was Wazoo suggesting she knows someone else is going to be murdered?" He picked up the dog.

Cyrus scrubbed at his face. "That had to be what she meant. But sometimes—a lot of the time—I think she says what comes into her head just to hear her own voice."

The dog climbed high on Roche's chest and licked his face. She was into checking out the insides of ears, noses and mouths. Roche wiped the back of his hand across his mouth, but planted a kiss between the critter's ears just the same.

"Now Wazoo smells the blood of someone dead while they're still alive," Spike said, mostly to himself. "I wish she'd take her *feelings* somewhere else. What d'you think, Roche?"

"I didn't expect to walk into a minefield around here," Roche said. "I wanted to walk through the Cashman place and see how big it was." His sneaky way of getting to the rectory and—Bleu—had turned into an idea with possibilities.

"There's a lot of property there," Cyrus said. He didn't sound interested. "It isn't even properly staked. I wonder who Mr. Cashman left it to."

"The owner shouldn't be hard to find," Roche said. He liked Madge's little Millie. She rested her head on his shoulder and sighed now and then. "Public records would have that information. That parcel is huge. I had no clue."

"Do we care?" Spike asked.

Roche grinned at him. "I think you've been taking surly pills, Sheriff."

Spike mumbled something, then said, "I went to see Kate Harper today." He looked at Roche. "Do you know her?"

Roche said, "No. I don't think so. Should I?"

"I don't know. She's the woman Ozaire Dupre's busy painting as the arch villain of the piece. His version of the story is that she

murdered Jim—or had him murdered—because he left her everything in his will and she wanted the money."

"But you think that's hogwash?"

"She's a decent woman," Cyrus said before Spike could respond.
"I need to visit her again myself. She was widowed young. Never re-
married, but she and Jim were good friends."

"Real good, apparently," Spike said. "He's left everything to her in
her will. So she said, anyway."

"That's what Ozaire told us, too," Roche said.

Cyrus shook his head. "People will talk. It doesn't mean anything."

"Ozaire wants to be sure I look into things there," Spike said, not
looking too serious. "She'd never be able to physically attack Jim
herself, that's for sure. And she didn't like being questioned. She did
say something interesting, though."

Roche let Madge's pooch drape herself over his shoulder. He was
anxious to see Bleu.

"She told me to think about unsolved incidents from the past, as
she called them. Or I think that's what she was suggestin'. And there
was a lot about how I'm suspicious of her because I'm a man in a
man's world and I'm picking on a poor woman."

"What did she mean?" Cyrus asked.

Spike wrinkled his nose. "Damned if I know. Except she was suggestin' something happened here in Toussaint that was never sorted out
and I ought to figure out what it was. She reckons there's someone else
in town with good reason not to want the school built and Jim Zachary
was too enthusiastic about the project for this person's comfort."

"She was suggesting she's got some knowledge of who killed Jim?"
Roche said.

"Who knows?" Spike said. "That's the way it sounded, but nothin'
I said would make her open up any more than that."

"I can't imagine what she meant," Cyrus said. "Could be, she's just mad and lashing out. It's not fair for some to suggest she'd get rid of her best friend for his money."

"It didn't make any sense to me." Spike looked from Roche to Cyrus. "Roche hasn't been here long enough. Can you think of something I didn't get to the bottom of, Cyrus?"

"No," Cyrus said at once. "Is that all you wanted to ask me about?"

"For now," Spike said, sounding irritable. "I'll get back to you if I come up with something else you might be able to help with."

"Fine," Cyrus said. "Let's continue this in the kitchen. Madge and Bleu will wonder what's goin' on."

"I'll join you once this has been picked up." Spike indicated the box of burned books.

Madge met Roche and Cyrus in the doorway to the kitchen, a finger to her lips. "Bleu's asleep," she whispered. "Come quietly. I can't let her stay that way or she'll never move her neck again, but I don't want her shocked awake."

Cyrus tiptoed just inside, but Roche followed Madge quietly until he saw Bleu, her head and arms resting on top of the kitchen table.

Her blond hair shone in what was left of the daylight. He moved closer and looked down on her slim neck. Everyone was vulnerable in sleep but she looked especially so.

Without waiting to see what Madge had in mind, he rubbed Bleu's back lightly and bent over her. She took a deep breath, turned her face to the side.

Her eyelashes flickered.

"Hey, sleepyhead," he whispered. "You need to be in bed."

Her eyes opened. She stared at him without lifting her head. Then jerked upright. "Oh, good heavens," she said, rubbing her face and running her fingers through her hair. "I must have gone to sleep. How funny."

The rest of them laughed. "It might be strange if you'd had any rest in the last almost two days," Madge said.

Bleu blinked and concentrated on Roche, which he didn't mind at all. "You've got a friend," she said, yawning and pointing at Millie.

He'd gotten used to the dog. "Just giving her a ride."

"I've got to make coffee for Spike," Cyrus said.

"And me," Bleu said. "I'll never make it home otherwise."

"I'll take you," Roche said promptly.

Bleu gave a lopsided smile. "Thank you, but where I go, my car goes. Leaving it behind last night caused enough trouble."

I don't know how much longer I can wait for you. And it isn't just more conversation I need.

"Let me hold Millie," Bleu said. "I'm going to have a dog one day. Michael never… I couldn't have one before." She got up, as if trying to cover her confusion, and stroked Millie.

He held quite still. This had to be a new beginning for him with Bleu. He would be angelic around her. The thought almost made him laugh. One way or another, she would learn to trust him, and he intended to make sure that was a good idea.

"Come on, baby," she said, trying to lift the dog away from Roche. Millie didn't cooperate.

"You'll just have to be masterful," he said, and smiled. If he could keep her close to him a little longer, he'd do whatever it took.

Cautiously, she looked behind his shoulder to see Millie's face.

Roche got a spine-locking brush of Bleu's breast across his arm— and the soft touch of her hair on the backs of his hands.

"Come on," Bleu wheedled.

If he looked up, Roche knew he'd catch Cyrus and Madge watching.

"I'd better take her," Madge said. "She embarrasses me. She's such a little slut."

What followed was an example of the pregnant pause before Madge said, "Why would I call her that? I've never called anyone that, ever."

"I'll get her," Bleu said. She held out her hands.

Millie pulled back a fraction.

"Be good," Bleu said. But she gave up on being discreet and lifted the dog. Her hips connected with Roche's body and he locked his knees. He enjoyed every second.

"Got you," Bleu said triumphantly and stepped away—to Roche's disappointment.

He glanced at her white blouse, through which he could see the suggestion of a bra that might be pink.

Anyone who looked at the lower regions of his anatomy would see he was a man in pain.

He turned away and sat at the far end of the table.

Cyrus carried mugs of coffee over, and a can of the cashews he was never without. Then he sat down, threw a nut in the air and caught it in his mouth. Roche looked at Madge and grinned.

He wondered if the two of them realized that their happiest smiles were for each other, that they came alive when they were together.

And he thought *he* had problems.

"So," Cyrus said. "What are you thinking about—with that Cashman property?"

Madge slid into a seat and Bleu sat down again, the dog cradled in her arms.

"I think it should be considered as a location for this new school you want," Roche said.

The other three gave him their attention.

"It doesn't belong to St. Cecil's," Cyrus pointed out. "And we've already got a site we can rebuild on."

Roche looked at Bleu. "Is there enough room for the school buildings there?"

"Marc Girard has been advising us," she said. Marc, married to Dr. Reb, owned an architectural firm in New Orleans. "He's got all the plat maps and he says we can make a start."

She didn't look happy.

"A start?" Cyrus said.

"The new building would be four times as big as the old one and should accommodate the children who might come for several years. But space could become a problem then. These are things I intend to present at the potlock over at Pappy's next week."

"What happens when we don't have enough space anymore?" Madge said.

"First we go to portables, and eventually we figure out how to expand more. We may have to consider acquiring land for a satellite campus."

Spike came in, helped himself to the coffee and joined the rest of them.

"We're talking about the school," Cyrus told him. "Looks like we've got big space problems before we even get started."

"So you start small and expand as you can," Spike said. "My Wendy says she wants the school built fast."

Wendy Devol, Spike's daughter by a first marriage, was around eight and didn't mince words.

"I haven't seen that Wendy for too long," Madge said. "I leave Rosebank before she's about in the morning and get back after she's in bed. I'll have to make sure I do get to see her, and David."

The expression on Spike's face became contented. He adored his children.

"I'm going to find out about the Cashman land," Roche said. "What do you intend to do about a multipurpose center, Bleu?"

"It's only been about ten days since I realized it was such an issue. I'm thinking about asking Marc to work on using the area where the parish hall is and build something a bit bigger, with two stories. What do you think?"

After a silence that seemed to stretch, Madge said, "The parish hall was built at the same time as the church. They're both pretty old. People want a new adult facility, but I think if we try to touch that hall, we'll find we've got preservationists breathing down our throats."

"I'd be one of them," Cyrus said. "Sorry, Bleu. And the idea of acquiring another parcel of land is great, but we'd never raise the money. This isn't a wealthy town. I wish what we already own was bigger. When the Church bought the parcel for St. Cecil's and the other buildings that went up, they didn't anticipate there would ever be such a need for growth."

"Maybe we should give the whole idea up," said Madge. "Jim's already dead and the note with the ashes was a threat."

"What note?" Bleu said.

"Just a silly note," Cyrus said.

Madge glared into her coffee. She reached for the cream and poured in more. "What it said meant the killer was threatening to burn the new school down and kill the children inside," she said.

Roche glanced at Spike and could see he was irritated at having his evidence chatted about.

"I expect Spike would like us to promise that what we've been talking about stays here," Roche said.

"I'd appreciate it if you didn't repeat anything you've heard," Spike said. "But you can't let someone bully you into abandoning your plans. The school must go ahead, Madge. Even if it didn't, we'd still have a murderer to catch."

The dog had fallen asleep again, this time draped over Bleu's shoulder. She supported Millie's bottom and stroked her gently. "He'll be caught," she said, sounding convinced.

"Let's hope it happens before someone else dies," Cyrus said.

Madge rested her chin in her hands. "Meanwhile, we'll be wondering about what Wazoo is or isn't smelling," she said.

"Fresh blood that's still pumping," Bleu said and rolled her eyes.

"Don't," Madge said and shuddered.

Cyrus offered her the can of nuts and she took several. Then she set them on the table; Roche figured she'd only accepted them to be polite.

Spike sighed and rubbed the back of his neck. He had his Stetson balanced on one knee. "Well," he said. "Me, I've got one big question to answer before I move on."

"Okay," Bleu said. "So tell us what big question."

"How did someone drop that box at the front door and get away so cleanly? So far, we've got nothing, and it'll be dark soon. The front of the house will have to be taped off, Cyrus."

"No problem," Cyrus told him. "I've got another big issue to deal with, too. We'd better get the word out that mass will be held in the parish hall until the church is available again."

"What kinds of things are you looking for out there?" Roche asked Spike.

"I'd take anything. Gum wrappers with big, fat fingerprints on 'em. A dropped wallet complete with ID." He made a grumbling sound. "I'm not even amusing myself. It's rained, there should be some footprints. My men didn't find any. No fibers or fragments of fabric anywhere. No hairs. No convenient puddles of body fluids. They scoured it. Nothing."

"There are footprints out there," Roche said.

"Yeah, yours." Spike shook his head. "You aren't so funny tonight, either."

"Mine are there, but they aren't the only ones. There are some that show in the soft ground just out from Cyrus's office—the side, not the front. I didn't think anything of it, except it seemed funny for them to come from that side and head up toward the lane, when it would be quicker to go straight out that way." He nodded toward Bonanza Alley.

Spike was on his feet. "The fewer people who take a look at this, the better. I'll have to get casts made of the prints. Let's hope there's something unique on the bottoms of his shoes."

Roche's stomach flipped. He hoped he wasn't starting a lot of trouble for someone completely innocent.

"Spike," he said. "The prints are from high heels. The footprints are a woman's."

Chapter

10

Bleu jumped when the door closed behind Roche. He had asked again to take her home, and she had refused.

She hadn't missed the long look he'd given her, or her own longing to say she'd go with him.

Cyrus and Madge had followed Spike back to the offices.

The only sound in the kitchen was the loud tick from an old clock on the wall.

Bleu went to a window overlooking Bonanza Alley. Roche's car was still there. He had paused to stare toward the bayou. Looking at him tightened her belly—and the muscles in her thighs. She remembered what had happened when she'd been alone with him earlier and her face burned. Roche had behaved as if he didn't know she was climaxing, but she didn't believe him.

It had felt so good, even if she had made a fool of herself.

The breeze ruffled Roche's hair. With his hands on his hips, every lean, muscular inch of him looked rigid.

Bleu turned away, wishing she'd been nicer to him before he left, that she'd made a move to arrange another time to be with him.

Too late now.

She didn't want to let him go. A breath caught in her throat. It seemed impossible, but she wanted to be alive again and with Roche.

When she glanced back outside, he was getting into his car.

Running, yanking the door to the yard open and leaving it to slam shut on its own, she dashed across the grass to the fence and pulled open the gate. Her sandals scrunched on the gravel parking strip and small rocks lodged under her bare feet.

"Roche," she called, but he had already started his engine.

In the middle of the alley, she stopped and let her hands fall to her sides. The car was moving.

"Roche," she said quietly, and felt sick with disappointment.

As his car passed, he glanced over his shoulder and saw her. The brakes squealed when he slammed them on and in seconds he was out of the vehicle and striding to meet her.

"I almost missed you," he said, breathing hard as if he'd been running. The hope in his eyes quickened Bleu's heart. "Changed your mind about that ride home?"

She shook her head and saw his shoulders drop slightly. "We were supposed to go out on a date the other evening," she said. "Well, not a date exactly—"

"I asked you out," he said, standing so close she had to look up at him. "That's called a date."

Bleu nodded. "It's probably been too long a day, but I wondered if you'd like to grab a meal with me a bit later. I think I need a nap first, and you probably do, too."

Roche stared at her silently.

She gave a small laugh and crossed her arms. "Of course you're too tired. Forget I said anything."

Her hair blew across her face and she pushed it away.

"You're asking me out?" Roche said, a slow smile spreading. "What do you have in mind?"

She smiled back. "I could make a supper reservation for us and where we go would be a surprise." It would be a surprise to her, too, since she didn't know anything about restaurants in the area. "There are a couple of places I've heard about up toward Lafayette." Her flash of bravery began to fade. "You think about it. If you want to go, give me a call."

"I'm calling," he said. "I want to go. Thanks."

Chapter
11

That evening

"I knew it," Roche said to Bleu. "You've got a secret life. I didn't know this place existed. But I don't get out much."

Her laugh was more embarrassed than amused. "You ought to change that," she said, her voice all but lost in the heavy blues beat from a small, gravelly group. "You know what a woman of the world I am—flitting around the countryside every night. If you're looking for the latest hot spot, just call me."

He put his elbows on the table in their booth and grinned at her—not that she was likely to see the finer points of his facial expression in the gloom. "Auntie's, huh? Interesting place. When's the last time you were here?"

She inclined her head. "Well—when I remember, I'll let you know."

Her choice made Bleu uncomfortable. Rather than ask for advice, she had picked a place out of the Lafayette telephone book. Fine dining and music sounded great, but now she wasn't sure exactly what it was supposed to mean. Little food seemed to be served.

"I like all the red," Roche said.

"It *is* very red in here," Bleu said. In fact, everything was red, including the lighting. Velvet-covered booths, tablecloths and napkins, walls, hanging glass lamps, carpets, the abbreviated sequined tuxedos worn by the waitstaff—male and female.

"I like the music, too," Roche said.

Bleu listened and nodded. "Me, too." Even if it *was* suggestive and heavily moody.

A waiter, his chest bare under his jacket, but with a bow tie in place, lighted a candle on the table. "Is this your first time at Auntie's?" he asked.

"Yes," Bleu said at once and bowed her head.

Roche laughed and echoed, "Yes." He asked her if she liked champagne and ordered a bottle when she said she did. Bart, who would be "looking after them," giggled and told them to "trust him," with "nibbles."

"I'm sorry," Bleu said when they were alone again. "I was trying to be sophisticated and find a nice place. This is awful."

"Don't be sorry," Roche said. "I want to be with you and I don't care where that is." He flexed muscles in his jaw. He couldn't seem to stop himself from being too honest around this woman.

Bleu looked sideways at him. Her eyes shone in the candlelight and there wasn't a hint of a smile on her face.

"Did I just say too much?"

"No," she said. "I'd have to be fool to think that was too much. I wanted to be with you, too. That's why I chased after you the way I did."

"D'you want to tell me what changed your mind about coming out with me? Or being anywhere at all with me, alone?"

Bart arrived with a champagne bucket, complete with bottle up to its neck in ice, and glasses. The nibbles were a small dish of nuts and another of pretzel sticks.

"How about some oysters to go with that?" Bart asked and winked at Roche.

"Yes," Bleu said. "We'd like that, wouldn't we?"

Roche nodded. If he suggested they go somewhere else, she would be mortified. And he'd meant what he said about only wanting to be with her. He prayed things were as sleazy as they were going to get.

The champagne wasn't bad. Roche felt almost ridiculously grateful, and pleased when he saw Bleu wrinkle her nose and look happy. He'd have to remember that bubbles relaxed her.

There were all kinds of bubbles...

Her dress—simple, white, sleeveless with a round neck and straight skirt—couldn't have looked better if it had been designed for her. Her only jewelry was a pair of crystal earrings that shot sparks of reflected red across her neck.

He drank deeply. Tonight, he was Mr. Model Date. He would not do anything but respond to her, with restraint. Tonight, he would prove how unthreatening he could be.

"This is good," Bleu said. Champagne wasn't something she'd had often, but she liked it. Roche, relaxed, more approachable than she ever remembered him, smiled back at her and managed to turn her heart more times than could be good for it.

He'd removed his black silk sport coat and his hair looked a little damp and very dark against an open-necked white shirt.

She would not start telling herself she didn't belong with a man like him.

Things were going to change with her. She would get past putting herself down and learn to feel desirable again. With enough guts, she could let go of her fear of getting close to a man—to this man.

"Oysters off your starboard side," Roche muttered.

She didn't have a chance to move her head before "Shelly" arrived, also without a shirt beneath her sequined jacket.

"I'm going to make these easy for you," Shelly said, leaning over the table until Bleu found the only safe place to look was at her own hands.

Shelly shucked oysters like a pro. "What else can I do for you?" she said.

"I can't think of a thing," Roche said, doing his best to avoid a view of naked breasts some plastic surgeon must have ordered special implants for. They were huge, with saucer-sized nipples.

He saw Bleu glance up and take a deep breath. Now, hers were the breasts he wanted to see naked.

"People don't know we specialize in couples," Shelly said.

Bleu frowned at her.

"You're fine where you are as long as you're comfortable. We insist our customers are comfortable. But when you're ready, so are we."

Stunned, Bleu had difficulty meeting Roche's eyes. "Is this a...*place?*" she asked when Shelly left.

"I'm not sure what it is," he said honestly. "But it's interesting." He carried one of her hands to his mouth and kissed it lightly. And he set it gently back on the table afterward.

"Yes, yes it is." She emptied her champagne and Bart appeared to refill the glass.

In the booth across from theirs, a couple settled in and wrapped their arms around each other. They kissed, and kissed. The man, beefy, with slick hair, pulled at his partner until he lifted her bottom from the seat. Unfazed, she knelt and pushed her hands into the back of his pants, pulled out his shirt and plunged her hands back inside.

Bleu glanced at Roche but he wasn't taking any notice of the performance. She felt a little dart of heat between her legs, crossed them at once and felt annoyed with herself.

"It's been a hell of a day," Roche said. "Did you sleep?"

They'd hardly spoken on the drive north and Bleu was relieved to feel looser, even if the couple next to them were embarrassing. "A bit. It felt good. How about you?"

He touched the tip of her chin and smiled. "Not a whole lot."

"Oh." She frowned. "If you're too tired—"

"I'm not," he said. "I didn't sleep because I was waiting to see you. Are we going to get to know each other, Bleu? No pressure?"

"I want to." It was true, why not tell him?

The couple in the other booth got champagne—no nibbles. Their waiter sat in with them, cozying up until the woman became a voluptuous, giggling sandwich filling. Whatever they discussed brought loud laughter and a lot of head nodding.

Giggles' boyfriend was a generous guy. When she gave the waiter a lingering kiss and something that made him squeal, "ooh," before he left, she was immediately welcomed back into another embrace.

"Why did you want us to get together tonight?" Roche asked.

She didn't know how much to say. "I haven't been fair to you. Or me. You don't need to hold a therapy session, but I am still getting over a bad marriage."

It touched him that she was honest. "You can talk to me about anything," he said. "Or nothing."

"I don't have a lot of confidence," she said, and hated the way it sounded. "That's not what I meant to say. I wasn't encouraged to be confident, but I'm too strong to let someone else destroy me. I'm getting back into living again and I like it." She gave him her brightest smile. And she meant what she said, darn it. Maybe she had a long way to go, but she was on her way. Coming out with him tonight proved that.

"You *are* strong," he said. She would be, he thought. These were the first steps and he admired her courage.

For himself, the increasing abandon of their neighbors was causing reactions he couldn't completely squelch. The pair needed a room and he had no doubt there were plenty available somewhere around here.

"You've never married," Bleu said. "You seem like someone who should have a wife and children."

He met her eyes steadily. "For years, there wasn't time. Then there wasn't anyone who interested me in the right way."

The woman next to them sat on her companion's lap. He encased her middle with his big hands and slipped them up until her breasts were half-exposed beneath a ruckled top. He limbered up his thumbs on her nipples and she writhed, gasping. Evidently bras were out of favor.

He ought, Roche thought, to get Bleu out of here. But if he made a big deal of it, she'd figure he'd been spending too much attention elsewhere or that he thought she was too naive to cope.

Bleu wished Roche would hold her hand. She spread her fingers on top of the table so that they came close to touching his wrist.

"You must have been young when you got married," Roche said.

"Yes." She must have been wrong when she'd been convinced Roche knew the details about Michael, but she didn't want to think about that now. A soft warmth had crept through her veins. Studiously, she avoided the antics at the next table but couldn't miss everything. For the second time tonight, bare breasts were on display and this time she supposed they were nice, nice enough for the man to look at them like gourmet ice-cream sundaes before sucking on one nipple then the other.

Bleu cleared her throat and moved a little closer to Roche.

"Would you like to leave?" he said. "It's getting late to find a meal, but we'd get coffee somewhere."

Because he thought she was a wimpy, fading flower with no experience? "It's comfortable here," she said. "The music's nice."

Roche knew she wasn't comfortable, but it wasn't his place to say so.

"Did Spike say anything important about his investigations?" Bleu asked. "Madge called me after I got home and said the three of you had been talking back in her office. She thinks Spike's got an idea about the killer." It was hard not to sound desperately hopeful.

"He's trying to think of some crime that was never solved. Here in Toussaint. He called it an incident, so I suppose he means a crime. I don't recall anything. How about you?"

"I've only been here a few weeks," she reminded him. "Nobody's said anything to me."

He spread his arms along the back of the booth and looked thoughtful.

Bleu looked at his solid chest, the crook of his shoulder, and had an urge to cuddle against him. He would put one of his arms around her and hold on. Then she'd tip her head back and he'd kiss her.

"There was a girl who went missing," Roche said slowly. "A teenager home from school on vacation. I think it turned out she'd run off with a boyfriend. I never heard she was found dead."

Bleu sighed. "Thank goodness. There's always so much trouble."

"Fortunately there isn't always a murder in St. Cecil's."

"Poor Jim." Bleu couldn't stand thinking about such a gentle man being exposed to horrendous violence.

"Bleu, I'd like us to go out," Roche said. "I know we are out. I mean, would you like to consider getting together now and then?"

She hid her smile.

"Don't answer until you're ready," he said.

Bleu rested her face against the back of the booth, the top of her head brushed the underside of his arm. "I would like that," she said quietly. She looked at his mouth. The outline was definite, the lower lip fuller than the top and the corners flipped up. She passed her tongue over her own mouth.

"That's great," he said, giving her chin a mock tap with a knuckle.

Noises next door turned from panting and grunting to escalating sounds of runaway excitement.

Bleu turned her head before she could stop herself. Giggles had her short skirt fashioned into a belt and her partner sagged in the booth while he bopped her up and down on his lap.

"Oh, dear," Bleu said weakly.

Roche took her by the hand and pulled her from their booth behind him. Bart appeared, all smiles to offer them "whatever their hearts desired," and Roche pushed some bills into his hand.

"Night," Roche said with a sloppy salute.

He strode outside with Bleu and settled her in his car.

Her pulse thudded in every place a pulse could thud. She wiggled a little and forced her breathing to settle down. When had she turned into a sex-crazed creature ready to react to any stimulus?

Roche got in beside her, and she sat with her knees primly together when she smiled at him. "I guess it takes all kinds," she said. "I don't think I'd make it as a concierge."

His smile charmed her—all the way from her brain, through every possible spot on the way to her toes. "That would depend on the clientele you were trying to satisfy. Let's get you home."

He patted her hand on her leg and she swallowed. Turning toward the passenger window, she let her eyes close. When had she last felt like this? Pliable, sensual and longing for a man's warmth and strength? Bitterness opened her eyes fast. Regardless of how long ago it had been, she hadn't been fulfilled.

They drove through a pleasant night. Roche smiled at her often. She felt his contentment. When they got to her place, she would get past all the inhibitions and ask him in. He wasn't rushing her along. She had nothing to fear from him and just to sit with him close beside her and share a comforting hour would feel so good.

"Tomorrow, I've got to catch up," she said, scrambling for anything at all to say.

"I'm sure. I'll be busy myself for the next couple of days. Out at the clinic. Things are still very slow in town."

"That'll change," she told him. She couldn't think of anything she'd like better than an excuse to sit and talk to Roche Savage, to have him listen to her, and look at her.

"It will in time," he said. "I admit I'm worried."

"About getting enough patients?" He surprised her.

"No, no. It's early yet to hope for progress, but someone killed Jim, and they were making a point."

"It's funny," she said. "But we could never find out who did it. What if it was someone passing through? Maybe robbing the collection boxes, and Jim caught them."

He glanced sideways at her. The dashboard light did nice things for his features. "Do you really think that?"

"No. Anyway, Sam Bush counts the money from the boxes and he'd have said if something was different."

"Try not to think about it all the time," he said.

They'd entered the streets of Toussaint and set off into the neighborhood that eventually petered out into the almost undeveloped area where Bleu lived.

If he asked her out tomorrow, Bleu intended to go. Not back to Auntie's or anywhere like it, though. She blushed at the thought. In her whole life she'd never seen anything like that.

She shifted in her seat again. A woman shouldn't get all sexy because of a thing like she'd just seen. Should she? Roche didn't seem affected by it.

He drove up the cul-de-sac, put on the emergency brake and got out.

Bleu let him come around and open her door—and help her get out. With a hand at the back of her waist, he ushered her up the front steps, took her key and opened the front door.

She faced him and looked up under the light on the wall. "I don't know what to say except, that was wild and I ought to be embarrassed."

He chuckled. "Chalk it up to *the education of Bleu*. Not exactly what you need, but part of life. Forget it. I really enjoyed being with you. Thank you."

"Thank you," she said and stepped a little closer. "You're really good company. Will you forgive me for standing you up? That was so childish of me. I think I got cold feet."

"Understandable," he said. "You didn't know if you could live up to my charm."

She bowed her head then looked at him through her lashes. "Something like that. Would you like to come in for that cup of coffee you suggested earlier?"

Roche rubbed her cheek with the back of a hand, then replaced his hand with his lips. He kissed her lightly and stood back. "It's been a long day. Get inside and lock up."

Her head buzzed. Goose bumps popped out on her legs. "Yes. Of course. Good night." Only then did she realize he hadn't even turned off his car engine.

"I'll talk to you soon," he said.

"I'll look forward to it."

"Night." He took a couple of downward steps.

Bleu went inside, locked the door and sat on the bottom step of the stairs. She crossed her arms and rocked. *Darn him, anyway.*

On the way back to Rosebank, Roche drove faster than was wise. Eventually, when he became aware of dark trees becoming a blur against a pewter sky, he forced the brake to the floor and fishtailed off the road and on to a rocky shoulder.

He didn't remember the last time restraint had cost him so much. She would have had him come in, and who knew what that would have led to?

"Oh, my God!"

It could have come to his getting carried away, persuading her into what would have been abandoned sex—he was worked up enough to get so wild he might or might not make her run, screaming, from him.

Okay. He was a saint. But he would have to give himself some breathing room or Saint Roche's halo would get confiscated.

Chapter
12

Early evening, two days later

"Would you like a glass of wine before you go?" Cyrus asked. "Or something else?"

"Wine would be lovely." Relief lightened Madge's heart. Cyrus was accepting that she had a date—and she *would* like a glass of wine just to relax with for a few minutes.

"When's Sig arriving?"

Madge looked at her watch. "He called and said he had a heavy clinic afternoon. He should be here in about forty-five minutes."

She watched Cyrus get up. It was special when a man felt familiar, but still managed to speed up your pulse. He was like that. In an old, green-check shirt and black pants, and wearing scuffed black loafers, he looked comfortable...and irresistible at the same time.

Madge smiled at herself. She had a bad case; she'd had it forever. And it wasn't as if she'd ever been a contrary sort. There had never been a time when she'd pined for something she couldn't have—except for Cyrus.

"Red or white?" he said, picking up a bottle standing at the back of a counter. "I think this is going to be a good one. It's a Cabernet Sauvignon—'76. I've been saving it."

She joined him at the counter. "What have you been saving it for?"

Above his collar, his neck turned a little red. "Something special. A celebration. I'm hoping tonight will be the start of something new and special for you."

He had a deep and rumbly voice, but it could still catch if he was emotional. It caught now, but he turned away and got out two glasses—two of the Waterford ones he'd told her an aunt had sent from Ireland when he was ordained.

Instead of following her instincts and protesting that he should not use the wine now, she said, "Thank you, Cyrus," and touched his back lightly.

"I've got an idea," he said, looking at her with suspiciously glittery blue eyes. "We had the old sitting room decorated because it's been a mess for years, but we still haven't used it. Let's inaugurate it now."

She smiled at him and nodded. Everything he said was about "we." Wazoo had been right to notice that she, Madge, also said it. How long ago had she, Madge, become a "we" with Cyrus?

Carrying both glasses, he led the way into the corridor outside the kitchen and turned right. He managed to open a door—this one refinished and glowing. The next project would be the entire corridor and front hall.

"It's so lovely," Madge said. She had better think so, since picking the fabrics, wall colors and furniture had all been left to her.

"I'm glad you put in the fans," Cyrus said.

He glanced at her sideways and they both laughed. Cyrus had thought the fans a frivolous waste of money at the time.

They sat down, one at either end of a couch covered with a red lotus-blossom design. Floor-to-ceiling drapes over the tall windows were striped and banded at the top with the same lotus blossoms. Madge sighed and worked her way farther into her corner of the couch.

"Look at you," Madge said suddenly. "I can read your mind. You think the money should have been spent on something else. But this room was falling apart."

Cyrus looked at her thoughtful brown eyes, her short, shiny, curly dark hair, and at that moment he would have signed for anything she wanted to do around here.

He felt the way she scrutinized him. There was no other word for it. Fate had dealt them a bitter lot, but then, it had also allowed them a lot of joy.

Madge rubbed her hands together and turned her face away from him. She didn't usually wear pants, but she had on jeans today, and a white blouse. Very nice they looked, too, although he always preferred her in a dress.

"Are you going to drink both glasses of wine?" she said, the corners of her mouth twitching.

"Oh. Sorry. I was taking another good look around in here. I think we should use it more. It's very comfortable and...*chic.* That's the word. My parents were *tres chic,* so I should know."

Madge gave him an odd look, and he realized he'd never mentioned his family before, except for his sister Celine, who lived with her husband, Jack Charbonnet, and their children, in New Orleans.

"Do you think I should run upstairs and get changed?" Madge asked. "Sig didn't say where he's taking me, but I did bring a dress with me."

She asked as if he were her brother or father. "Yes," he said, and his throat hurt. "Go do it, then maybe we'll still have a few more quiet minutes. I want to talk to you about the school and the center.

I'd be a liar if I said I wasn't concerned. But we're goin' to get it done. Maybe we'll have to think smaller is all."

"Cyrus…" She wanted to talk about the heaviness pressing in on everyone in town. At the same time she wished she could shut it out. "It's been three days and there's nothing. Not a word about the case going forward."

He sucked in his bottom lip. "Yes. From the complaints, you'd think people were mad at being questioned, but I think they're grateful for any sign that official wheels are turning."

Spike and his people continued to go door to door, questioning, searching for any small fragment that might lead to a break in the case. "Bleu's very quiet, isn't she?"

His expression became speculative. "Very. Does she seem as if she's only worried about the parish? And Jim, of course. Or do you think there's something else?"

"Nothing gets past you," Madge said. "Of course there's something—or someone—else. Roche." The idea worried her.

"They aren't talking about it to anyone else," Cyrus said. "We'll find out if we're supposed to."

"I don't think—"

"Get changed," he said. "Then you can make everything around here seem so plausible, I'll wonder why I ever worried at all."

"Exactly." She put her glass beside his on a brass table.

Madge left quickly. She wasn't a woman who needed a lot of fuss to make herself look lovely.

He got up and walked to a window. Colored lights from a long-ago party remained strung in the trees. Madge liked them, so they stayed, and he made sure any burned-out bulbs were replaced.

Madge had talked about how pretty a Christmas tree would look in here this year.

Families had Christmas trees. Priests didn't.

He was feeling sorry for himself, and God deserved better than that from him. When he took his vows, he committed his life to the Church and he didn't regret his decision.

If Sig Smith was the one for Madge, he had better treat her the way she deserved to be treated. At least the man was committed to Roche's clinic in Toussaint and seemed to like living in the town. And Roche said Sig was reliable. Roche trusted Sig Smith, and that should be enough for Cyrus.

It might be wrong, but Cyrus knew he wouldn't relax until he could see that Madge was happy with…another man. She needed marriage and children. Madge loved children.

There were other things he should be thinking about, like the senseless murder of a good man. With the exception of Ozaire, no one had a notion who had killed Jim. Or, if they did, they weren't sharing their thoughts.

Spike and his deputies must have interviewed every person in this town by now and learned nothing substantial. He intended to repeat the rounds of questioning and only grew more grim-faced and determined.

The phone rang, startling Cyrus. He picked up. "Father Cyrus Payne," he said.

"Father, this is serious," a man said. "I don't understand why there ain't nothin' been done to take the suspect into custody."

"Who is this?" Cyrus said.

"Why, it's Ozaire. You know me, Father."

Cyrus sighed and slid to sit on the couch again. "Yes, I do. How are you, Ozaire?"

"Mad, that's how I am. Excuse me for sayin' so, Father. What's the matter with Spike Devol? He's got all the proof he needs. What's he waiting for?"

An unpleasant feeling gripped Cyrus's stomach. Nothing stayed secret around here. "What would that be?"

"You just bein' difficult," Ozaire said. "Excuse me for sayin' so, Father. I know all about those footprints. A woman's footprints. I already told you what Kate Harper said about Jim. I told Spike, too, and I'm sure he talked to her. She needs to be picked up."

"And you, Ozaire, need to start using your head." Cyrus breathed deeply and tried to calm his thudding heart. "Who told you about the prints?"

"I've got my sources."

"Of course you do. I'm told Kate Harper has arthritis. She isn't someone who could climb around in high-heeled shoes."

Ozaire cackled. "Shows what you know. And shows how much you notice, too. Miz Harper, she loves to dance. Lil told me that's one of the things she had against poor Jim. He didn't dance. And the arthritis is in her neck, not her feet—if it's anywhere at all. You better get a good look at her shoes. There's some around here calls her Imelda."

Madge came through the door, her head tilted to one side while she put some sort of shiny thing in her hair.

"This is what I want you to do, Ozaire," Cyrus said. "Go to see Spike again and ask him your questions directly."

"But I thought you'd—"

"You thought I'd carry these tales of yours to Spike? I can't do that. He'll want to hear from you himself. I'm busy here, Ozaire. Look—"

"I'm not sayin' she did it herself," Ozaire interrupted. "Someone needs to look into any strangers in town. I reckon Kate hired herself a hit man."

Cyrus closed his eyes and made himself wait a moment. Then he said, "Thank you for calling, Ozaire. Look after yourself and God bless you."

When he put down the phone and looked up, Madge frowned at him. "What was all that?"

"Ozaire is still trying to convict Kate Harper of murder. Tomorrow, I'm going to visit her again, myself. She's got to know there are very few people who believe these crazy stories. And she'll have heard them by now, I'm afraid."

"She surely will," Madge said. She walked to the table and picked up her glass. She gave Cyrus his. "You're going to see her tomorrow, aren't you?"

He nodded.

"I'll come with you," Madge said. "I'm overdue to see her, anyway. Now let's have those few quiet minutes."

He tipped up his glass and swallowed some of the wine. It flooded him with warmth and he wished he could hold on to that.

What Madge had put in her hair was a comb. Along the top there were tiny blue crystals set very close together, covering the bar. The comb pulled her hair back at one side.

"I like your hair like that," he said. "And the comb. And the earrings!" He laughed. "Sapphire earrings look good on you."

"They're fake," she said, but she smiled with pleasure. "Pretty good, though."

Madge never wore much makeup. She didn't have a lot on tonight, but her eyelashes, always thick, looked even thicker and darker and she wore lipstick, a pinkish brown that showed off how pretty her full mouth was.

"Now you're checking out the makeup," she said. "Is it too much?"

"Oh, no. It's just right."

Her laugh made him smile. "As if you'd know anything about makeup," she said.

He gave her a withering look. "I know enough to recognize when a woman's turned herself into a clown or just added some nice color. You're in that group, the nice-color group."

"Thank you."

"And I've never seen you in a better dress." Shiny blue silk, the skirt fitted quite tightly and finished a couple of inches above the knee. The top was one of those halter things that crossed over in front and went around the neck, leaving her back bare. "Just...Sig Smith is a lucky man and he'd better appreciate it."

Madge laughed. "Are you sure you don't have a shotgun hidden away around here?"

"If I needed a shotgun, I probably couldn't wait to cock it before I pummeled the life out of Sig Smith."

Unfortunately, he meant every word he said and it was time to control himself. "Sit down," he said, eyeing her shoes. "And don't fall over in those things."

The heels of her shoes were high and narrow; thin straps fastened around her slim ankles.

He didn't want her to go out with Sig Smith, or any other man. Men were all instinct, and she would have the kind of effect on Sig that would have his instincts doing cartwheels.

Madge crossed her legs.

"Do you like the wine?" Cyrus asked. He concentrated on his own glass, but not before he'd seen her skirt rise high on her thighs, and looked at the vulnerable underside of her leg above one knee. Her shoulders and arms were smooth.

"It's good wine," Madge said. She looked too serious. "I completely forgot to ask if Millie is okay here with you overnight."

"I like her here," he said honestly. He liked the gentle warmth from the little body curled against him in his bed. "You just have a good time."

"What do you think about Roche's idea to see about the Cashman land?" Madge asked.

"It would be a great idea if St. Cecil's had any way of raising the money to buy it. If it's even for sale. But it's impossible."

"Probably," said Madge. "But I would like to know who owns that parcel, wouldn't you? I never thought about it before, but now it's a mystery. I don't know of anyone called Cashman. You know how I like to solve mysteries."

"I imagine Roche intends to do that," he said. With every second, he struggled between wanting her to stay and wishing she would go quickly so he couldn't look at her anymore or think about Sig Smith's hand at her waist, his thumb resting on bare skin.

He would want to kiss and hold her.

He would want more than that.

Cyrus looked away. He bent forward and propped his elbows on his knees.

"What is it?" Madge asked.

"Nothing." Now he sounded like a petulant teenager. "It's been a long, hard day. I'll try to catch up on some sleep after you leave."

"You should." She got up and sat down again, near to him. "You keep going as if you don't have the needs other people have. But you do, my friend." She rubbed her fingertips up and down his spine.

She didn't have any idea what she did when she touched him like that.

"I know when I'm pushing too hard," he told her. "I have ordinary needs that get in the way when I want to keep going. But I do know when I'm worn out. Don't worry about me."

"I do. I always will."

He checked his watch. "Shouldn't Sig be here?"

"Any time now," she said. "Unless he's got cold feet."

"Fat chance." Cyrus looked back at her. She wore a very light, lemon-scented perfume. "Where's Millie?"

"I fibbed." Madge winced. "I didn't forget to ask you if she could stay, I just took you for granted. She's on your bed. I told her she was staying with you and she went right up there."

Cyrus slept in a simple room on the third floor. It had been built beneath the rafters of the house and had a single dormer window. He felt peaceful there—most of the time. "You can take me for granted. You should hear what Millie and I say about you when you're not around."

She giggled, then hitched at the bodice of her dress.

"Is that thing behind your neck going to stay?" The bow she'd tied seemed ready to unravel.

Madge turned away from him. "Make sure it will. Put a knot in it, then tie the bow."

Bows were not Cyrus's forte but he dutifully undid the one that was ready to come undone, looked over her shoulders to make sure he had the fabric even and straight. He felt the weight of her breasts and might as well have been kicked in the gut.

"Do you want me to do it?" Madge raised her arms, showing the side of a breast. How pale the skin was there.

"I can do it." Once he concentrated he got a fresh knot tied with little problem. "Maybe I should just put the ends flat. The bow sticks up a lot on top of the double knot."

"Good idea."

Cyrus spread the ends of the ties against her back, smoothing away wrinkles. This should feel forbidden to him, but it didn't. Such a simple, but intimate gesture seemed natural, right.

"That looks okay." He tweaked one last time, let his fingertips drift down over her shoulder blades, and moved away. He picked up his wine again.

"Thank you." Madge still faced away from him.

The front doorbell rang and Cyrus sprang to his feet. "That'll be Sig."

"Stay here," Madge said, standing herself. "You don't have to greet someone here to see me."

"It's more appropriate," Cyrus told her, waving her back onto the couch. "Sit there and sip your wine. Look nonchalant. Not a bit eager. It won't hurt for him to know I'm responsible for you."

"You're not," Madge said, but she sat down yet again.

"You spend most of your time here with me. You have no male relatives to look after you. I *am* responsible for you. That's the way it is."

Chapter
13

He left the room before Madge could get another word in. Her head spun a little and she wasn't sure if it was the partial glass of wine on an empty stomach—unlikely—or the past half-hour in Cyrus's company. The answer was a no-brainer. He watched over her like a protective father, or brother...or something else. He had become her family. A family of two members who had started to hurt each other.

She heard voices approaching. A laugh. The deep tones of two men.

"Hi." Sig Smith came into the room and walked straight toward her. He gave her a white box tied up with gold ribbon. "You don't have to wear this if you don't like it. But it smells nice anyway."

A little above medium height, buff, as they said, with a long, sun-bleached crew cut, very dark eyebrows and disconcertingly piercing gray eyes, Sig shifted from foot to foot a couple of times before he settled and smiled at her. That smile would be enough to stop most women in their tracks. Madge enjoyed it, until she noticed Cyrus's expression.

Her boss, her friend, had never looked so conflicted or so sad. She wanted to see Sig out, to tell Cyrus she'd made a mistake and wasn't interested in any kind of male partner after all.

Cyrus felt her eyes on him and flashed her a smile.

No other man's smile competed with Cyrus's.

"Come on," Sig said. "At least take a look at it. Your dog can wear it on his collar if it seems too much like something meant for a prom."

"She," Cyrus said.

The cool sound of his voice sent Madge's stomach toward her feet. Sig raised a brow.

"Madge's papillon is named Millie. She's a girl."

"Ah." Sig grimaced. "Sorry about that. I haven't really met Millie."

Quickly, Madge opened the white box and removed a gardenia corsage from a bed of green. She smelled the blossoms and closed her eyes. "They have to be the most beautiful-smelling flowers."

Sig took the corsage from her, pulled a pearl-studded pin from the back and placed the flowers on the left side of her bodice, just below the collarbone. Very carefully, he put two fingers behind the dress, against her skin and bent close to secure the pin through the florist's tape.

Once more she glanced at Cyrus, and this time she felt ill. His blue eyes could turn navy sometimes, usually when he was unhappy about something. They were navy blue tonight. He watched Sig with the closest thing to hate she had ever seen on Cyrus's face.

Cyrus didn't hate anyone.

This was her fault, and he would suffer because he'd blame himself for reactions he had sworn never to allow himself.

"I thought I'd take Madge to the new place, the supper club, Claude's. Would you like that, Madge?"

"I've never been there, but I've heard it's lovely." The new club had been opened a few miles east of Rosebank and the Savages' clinic. It was said to be very popular and very expensive.

"I expect you know all about our trouble here at St. Cecil's," Cyrus said, as if he hadn't heard Sig mention the club.

"Yes, indeed." Sig nodded. "Jim Zachary was a really good man."

"How would you know?" Cyrus asked, sounding unreasonably sharp.

"I don't normally speak about these things, but I guess it doesn't matter now. Anyway, you were Jim's priest. He was a patient of ours. Roche and I thought highly of him."

"Roche never mentioned treating him," Cyrus said.

Sig's dark brows shot up. "Which probably means I shouldn't have, either."

"We won't mention it, will we, Cyrus?" Madge said.

"Not unless it becomes necessary," Cyrus said. He wouldn't look at her. "You live in Toussaint, don't you, Sig?"

"I do, yes. Next door to the clinic on Cotton Street."

"That's what I thought," Cyrus said. "Just bring Madge back by here after dinner, and I'll take her home."

Madge hoped she wasn't as red as she felt. Saying anything at all would be a mistake.

"Wouldn't think of it," Sig said. "I can come right past Rosebank on my way back to Toussaint."

Cyrus was quiet a moment. "Yes. Well, I'll come and get you in the morning, Madge. They're taking their time with your car."

"They finished it today," she told him. "And they took it home for me. How's that for service?"

"It's good service," Cyrus said. He gave a forced smile and slapped his hands together. "Well, off you go, you two. Hope you got a reservation, Sig. They do say that place is busy."

"Yes, I did that."

"Good man." Cyrus thumped Sig on the back and urged him and Madge toward the front door like a pair of high schoolers.

Sig opened the door for Madge and she looked back at Cyrus. He gave her a wave and started to turn away. "See you tomorrow. Have a good time." Then he turned toward her again. "What about Millie? You'll probably want to stop and get her before you go home. Sig will need to get on, so I'll take you back."

She needed to cry. And she didn't want to go out. "Millie will be good, Cyrus. Her crate's in my office. If she get's rambunctious, just put her in there for the night."

Cyrus nodded. And felt a complete fool. But more than feeling like a fool, he had pains in his gut and the start of a sweat at his hairline, even though he was icy. "Of course Millie will be fine," he said, forcing a big smile. "We're going to practice bad habits until you get in tomorrow."

Madge gave him a puzzled look, but smiled when he did, and Sig ushered her outside.

Until he heard a car engine come to life, Cyrus stayed where he was, his heart beating hard.

The sound of the car faded into the distance, and he returned to the sitting room. He went to a window and looked out into the darkness of the backyard. Dark but for Madge's fairy lights and, more distantly, moonlight on the bayou.

Did a life alone make a man a better priest?

His own question shocked him.

Alone was the way he was, the way he was supposed to be and the way he would remain.

What he must do was obvious. No matter what it cost him, he would stay in Toussaint until Madge was settled and safe, then he'd ask for reassignment. After a sabbatical.

He didn't know if he could be the one to perform the marriage ceremony, but if that's what she wanted, he'd try.

When he turned toward the room, he ran into the back of the couch and paused to calm down. He was getting ahead of himself.

Quickly, he gathered the two glasses—still not empty—and took them to the kitchen in one hand.

Once more, he felt drawn to the window.

He faced what he'd been trying to avoid. What if this crazy killer decided that murdering Madge would be the way to stop the project? Murdering her and perhaps throwing her body in the bayou.

He should feel the same about the possibility of anyone getting harmed.

Anyone wasn't his Madge.

The sweat on his brow broke free and trickled down the sides of his face. The colored lights outside shot prisms in every direction and he looked at them as if through rain beating on glass.

There wouldn't be another attack until—and unless—the madman realized the project wasn't going to stop.

He could stop it, Cyrus thought. He'd have to make a special request now that the project was approved, but a man's death would be all the justification he needed. Not that Spike and his people were convinced Jim died because of the school. One of their theories was that the brochure had been meant to divert them from the real motive.

He could scarcely breath. Smith had looked handsome and perfectly dressed. He and Madge made a nice couple. The man looked at her...he looked at her as if he couldn't and didn't want to see anything else.

Isn't that what I want for Madge? Someone to adore her?

Pulling air in through his mouth, he approached the deep old enamel sinks. "Damn it," he said. Then he shouted. "Damn it, God. You ask too much."

A squeaky sound vaguely touched his mind, but now the kitchen turned gray. He passed the back of a shaky hand across his brow.

"No!" he yelled, and hurled the glasses into the nearest sink, smashing them into an explosion of crystal shards.

Cyrus took several steps backward, his head hanging down.

He heard the squeaking again and looked for the source.

Under the table, the glint of her black eyes scarcely visible, he saw Millie.

Grabbing a dish cloth, he wiped his face and threw the cloth aside again. Now he was so useless, he was into frightening five-pound dogs.

"Come here, girl," he said, stooping.

Millie zipped out and leaped into his arms.

Cyrus held her shivering body against him and took off along the corridor to the stairs. He didn't stop running until he reached his austere room under the eaves and fell to his back on the bed. He left the lights off and lay there, staring at the ceiling with the dog curled up on his chest.

Chapter

14

At the same time

Bleu pulled her Honda all the way into the carport. That way Roche would have plenty of room to park in the driveway behind her.

She pushed open her door and barely stopped it from slamming wide open and into an old bike left by some previous occupant of the townhouse. Excitement fluttered in her belly. If she didn't calm down, Roche would see how much it meant to her to see him after two days. That, or she'd make an idiot of herself in some other way.

Usually she avoided getting home after dark, but she'd spent the afternoon at Sam Bush's office and they'd worked late. At least he hadn't asked her out again, as she had feared he might. Sam was a lonely man. It had to be hard for him not to be free even though his wife had taken off.

Bleu liked Sam but he wasn't her type.

The light outside the front door had burned out. She unlocked the front door, put her bag down to hold it open and reached to unscrew the dead bulb.

As soon as she touched it, it flashed on and she jumped. Immediately, the light went out again, and she barely stopped the globe from falling. With a shaky sigh, she screwed it back in. She was too jumpy these days.

Roche would arrive in less than an hour—barely time for her to shower and be ready. And she had to decide what to wear for a date at home. He was cooking dinner!

Bleu smiled, but her tummy twisted. She shut the front door and ran upstairs to her bedroom. The mattress she slept on was made, and her green cotton quilt helped make up for the Spartan surroundings, including the lack of an actual bed. A tall, unfinished chest of drawers, two green-striped carpets and a straight-backed wooden chair made up the rest of the decor.

She threw her purse on the mattress and flung open a closet door. Somewhere, she had a pair of blue silk pants she hadn't worn since they were cleaned.

There they were. Carefully, Bleu put them down beside her purse.

Roche had called each day since the infamous date at Auntie's. Bleu flinched at the thought of the place being her own choice. When she was feeling sensible, she could laugh at herself and the spectacle they'd witnessed. She wasn't quite laughing now.

From the chest of drawers, she took a cotton sweater in a paler blue than the pants and dropped it on the mattress, too. Talking to Roche—he'd called more than once on each of the past two days—and starting to feel as if they were close had excited her.

His voice tightened her all over. Just the sound of him made her pulse race. But then she relaxed and felt warm and safe—and longed to be with him. There wasn't much mystery about all this. She'd started falling in love with him.

She slammed the drawer shut and leaned her weight on the chest.

Why should she be surprised that she reacted like a girl with a first boyfriend, dreamily imagining that this was a forever thing? Experience wasn't her middle name.

A violent thud came from behind her. Bleu shot around, her heart in her throat, blood pounding in her ears.

The noise came from the bathroom.

Uncontrollable shaking took over.

Another bang.

A tearing sound.

Bleu caught a toe in the nearest rug, stumbled sideways catching at emptiness and fell against the closet, her shoulder landing hard enough to rattle the doors.

Angry, deep-throated grunts grew louder.

The bathroom lay between her and the top of the stairs. She'd never make it out of the bedroom if someone opened that bathroom door and came for her.

Her cell was in the bag on the mattress.

Everything was too far away to help her.

And she couldn't seem to move.

The clock radio on the seat of her one chair blasted on. Loud enough so she could hear it when she was downstairs, yesterday she had thought to put it on a timer for safety reasons. Anyone managing to get into the house when she was at home in the evening would hear the noise and think there was someone up here.

Maybe they would.

Sweat drizzled down the sides of her face and the middle of her back.

Get the phone.

Grunts turned to hissing, then high-pitched howling and a crazed scratching on the other side of the bathroom door.

The tension ebbed. Bleu still shook but she giggled and felt ridiculous. A *cat* was shut in the bathroom, probably the big tabby that liked to sun himself outside her kitchen door.

He would be wild and dangerous when she let him out.

On her toes, she crossed the room. With her back to the wall, she reached for the bathroom door handle, turned it sharply and pushed.

Shrieking, the tabby emerged, first hunched down and spitting, then leaping and throwing himself downstairs, hissing with fury all the way.

Bleu wanted him out of the house. Now. She stepped cautiously down after him, listening so hard her ears popped, and walked into the one big room downstairs.

The end of the cat's tail disappeared through an open window above the sink, and the instant quiet drained any fight Bleu had left. She managed to get herself to that window and shut it tight.

This would teach her to be more careful. She always made sure all windows and doors were secure before she left in the morning, but this time she couldn't have checked that the catch was all the way down.

Now she really had to hurry, and on weak legs, Bleu rushed back the way she'd come. Last night, she had cleaned every inch of the place, and the flowers on her little table still looked fresh.

Her cell phone rang before she made it up the last couple of steps, but she reached her bag in time to answer.

"Hello," she said, not meaning to sound so frazzled.

"Are you okay?" It was Roche.

"Great," she lied, aware of a silly smile on her face. "Looking forward to seeing you." Now, a cool woman didn't blurt that out.

He didn't answer, or not immediately. When he did, he said, "I am so sorry, Bleu. This is awful, but I can't get there."

Her throat ached. Then she felt a little sick, and her eyes burned.

Ridiculous. Things happened. Disappointments happened all the time. "Boo," she said. "That's a shame. You've been working really hard, haven't you?" Unless he said otherwise, she would choose to believe that work was keeping him from their evening together.

"I have," he said. "But I didn't expect this one. I'll explain better when I see you."

Her breathing relaxed a bit. "I'll be interested." Psychiatry had begun to really intrigue her. Or perhaps she was hoping to find answers about herself. "What time do you think you'll get away?" It didn't matter if he was late.

"Not tonight, Bleu. I'm going to have to stand by. Are you going to forgive me?"

"There's nothing to forgive," she said and forced a laugh. "You're a busy man. Don't worry about me, I've got plenty of chores to catch up on." And she wasn't proud that she felt weak and like having a good cry.

Darn that cat.

"Thank you," Roche said. "I'm really bummed out. I'm glad you're more grown up than me."

He was kidding her, but she was glad he didn't know just how disappointed she was. "I'm a baby," she said. "But I'm not going to cry without an audience."

They both laughed.

"Is it all right if I call you first thing?" Roche said. "Are you going to the rectory?"

"Yes, and yes," she said.

"What time are you getting there?"

"Before you'll be ready to get up," she told him. "Just call my cell when you feel like it. Good luck tonight." Now she wanted to get off the phone and be miserable all on her own.

"Expect an early ring," he said.

Bleu smiled. "Okay, I'll do that."

"Tomorrow, then?"

It took her a few second to get a breath before she said, "Tomorrow. I'll look forward to it. Good night."

"Good night," he said, and they hung up.

Pull yourself together and grow up. After Michael, weakness had been the first item on her list of emotions that had to go.

Back upstairs she went. She wasn't interested in eating dinner anymore.

She hadn't told Roche about the cat, because he would have grilled her on how it got in and she didn't want to say she'd forgotten to close one of the windows.

The clothes she had chosen were quickly put away, and she pulled out her favorite pajamas instead.

Instead of a quick shower, she would take a long, hot bath in mountains of bubbles and read a book until she turned into a prune.

Locked in the bathroom, she checked for scratches on the back of the door and grimaced. The paintbrush would have to come out. The poor cat had terrified himself by shutting himself in.

The start of a headache niggled between her brows. The cat could have run inside through the front door while she was fixing the outside light.

She stripped off her clothes.

Air from the fan sent the shower curtain billowing inward. The current felt good. Bleu turned the faucets on and grabbed the edge of the curtain to pull it out.

On the bottom of the tub, in the first rivulet of water to shine its way over the porcelain, a pinkish-red streak wound a path.

Bleu gripped the curtain so tightly, a ring popped off the rod.

With a yank, she bared the tub.

In the bottom, with its head missing, lay the body of a chicken.

Chapter
15

Late that night

A high, clear moon silvered the trees on either side of the cul-de-sac. Roche took measured steps up Cypress Place. Carrying a peace offering, he had left his car around the corner so he wouldn't risk waking Bleu if her townhouse was in darkness. If it was, he'd leave.

There were lights burning on the lower floor.

A wiser man wouldn't feel so hopeful. In every indicator, he read that she seemed to be opening up to him, but he couldn't be sure that what she felt was even close to the way he wanted her.

A sensible man wouldn't be anywhere near her place at this time of night, but he wasn't sensible, only beyond being tired, and on fire to see Bleu.

Either she liked him or wanted to like him. He knew the signs; and he knew the signs that someone had been damaged. Bleu had been badly broken by some goon, but Roche had always felt confident he could fix anyone, given enough time.

He could fix Bleu, as long as he managed to keep the lid on his own little issue.

Keep the lid on the wild stuff, not on sex altogether. It doesn't mean endless abstinence, only restraint. I know what she could enjoy if she'd relax enough. No, not just enjoy. Holding back costs, but I've got to keep to the plan. If fate smiles on me—I'll blow your mind, Bleu.

In her driveway, he realized the unthinkable: he had the start of cold feet. Intruding at this time of night would throw her off balance—if she didn't die from shock first.

Roche backed down the driveway.

If he gave her a quick call and said he was outside, she'd want to at least say, "Hi."

She might think he was a crazed predator.

Maybe he didn't want to think along those lines.

Her number was programed. Juggling his packages, he gave the thumb to the necessary button, slammed the phone to his ear and looked for the Little Dipper.

Her whispered, "yes," came just as he was about to hang up.

"Are you asleep?" he whispered back.

Silence.

"I mean, did I wake you up?"

"Is this Roche?"

"How many men call you in the middle of the night?" he said at normal pitch.

"I didn't mean… No, I'm sorry, it's just that you didn't say who you are."

He listened to the tone of her voice and took note of each word she said. "Are you afraid of me?"

Her throat clicked. "No, of course not."

"Should *you* be apologizing because I did something as dumb as to call you at this hour?"

She didn't answer.

"*No.* And that's exactly what *you* should say. No, Roche. You're a damned nuisance and you wouldn't know 'appropriate' if it hit you in broad daylight. *I'm* sorry, Bleu. Now get to sleep, and I'll go home and behave myself." Sheesh, what a goddamn idiot he could be.

"No," she said quickly—and too anxiously, he thought. He heard her draw in a breath before she added, "You said you weren't coming, so you surprised me, is all. Where are you?"

"I'm...in your driveway. But I'm leaving and I really am sorry for interrupting you."

"No, don't go!" She breathed harder. "Would you like some...coffee? Or I do have some bottles of that lemonade with alcohol in it. They were in a basket from some ladies who welcomed me to the neighborhood. I forgot to buy more wine."

Roche chewed a hangnail. Dr. Roche Savage—the psychiatrist—stood in a woman's driveway after midnight, chewing a hangnail and having a long conversation with her on the phone.

"I just realized how ridiculous it was for me to come," he said. "Forgive me and I'll call at a more—"

"I'm glad you were stupid enough to come," she said, and he could hear...*desperation* in her voice? That couldn't be.

"You and I make quite the pair," she continued. "Are you sure you didn't go into psychiatry because *you've* got something emotional that needs fixing?"

"I thought that was the only reason for going into psychiatry," he said. *If she only knew.*

He laughed, but Bleu didn't.

The front door opened and she stood, a silhouette in the light.

"Come and have—" She let her hand and the phone, fall to her side. "Come on in and talk to me," she said loudly.

Relief actually weakened Bleu's knees. She clenched her hands but wanted, more than anything, to run and hold on to him.

Roche jogged all the way to her front door. For a moment, he stood there, looking down into her face. She wanted to cry and laugh at the same time. The cat, and the horrible chicken, had terrified her and, even though the whole thing had to be a nasty coincidence, she couldn't quite shake her dread.

"Straight on in," she said. "You know the way."

He did. And straight on in he went, but she could have sworn he considered kissing her before he did.

"I've been taking catnaps," she said behind him. "I can't stay asleep, though." Cats killed chickens; they killed much bigger prey than chickens.

"You're unsettled, that's why." He carried a case of wine. Also, dangling from his fingers, were two bags filled with groceries. He put the case on the floor, some cheese in the refrigerator and left the rest of what was in the sacks on a counter.

"You didn't need to bring anything here," Bleu said, and she heard how awkward she sounded.

"Nope. I didn't need to, but I wanted to. We may need a snack, and the wine is for when I visit. And I still have to cook you dinner soon, remember?"

She followed an urge to step outside. The moon lighted the landscape, but she didn't see anything move. Roche might be sympathetic if she told him what had happened, but he'd probably write her off as unbalanced if he found out she wondered if someone had deliberately set up the scene she found in her bathroom.

"What are you looking for?" he said from the kitchen.

"Nothing," she almost shouted and came into the house again.

From his expression, she knew that she hadn't covered the apprehension on her face quickly enough. She would not risk giving him a reason to question her stability.

Roche looked at Bleu carefully.

"I'll let you to put these things where they go," he told her.

She nodded, then shut the door and locked it.

How could he blame her for being jumpy? He didn't.

"Have you heard anything?" she asked, joining him in the kitchen. "Do the police have any leads yet?" A blue cotton T-shirt over what appeared to be a pair of pink-check pajamas looked cute on her. He hadn't noticed before that she had small feet and she painted her toenails. He did notice that she wore a bra. That was a shame.

"Have you?" she said.

Roche stared at her for an instant and said, "No one's been arrested, as far as I know." From what he saw and felt, she was a lot more than jumpy.

"No," she said, looking into the distance. "I didn't think so."

"It'll happen," he told her, and hoped they would like what happened.

"I was thinking about that land," Bleu said. "Cashman's. It's been on my mind."

He watched hope spark in her eyes and was glad he had at least something to tell her. "You really want something to come of that, don't you?" he asked.

"I had a dream," she said and her smile turned down. "I fell asleep on my Coca Cola banquette—"

"How would you do that?" Roche asked. "It's curved and there's a table sticking up."

"You kind of burrow along the seat from one end and there you are. The table overhangs you. It's a bit like camping out."

"Mm." He nodded and looked at the Coca Cola booth in the corner, still working for its living. "Lying on plastic sounds sticky. Don't you have a bed?"

"Yes, but it's upstairs."

"Is that a problem?" he asked.

She hunched her shoulders. "I prefer being down here with all the lights on."

Her honesty gave him confidence. He needed to have her trust.

"Tell me about your dream," he said.

"It was stupid. Someone came along and gave me the deed to the land so I could give it to the church. I kept thanking them, over and over. Only I don't know who it was."

Carefully, Roche held her elbow and walked her to the round table. Once she was seated, he went into the kitchen again and started opening and closing doors.

She didn't say a thing. Just sat there and watched with a little smile on her face.

Lemonade with alcohol in it.

Roche would have preferred one of the wines he'd brought, but hard lemonade it would be.

He opened the refrigerator again and there it was. With smooth efficiency, he swept out two bottles, unscrewed the pop-off tops with his bare hands and used two glasses from a draining rack.

Paper towels would serve just fine as napkins. He tore off two sheets and folded each one into four. These he put on the table with the glasses on top. "There," he said, and slid into the chair facing her. "Let's see how it tastes."

The stuff was strong. Roche liked it.

So, evidently, did Bleu. She drank down half the glass without stopping.

"That's refreshing," she said, inspecting the label. "Mm, I love lemonade. I'm glad you came."

Sometimes it was best just to let someone talk. Bleu was lonely and scared—that's why she hadn't gone upstairs to bed—and she was grateful for company, even his.

"You're quiet," she said.

"Just thinking," he said.

"About what?" Bleu said.

"Did you know that women always ask that question, but most men never do. Men think, 'She's thinking. Oh, good, that means I don't have to talk.' Then women get mad because the men don't say anything."

Bleu frowned. "So, did you just talk...or maybe what you said doesn't count. I don't think it counts as talking."

The lemonade was relaxing her. Roche made sure his expression was serious. "Yes, it does count. I wanted you to know I had that thought about men's as well as women's reactions. But I've got other things to say. I'm concerned about you, Bleu. Out here on your own, when there's a murderer on the loose."

"That's so nice of you to care." She smiled, then turned somber. "I keep thinking about Jim Zachary. I see him in that pew. Then I try to shut it out. Do you really think he died because of the new school?"

"It looked that way," Roche said.

"There's talk about the school being a diversion by someone who just wanted to kill Jim," Bleu said.

He could see how badly she wanted to believe the grapevine. "Possibly," he said.

They looked steadily at each other.

A window frame made the snapping sound that could come with settling in fairly new construction.

Watching Bleu, he frowned. She searched the kitchen and living room, turned all the way around in her chair, and when she faced him again, he saw the heavy pulse in her throat. She had been holding her breath and let it out in a rush, attempting a neutral expression at the same time.

Her effort didn't work.

"Are you okay?" he asked. "You're leaping out of your skin."

"I'm fine," she announced, her mouth in a straight line.

In other words *don't press me.*

"You don't think Jim's murder was a diversion, do you?"

"I think we're on the outside of this one," Roche said. And he detested not being able to get his hands on all the puzzle pieces Spike might already have.

"That part irks me, too," Bleu said. She turned her glass in circles on the tabletop. "You and I could be useful. We're both puzzle and problem solvers. Did you actually get a peek at the note?"

"The one with the box?" He shook his head, no. "But they admitted it threatened future school children. I'd like to know what was written, word-for-word."

"The original school burned," Bleu said. "A long time ago. Cyrus came years and years after it happened. No one talks about it."

"People put things behind them, even big things. Sometimes they bury the things they fear the most."

"I guess," Bleu said. "But the remains of the walls are there and they're scorched. Anyway, who knows why people do what they do?"

She fiddled with the edge of the table and watched her own fingers.

"Madge saw the note when the box was delivered," Roche said. He looked away.

"Yes…no!" Her laugh surprised him. "No, sir, I will not try to make my cousin squeal to me."

He raised both hands and tried to appear innocent. "Absolutely not," he said. "You're a woman of honor. Of course you wouldn't do that. Would you?"

Bleu leaned across the table and poked his arm. "Shame on you."

He cocked an eyebrow. "Even if the whole story is that someone doesn't want the school—" he covered her hand on the table "—turning our backs on the project isn't the answer. It's never the answer to let a bully win. He only bullies some more the next time he wants something."

"Madge said she and Cyrus were going to visit Kate Harper tomorrow. I might go, too."

Roche thought about that. "Why?"

"Why am I going? Because I want to see if there's anything about Mrs. Harper that wiggles my sniffer. I understand they've taken casts of those footprints outside the rectory. They belong to a woman for sure."

Wiggles my sniffer? "Does your sniffer tend to wiggle if—"

"Yes, it does," Bleu said, and she wasn't smiling anymore. "Absolutely. And I don't take that lightly."

"You think you have some sort of second sight, or sense, or whatever?"

"I'm not discussing that anymore," Bleu said. She pushed her hair back, gathered it up and held it at her crown.

He didn't like this townhouse. And he didn't like it that she was living such a spare life—not that a simple existence was a terrible thing. But he was convinced that Bleu barely managed on what she had.

"Wazoo's a bad influence on you," he said.

She shook her finger at him. "Watch it, or I'll tell Annie. You know she think's Wazoo's special. I'm going to see her at Pappy's, at the fund-raiser."

"Don't you worry, ma'am, I won't be saying a word there. In fact, Wazoo's done more than one good turn for my family. So even if I weren't scared of my sister-in-law, that twin of mine is someone I don't want to argue with."

"Max is your twin?" She frowned. "Of course he is. You're so alike. Why didn't I think of that before?"

"Probably because he looks so much older than I do," Roche said.

They both laughed, then fell silent.

"Did you ever even get close to marrying?" Bleu said. "I'm sorry. That's not something a lady's supposed to ask."

"You just did," he said. "So I guess some ladies do. Nope, not even close. Was your divorce really difficult?"

She laced her fingers together and made circles with her thumbs. "If I tell you, two people in Toussaint will know."

"Who's the other one?"

"My cousin, Madge. She knew Michael."

"Your husband?" And a man Roche wanted to meet.

"Mm. He's dead."

Roche reached across the table and raised her chin. He kept his finger there until she looked at him. "I'm sorry," he said. "You're grieving, aren't you?" He could forgive himself for the mistake, but he regretted making it just the same.

Bleu stood up. "I'm not grieving, because I'm not a nice person. I've moved on, and that isn't right—not right to feel glad Michael's gone, I mean. I'm glad. When I heard he was dead, I felt excited. I was happy. There must be something wrong with me." She blinked rapidly.

Roche sat back in his chair and studied her with his head to one side. "You're saying what you think you ought to say. The socially acceptable things. It's a shame you can't miss your husband, but it's not wrong that you don't. How long ago did he die?" Bleu's behavior started to make some sense.

"Several years," she said. "I've forgotten how long."

"Were you with him when he died?"

"He was in a holding cell, waiting to be arraigned for dealing drugs."

Roche frowned and kept quiet. He couldn't picture Bleu with a drug dealer, or imagine why a man like that would choose someone like her.

On the other hand, maybe he could. He could visualize how vulnerable she must have been a few years earlier. She'd learned to be tougher, but she was still vulnerable.

Bleu took another swallow of her lemonade. "Someone shot him. They never found out who. Even if someone wanted to talk, they'd be scared in that setup."

"But—"

"I don't like talking about it. They thought he had murdered someone, too. But he went to church all the time. He was president of the parish counsel. Everyone thought he was perfect and I was lucky." She focused on him, her expression horrified. "I didn't know anything about the drugs."

"I'm so sorry," he told her and stood up. "You've just been through a lot of trauma with this local murder and you're on edge. It's good to let everything out sometimes."

She shook her head. "No, it isn't. I'm not supposed to."

"Do you want to know what I found out about that land so far?" He needed to steer her away from what upset her so much.

Bleu rubbed her face, then gave him a thin smile. "Of course. But I shouldn't have started right in talking about that instead of Jim. I don't know what came over me."

"You don't want to think about Jim," he said. "It's okay, you're human. I was told someone actually lived in the woods on that land. Probably for a long time. Cashman *was* the man's name. I haven't gotten as far as I'd like with it, but there's supposed to be a shack where he lived. He got sick at about a hundred and ten years old and went off somewhere. The end."

"It can't be the end. What about his heirs?"

Roche pulled up his shoulders. "A search will be done to find the next of kin."

She pouted a bit, which was the last thing he expected her to do. "That means some greedy heirs will pop up and want zillions of dollars for it." She paused. "There's only one thing for it—I'll have to sell my Honda."

To smile or not to smile?

Not to smile.

"Bleu," he said quietly. "How many students do you expect to have at the school?"

"Around a hundred to start. They'll come from quite a wide area."

"That's what I thought. And it may take some years for the numbers to get really significant."

"Yes," she said.

"So I wouldn't worry about having enough space right away. Just do what I'm told you do so well—win hearts and minds and raise money."

"Good idea." She finished her lemonade and tilted her face up to his. "I do like my little bit of drama sometimes."

The only way he was keeping himself from touching her was by not allowing himself to look at her too much. He didn't know how long he could trust himself not to make a move.

"I'm nervous about the party and looking forward to it at the same time," Bleu said. "I really did think about putting it off, but Cyrus wants us to keep everything on schedule. I'm grateful to Pappy for offering the restaurant for the evening. It'll be easier to hold the potluck there. He said we should dance, too, and loosen people up. He said that, not me. He told Annie to tell me. I've never met him.

'Loosen them up so they give more,' that's what he said." She raised her eyebrows high. "Pappy's having the Swamp Doggies there to play, too."

"I didn't know Pappy was a Catholic," Roche said.

"Cyrus doesn't think he is, but...oh, well. I've sent him loads of thanks, but I won't let him give us the food. I made a lot of calls asking people to bring dishes."

Roche finished his own hard lemonade. "Would you like another one of these?" he said.

"Oh, no, thank you. I think there's more alcohol in these than you think. But you have one."

He did. "Do you mean you told Pappy you didn't want his food because you'd rather have people trail out there with dishes of stuff?"

"No! I said I couldn't take so much advantage of his kindness."

Roche decided he'd ask Max's wife, Annie, what she thought about that. She ruled Pappy's. He doubted if having people run in and out of the kitchen asking to put things in the oven would go over too well. As the manager of the place, she ran a tight, successful ship. About now, she'd be thinking about lawsuits if someone slipped on something they dropped on the floor.

"It's after one in the morning!" Bleu stared at her watch. "You're going to be so tired."

He didn't bother with the glass this time. "So are you. But we weren't doing so well at sleeping."

"No." She looked around the room. "This place is pretty dreary. I try not to look at it too closely. I get depressed if I think about it."

He liked nice places, but didn't worry about them one way or the other. "It's functional," he said, wondering how she would react if he asked her to let him arrange a better place. "It's easy to keep clean." Any offers like that would have her thinking he had designs on her.

Designs was a weak work for what he wanted with Bleu.

What Bleu wouldn't tell Roche was that the almost-empty room embarrassed her. She'd never seen where he lived, but it would be comfortable, she was sure of that.

"There's three floors here?" Roche said.

She looked at him sharply. "The attic isn't finished. I think the builder ran out of money."

"So this is your living room, as well as your dining room and kitchen?"

"Yes." His questions made her fidgety. "A great room, I guess."

He looked toward her booth. "You need a couch. And maybe a chair. A couple of tables and lamps. That's all it would need."

In other words, he agreed that she lived in a dump. "I'll get them one of these days. If I stay here." And if she either came into money from a relative she didn't know she had, or managed to find some used furniture she could bear.

"But you have a bedroom above this?"

Her heart turned over really quickly. "Yes." After getting rid of the dead bird, she had scrubbed the tub with bleach until her knuckles hurt.

"Of course you do."

While he put her through the interrogation, he drank his lemonade from the bottle. He was such a…renegade in appearance. He had another T-shirt on, white again, and jeans. She wondered if he wore jeans when he worked. That wouldn't seem very professional.

"Are you tired?" he said. "You must be."

"Dog tired," she told him. "But I don't want to go up there. I'll drop off down here after you leave." And once again, she had said too much.

Roche frowned at her. "You shouldn't have to be afraid where you live. That's not right."

Bleu sighed. "I know, but I haven't figured out what to do about it. I thought about locking everything up and going upstairs as soon as I get home each day. I can't do that. It would be like marooning myself on an island, only the water would be the stairs."

She looked toward the stairs—a few feet from the front door. Partway up they were hidden by one of the walls of this room. When you looked up there, it was all shadows.

When she'd been a child, going upstairs at night had scared her, then she'd gotten over the feeling. But while they'd been married, Michael had made sure the shadows and the waiting scary things came back.

Michael became one of her scary things—the scariest one of all. And in her mind he was still around, his memory undercutting her confidence, reminding her she wasn't what men wanted, once they had her.

"A cat came in through a window today, then got shut in my bathroom," she blurted out. "Scared me, I can tell you. I thought someone was in there going mad and ready to jump out and grab me."

"A cat?" He screwed up his eyes. "What cat?"

She told him about the tabby and what had happened earlier—minus the dead chicken.

Roche went immediately to the kitchen. "Which window?" he said.

"Right," she said. "Behind the sink."

He peered at the catch. "You must have left it open."

"Yes," she said quietly, and felt caught. "But he could have gotten in through the front door. I had to stop and screw the lightbulb back in. The door was blocked open for a few minutes. He could have sneaked past." But not, she knew, in the wake of a terrified chicken.

"You can't afford to make mistakes like that now," he told her, and she had to look away from his angry eyes. "Promise me you'll go over every latch in this place, every time you come in or go out. Better yet—only open windows upstairs."

"Okay." She wouldn't want to cross him when he was furious, and he was furious at this moment.

"Let me get you a room at Rosebank," Roche said. His flattened lips were white.

Looking into his face was dangerous. Even glancing at his tall, well-made body made her stir. She hadn't forgotten what had happened when they'd been together here before. Only the way he'd brushed off her responses in the past kept her from apologizing again.

"Bleu," he said. "I can't leave you here like this."

"It's too late for me to get a room at Rosebank. I'd wake people up."

He moved rapidly, enclosed the back of her neck in one of his hands. "Okay, I'm taking charge." When he turned her away from him, short of putting up a ridiculous fight, she had no choice but to let him push her along in front of him, toward the stairs.

At the bottom, he stopped and ran his warm hand down to her waist. He gave her a gentle shove. "Up you go and you'd better be asleep fast."

Of course, he didn't know the kind of fear she felt up there.

"I'll be down here," he said. "I'm tired enough to sleep on the carpet."

"Oh, no you don't. Good night, Roche. You're a kind man, but go home."

"Get up there," he said, pointing upstairs and giving her an unconvincing frown. "Now."

"*No.* Thank you for caring, but no. I feel totally ridiculous now and that'll help make me brave. Good night. And thank you for coming—you've helped me a lot." Determination not to look like a fool probably made most people tougher. Bleu wasn't tough and didn't feel tough. Embarrassment made her want to disappear.

With his arms crossed and his weight on one leg, he stared at her—militantly. Finally he sniffed and said, "Fine. I'll go."

She nodded, and he opened the front door.

A rush of wind surprised her. The weather was changing.

He just stood there.

Bleu cleared her throat, which didn't do a thing to stop her heart from jumping around. "Drive carefully," she said.

Roche didn't move or answer.

"Y'know, Spike hasn't had long to work on the case," she said. "But we'll probably hear something tomorrow. Call me if you find out first."

He closed the door softly. "I'm not leaving unless you can manage to throw me out. You could ask Spike to do it for you, but that might not look so good for either of us."

"This is ridiculous."

"Uh-huh," he said. "And it's getting later. Time has a way of doing that. Why don't you go back to camping in your Coke booth? I'll stretch out on the floor. I've had plenty of practice."

Bleu didn't believe him. And she didn't know what to say next.

"Or I'll take the booth and you lie on the floor," he said with a faintly evil smile.

"Some people would say you're torturing me," she said.

"That's a nice thing to tell me." He grimaced, turned the corners of his mouth way down. "I'll just make myself comfortable while you decide which four-star bed you want."

In one fluid motion, he dropped to the floor and lay flat on his back with his arms crossed under his head.

More amused than angry, more jumpy than afraid of him being there, she said, "I'm not talking to you anymore tonight." She opened a cupboard and hauled out the thin duvet and two pillows she used in winter—and when she holed up down here. "There." She dropped them on top of him. "Sweet dreams."

Her heart pounded in her throat now and she felt sick. In the few seconds she watched him, he didn't move a muscle under the pile of bedding.

"Good, then," she said, and pounded upstairs. "I hope you get rug burns."

Chapter
16

Rain and thunder woke him up.

Drops glittered on the windows, slapped harder and faster until they ran together in a wash. The thunder wasn't too far off.

He could see the clock on the microwave—3:40. Hardly any sleep. He hoped Bleu wouldn't be woken up by the cacophony.

Roche pushed up to his elbows and smiled slightly. She might not have believed him, but this wasn't the first time he'd slept on a carpet. Tonight, he preferred it to that five-star hotel.

What if she was afraid of thunder and lightning? A lot of people were, particularly if they suffered from panic attacks or were simply overly fearful and sensitive. He thought Bleu was highly sensitive, not an easy condition to control without a lot of work.

Thunder rolled, and rolled.

Seconds later lightning split the sky, from as far as he could see into the heavens, to the land. It made its cut like the scar from a jagged blade.

He got a quick image of the wound in Jim Zachary's neck. Bleu would see that vividly for longer than he would.

The crackling faded away, and the rain sounded louder.

Roche got up and took the pillows and coverlet with him. He went to the bottom of the stairs, dropped to his knees and drew the blanket around him.

Dwelling on the deepest reason for his being there disturbed him—confident sophisticate that he was… Was Bleu the kind of challenge that aroused his hunter instincts? He'd never thought of himself as the conqueror type!

He lay down, pulled the pillow beneath his head, glanced up and started.

"Bleu," he said, and sat up again. "What are you doing?"

She lay curled up on the top step, and he could see that her eyes were open.

"Go to sleep," she said and rolled over, showing him her back.

If he went up there, he would be taking advantage of her. If she let him go to her, it would be out of her need for comfort.

Could he comfort her? Could he be near her and not test to see if she would respond to him?

He lay down again and closed his eyes.

Shit, if she fell asleep and rolled over again, she'd fall down the stairs.

Scuffling followed and he opened one eye a little.

Bleu looked down at him again. She put a hand under her cheek and watched him.

"Don't panic," he said. "I'm getting up. If you think you can manage not to freak out, I'll come up there and you can get back in bed. I like being on the floor, and one spot is as good as another."

"I'm going to be embarrassed over this for the rest of my life," Bleu said. "*Please,* go home now."

"Sure, and find out tomorrow how you fell down here and broke your neck."

"You're superstitious," she said.

"Huh?" He'd never been accused of that before.

"You're afraid if you leave me, something will happen and then you'll have to live with all the 'what ifs.' Mostly, 'What if I'd stayed—it wouldn't have happened.'"

He thought about it. "There's some of that. Look, I could sit outside in my car, if it'll make you feel better."

"It won't."

"Okay, put up with me till morning and tomorrow I'll talk to Spike about a twenty-four-hour surveillance setup. He can help us find the right people for that."

She sat up again. "I can't afford that sort of thing and, before you offer to pay for it, I would never let you." After a pause, she said, "You are one terrific man. And I hope you don't have rug burns. That was a stupid thing to say."

"If you said it, it was. I didn't hear you."

Bleu pulled her legs beneath her. Coming off as immature irked her, but some things were more than hard to overcome.

"Roche?" She *would* get past this irrational suspicion of all men. "It's nice to have you here. I know I'm safer with you." A huge breath didn't calm her down. "If you're comfortable with the idea, why don't you come up here and lie down? I'm going to feel even worse tomorrow, if you haven't slept all night. I just don't want you on the floor anymore—it's awful."

Roche thought about it for a long time. He hadn't been invited because she was ready for him to make love to her, just to sleep. Lying with her would be so nice, but he wasn't completely sure of his iron control.

"You don't have to come up," she said. His silence told her he didn't want to accept her invitation. How awful.

"Shall I bring this bedding?"

Rational thought abandoned Bleu. "Um…a pillow."

By the time he reached the top, she stood beside a mattress on the floor. Even in the gloom, he could see how wide her eyes were.

Sure he could be close to her and not turn into an animal. He breathed through his nose.

He had always chosen his partners carefully. *No fragile flowers in that bunch.* He couldn't control his thoughts of how it would be to share hot nights, and days, with Bleu.

Downstairs, that's where he should have stayed.

"Roche?" Bleu said softly.

"Uh-huh."

"Nothing."

"Where do you want me?" he said. Oh, hell, if only she really knew.

"Which side of the bed do you prefer?"

Something like a small scream sounded in his head. "Ladies first." His nerves pounded. "You choose. I'll take what's left." The mounting excitement would be a bear to control.

A diminutive figure, her hair catching speckles of light, Bleu went silently to the side of the bed nearest the window. She slid beneath a sheet on the mattress, wiggled and wriggled and pounded her pillow, then became utterly still.

Roche walked carefully to the vacant side and lowered himself to sit on the edge.

Bleu sighed. She tried to hold her breath, then made sure she breathed regularly.

Inch by inch, she pushed to a more central position on her portion.

Her stomach clenched, and she couldn't make a muscle in her body relax.

Slowly, with the sheet over her face, she rolled onto her back, stretched out her legs and folded her hands on her tummy. Now she'd appear relaxed.

There were some patients out there, Roche thought, who were enjoying explosive sex lives because he had taught them how to pleasure a partner by putting his or her needs first. He could have all that. Sure, he could.

Wind joined the rain and a howl set up. The window panes rattled.

He heard Bleu sigh.

She'd stopped moving behind him, and the silence jostled at his eardrums. The only sound he heard clearly was his own very shallow breathing. Shortly, he'd find out if this development would make or break his hopes.

Roche put the pillow he'd carried upstairs on the bed, shucked his jeans and got in beside her. "We're grownups," he told her. "There's nothing to feel anxious about. Relax, Bleu. I intend to." *Lying could become a habit...fast.*

Bleu lay so still, she might have been dead. He slid his eyes sideways to look at her, a bump under the white sheet. God, she even looked like a corpse.

"Roche?"

He jumped. "Mm. You all right?"

"Great." They lay, side by side, outstretched and unmoving with a few virginal inches of space between them. "We'll both sleep better now." *Lying can be justified.*

"I'll feel safe." She'd like to. His strong body gave her security, but "safe" would have to be worked on.

He could tell she was holding too still. And she trembled lightly but steadily.

"I'm going to move," he said. "Don't jump and don't run. For God's sake, don't run away. I don't think I could take that."

Carefully, he turned onto his side, facing her.

"I'm not going to run." She could feel him watching her. "I don't have anywhere to run to."

Roche wished she hadn't added that.

"Relax," he said. "You're stiff."

"Yeah."

"I don't blame you. If I were in bed with a maniac, I'd be stiff, too."

She laughed, and his muscles softened a little. Once in a while, a gamble paid off.

"Glad I could amuse you," he said.

Slowly, he smoothed her shoulder. Again and again, he swept from her neck to her wrist and back again.

Bleu didn't make a sound.

From her wrist, he shifted his hand to her tummy, touching her lightly. "Let yourself go," he said into her ear.

"We're supposed to be sleeping," she told him, fully aware that when she'd asked him up here, she'd been ready for a dangerous experiment. He wanted to make love to her and she wanted it, too. She just didn't know if she could do it.

Roche rubbed circles on her belly. Layers of fabric separated him from her skin, but his hand might as well have been on her naked flesh.

Roche wanted to move down her legs, but it was too soon.

When he kissed her shoulder, then opened his mouth enough to damped her T-shirt and pajama top, she turned rigid again.

Why not try practicing what he preached? Take it slowly, build her pleasure, make it about her...and hope he could find satisfaction.

Thunder sounded again.

She shifted closer to him.

Roche inched downward in the bed slightly. Some things couldn't be softened or hidden—not until they were ready.

He knew the difference between his feelings for women in the past and what was happening to him with Bleu.

It scared the hell out of him. Before, it had always been physical— a need to be met, then move on. Just smile and be grateful for the outlet. With Bleu, his mind, his brain, his emotions were involved. He cared about her feelings and how it would be for her if they were intimate—and afterward.

"You still okay?" he asked her. "Storms bother you, don't they?" She felt incredible to him. He could settle for this for a long time if he had to.

"Sometimes." In fact she enjoyed the thrill of realizing the weather's force. "How do you think Cyrus would feel about us—like this?" she said.

"Jealous."

She landed a pointed elbow in his side. "That's not the way you talk about a priest."

"The priest in question is a man in every sense of the word, if I ever saw one. I wouldn't want to live with his pain."

"It's sad," Bleu said. "I think he loves Madge and she loves him."

"You won't get any gold stars for that deduction," he told her. "It's obvious, and I hate it for both of them."

Thunder rumbled overhead, and a moment later, lightning seemed to shoot directly at the window.

Bleu pulled the cover over her head and squirmed until her face rested in the hollow of Roche's shoulder. Automatically, she raised a knee across his thighs.

Her breasts got heavy. The nipples burned. He kept on rubbing, sliding back and forth from hipbone to hipbone and occasionally squeezing her hip.

Swallowing, swallowing again, she grew hot. He was a hard man in every way.

The noise faded, and after several deep breaths, she made to move away again.

He held her where she was, and she became a statue.

"Comforting each other is no sin," he told her. "I don't know what happened to you in the past. I hope you'll explain it one day. In the meantime, would you hate it if we spent a little time in each other's arms?"

Would she? The answer was a no-brainer. Bleu's throat felt as if a chunk of wood had been stuck there.

"I couldn't hate being with you," she said, wondering if he would hear her.

He did. "Thank you," he said. "I've got a lot to find out about trusting and learning.... I want to learn to be what a woman needs. To be what you need."

She swallowed and wondered if she could be what *he* needed. Oh, but he felt so good. Big, solid, warm and protective. She had never had any of those things.

"What are you thinking?" she said. "Why is it important to please me?"

"It just is. And you're gentle—different from women I've known. You need to teach me to be gentle."

She rested her head back on his shoulder and couldn't believe she was here at all.

Roche pulled her into his arms. He smoothed the front of her neck, and her breastbone—again and again. He lulled her. With his other hand, he slipped just inside the bottom of her T-shirt and made soft circles with his palm. Bleu felt she was melting.

"I wouldn't push you if you wanted to stop," he said. "Do you believe me?"

"I guess so."

"The instant you want me to, I'll stop."

She knew what he wanted. Michael had warned her that all men wanted it and they would be even rougher than he was. She shuddered, not knowing how that could be possible. He had been so rough. Once he came home very late and she'd been almost asleep. He'd stripped back the bedcovers, torn off her clothes and had sex, violently, with no finesse. Only minutes later, she landed on the floor, where he threw her before launching himself on top and beating her upper arms and body until she could scarcely move.

"What is it?" Roche kissed her ear and ran his tongue through the folds.

"An old memory," she said. "I'm not going to think about it anymore."

"Good. Try to copy what I do. I'm going to turn your back toward me. I'll move a little, my hips, my waist. Spooning isn't given enough credit. I want you to rock and roll with me in this bed, only we don't want to wake the neighbors."

While he spoke, he rotated her. How easily he put her body where he wanted it.

She stopped herself from saying she didn't have any neighbors, and turned even hotter when she felt his pelvis against her bottom, pushing her forward, then his hand spreading low on her belly, pressing her to him as he rocked his lower body back.

Between her legs, she was wet at once. Wet and contracting.

He was hard, and this was no small man.

The rocking continued, still slow but with more insistence.

"Face me again?" he said, and she didn't give herself time to think before twisting around.

Roche put his mouth against hers. Kissing. He kissed her, moved to flit his lips across hers, his face in one direction, then another, until she started to copy him.

The hardened tips of her breasts met his chest and the faint brushing seared her skin.

Her thighs molded to his, her belly to his, and the restrained undulation of his pelvis into hers amazed Bleu.

Effortlessly, he heated her to boiling.

"Bleu," he said against her neck. "I care about you."

She couldn't respond.

"I don't expect you to say anything," he told her. "I'd like to feel your skin against mine—all over. If you can't do that, say so. If you think you can but then you change your mind, fine."

He had to feel her trembling. "I can," she said and closed her eyes tight. She didn't know how she should do what he asked.

"Here goes," he said and pulled his T-shirt over his head.

She could see him looking at her and edged her top up a few inches. And a few more inches. Bleu exhaled and took the shirt off.

Now he might change, she thought. He could shout and tell her she was bad. He could hit out at her, bruise her skin where her clothes would hide the marks. Convulsively, she folded her arms across her breasts.

Roche took off his shorts.

Her breathing shallow, Bleu scrunched up to work off her pajama bottoms and panties. She pushed all of her clothes down inside the bed in case she needed to get them quickly.

"Now it's trial by fire." His voice had turned to that gravelly sound. "Come to me."

Bleu's face tingled. With one hand she tentatively rubbed his chest, threaded her fingers through the hair.

"A bit closer," Roche said and slid his hands around her waist.

He didn't need to be told how difficult this was for her. He could feel it. But if she didn't want to be with him, she wouldn't be and he held their future together in his hands.

He eased her rigid body tight against him. "You feel so good," he told her.

Sliding his knees up to grip her hips on either side, he started to move their bodies as one. She reacted by shooting her arms around his neck and holding on. Her breasts flattened to his chest. Bleu gasped when he gently bent her backward, opening her mouth wide with his, grazing her teeth, then reversed the arch of their bodies by pulling her by the back of the neck until her face was above his, her back curved forward.

Bleu settled into his rhythm and had to breathe through her mouth when she felt him spring between her thighs, between the slickness there.

He was smooth, and hot, and hard, and every place his penis touched, her flesh answered.

"You okay?" he said, wrapping her body closer when she'd thought that wasn't possible. "Can you put your leg on top of mine?"

"Yes," she said. "Are *you* okay?"

She thought he chuckled but couldn't be certain.

"I'm great," he said.

Aware of how she opened herself to him, Bleu put her top leg over his, curled her knee over his hip.

"So sweet," he said against her neck, and she felt how his hands weren't as steady as they had been.

"I'm not going all the way inside you," he said.

Her brain clamored and she thought her blood stopped flowing.

With one hand, he held his penis and slid it over her pelvic bone. Velvet and iron, he encountered her, rocked a small way into her, and slipped out.

Bleu wound her wrists together, ground bone on bone behind his neck.

He started to enter her, only to rotate partway out again, and again.

She kissed him and he used his tongue, in and out at the same slow pace as his penis massaged the entrance to her body.

He was different. This was different.

The sensation she remembered from the other day, only so much more intense, began to pulse. Their hips rolled together, her breasts brushed over his chest, she reached between them to hold any part she could, and the pulse took over. Thudding, swelling.

She tried to clamp him close, then to force him into her. He continued to guide the rhythm.

Back and forth.

Back and forth.

Bleu heard her own cry. It whirled with the wind and rain, and her release was a fierce, fabulous dart throughout her. Wide, spreading.

Roche didn't stop moving and her climax blossomed again. She curled into him, dug her fingers into his buttocks, and the muscle didn't give at all.

"More?" he whispered.

"Yes."

He lifted her, turned on his back and settled her in his lap. "Hold my shoulders."

She held on and he pushed her legs behind her until they lay thigh to thigh, belly to belly.

He pushed her hips higher until her breasts touched his face.

"Roche!"

He ran his tongue in circles over one breast. Bleu tried to find something safe to hold on to and only found his hair.

Somewhere deep, she thought it was in her head, lurked fear. She would be punished for this. Enjoying what Roche was doing with her. Michael said only sluts enjoyed anything to do with having a man close to their bodies.

She squeezed her eyes shut, tried to close her thoughts away.

Roche's tongue wound around her nipple and she barely stopped herself from shrieking again.

He sucked and Bleu felt boneless. She curled heavily over him.

Tipping his head back, he kissed her mouth, long and slow. While they kissed, he lowered her, breast to chest, belly to belly, and, finally, pelvis to pelvis.

"Now you take charge," he whispered. "I won't let you fall."

Bleu planted her knees either side of him, found and held him with both hands and slipped his smooth flesh over that frontal place where the sweet pain began for her.

This time she was weak in his arms. He entered, once, twice, three times, with long, slow strokes.

He forced his head into the pillow and Bleu saw the veins in his neck distend, the sweat shimmer on his skin. He felt slippery, but so did she.

Again, her body opened to him and she felt as if little pieces of herself flew away, leaving her revealed and vulnerable.

Four, five. Roche's hips swung while his back arched away from her, and he held her breasts. He emptied the substance of his sexuality into her.

Chapter
17

Very early the following morning

Justice was not always patient.

He had misjudged his entry into the house, heightened his excitement by waiting, but waited too long. The little trick to throw her off balance had amused him—especially watching the chicken run and flap after he'd severed its head. He would have gone in soon afterward, before Roche Savage was due to arrive, only a call to the clinic had confirmed Justice's suspicions. As he'd suspected when he saw her pass a window wearing pajamas, Roche had changed his mind about coming.

He wasn't supposed to come at all after that, damn it. Tonight, he should have been staying at the clinic. Instead he had showed up late, almost at the moment when Justice would have let himself in through the kitchen door for the second time. The first time had been with the carcass and the cat. He had scratches as mementos.

How much longer could he wait while Savage fucked Bleu's brains out? The shrink's first morning appointment at his place on Cotton

Street was at six. The good doctor accommodated those coming off a night shift. "Such a lovely man," an assistant had told him, Justice, on the phone. "He doesn't like a patient to go to bed all in a muddle."

Come on, come on. The man would have to go to Rosebank before he saw patients, wouldn't he? Surely that had not been a miscalculation.

What if they were still at it, sweating and banging up there, the time forgotten? Once it got light, the plan would become too dangerous.

He, Justice, had learned all about Roche Savage. *Dr.* Savage's history wasn't mentioned locally. Because of one act of bravery, the town had made him a hero. They all spoke of how Roche had saved the lives of both his brother and his brother's wife. Only a handful knew about their *hero's* cruel perversion. Just one had witnessed an exhibition that revealed he could be an animal when he was with a woman. The woman in question was dead now. How convenient. Although, of course, Roche Savage had no part of that death.

But Roche had to get out of Bleu's place *now.*

Come on, boy. Enough for one night. Thanks for warming her up. It's my turn now.

He would make her beg for him. Soon enough, she'd tell him he was the best she'd ever been with. And she'd be right. Why have an enthusiastic amateur when she could have the consummate professional?

He laughed quietly, looking toward the front of the townhouse through a knothole in the carport siding. Rain hammered the roof over his head and sliced through light from that single fixture outside the townhouse front door. It would have been better to break the bulb when he'd loosened it, but he had wanted to see her jump when it came away in her hand.

She would have been so perfectly off balance if he hadn't hung around to build the thrill.

Using the tiny beam from a laser light, he had found a storage room at the back of the carport and shut himself in. Around him were remnants of hardware left by the landlord. A step in the wrong direction could bring mismatched boards crashing around him. Tools hung by hooks from pegboard on one wall, and paint cans glinted in an uneven stack.

The aroma of dust, rust and oil from a metal drum didn't make him any happier.

Shit. Was that…no, the sky was not lighter yet, or only very faintly. The front house light cast a brightening aura and the rain reflected its shine. That house was as dark as it had been for the last hour, since a downstairs lamp finally went out.

The carport roof leaked. Not a lot, but enough to land the occasional splat on his head, or into the big open drum beside him. More water seeped in around a badly fitting door in the back wall.

He put a hand into his pocket and massaged the soft, sleek Italian knife he loved more than he'd ever loved anything. If things went well, she'd feel the blade. Marks for all time, that's what he'd make. Even if that time was very short.

Bleu Laveau was small. He would stab deep, again, and again. Her screams would come when she saw what he intended to do to her. The first slice would shock her into gurgling despair. The second might kill her, but why should he let that stop his fun?

How long he spent with her would be up to the sunrise.

Chapter
18

Predawn the same day

Propped against the wall, Bleu watched Roche roll onto his back, his face turned away from her.

The night had become an unreal memory.

A sheen from water on the uncurtained windows swirled across the white sheet around the man's hips. His skin gleamed.

She didn't know how long she had slept, but it couldn't have been long.

She had fished her pajamas from inside the bed and slipped into them, careful not to awaken Roche.

The clothes made her feel safer.

Good women don't flaunt their naked bodies. She held her throat, and tried to relax her tightening muscles. Michael had insisted she be dressed in bed, even if he had torn at her nightgown and bruised her skin each time he reached for her in the dark.

Never in the light. She almost smiled and the tune, "Never on a

Sunday," roamed her mind. That had been true, too. When she had been married, she'd craved Sundays and daylight because Michael never approached her at those times.

"Hey, green eyes."

She started and looked at Roche's shadowy face. Her tummy turned and she felt jumpy. "You slept," she said. "You seemed peaceful."

"Oh, yeah," he said, his voice rough.

Roche reached for her. She wouldn't let herself refuse him. He pulled her down into the bed until he could hold her against him and wrap the sheet over her, too.

"Little pajama miss," he said, ranging a hand over her back. "A kiss, please."

Bleu watched his face while they kissed. His eyes were shut tightly. She couldn't close hers. She was fragmenting again, freezing up as faint light crept into the room. They kissed, and Roche turned her to her back, rested on his elbows and held her still with his fingers in her hair.

He wrapped a naked leg over both of hers and she felt how hard he was again. Awkwardly, she patted his back and smoothed his hair.

"Come with me," he said against her cheek.

Roche didn't give her any choice. For a big man, he could move very fast. Almost instantly on his knees, he scooped her up by a hand under her shoulders and another under her knees.

"Put me down," she said, pushing against his chest.

He ignored her but went only as far as a large, wall-mounted mirror and set her down. "There," he said. "You're down. Now stay put until I tell you otherwise."

"Ew," she said, catching sight of herself in the rumpled pink pajamas. "This is mean." Her hair was tousled, her face too pale and her eyes so dark they seemed all pupil.

"Look at yourself," Roche whispered into her ear.

"You're mean."

"I know a good thing when I see it. Look. Now."

She raised her gaze to the mirror again and trembled. Standing behind and slightly to the right of her, Roche's entire naked right side was visible all the way from his intent face, past broad shoulders, slim hips, the dark shadows at his groin and down his muscular leg.

"You cover yourself up," he said quietly. "Why is that?"

She opened her mouth but couldn't make herself tell him.

"It's okay," he said, softly rubbing the sides of her neck. "I think I know. When you're naked you feel vulnerable, is that it?"

Her heart beat harder but she gave a single nod.

"Have you been humiliated in the past?"

She nodded again.

Roche slipped a hand beneath the front of her pajama top and stroked her ribcage. He slid just inside her pants to smooth her stomach and massaged upward until he stopped a breath away from her breasts.

"You're beautiful. You never have to feel self-conscious about your body. Let me show you."

She stiffened and Roche kissed the spot where her neck met her shoulder. "You're okay," he murmured.

Unerringly, he undid the buttons on her top and slowly separated the front. She tried to turn in his arms. Roche wouldn't allow it. He held her still and revealed her breasts.

High and very white, they showed clearly in the mirror. He flattened his palms over her nipples and made circles until the little muscles at the entrance to her body jerked tight and she flinched at the sensation.

Cautiously, she put a hand on his thigh and her breath shortened when Roche groaned.

Slowly, he pulled the pajama top from her shoulders and let it fall. Bleu made fists to stop herself from grabbing for cover.

"Who told you it's wrong to enjoy your body?" he asked.

Bleu shook her head.

Her back rested against his chest and he cupped her breasts. She tingled and burned, and she trembled. His thumbs, circling her nipples, did what he intended them to do. She dropped the back of her head against his shoulder and pinched her eyes tight shut.

Roche kissed her neck. He dropped gradually to his knees, kissing her spine again and again with firm, parted lips. And he ran his flattened hands down her body, catching the waist of her pants and pulling them to her feet.

He kissed the little dip at the base of her spine, licked and nipped her there and Bleu wobbled, tried unsuccessfully to grab him.

His fingers between her thighs, delving into the slick folds there, made Bleu glowing hot. She allowed herself another look in the mirror, and her skin flamed. The sight of his moving hands, tanned against her pallor, turned her blood to water. She breathed through her mouth.

She stared at herself, at him curled around her, pleasuring her. The woman in the mirror seemed a stranger, the man a dark and powerful force.

A climax began its shooting arch. She tossed her head and body and flailed to touch him wherever she could reach.

"It's good," he murmured. "You are so good. Go with it. There's so much more."

He spun her to face him and she moaned. "Don't stop, please." She couldn't bear it.

Roche didn't stop. At once he reached to part her again, and stroke her again, and when she could barely hold back a scream, he bent his legs then slid himself hard inside her, lifted her to ride his hips.

The strength of each thrust bounced her on his hips. She clutched his hair. He sucked on a breast.

And they both gave in to spasm after spasm until Roche lowered her to lie on the floor and covered her, still sending himself deep inside, slowly now, grunting, then catching her moans in his mouth.

They lay there, wrapped so close they were one. Bleu kissed his face. She panted, locked her ankles behind his buttocks and reveled in the sensations of having him as connected to her as she could get him.

"Did Michael make you think you should keep yourself covered?" he asked very quietly.

Bleu held him even tighter. "All that's over," she said. "I'm better now."

Was she? he wondered. She was wonderful. He felt more sated that he could have imagined on any dark night filled with lone sexual longing. This woman would change him. She already had. But she wasn't "better now," just improving. God, was she improving! He bit the lobe of her ear and she batted weakly at him.

With effort, he stood and pulled her to her feet. And he kissed her, amazed at the tenderness he felt, tenderness that didn't mask how his body began to quicken again.

Her arms raised high and surrounding his neck, her breasts, belly and thighs molded to him, she kissed him back with almost ferocious determination.

"Look again," he told her, easing her face toward the mirror. "Tell me it's a good idea to cover a body like yours."

She did look, her eyes just clearing an upraised arm. "Yours should never be covered," she said, and laughed. For a moment she stared at their naked, intertwined bodies, but then she pressed her face against him and held on tight.

"You're so sexy, Bleu."

"Only with you. See how we are?"

He saw—again—and braced against a raw jolt. "Back to bed." Without giving her a chance for an opinion, he slid them both beneath the sheet and kept on holding her. "Are you as beat as I am?"

"Mmm."

Stroking her hair, he dropped his head onto her shoulder and said, "I'm afraid to ask what time it is."

"I'm not sure. The alarm on the radio doesn't work. I don't sleep a lot, so I don't need one."

"Is it getting light?" He kept his eyes hidden.

"Yes." Shades of gray grew paler and paler, chased darkness out of the corners. "You've got to be somewhere?" She couldn't bear for him to go.

"I don't want to leave you." On his elbows again, he looked down into her face. "Are you sick of me now?"

"What?" She swallowed. "Yes, absolutely sick of you." If she had ever seen a man in her dreams, Roche would have been that man. Why couldn't she have met him a long time ago, before Michael?

His hand on her breast felt too good. There were reactions that had lives of their own. Bleu arched her back toward him. Those shades of gray were disappearing and she saw the concentration in his very blue eyes. Beard darkened his jaw and showed even darker where the shallow cleft dipped in his chin.

There should be curtains at the windows. She hadn't bothered because they cost a lot and she had no neighbors. The landlord had insisted the place was unfurnished and he didn't have to provide window coverings.

"Bleu," Roche whispered against her breast. He took her nipple between his teeth and shook lightly before he sucked.

The result was electric.

"Roche," she said, combing his mussed hair with her fingers, convulsing at the sensations he made and holding his face hard to her breast.

"Mmm?"

Bleu responded elsewhere.

She shouldn't let this happen again, not yet. They needed a little space first.

"I think you're getting late," she said.

He continued, deeply engrossed in what he was doing.

If the sky weren't overcast and rain falling again, much more light would have come into the room.

Bleu breathed hard, but she turned her head sideways to look at his watch. "It's well after five," she said.

He burrowed his face into her neck and grew heavy on top of her. "It can't be."

"It is."

He sprang to sit on the edge of the mattress. "Hell," he said, and stood up, naked and breathtaking. "I've got to go, sweet."

"The shower—"

"I can shower and change at the office," he said. "Fortunately, I have my own entrance into the building." He had started dressing.

When he'd pulled his shirt over his head, he stopped and stared at her. "Don't you forget last night. Or this morning. You understand?"

"I couldn't," she said honestly.

He didn't smile. "Good. I need to see you tonight."

Bleu nodded and felt herself blush. She couldn't have said no.

"It'll be a longer night this time," he told her. "I'll come and get you. What time do you get home?"

"Around six, unless work keeps me."

"I'll be here at six, unless you call me. But if it has to be later, I'll wait for you," he said.

"You'd better go."

"Bye," he said, sticking his feet into his shoes and stuffing things into his pockets. "Later."

"Later."

By the time she heard the front door close, Bleu had sneaked from the mattress to retrieve her pajamas and put them on. In bed once more, she closed her eyes, even though she didn't expect to sleep.

Scared shouldn't be the first thing that came to mind when a man left a woman he'd made love to, and wanted to make love to many more times.

But he was, Roche thought, scared sick. The sex had been amazing, but he'd planned the way it would go. He hadn't even known if he would be able to hold on and stay cool. Cool hadn't happened, but he had kept himself in check.

If he told himself he wouldn't try to educate her a little more each time they were together, he'd be a liar. Educate? He lengthened his stride to reach the bottom of the cul-de-sac. What he had in mind wasn't taught in any course he knew of. You had to be a natural to get it right.

Damn, she was like honey, sweet and sexy-sticky, and she was supple. He could bend her body wherever he wanted it to go.

Watching her in the mirror had driven him wild. And he felt wild all over again.

He aimed his key at the BMW. A more serviceable vehicle was what he should have around here. This week he'd look for something. That car of Bleu's was living on borrowed time. Maybe she'd accept the BMW.

Sure, she would. He could tell her he wanted to wait to sell it until he could be somewhere with a good dealer. Make it a loaner.

Take it slow and easy, buddy. The woman isn't for sale.

He couldn't let anyone see him. "Mess" didn't cover it. Behind the wheel, he sat with one foot outside on the rough road while he started the car. He wanted fresh air before this day turned muggy. The rain had stopped at last and already a faint vaporous layer collected over the ground.

Roche reached to pull the door shut.

He stopped, and listened.

A dull boom. Like something exploding in a confined space. Or maybe a big bang muffled by layers of…layers of what?

The sound didn't last more than seconds and he had no idea where it came from.

He closed the car door and adjusted his mirrors.

Smoke rose in a smutty plume behind him. It rose from Cypress Place.

He leaped from the car and took off the way he'd come. The instant he got around the corner his head started to pound and his palms sweated.

The smoke poured from the carport up the side of Bleu's townhouse. While he ran, he saw a bush catch fire and crackle to nothing.

Thank God everything was wet.

An acrid, oily scent streamed energy through him. There could be all kinds of flammable materials in that carport. Paint, thinner, old brushes, oily rags.

The smoke got thicker and engulfed the side of the house. Flames licked at the carport—and Bleu's car.

Damn it, the car would go up.

"Bleu," he yelled, gasping as smoke reached him. He got to the driveway, dashed to, then up the front steps. Shit, he'd locked the front door—of course he had.

He stepped back and looked up at the bedroom window. "Bleu! For God's sake. *Bleu!*"

Damn, Max. His twin had nagged Roche into not carrying a weapon anymore. He sure as hell needed it to deal with the lock.

Choking, he gave himself room, threw his body at the door and felt a rush of hope when it creaked on its hinges.

A few steps away, then he repeated the process, leaving the ground when he hurled himself against the cheap wood. This time it splintered—not on the handle side, but where the screws in the hinges were letting go.

The sound of sirens shocked him. He hadn't taken the time to call anyone.

A third assault on the door tore the top hinge from the wood. He jumped, hitting the thing with both feet and all of his weight.

He landed inside, flat on his back on top of the door.

"Roche!"

There she was. At the top of the damn stairs. *She's more afraid of who might come through the door than she is of the fire.*

"Come to me," he yelled, starting up the stairs.

Wearing her baggy pajamas again and looking almost childlike, she got to her feet and took a downward step, her eyes locked on his.

Black smoke streamed through the open door.

He grabbed her from the stairs, threw her over a shoulder and went out over the rocking, fallen door.

The local fire truck, its crew working as fast as they could given their old equipment, ran toward the building, hoses unwinding as they went. Water drizzled at first, then shot out in a brave stream.

Another truck roared into the cul-de-sac, this one with the St. Martinville insignia on its side.

"Thank God for rapid response teams," he said.

Bleu coughed. "You can put me down," she said quietly.

"Farther away, first."

A cruiser joined the trucks, followed by another.

Spike got out of the first one, tipped his Stetson over his eyes and plodded toward them. "Stick around, if you don't mind," he said to Roche.

More familiar bodies in slick-sleeved khaki uniforms and straw Stetsons came their way at a run, and passed by, but not without hard glances. They went into a huddle with Spike a few yards away, then separated and spread out in different directions.

Carefully, Roche put Bleu's feet on the ground.

If anything, the smell got worse and the smoke, blacker.

Roche scratched his forehead and rubbed at his stubbly chin.

Spike joined them again. "Hard night?" Spike said, immediately looking away.

Roche put an arm around Bleu and rolled her in so her face was hidden against his chest. "Save it," he told Spike. "Sometimes less is more."

Spike's eyes slid toward him and there was no doubt the man was exhausted. "This damn town is falling apart," he said. "Got any neat little platitudes for that?"

"Nope." But Roche didn't apologize for what he'd said. "How did you all know about the fire so fast?"

"A call came in. To the fire station and to us."

"I didn't make any calls," Roche said. "I was around the corner and in my car when I heard something go up. Did anyone get a trace on the calls?"

"Save me," Spike said. "Everyone's a cop these days. This is Toussaint, Louisiana, not New York City. Maybe we've got something, maybe we haven't."

"Doesn't have to be New York…" Roche decided not to finish. "Someone in Crawfish Alley must have called. That's the closest street."

"How long ago did this start?" Spike asked. With the St. Martinville crew on scene, the problem was all but over. Occasional cracks and pops came from the carport, following by more smoke, but the whole thing was calming down. Hoses snaked in every direction, and men who hadn't taken the time to clamp the tops of their flapping boots shut, moved rapidly but not as if they were worried about a thing.

"Minutes," Roche said.

"You sure you didn't call?" Spike said.

"Sure, I'm sure," Roche said. "Like I said, I was getting into my car down there." He hooked a thumb toward the bottom of the street. "There was a thud like something went up under a heap of blankets. I almost didn't come back."

"That right?" Spike said, eyeing him. "Did you hear the fire sirens before you decided to get out of your car again and come back? It wouldn't have looked good if you drove away. Someone might have come to the wrong conclusion."

Damn it, the man was suggesting Roche could have had something to do with the fire. "Nice police work," was all he let himself say.

"Like fire, do you?" Spike said, grinding out the words. "Is this a warmup for the little kids…no pun intended."

Roche pressed his lips together.

Bleu pushed against his chest and faced Spike. "Spike, you say some nasty things sometimes. Roche didn't set fire to the carport and run away. If he did, he certainly wouldn't call for help and come back. Use your head. How about whoever did set that fire placed the call and hoped Roche would be blamed? Check Roche's cell-phone records and you'll see he didn't call you."

Roche enjoyed the way she rushed to his defense. He noted the interesting color in Spike's cheeks.

"No one goes in there till the chief gets here," he yelled, indicating the carport. "I'd still like you two over at the station," he added to Roche and Bleu.

"I need to get dressed," Bleu said.

She trembled and Roche wanted to punch Spike, who behaved as if he hadn't heard her.

"I've got a coat in the back of my car," Roche said into her ear. "Don't worry. It'll just look like you got woken up suddenly by the fire."

She wrinkled her nose. "And what's your excuse?"

He laughed. "If I need one, I'll have one. I don't think anyone's going to notice a thing."

"You can't go back into that house until they're sure the fire's out, Miz Laveau," Spike said. "It's just a precaution."

Roche didn't miss the formality. "Can we stop by my office on the way to the station?" he asked. "There's a shower there and my assistant will come up with some clothes for Bleu."

Spike raised one brow until it disappeared into his hat. "Why not? You're on your own recognizance. You've got time to clean up. Pick up doughnuts or something on the way. I'm starving. And pray there's still hot coffee in my office."

Roche saluted. "You've got it."

Bleu was barefoot. He looked down. "Fireman's lift or piggyback?"

"I can walk."

He caught her around the back and picked her up from beneath her knees. Spike glanced at him and shook his head in that, *"Women,"* way that conveyed understanding between men.

A fireman scuffed from the carport, the tops of his boots flapping. "Hey up, Sheriff," he said. "We've about got it done. At least the old junker didn't go up. Looks like hell, though. Smells worse. We'll have to open a wall just to make sure we're not missing something."

Roche pretended to be concentrating on something else.

"Thanks for the good work," Spike said.

"Look at this," the fireman said. He held up a flint fire starter, the melted, misshapen red handle wrapped in a rag. "The chief's gonna be interested in this one. I reckon this is what got things started. It was in an old oil drum. Couldn't have done the job on its own."

Chapter
19

"I thought she got rid of that thing the last time she smashed it," Spike said.

Roche, with Bleu at his side, had only taken a few steps down the cul-de-sac when a dark blue van appeared. Dented and scraped, emblazoned on its sides were ringed planets, signs of the zodiac and a list of Wazoo's services in a block down the center.

Illustrator, makeup consultant, waitress, pet psychologist, housekeeper, expert on matters black and white, potions—or what you will, advertising executive, dancer and exorcist.

The little gathering in the cul-de-sac was seeing the good side of the vehicle. The other looked as if a giant ice-cream scoop had taken a passing dig at it.

"How would she know to come here?" Bleu said. Wazoo intrigued her; the woman had a way of showing up at odd times and in odd places.

Roche shook his head. "She probably monitors radio transmissions."

To Bleu, although he hinted at disapproval, he actually seemed okay with whatever Wazoo did.

Spike bent forward so the brim of his hat completely obscured his face. "She's got a radio." He flicked a piece of ash from his well-creased short sleeve.

Roche waited for Wazoo to appear and frowned. "She's not alone in the van." Darkly tinted windows made it hard to see inside. Someone moved beside the driver.

"Nope." Spike leaned forward, trying to see through the windshield.

"Is that Nat Archer with her?" Roche said. "Madge mentioned Wazoo threatened to get him in here."

"Damn her hide, anyway," Spike said, squinting toward the van. "Like I need an NOPD homicide cop sniffing around. Or any idle meddlers like Wazoo."

Nat Archer and Jilly's husband, Guy Gautreaux, used to be partners on the homicide squad in New Orleans. They still helped each other out when they wanted to know their backs were totally covered.

"You know she's protective of you," Roche told Spike. "She's trying to help. That's the only reason she'd get Nat to come."

Spike looked at him sideways, one side of his mouth tipped up. "The only reason? I think that crazy man would marry our town loon if she'd have him."

"Hush," Bleu said.

The van door creaked open on the driver's side. The wider Wazoo pushed it, the louder the sound of metal screeching on metal became.

Vertically challenged, she slid to the ground and closed the door with a mighty fling. Purple was the color of the day, with black, naturally. She resembled an exotic butterfly in motion—an angry butterfly.

"Is there fog crawling up the front of that wreck?" Roche said.

Bleu leaned to see around Wazoo. Vapor oozed over the hood of the van.

"Bum radiator," Spike said. "That's steam. Even leak stopper won't work anymore. She carries water with her for when it really runs out the bottom."

"This where you live, Bleu Laveau?" Wazoo called out.

"Yes," Bleu said. "Nice to see you." Even to her the greeting sounded banal, but everyone made conversation sometimes.

"Well, I surely can't say the same about you," Wazoo said, marching uphill toward the group. "A fire. Of course, a fire. We got a box of burned books, didn't we? We know there's someone around who likes fires." She pointed from Roche to Spike and nodded at Bleu. "This girl, she's likely to be the next one in the church—for her funeral. So you better be watchin'." She looked over her shoulder and planted her hands on her hips.

Bleu's pajamas were too warm. She needed to buy some new ones—not that she intended to spend a lot of time wearing them out here. A glowing orb in the sky, the sun, and all the gorgeous golden trim on parting clouds wouldn't seem so lovely in an hour.

Wazoo stood right where she was until a woman appeared on the passenger side of her vehicle.

"That's not Nat," Spike said.

Wazoo shot him a pitying glance. "No shit?"

"What is Mary Pinney doing here?" Bleu's top stuck to her skin. She had nowhere to hide from anyone who chose to come for the show.

Mary and her husband, George, whom most people had never seen, lived in rented rooms at Jim Zachary's place. Mary managed Hungry Eyes, the café and bookstore at the far end of Main Street. As one of her many jobs, Wazoo had helped out there for years.

"Don't you get uppity," Wazoo said to Bleu. "I know it's only because you've had a shock, but you need to get over it. We were on our way to open up Hungry Eyes. Followed one of Spike's cruisers here. Mary's concerned for you, too. You know how interested she is in a teaching job at the new school if it's built. All these bad things happenin' weigh on her."

Bleu knew all about Mary's interest in the school, but didn't see why that gave her the right or a reason to be here.

"Hoo mama," Wazoo said, watching Mary close her door and come around the front of the van. "That girl gotta have hidden depths. Have you met her husband?"

"No." And Bleu wasn't interested.

"Wait till you do see him. When he was made, whoever did it smiled, big-time. There's things we can't see, given the rules about wearing clothes, but we got imaginations—"

"Wazoo," Spike said, trying to look stern.

"When can I go back inside the house?" Bleu asked him. "It looks like it's only the carport and the siding that got damaged. Mostly the carport." She stared in that direction. "Well, darn it anyway. My car's a mess."

"It didn't blow up," Wazoo said. "You should be givin' thanks, girl. What's a bit of soot among friends? Most of it will wash off. If you're so inclined. I kind of like character to a vehicle myself. Now, are you hearing me?"

Bleu nodded yes.

"*Never relax, not for one second, silly girl.* Stands to reason, if the new school made someone mad enough to kill poor Jim, then you're an ugly pimple on the killer's skin. He wants to squeeze you out. Got that?"

"Lovely description," Bleu said. "Thanks for the warning."

"Bleu isn't alone," Roche said. "She's being looked after."

Wazoo looked up at him from beneath thick eyelashes. "I'm just sure she is. My, the gods were payin' someone off when they made the Savage twins, too. You are a wet dream, boy."

Bleu wanted to disappear.

Roche laughed. "Thank you, Wazoo," he said, and that was the end of it.

Bleu stopped looking at Wazoo. She had met Mary Pinney at the parish hall meeting, but with the crowd and all the questions, there hadn't been time to study the woman. Pointed inquiries about when teachers would be hired did catch Bleu off guard, but she had put the pushy approach down to eagerness.

Tall, tanned, muscular, her long dark hair scraped back into a thick coil, Mary made Bleu want to say that she didn't see much hidden about her potential depths. There was a physicality there, even given a calm, fine-boned face and clear blue eyes.

"Hidden depths," Bleu muttered under her breath.

"You've got that right," Wazoo whispered in her ear. "She's a nudist, y'know. Doesn't wear a stitch when she's home. Cooks, cleans, does everything in the skin she was born with."

"How do you know?" Bleu said from the corner of her mouth, doing a poor job of hiding a grin.

Wazoo gave her an arch look and tossed her masses of curly black hair. "I've got my sources," she said archly. "You'd be surprised what I know."

Bleu let it go.

"Wow," Roche said. "I don't think Miz Pinney gets around much or I'd have seen her." He cast Bleu a sidelong glance, a provocative grin. She kept her expression blank.

"What's she doin'?" Spike said.

"Stretches," Wazoo said. "She keeps very fit. She always stretches when she's been sitting."

Roche looked the woman over and muttered something that sounded to Bleu like, "Obsessive, compulsive."

Wazoo didn't notice.

There wasn't any more time before Mary Pinney came their way, her walk resembling that of a big, graceful cat. Bleu couldn't visualize her teaching young children, although she supposed that serene, almost empty air could be useful in some situations. A gauzy white poet's shirt hung from her shoulders, worn over soft, white linen shorts—very short. With the sun behind her, her lithe body, including notable, uptilted and naked breasts, was outlined inside the shirt. Her feet were bare.

She raised a hand. "Good day to you. Bleu, I am so sorry for your trouble. You let me know right away if I can do anything to help you." Her rich voice carried clearly across the cul-de-sac.

Realizing her mouth was open, Bleu closed it at once. She nodded at Mary.

"Jeez," Spike said, not quite under his breath.

"Do we think someone came here just to set a fire?" Mary Pinney asked loudly.

Wazoo squinted toward the house. "Maybe. But it should have been easy to burn the place to the ground."

"If his only goal was to burn Bleu's townhouse down, he'd have done it properly," Roche said.

"He must have figured she was home," Mary Pinney said. "He could have rung the doorbell if he wanted to. Or broken in. Something must have stopped him."

"Roche was with me," Bleu said, feeling defiant. "Someone could have come here expecting to find me alone and talk me out of continuing to work on the school project. They'd have waited for Roche to leave. Only...he was with me all night."

"She was upset," Roche said. "I couldn't leave her like that."

"You were so kind," she said, looking up at him. "It hasn't been easy lately."

"Uh-huh," Wazoo said. She looked Roche over. "I know a kind man when I see one and I'm seein' a *real* kind man now. I expect he got into your mind—that's what people pay him to do—and he smoothed out all your troubles. I bet he soothed your troubles away until you couldn't remember a thing about them."

The heat Bleu felt wasn't because the day was getting hotter and stickier with every moment.

"You shouldn't say things like that," Roche said. "Flattery makes me shy."

"You're quiet, Sheriff," Mary said. "What are you thinking? That this was just practice for all the little children he threatened to kill?"

"Who told you that?" Spike swung back. He colored and glared toward Wazoo. "Don't say that again, to anyone."

"Oh, no," Bleu said. Her eyes widened and grew dark. "This is awful. How did they find out?"

Roche followed the direction of her horrified stare and winced. He saw Father Cyrus's dusty, dark red Impala station wagon floating up the road. Its shocks were blown again and the vehicle resembled an ungraceful liner. Cyrus refused to replace the vehicle and only Ozaire Dupre's ingenuity kept it running.

"Why is he here? I'll never be able to look at him again," Bleu said.

"Just don't let him block the emergency vehicles in," Spike said.

Yellow tape flapped between stakes one of the officers had driven into the ground across the entire frontage of the property. The firemen were still busy, and Roche heard the distinctive sound of an axe splintering wood. They were opening singed walls in case any embers lurked inside, waiting to spurt into another fire.

Cyrus parked and got out, followed by Madge and, to Roche's annoyance, Sam Bush. He didn't like the man, didn't like the way he hung around Madge. And he gritted his teeth whenever Sam looked at Bleu.

What was the difference between a man like that, who didn't hide his obsession with women, and Roche? There *was* a difference, damn it. He might be physically attracted to any sexy female that roused his erotic factor, but he stopped his mind from engaging and taking action, and made sure he didn't signal his reactions. And he never pushed for what a female made him want...unless fate threw a desirable and willing partner into his arms.

Fate had definitely brought Bleu to him. He looked at her. Right now, he wanted her again, and he only wanted her. For the first time in his life he lusted for one woman alone and the idea unnerved him.

Roche liked looking at Bleu. Her eyes were a clear green and honest. Her sudden smiles and laughs tightened his muscles, and he enjoyed the sensation. When he wasn't around her, he wanted to be.

"Roche?"

He jumped and faced Cyrus. "Hey. We've got to stop having these morning meetings."

Cyrus didn't look amused. "You're right." If he noticed what Bleu wore, he showed no sign of it.

Sam Bush was another matter. He narrowed his eyes to look Bleu over from head to foot, taking too long over points in between. Roche knew Sam's kind. He would have no finesse with a woman, take no time. Just squeeze and strain, thrust, sweat, tell lies behind closed doors, then roll off and fall asleep.

How did he know the way Sam was with women? Roche detested himself for thinking like a man who hadn't spent years learning to listen and not make judgments.

Sam's only sin was that he liked to look at a lovely woman. That didn't make him a monster.

Sam approached him now, and they moved a few feet away from the others. "Have you given any thought to what they're saying about Kate Harper?" Sam said.

"Not a lot," Roche said honestly. "She seems like a nice woman to me."

"She is," Sam said. He had very serious gray eyes and right now they were concerned. "And no way could she have killed Jim Zachary."

"I wouldn't know, but I doubt it," Roche said. "People want a name and a face to pin the blame on."

"That's because they're scared," Sam said. "I'm uneasy. Not for me—I can take care of myself. But for people like Madge and Bleu and the other women in town. And any men who are vulnerable, obviously." He inclined his head toward the townhouse. "We heard they think this fire was set."

"I think that's what we'll find out," Roche said.

"It could be an accident," Cyrus put in, but without conviction.

"He's killed once," Sam said, as much to himself as to Roche. "If we don't get him, he'll do it again."

Roche swallowed and glanced back at Bleu. There was little point arguing that Jim's killer and whoever came here this morning weren't the same person. What if the fire had really taken hold? What if she'd been killed? He couldn't make himself think about it too deeply.

"Cyrus." Spike beckoned for the priest, and they talked quietly together.

Glancing around, Cyrus indicated he wanted Sam to join them and they went into a huddle. Probably Spike was bringing them up to date. Roche wandered back to the women.

"Are they talking about me?" Bleu said, sounding worried. "They don't have to follow me around all the time. I couldn't stand that."

"No," Roche said. "Not necessarily them, and not all the time, but someone has to look out for you. We'll take it in turns." As many turns as possible would be his. He contemplated how he could keep Bleu somewhere close at all times. He couldn't. His patient load had picked up and he couldn't neglect people.

"It's too much trouble," Bleu said. "I'll be careful, but other people can't be worrying about me. I don't want them to. Whoever was here wanted to scare me. So I *am* scared. That should give him his jollies."

Standing beside her cousin, Madge took hold of her hand and leaned against her. "You are a walkin' stick of dynamite. Move into the rectory. That way we can make sure you're never on your own. Cyrus won't let anything happen to you."

"Thanks," Bleu said. "I could also quit and let myself get run out of town, but I'm not going to. I'm calling an alarm company. I'm going to have sensors, not just in the house, but in the yard. I can put it on a credit card."

Roche heard what she said, but didn't comment.

"As soon as I can, I'll get my dog. Lil's Ozaire can help with that—everyone says he's an expert. And I'll get a gun. I know how to shoot."

Madge met Roche's eyes. He could tell she was worried, but didn't know what to say.

"First the alarms," Roche said. "We'll get someone over to replace the door."

"It just needs fixing," Bleu said, frowning.

Roche figured she was adding up the expenses. "I broke it, I'll get it fixed. I want something heavy-duty."

Madge gave him a serious nod. "Of course," she said. "What's Mary Pinney doin' here?" She finished in a whisper.

"She came with Wazoo," Bleu told her, glancing toward Wazoo and Mary.

"Mary usually keeps to herself. We don't see much of her, or we didn't until she got wind of the school. She's a teacher. She wants—"

"To teach at St. Cecil's," Roche said at once. "I've been told. Who called you about the fire?"

Madge frowned. "We'll have to ask Cyrus. We were getting ready for an early meeting when the phone rang."

Sam Bush ambled up to join them. "Spike told us what they know about the fire so far," he said. "Not so much, except they think it was set."

"At least we know we're looking for a man," Roche said. "That's something. No woman could have killed the way Jim Zachary was killed." He couldn't explain the woman's footprints outside the rectory, but still didn't connect the crime to a female.

Wazoo walked up in time to hear, and give him a pitying look. "You, dreamer man, haven't seen a real angry woman."

Arguing wasn't Roche's way. "Perhaps not." He had dealt with more anger, male and female, than most people could even imagine.

"Roche and I were talking about this," Sam said. "Jim Zachary had a lady friend and there are some in town who would like to pin it all on her because she inherits his money. We don't believe it."

"I know all about Kate Harper," Wazoo said.

Roche waited for her to continue, but she didn't.

Firemen retracted their hoses, but he could see deputies continuing to comb the hillside behind the townhouses.

"No one goes in the carport," one of the firemen shouted. "The chief's held up. He won't want it trashed by civilians."

"Gotcha," Spike shouted back.

An officer had taken the emergency brake off Bleu's car. With the driver's door open, he used a foot on the steep driveway to start moving the vehicle downhill and away from the carport. He trod on the brake and yelled, "Let me get this down the bottom, then we can turn a hose on it. Get the soot off and it'll look fine." He turned the key in the ignition and the engine turned over normally.

"She'll be grateful to have her car," Roche said. "Bleu doesn't like relying on other people for anything, including rides."

Black smoke poured out around the engine compartment.

An explosion splintered glass and sent pieces of the car flying.

"Bleu got lucky," Wazoo said.

Chapter
20

After lunch the same day

Bleu stood on the path beside Bayou Teche, with St. Cecil's behind her and the thick, chrome-green waters running glossy and slow, in front.

Spikes of pale purple flowers bobbed atop floating blankets of dark, waxy water hyacinth leaves. Beside her, an old willow trailed branches that jiggled with the current.

And the sun had grown as hot as promised. Her damp skin cooled with each tiny current of air.

If she closed her eyes, she saw pieces of her car shooting through flames, and the fireman, Kevin Rains, sprawled on the ground, covered with soot and not moving.

Running away was too easy. She loved life and wanted to love people. Even Michael hadn't killed the best parts of her. Roche was her passion. He was also her pain, but she would not allow herself to withdraw, so that she would never know what might have been with the two of them. The two of them had already had too much, and she had come too far.

Her cheeks burned. Her body flushed.

Kevin Rains had suffered for trying to do a good deed. He had been about to wash her car. A kindness that sent him to the hospital. Roche had driven there with Bleu, where they'd been able to talk to Kevin almost immediately. Once his broken wrist mended and the burns on his neck healed, he would be fine. Still, guilt tormented Bleu.

"Don't jump," a male voice shouted.

Bleu turned to see Sam Bush pushing open the little gate at the bottom of the rectory garden. "Hi." She shaded her eyes to watch him. He had been kind today, and concerned.

"You've been down here a long time," he said. The white shirt and conservative gray slacks he almost always wore were evidently his nod to his profession.

"It's calm here," she said. "And beautiful."

He grunted.

Alive, that was the first word that came to Bleu about Sam. Intelligent, interested, fit, vibrant and stubborn also came to mind. She smiled at him. "Say you aren't on duty."

"On duty?"

"Guarding me."

He laughed, and she noticed for the first time that laughter didn't erase the seriousness from his eyes.

"Well?" she pressed him.

"Give us all a break," he said, pulling his shoulders up. "You can't expect anyone to relax until this joker's caught."

"I guess not." A twist in her stomach chased away a light moment. Once more she looked across the bayou. "Have you ever been in a pirogue?" The long, narrow wooden boats—their captain and crew, a single man or woman balanced on their feet and plying a long paddle to and fro—plied back and forth from swamp dwellings.

"Sure I have," Sam said. "Lots of times. They look as if they belong in another century."

"Mmm-hmm. Another world, really. You don't need to babysit me."

He stood beside her, his hands in his pockets. "Maybe it feels good to be needed."

Bleu looked at him sharply. She didn't know what to say.

Sam flashed her a smile. "Must be all this quiet, and the company of a lovely lady—I'm turning wistful. That, or I'm a lonely man."

"Are you?" she said. She had never really thought much about him, other than that he was good at his job.

He shook his head. "Not really. But this isn't about me. You and Roche are getting close, aren't you?"

As if he hadn't already witnessed the answer to that question today. "I like him very much."

"Decent guy. Accomplished, too."

"Yes. I know about your wife—how she left."

The corner of his mouth turned down. "I wish that was history."

"It will be in time." With luck, all bad memories became history. "We get used to things and move on."

"I intend to do that." He focused too hard on a heaving bed of hyacinth.

Bleu swallowed. "Is something wrong?"

"No!"

Now he'd think she was prying. "I didn't really think so."

"How well do you know Madge?" he asked.

The question caught her off guard. She hadn't missed his interest in her cousin. "She's my favorite cousin."

Sam slapped the heel of a hand into his brow. "What a dumb question. For a moment I forgot you were related. Forget I asked."

"We spent a lot of time together when we were kids. I used to stay with her family on school vacations. She's really special."

"Yes."

Bleu stuck her thumbs into the pockets of her tan pants. Saying nothing could make him awkward. On the other hand, anything she said could be wrong.

"I like Madge," Sam said. "Looks as if I've waited too long to let her know how much."

She waited for him to continue.

"She's getting involved with Sig Smith, isn't she?"

"I don't know," she told him honestly. "We haven't talked about it." All Bleu knew was that Madge and Sig had gone out.

"I've already said too much. Roche called Cyrus to make sure you were in someone's sights."

She stared at her pink toenails, visible in strappy brown sandals. For some reason, Roche really did care about her. Who knew how much, but it was time to learn to take good things in both hands without second-guessing what would come next. She'd try.

"Your front door's being repaired," Sam said. "But don't be surprised if Madge and Cyrus keep pushing you to stay here. Don't you think you should?"

"No. I'm grateful about the door, but it's my job to learn to live alone."

She felt his eyes on her.

"I mean, I've usually had people around me, but now I don't and I like that."

"If you say so." He looked at his watch. "Madge said she and Cyrus are leaving for Kate Harper's place shortly. I think they hope you'll go with them."

"I want to." She put a hand on his arm. "Thanks for coming down, Sam. Are you coming out to Pappy's for the fund drive?"

He raised an eyebrow.

Bleu laughed. "Did I call it a fund drive? I'm slipping. I meant for the information and commitment potluck."

"I wouldn't miss it." He got that distant air about him again. "We used to go out there and dance to the Swamp Doggies. Betty was some two-stepper."

"I bet you're good at it yourself," she said quickly.

"Promise me a dance and I'll show you," he said.

"You've got it." Movement caught her attention. "Madge is waving up there."

Sam spun to look uphill, but he smoothed his expression rapidly and waved Bleu ahead of him.

"Hey," Bleu shouted. "I'm coming." She broke into a run and pounded through the garden until she arrived, panting, at the kitchen door.

"Cyrus and I are leaving for Kate Harper's," Madge said. "Do you still want to come?"

"Yes," Bleu said. She turned as Sam arrived behind her. "Thanks for keeping me company."

He shrugged, looking at Madge. "That woman's had a hard time," he said. "Kate, I mean. She and Jim were close for a long time. I hope Spike isn't taking any notice of the kind of stuff Ozaire's been spreading."

Reading Madge's expression wasn't easy, not when she looked at Sam. "Spike's a kind man," she said. "And I guess his dad told Ozaire off. Said he'd lose his part-time job out at the station if he didn't keep his mouth shut."

Spike's dad, Homer Devol, ran the gas station, convenience store and boat launch on the outskirts of Toussaint. Ozaire helped out part-time. Homer didn't mince words or get shy about his opinions.

"That should help," Sam said. "I'd better get back to my office."

"Sure," Madge said. "Come on, Bleu. Lil packed some cookies for us to take to Kate."

Bleu heard Sam walking behind her. He left without another word. "Madge," she whispered. "Say goodbye to Sam. He's a good guy."

"I know," Madge said. She raised her voice. "Bye, Sam. Take it easy."

He looked back at her, and she waved. Sam hesitated, raised a hand and walked on.

"I feel sorry for him," Bleu said.

"He hasn't had it easy," Madge said. "But I...I hope he meets someone who can be what he needs."

"And that isn't you?"

"It isn't," Madge said. "I don't think I can be what anyone needs."

Before Bleu could respond, Madge had hurried into the kitchen. She picked up a basket lined and covered with blue-spotted white cloths. "Goodies for Kate," she said. "We'll let Cyrus know we're ready to go. Roche called to check on you—again—and I told him we'd be gone for a couple of hours at the most."

He should be concentrating on his patients, Bleu thought, but still she smiled.

In Madge's comfortably worn office, where piano blues played loudly enough on the old sound system to be heard, but softly enough to allow conversation, Bleu went to the desk and checked to see if there was any mail for her.

"Five envelopes," Madge said behind her. "Let me check on Cyrus while you open them. He's writing his homily. You know how much he struggles not to let them get too long."

Everyone knew.

Everyone knew Cyrus failed most of the time and rarely kept one of his passionate talks shorter than forty minutes.

While she waited, Bleu opened her mail. Five checks, four of them nice, and accompanied by friendly notes, and one large enough to make her eyes bug. That one was signed by Reb Girard, the town doctor. Reb's family had lived in Toussaint just about forever. Her father had been the local doctor before her. Now she was married to childhood friend, Marc Girard, an architect, and they had two children. Money couldn't be a problem, but the check still made Bleu want to sing and dance.

Instead, she flopped into Madge's red-and-white-striped over-stuffed chair and stretched out her legs. A horrible day was showing promise. Kevin Rains, despite taking the fall for her, would be at home by now—if he wasn't back at the firehouse. Apparently the fire had caused damage no one saw until it was too late. Bleu doubted she'd ever get into another car with quite as much confidence again.

Her cell phone rang in her pocket and she pulled it out. "Hello."

"It's Roche."

She hadn't thought to check the readout. "Yes," she said. Darn it anyway, why did she get tongue-tied around him? "I just got in some nice donation checks."

"That's great," he said. "Bleu, you haven't forgotten about tonight, have you?"

Tonight. "I might have to beg off and do some cleanup," she said. She heard the wobble in her voice. "There's a lot to be done. I'd be wrong if I didn't look into making the place as safe as I can. Not that I think this person will strike in the same place twice."

"Cleanup is a great idea," he said. "I'll bring my rubber gloves."

It took her an instant to register what he'd said and laugh. "You've already done too much for me. Driving me around and everything." She had yet to decide what to do about a car.

His voice lowered. "I couldn't do too much for you. Don't fight me on this. A promise is a promise and you said we had a date tonight. If we spend it washing walls, that's good with me."

She thought about it. Wanting to see him didn't make it easier to be objective. "Okay. Thanks. I hope you've got an apron, too."

"You'd be surprised what I've got," he said.

Bleu didn't pursue that. "I'll see you later, then?"

"Later." He was still on the line, listening, when she hung up softly.

Millie whipped from beneath the desk, for all the world as if she'd only just noticed Bleu's presence, and leaped onto her lap. Two turnarounds and the sleek black-and-white fur ball settled in.

"You've got a real case on Roche."

At the sound of Madge entering the room, Bleu craned to see over her shoulder. She was not comforted by the serious expression on her cousin's face.

"He's easy on the eyes," Madge continued. She closed the door softly and went to lean against her desk. "Both of the Savage brothers are."

"True," Bleu said, as lightly as she could. "Is it just me or is it stuffy in here?"

Madge skirted the desk and opened a window. Nasturtiums bobbled their gold-and-copper heads, some slipping through the open crack as if trying to get inside.

For a moment, Madge stood there, gazing out and absentmindedly gripping the edge of the window frame.

"What's the matter?" Tension got thicker by the second, and Bleu felt a little sick.

The lazy piano filled the silences between them. The dog lifted her head and looked from Bleu to Madge. Her nose twitched, but she sighed and closed her eyes.

"I'm going to get a dog as soon as I can," Bleu said, making conversation. "I think it would be good company. I always had one as a kid."

"I know," Madge said. "Why wait? Get a good watch dog."

"I intend to," Bleu told her, more sharply than she intended. "I'll have to wait a bit till I can afford it. Most of all, I want a good buddy. I don't intend to spend a lot of time being scared."

"You're changing," Madge said, quietly. "You're not so gentle. Why is that?"

Was she being told off for trying to take command of her life? "I'm the same old Bleu, just older and wiser. Do you think I should have stayed beaten down and scared forever?"

"You know I don't." Madge sounded angry, but Bleu didn't take it personally. Something was on Madge's mind and it wasn't whether or not Bleu was growing more independent. "Sorry. I'm a bit uptight. Cyrus will be a few more minutes, and I should say some things to you. I've already put them off too long."

Bleu swallowed, but she made sure she looked interested and approachable. "Then don't put them off any longer. We've always been able to talk to each other."

"We haven't spent a lot of adult time together. You know what I mean? I'm sure you've got your thoughts about the way I'm living my life. I know it's not too tidy, but I'm doing my best."

"I know you are," Bleu said quietly. "You're a special woman. You've always tried to do the best for everyone. I want things to work out for you—in the way you want them to work out. Do you like Sig Smith? You went out for dinner with him."

Madge's expression closed. "Yes. We had a pleasant evening. Thanks for asking."

But I don't want to talk about it? "I'm glad."

"What do you know about Roche Savage?" Madge said.

Taken aback by the directness, Bleu gave herself time to think, time not to say what she might regret later. "I know what most people know," she said. "And from my own experience, I think he's pretty special."

"That's what I was afraid of."

Bleu felt a little cold. She ran her fingers through Millie's fur, and the dog all but purred.

"I didn't mean that the way it sounded," Madge said. "All I've got is hearsay but not too much has been said to refute it."

"You're using big words. They make me nervous."

Madge sunk her hands deep in the pockets of a pink check dress and pulled the tulip-shaped skirt tighter about her curvy hips. "I won't win any prizes for diplomacy."

Sweat formed on Bleu's palms. "Just tell me what's on your mind. You're scaring me."

"Shoot," Madge said, with a lot of feeling. "Who knows how much is real and how much is just Lil gossiping? I'd almost forgotten about it."

Bleu resisted the temptation to stand up. There was no need to be confrontational. "Why not tell me what you heard?"

"I shouldn't have said anythin'." Madge's face flamed. "Be careful, that's all. People can seem one way and be another."

"Yes, they can. But you're not going to leave me with that kind of hint."

Madge puffed up her cheeks. She retrieved her dog and hugged the animal close. "Don't you think Roche is a bit worldly for you?"

"Not that I've noticed." Which wasn't at all true. "You know I had a bad time when I was married. *That* was too worldly for me."

Madge wouldn't meet her eyes. "Michael was a criminal."

"Yes. But before we knew that—"

"I meant the way he treated you was criminal."

Bleu did stand up then. "It was, but I shouldn't have told you about it. You don't need to deal with my troubles."

"Why?" Madge came closer. "We don't have any other available family. I want to be here for you. I know you'd stand by me."

"I would." Bleu looked into Madge's dark eyes and saw how troubled she was. "But there is something you're worrying about— about Roche. Isn't there?"

"He's not your type."

"Why?" Getting angry or defensive wouldn't help anything. "I'm not his social equal, if that's what you mean, but it doesn't seem to bother him."

"That's not what I meant. He's a lot more experienced than you."

"How would you know?" The rising pitch of her own voice embarrassed Bleu. "You mean well, but you're talking about things you can't know. Is it because Roche and I come from such different backgrounds? I'm poor and he's rich?"

"You weren't always so poor. Michael did that to you. You know I don't think about money, Bleu."

"Have you ever thought you should spend more time thinking about yourself?" Bleu asked. "You could work on straightening out the mess you're in and leave me to deal with my own life."

"That's mean," Madge said. "You aren't like that. It's because you don't feel good about yourself."

Bleu resisted the temptation to snap back again. "You could be right. Let's not talk about this anymore. You want the best for me. Thank you."

"Has..." The flush that remained on Madge's skin turned much darker. "Has he tried to...you know."

"Why don't you go ahead and ask what you want to know?"

Silence lengthened after that. Bleu could hear the beat of her own heart.

She jumped at the sound of a bird hitting the window. Millie gave a bark and the creature flew away again. Bleu rubbed her palms together. She was sweating.

"Something happened a couple of years back," Madge said. She appeared close to tears. "Lil's the one who saw it. A lot of strange things were happening, and she was out at night looking for something."

"Saw what?" Bleu couldn't smile or pretend anymore. "If you've got something to tell me, do it."

"I only want you to be careful and—"

"Tell me!"

Setting Millie down, Madge took hold of one of Bleu's hands. "I wasn't there. I'm saying what I was told. Cyrus would hate it if he knew I was telling you, but you're not his cousin."

"I don't think Cyrus would willingly let me be in danger," she said.

"He wouldn't. But sometimes he either doesn't believe things, or doesn't really hear them. This was out at the Green Veil clinic when it was just finished. Before Max started having patients there."

"Okay."

"It was at night. In the dark. Like I said, Lil was looking for something around Rosebank. Green Veil's next door."

"I know," Bleu said quietly.

"The lights were all on at Green Veil, which was unusual then. Lil walked over that way and saw something."

Bleu nodded.

"There's a reception area in front. It's big and the windows go all the way up to the first floor. Roche was with a woman in the foyer. He chased her and grabbed her."

Nerves jumped in Bleu's tummy. She had to listen, but she didn't want to.

"That's all," Madge said, pushing her hair back. "He was a bit aggressive with her. So I want you to make sure you're okay with him."

Bleu stared at Madge. "That's not all, is it?"

Slowly, Madge shook her head, no. "The woman's clothes were torn."

"Oh." Bleu covered her mouth.

"Her skirts went up and she didn't have anything on underneath. Lil said there was sex. And it was rough."

If she could make this whole conversation go away, she would. Bleu took deep breaths. "Lil's sure this was Roche? Who was the woman?"

Madge's eyes slid away. "She isn't around here anymore. I shouldn't name names. All I can say is what Lil reckoned. She dramatizes, but I would be wrong not to say this. Bleu, she talked about rape."

Chapter
21

Every breath Bleu took felt thick and old. The weight on her chest only got heavier. Her first instinct after Madge's announcement had been to get out of coming to Kate Harper's, but staying on her own at the rectory was a bad, bad idea.

"It's nice of you two to come along," Cyrus said. He tucked a trailing vine of pale pink roses back into an arbor over the gate leading to Kate's pretty white house.

"I thought Kate would call the rectory again by now," Madge said. "Don't you think it's strange she hasn't?"

Cyrus closed the wooden gate behind the three of them. "We did speak again today. I called her. She was sad, but restrained—the way you'd expect her to be."

"Kate's old world," Madge said to Bleu. "Proper in a way. I don't suppose she's too comfortable letting people see how she feels."

"Are you sure I should be here?" Bleu asked. "She's only met me a couple of times."

"Yes," Cyrus said. "Jim liked you a lot and he was enthusiastic about the school and the possibility of a senior center. You knew him, and Kate will appreciate it that you can talk about him."

Bleu smiled at Cyrus and followed along the gravel path.

What she couldn't ignore was Madge's agitation. When they looked at each other, Madge constantly appeared about to say something, but never did.

Several wide steps up to a screened porch, also loaded with roses, let them see that the front door was open. Cyrus rang the bell.

Not a sound came from inside the two-story house.

"Oh, dear," Madge said. "Poor Kate. If she wants to be alone, we shouldn't intrude."

"She likes her gardens," Cyrus said. "She could be out back."

They trailed in ragged file onto a fork in the path which looked as if it led around the house. Cyrus walked ahead.

His well-washed check shirt didn't look priestlike. Bleu thought, as she so often did, that he could be any woman's vital husband, the father of rambunctious children. When he glanced back, it was directly at Madge and his smile flashed just for her.

"Bleu," Madge whispered. "I don't think I should have told you what I did. I haven't heard anything else about Roche—nothing worrying."

"You did the right thing," Bleu said. Her eyes stung. It was impossible not to think of being in bed with him, his gentle power and the way he'd excited her made her feel complete. There had been nothing rough or scary about him.

"I only want the best for you," Madge said.

"I know," Bleu said, and she did. "Don't worry. It's in my hands now."

Madge hesitated. "You probably won't see him again, will you? That doesn't seem completely fair. Lil always makes a lot out of a little. I'm sure she saw Roche with someone, but it didn't have to be exactly the way she said."

Cyrus had stopped in front of them.

"Not now," Bleu said. She didn't know what she would do about Roche.

Laughter came from behind the house. Cyrus reached the end of the side wall and called out, "Kate? You here?"

More laughter rose. A man and a woman laughing together. Bleu frowned and listened hard. A shared moment. A conspiratorial pleasure.

"She's already got company," Madge said, joining Cyrus.

Her cousin had only heard laughter, not something secretive or forbidden. Bleu decided her imagination was wayward.

The three of them went forward until they saw a beautiful garden. Lush hedges and shrubs, banks of brilliant flowers, a perfectly mowed lawn that stretched into groves of fruit trees.

Bleu didn't see anyone there.

"That's Jim's house over there," Madge said, pointing. "I heard he left that to Kate, too. At least she'll be really well-fixed."

Built of split logs on stilts, Jim's house probably covered four thousand square feet.

Set too far back to be seen from the road, trees all but hid it on all sides except for the one that faced Kate's property.

"I didn't expect anything quite so grand," Bleu said.

"Jim's house, you mean?" Cyrus asked. "Or this one?"

She blew at a hair caught on her lips. "Both, I guess."

"Should we come back?" Madge said, already backing away.

"Kate!" Cyrus headed for an archway cut in a tall hedge ahead of them.

He ducked to go through and Bleu followed him.

"Who's that?" Madge asked when she joined them.

Kate sat in a white wood chaise, facing away from them. Beside her on a stool, a man with a lot of curly brown hair talked quietly, his arms wrapped around his knees. A pale denim shirt stretched over his hunched back. Bleu thought he must be tall. He was certainly well-built.

Kate held a glass toward him and he picked up a jug from a tray on the grass and poured. Then he poured for himself, and they laughed again, their heads close together.

"Maybe another time." Cyrus swung around and the hardness in his face shocked Bleu.

"Father Cyrus, is that you?"

Bleu saw Kate stand up.

The man also got to his feet. He moved a couple of steps away from her.

"Father? You will not go away without talkin' to me. Whatever next? George, get more chairs, and glasses for tea."

George, unsmiling, left at once.

"Hello, Kate," Cyrus said, turning around again. "I didn't want to interrupt."

"That's George Pinney," Madge said, her voice low. "He and his wife have rooms in Jim's house. George helps…helped Jim with things around the two properties. Mary manages Hungry Eyes. I don't really know them well."

Bleu and Madge glanced at one another.

"I've met Mary," Bleu said, wishing it hadn't been while she was in her pajamas. "But you know that."

She called out to Kate, "Don't go to any trouble, Mrs. Harper. We only want to know how you are."

"And let you know how the case is progressing," Cyrus added.

Kate held a starched lace fan. She flipped it open and wafted it very rapidly before her face. Over the top, she stared at them with pale blue eyes. Red hair curled beneath a broad-brimmed straw hat.

George Pinney came back with folding chairs slung behind one shoulder. He had little difficulty holding three in one hand. In the other, he carried glasses.

Quickly, he set up the chairs, lifted the tray from the grass to the stool he'd abandoned and poured for everyone. Then he stood away a little, wiping his hands on his dark pants.

"This is George," Kate said, looking up at the man from beneath the brim of her hat. "I don't know what I'd be doing without him and Mary. If I had to sit here all the time imagining my poor Jimmy lyin' dead in the church, why, I think I'd just curl up and die. At least I could go to join Jimmy then."

Bleu pursed her lips to stop a grin. This wasn't supposed to be funny.

"Kate," Cyrus said. "You know Jim's body hasn't been released—"

"No!" Kate completely hid her face with the fan. She shook her head and the hat brim wobbled. "Don't, please, I can't bear it. Who would do such a thing to a sweet, innocent man who never hurt a fly? I ask you, who would do that?"

"Someone who has lost his way in life," Cyrus said gently. "We're here for you. The whole town is here for you."

"Not the whole town," Kate said.

Cyrus shook his head. "Don't think about any of that. Whatever you need, you've got it. We'll make sure of it."

Kate sniffed. "Thank you, Father."

"Do you need something now?" Cyrus asked.

Bleu watched his honest face, looked at Madge watching him, too, and felt so sad.

"What I need is for some people in this town to stop sayin' terrible things about me." Kate dropped the fan in her lap and raised her pointed chin. She had a smooth, heart-shaped face, pale against her red hair, and now her spirit brought her back up straight. "I do know what's been suggested. Jim and I have kept company for some years. We aren't—weren't—children, but our intentions were pure."

"Of course they were," Cyrus said.

"Weren't they, George?" Kate said. "You and Mary have been here. You're my witnesses that Jim and I had a chaste friendship. We were two lonely people who helped each other get through life. He made sure I was looked after. I kept him company."

Bleu thought about the dinners she had cooked for him. She smiled at the woman. "And you made sure he didn't starve," she said. "You do remember me, Mrs. Harper. I'm Bleu Laveau. I so liked Jim—he was the best-tempered man."

Kate's white lace dress settled gracefully around her. Even her neck and the skin revealed between crisp lapels showed little sign of age.

"Jim Zachary would do anything for me," Kate said, apparently not hearing what Bleu said. "George here did all the shoppin' and Mary cooked our meals. Jim's and mine, that is. We ate here. They ate over there." She pointed a pale orange fingernail toward Jim Zachary's house.

"That must have been a great comfort to you," Madge said. She set the basket of baked goodies down near Kate.

Bleu took inventory of the woman. She wasn't old, or even elderly. Early fifties at the most. And she showed no sign of arthritis that Bleu could see.

"What are you goin' to do about this nonsense talk?" Kate asked Cyrus.

High-heeled pumps showed off a pair of slim ankles.

"If someone says something they shouldn't, I'll be sure to have a chat," Cyrus told her. "But you don't have to worry about that. You've got other things on your mind."

"I surely do," Kate said. Her mouth trembled. "I laugh because I don't want to cry. I talk as if I'm angry because it stops me from screamin'. I dress myself up and put on makeup because there's no way I'm going to let folks in this town, the ones who don't like me, chatter about how I'm lettin' myself go. Jim wouldn't like it and neither do I."

"I admire you for that," Madge said. "I don't know if I could be as strong."

Bleu couldn't keep her eyes off Kate's shoes. They didn't look very big, but neither were they tiny. Were they large enough to make the footprints outside the rectory?

Now she was being a fool. No way would this fastidious woman climb around in the mud—or pack filthy burned books into a box and wrap it up like a wedding gift. And Jim would have had to put his head down on the pew and hold still while Kate stabbed that knife through his neck.

Bleu swallowed several times.

Even then, it was doubtful Kate could have got the blade to go in, skewer the bench, then pull the thing out.

Nausea washed over Bleu.

Two tears slipped from the corners of Kate's eyes. "I told him not to get involved," she whispered.

Cyrus caught Bleu's eye and shook his head slightly. "Whoever did that to Jim wasn't rational," he said. "I think it was a random thing."

"No, Father. My Jim died because he was too good and because he always championed the underdog." Her china-blue gaze settled, without malice, on Bleu. "He told me how angry he was that people didn't treat you well, Bleu. He thought the new school was a wonderful idea, and the senior center, well, he couldn't stop talkin' about that. He wanted there to be a place for the old people to go.

He talked about hiring a nurse to be there just in case, and makin' the place handicapped accessible. There would be plenty of room in the end, that's what he said. Although I never could figure out how." She raised her shoulders and she held her glass out.

George Pinney scrambled to refill her iced tea and Kate drank, raising her delicate white throat.

"Poor George," Kate said. "He lost his job, you know."

"Now, Miz Harper," George said, his face darkening. "No need to bother people with my little troubles, not when there's much bigger things to worry about."

"I think it embarrasses him if I talk about it," Kate said, as if the man couldn't hear every word of her conversation. "He used to be quite somethin'. Worked for a law firm in N'awlins, not that I know anythin' about things like that. Now look at him. And Mary's away all day workin' at that café. Not a suitable job for an educated woman at all."

Bleu's attention repeatedly wandered. She didn't think she liked Kate Harper and felt sorry for George Pinney, who must need whatever he earned working around the two houses or he would never tolerate being humiliated by Kate.

"I'm going to have to get back," Cyrus said. "But I did want to cover a few things with you first, Kate."

"Of course, Father." She leaned forward and slipped a slim hand into one of his big, tanned ones. "You can make me feel safe and that's a blessin'."

"Would you rather we spoke alone?"

"Why?" Kate stared around. "Are you goin' to say somethin' that people who care about me can't hear?"

"Not a thing." Cyrus smiled at her and his chest expanded with the big breath he took. "Are you okay for money? I mean do you have enough for your running expenses?"

Kate nodded. "Thank you for askin'. Some would shy away from a delicate subject like that. I know my late husband didn't provide for me, but other members of my family did and I'll manage. I didn't want Jim to leave me anythin', but he wouldn't hear of anythin' else. It'll be a while before things can be settled, but then—" she looked away "—then I'll be a rich woman. Rich with no one to share anythin' with. I'd give up everythin' I have if I could get Jim back."

"I know you would," Cyrus said.

Madge and Bleu looked at each other and quickly away again. Cyrus was serious. The woman was sucking him right in with the helpless-victim act. Why did men fall for that?

"Do you know if Jim has any other relatives?" Cyrus asked. He had told Madge and Bleu that Spike wanted him to ask these questions so Spike wouldn't have to.

"If he did have any, he never mentioned them," Kate said.

"When the coroner is finished with his...work, Jim's funeral will have to be arranged. I know you aren't related to him, but since the two of you were close, if there aren't any relatives, you should be the one to decide how things are done. If you want to, of course."

Kate put her feet on the chaise again. She folded her hands in her lap and looked far away.

"Kate?" Cyrus said.

"Don't press me," she said. "I can't bear it. Madge, you arrange everything and let me know the details. You're used to these things. He liked a rose in his buttonhole. There's to be a fresh one for the viewin'. And plenty of food for after the service. Champagne so we can toast Jim.

"Make sure I'm in the front pew and I'll walk behind the casket. That's the least I can do for him."

Bleu eyed the shoes one more time. Just because the prints Roche found might have been too big didn't mean a thing. With the mud being wet, a person's feet could have slipped and made the prints bigger.

"I'll talk to y'all another time," Kate said.

Cyrus got up at once, and Bleu followed with Madge.

Unexpectedly, Kate turned sharp eyes on Bleu. "Enough damage has been done because of this silly scheme of yours."

Bleu's skin prickled.

"A fancy school in a little place like this? Such airs. And who's going to afford to send their children there, I'd like to know?"

"Kate," Cyrus put in quickly. "Bleu didn't decide we should have a school, the parishioners did—or many of them. Bleu's only here because we asked her to come and help us."

"Give it up, before someone else dies," Kate said, still focused on Bleu. "It's a cursed idea. You weren't here and I was just a child, but that old school went up in flames and a lot of children died. Burned to death. Trapped in that little hall in there. They were singin' in the mornin', their little faces turned up like flowers to the sun. And they all died."

Madge made a strangled sound.

"Kate, Kate," Cyrus said. "No one talks about it. I didn't even know there had been deaths. How terrible."

Tears brimmed in her eyes. "Don't you go buildin' another school. Hear me, girl? Not again—or I know terrible things are goin' to happen. They already did, didn't they?" She leaned forward, as if begging for understanding.

"Hush," Bleu said. Before she could stop herself, she put a hand on the woman's cheek.

Kate pressed her own fingers over Bleu's and kissed her palm.

Revulsion cramped Bleu's stomach but she didn't pull away.

"I'll tell you how I know," Kate said, crying openly. "I was late for school that day. When I got there, the place was all smoke and flames and people tryin' to save the little children. The mothers and fathers cryin' and screamin'. But I was late, so I was fine. The whole area knew about it, but that generation's all but gone now. People came from all over to help. I can still see all the parents tryin' to rescue their babies.

"I walked home just sobbin' all the way. I walked home alone. Nobody came lookin' for me."

Chapter
22

Roche leaned on the hood of his car with his ankles crossed.

He had better look more nonchalant than he felt. Sam Bush told him Bleu had gone with Cyrus and Madge to see Kate Harper and Roche decided he would come to Kate's and wait for Bleu.

Given the changes between them, the uncertain feeling he had didn't make a lot of sense, except that Bleu had stood him up before and he was afraid that, after the morning's drama, she might do it again.

He had to see her.

Another half hour passed before he saw Madge lead the way from the side of the house with Cyrus and Bleu behind her. All three looked at their feet, and their faces didn't give him confidence that he'd get a happy greeting.

But his excuse for showing up was in the can, and it was good.

Bleu saw him first but didn't wave. He did.

She must have said something, because the others looked in his direction and Cyrus did raise a hand.

"Hey," he said when they got closer. "Sam told me Bleu was

here. I figured since it was past time for her to go home, I'd stop by and take her."

Cyrus said, "Good. She needs to get out of here." He pulled his eyebrows down. "It's been difficult."

"I should go back to the rectory and finish up some things," Bleu said.

Roche kept the smile on his face, but his jaws locked. *Sure you should. And you intend to duck out on me again, don't you?*

"Absolutely not," Cyrus told her. "You've had a long, hard day, and I don't want you back at the rectory. Madge or I will come and get you after morning mass tomorrow."

"No need," Bleu said. "I'm getting a bicycle."

"The hell you are." *Damn it,* Roche thought. His unruly mouth got him every time. "I mean, I don't think that's a good idea."

"Fortunately, it isn't a decision you have to make," Bleu said. "I'll be fine. I'll get something from the insurance on my car. When I can, I'll get another one. Ozaire Dupre told me he can find good second-hand ones. He might already have found me a bike, and he knows about a dog he thinks I'd love, too. Only I can't get one yet."

"Ozaire's a regular one-man procurement machine," Roche said. "I hope you didn't pay him for a bike before seeing it. He probably pulled it out of the bayou."

"What did he do to you?" Bleu said. "He's been nice to me."

Roche looked at the toes of his shoes. "Ozaire's got a lot of good points." He decided not to bring up the man's willingness to assassinate someone's character when he had no proof.

"Why don't you come back with us, Bleu?" Madge asked. She put an arm around Bleu's shoulders. "I'll take you to Rosebank with me, and you can really rest. You'll need to air your place out before you sleep there."

Roche crossed his arms and watched Madge. She wouldn't look at him. "That ozone stuff does great things," he said. "The fire department sprayed it all over so there's no smell. And the door's been fixed."

Bleu's eyes glittered as if she might cry. "Thank you," she said.

He didn't want gratitude, but he did want to know why Madge was getting in the middle.

"I think Kate is deeply upset," Cyrus said. "I'll counsel her if she'll let me, but perhaps she'll come and talk to you, Roche. We expect grief, but one moment she's in denial about Jim's death and the next she's angry and confrontational about it."

"I'll see if I can make an excuse to talk to her," Roche said. Bleu was staring at him. "I could get Dr. Reb to take me with her. She probably plans on coming over here anyway."

"Good idea." Cyrus slapped his shoulder. "See if you can get Bleu to eat something. I don't think I've seen her have a meal all day."

"She's taking me out to dinner," Roche said, smiling at each of them. "We're going for Chinese takeout."

Cyrus laughed and glanced at Madge. "I might see if Madge will share a lonely priest's chicken pie," he said. "Lil Dupre prides herself on the ones she makes for me."

"That sounds wonderful," Madge said, all smiles. She sobered at once. "There's plenty there for you, Bleu."

A confused light entered Cyrus's eyes. "Bleu and Roche are eating together," he said. "We'd best get back."

All the way to Cyrus's car, Madge repeatedly craned to see Bleu and Roche.

"What's up with Madge?" Roche said. He settled a hand on Bleu's back but she hurried to his car, away from his touch.

When they were side by side in the front seat of the BMW, he said, "I've got the food in the trunk. I didn't think you'd feel like stopping."

She turned her face from him and kept it averted, while he drove away negotiating the narrow, mostly unimproved roads in the area where Kate lived.

A pinkish-gray haze hung in the distance. Waiting for Bleu, he'd been aware of how heavy the air felt, but the moisture that formed on his back had little to do with that. "How was your day?" he asked. *Lame.*

"Not so good. But there wasn't any reason it should be." She face forward and lifted her chin. The humidity had curled her hair.

"I was serious about what I got for dinner," he told her. "There's a new Chinese place on Main Street."

She showed no interest.

"I meant what I said about the ozone spray, too. That stuff's a miracle. The fire didn't actually go through the wall of the house, but plenty of smoke got in."

"Thank you for coming back for me this morning," she said. "I'm sorry I did my panic thing. I never know when it'll happen. When it does, I can't seem to move. You ought to know about that."

"No big deal." He glanced sideways, and she was looking at him. Roche nodded and said, "I'm grateful I didn't leave your place any earlier this morning. I might have been too far away to know what had happened."

She didn't say anything.

"Did I hear right, that you'll consider teaching at the new school?"

"If there ever is one," Bleu said.

"There will be."

"Not if Kate Harper has her way."

"Meaning?" he said.

"Oh, nothing. She's understandably upset about Jim and thinks he was killed because he supported the school. She doesn't want it built at all."

"She won't have any say in that," Roche said. "Not that I blame her for her conclusions."

"Her conclusions are right," Bleu said. "It's obvious."

"I can't argue with you," he told her. "But Cyrus isn't going to roll over and play dead because someone's involved in a dangerous game."

"That was an unfortunate choice of words," she said.

"You're sniping."

The words left his mouth without passing his brain.

Bleu clammed up.

"I shouldn't have said that," he told her. "But you asked for it."

"Now who's sniping?" Bleu said.

They drove in silence for the next fifteen minutes. Businesses had closed for the evening on Main Street, and the lowering sun threw long shadows from tree trunks.

At the end of Crawfish Alley, Dr. Reb Girard brought her Land Rover to a halt at a stop sight and she waved, her red hair glinting in the light. Reb practiced from the house on the alley where her father had practiced before her.

"She's something," Roche said, feeling daring. "She loves medicine. If she didn't she could stay out at Cloud's End and host garden parties. Marc has plenty for both of them." Marc Girard, a successful architect, had inherited a good deal of the commercial real estate in the town. Cloud's End was the Girards' impressive home just outside Toussaint.

"You should understand how dedicated some people are to their professions," Bleu said.

He just stopped himself from slamming on the brakes. This would be easier if he had not started needing to see Bleu these days, to be with her. Arguing wasn't something he did well, but he would find out what was going through her head.

In the townhouse driveway, he parked far enough down for her to see how untouched the place looked. The team from Green Veil had put in some productive hours.

Bleu cleared her throat. "Look at this," she said. "I can't believe it."

"The crew we use at Green Veil do good work. There's always plenty to be done out there."

"The front door... It's new."

"Thanks to me, the old one got pretty badly abused," he said.

"They cleaned up the garage? And my car's been taken away?"

"It's totaled. The car went to the insurance adjuster. But you already know that. I don't think the cleanup took as much as you think it did. Smoke damage often looks worse than it is."

If she let him know he wasn't welcome to come in, he would argue. Wouldn't he?

"Thank you, Roche."

"You already did that bit," he told her. "I'll get our dinner out of the trunk. I put it there so it wouldn't smell in the car."

"Roche..."

He let her pause go on. This time he wouldn't fill any gaps for her.

She ran her fingers through her hair. The white blouse and tan pants she wore were simple. On her, they were classy and sexy.

"You did tell me we had a date tonight," he said. So he'd given up and filled in some of the silence—he was human.

"I know." She turned a little ring with a pearl in it around and around on her right hand.

"Let's go." He sprang the trunk and got out of the car. Praying she would lighten up, and that they'd be able to relax together, he grabbed the bags and slammed the trunk.

She was out of the car, but at least she hadn't scurried up the steps to get away from him.

He smiled at her.

Bleu smiled back, quickly, and looked at the ground.

Was it guilt? Was that it? She felt guilty for sleeping with him, having sex with him—and enjoying it? He had no doubt Bleu had loved the sex. He had also clued in to the reticence she had worked through.

He caught up with her at the bottom of the steps to the front door. "Wait," he said. "Look at me, Bleu."

She didn't.

Roche shifted all the bags into one arm and held her elbow, pulled her to face him.

Her expression shook him. Tears shone along her eyelids and her mouth trembled. She stood very straight, very stiff.

"What's wrong with you?" he asked. "I thought—"

"You thought I'd never find out about you?" Bleu said. "Is that what you thought?"

Chapter
23

At the same time

He worked alone.

The idea of having a partner—even if only until he didn't need one anymore—made him edgy. If you let someone inside, they made demands. And they made mistakes.

Justice didn't tolerate mistakes. They were too dangerous.

From where he stood, he could see the bayou without anyone seeing him. He was hidden by the trees. Watching traffic on the water calmed him, focused him. He liked thinking about the gators in there—and the cottonmouths. He had a particular fondness for the snakes. What would it be like to carry an instrument of agonizing destruction with you?

The snakes had possibilities.

He had to stop the rage at his failure that morning. Rage was better gathered in and turned outward again.

Setting the fire had only complicated things. He should have sucked up his anger that Roche didn't leave in time, and gone back later, or tomorrow. If the fire chief had the right resources, they'd figure out what he'd done. Then there would be a hunt, and he'd be the hunted. Not that they'd ever find out who he was.

Killing Bleu would be the fastest way to get what he wanted. Or it would be a good start.

The other one would have to go, too, but not until he got what he wanted from her.

He had picked his next diversion. When the authorities needed to be confused, there was nothing like a fresh kill to do the job.

Chapter
24

Roche didn't talk to her, didn't answer the question she shouldn't have asked, didn't look at her.

He opened the new front door. Heavy, carved from oak; a glass fanlight at the top reminded her of a white-crystal peacock's tail.

As soon as she went inside the townhouse, he followed and dropped keys into her hand. He walked to the kitchen and put the bags on a counter.

Bleu's breath began to catch. She couldn't fill her lungs, her ribs ached. How could she have thought these episodes were over?

His face was expressionless. "There are locks on the windows now," he said and raised a blind to show her. "They slide on these tracks. Easy to operate and very safe." He dropped more keys beside the bags. "The back door's been replaced, too. The place in the siding where the firefighters checked inside the wall is also patched."

When she began to shake, Bleu couldn't do a thing to stop her teeth from chattering or her knees from jerking.

"You don't have to worry about this place being tight anymore."

With his hands in the pockets of his jeans and a dark green shirt tucked loosely inside at the waist, he moved as if he were relaxed. Bleu knew a sham when she saw one.

"You are very kind," she said. "Thank you."

"I don't want you to thank me. An alarm system's been ordered. They'll show up tomorrow, and we've already made sure someone other than you will be here when it's installed."

Sweat ran on her palms. She breathed through her mouth, desperate not to throw up. "The bills," she said. "Please—"

"We'll discuss bills at another time. You insist you're going to stay here, even though whoever the cops are trying to hunt down knows you live in this place. It needs to be as safe as it can be."

When she needed control more than she ever had, she was losing it completely. "It's not your responsibility."

"I've made it mine. What's been done isn't charity—the owner wants it this way. Are you hungry?"

Hungry? "No, thank you. Not yet."

"Good. Neither am I. What's the matter with you?" He came closer. "Are you going to collapse on me? If you are, let me know and I'll call an aid car."

She shook her head, shocked by his toughness.

"Take a deep breath," he said, never moving his eyes from her.

Bleu did her best. Her hands turned icy.

"Another one," he said. "And another. Do you like the front door?"

She clasped her hands and looked at the door. "Nice." The next breath came more easily. "It's really beautiful."

"Sit," he said, turning a chair around at the table. When she didn't move, he said, "Sit down now, before you fall down."

She did as she was told and her heart slowed.

Roche walked behind her into the kitchen and turned the faucet on. When he returned, it was with a glass of water and ice. "This'll help," he said. "Hold it with both hands."

She drank, letting her eyes close, then rolled the cold glass across her forehead. "Sorry about that," she said.

"Panic attack," he said and he wasn't asking her a question. "If you feel it starting up again, warn me."

"It won't. I'm not good company. I appreciate all you've done to help me, but I'd like to be alone. Tomorrow we'll talk. Forgive me, please."

He pulled out another chair and sat down facing her. "Not so fast," he said. "When was the last time that happened to you? The panic?"

"You sound like a doctor."

"I am a doctor."

She looked at him. "You're a psychiatrist."

"I went through the same training as any other doctor and there's nothing wrong with my memory."

He sounded matter-of-fact, not brusque or judgmental.

"I told you. It hasn't happened for a long time. A couple of years, probably."

"Do you think it was the fire that stressed you?" He leaned forward and rested his elbows on his knees. "You dealt with Jim Zachary's death without falling apart. If anything should have made you panic, that was it."

She wanted to snap back that she wasn't falling apart, but a few minutes ago she had been.

"I'm strong," she said. "Really I am. I had to be, so I learned how." Her voice sounded steady enough.

"Uh-huh."

"It was probably because of everything that's happened today," she said, not believing a word of it. "Going to see Kate Harper wasn't a good idea. She's upset and not herself."

"Not herself how?"

She still wanted to share everything with him. "She was with George Pinney, Mary's husband, who looks after her property and Jim's. They were laughing together and it seemed so strange, like Jim wasn't dead and everything was normal. It even upset Cyrus. I saw it in his eyes. Probably wasn't anything, but—" she shrugged "—I think I could make something out of absolutely nothing right now."

Roche steepled his fingers beneath his chin. "Our first instincts are more often right than wrong. I hope it was nothing, but I'm with you—sounds bizarre."

They stayed where they were, facing each other, their eyes meeting, looking speculative, shifting away. Bleu longed for the strain to break. She needed a storm, the kind that washed away everything in its wake—and in this case, cleared away her doubts about this man she wanted so very much.

"You can let me have it now," Roche said. "What is it that I thought you'd never find out?"

Bleu sat on her hands and bowed her head.

"Don't hide your face from me," he said. "You're angry. You don't owe me a thing, but I'd appreciate it if you'd let me know what I've done wrong."

She popped to her feet and stood there, looking down into his face. "I shouldn't have said anything. There's no reason why I should have. You've never done anything bad to me."

Very slowly, he drew in a breath. "Just tell me." He thought he knew.

"Is it true that you did something awful to a woman once?"

Roche slumped. He rubbed a hand over his face. "Like what?"

She turned to walk away, but he caught her wrist and pulled her back. "Sit down," he said. "We can deal with this, whatever it is."

"Is it true that you like rough sex?"

Roche flexed his fingers. That wasn't the term he'd expected from her. "Why would you ask me a thing like that? After being with me?"

Bleu sat on the edge of her chair and leaned toward him. "You were sweet. And sexy. I've never felt that way, excited, but…it was right."

"Who told you I like rough sex?"

"Do you?"

He couldn't look away from her slightly parted lips. "Damn it. I'd like to know who talked to you about it."

"Answer me."

She wasn't shrinking. Something about that pleased him. Could be, it excited him, too.

"I'll answer you. The night with you was incredible. I want many more nights like that. Rough sex—no, I don't particularly like rough sex. But I could probably be described as sexually adventurous. Inventive. I get bored and like to try new things. Is that so terrible?"

Her blanched face took on a shiny, almost transparent look. "I don't know what it means," she whispered.

Anger stirred. "It means I could decide I want to make love standing on my head." He knew he should give himself time to calm down, but he wasn't Superman. "That wouldn't necessarily mean *you'd* have to be standing on *your* head, but it might."

She blinked and sucked in the corners of her mouth.

"What do you think about that?"

"I don't," she told him.

"Who talked to you about me?"

"There was one time that was different, wasn't there?" she said. "A time at Green Veil when…you were seen through the windows in front."

"Really? Okay, yes. It's a good thing your spy didn't get to see what happened upstairs in the gym before that. The lady was athletic."

"Don't." She looked as if he'd grown horns.

"Don't what? Don't tell you what you want to know? You asked. Let me see. We rode exercise bikes that night. I doubt if they'd been ridden quite that way before. Then we used one of the hot mud rooms. Everything gets really slippery—and messy. But who cares about mess in the heat of the moment—so to speak?"

He could see her hold herself stiff and force back tears. "That sounds adventurous all right," she said with a forced little laugh.

"What happened down in reception afterward was probably a mistake, but she decided we weren't finished yet. If I'd been less...hot?...I wouldn't have let that happen. Anything else you want to know?"

Bleu coughed. "Did you rape her?"

Iced water, doused over him from head to foot, wouldn't have shaken him more. Roche stood up. Vaguely, he wished he hadn't because he didn't want to make her feel threatened, and from his vantage point he could only look way down on her.

"If you have to ask the question, then I must have," he told her. "How does it feel to be alone with a rapist?"

"I don't think you are," Bleu said. "But I wanted you to tell me it wasn't true."

"Like a child," he said. "Make it all right, Daddy. Tell me it's all sugar and spice and no slugs."

"Don't." She raised her hands, curled into fists. "I didn't handle that well, but you're really not handling it well, either. Something happened, Roche, you've already admitted it."

"And I told you—or I'm telling you now—it was the woman's idea. Only you couldn't even imagine a thing like that, could you? What happened to you? Who damaged you so badly you're terrified of sex? Your dead husband?"

"Stop it!"

He should, and he knew it. But for once he wasn't holding his temper in check. He couldn't believe she doubted him.

"I'm sorry," she said.

Roche turned his back and put distance between them. His temples pounded. "Are you?" He slammed his fists down on the counter. "Do you believe I would rape a woman?"

"No."

He could hardly hear her. Again he punished the counter. His hands throbbed.

"Violence frightens me," she said. "Please don't be angry."

"Violence?" He looked over his shoulder at her and laughed. "What would you know about violence?"

Her hands fell to her sides. "I know about it," was all she said.

"I didn't rape her."

Not technically. Lee had wanted it. She'd come looking for him and goaded him into having sex with her. And it was sex. What they had done had nothing to do with love.

She came looking for dangerous excitement, but she got a lot more than she planned.

Chapter
25

Late that evening

Madge chafed her arms. The air-conditioning ran in Sig's car, but that wasn't what made her cold. The chill came from inside her body and raised goose bumps on her skin.

Sig had been waiting at St. Cecil's when she got back from Kate's place. He wanted to take her out again, tonight, and looked hopeful enough to make her smile. When she'd started to say she already had plans, Cyrus told Sig that a chicken pie was no reason to give up a night out and she had felt obligated to go with him.

"I like being with you," Sig said.

"Thank you."

She knew he was waiting for her to tell him she liked being with him, too. Sig Smith was a decent man. Smart, funny, kind and attractive. What woman could want more?

She did.

"What did you think of the restaurant?" he asked.

Madge had scarcely noticed either her surroundings or what she ate. "Lovely," she said. He'd taken her to a jazz club in Lafayette where the food had almost as good a reputation as the music.

"You're tired," he said. "I shouldn't have sprung the invitation on you so late."

"You're a busy man. Sometimes busy people don't have a lot of time for plannin'."

He put a hand on top of hers—on her knee. "D'you know, I've never heard you say anything unkind about anyone? And you put everyone else first. It's sweet, but I worry you could get taken advantage of."

Not pulling her hand away was hard. "Thank you. No need to worry about me. I've been on my own a long time, and I do a good job of looking after myself."

He patted her fingers and returned his hand to the wheel.

"Can I ask you something?" he said.

Madge wanted to be home, shut away, sleeping and not thinking. "If you like."

"We haven't gotten into anything very personal. I've never been married. How about you?"

She almost laughed. "No. I thought everyone knew that."

"I don't know the people who would. Have you ever thought of settling down?"

"Not really." The real answer was too complicated and not something she would share, anyway.

"Why is that?"

Just let me get home.

When she didn't answer, he said, "You don't want to talk about this."

She shrugged and ran her fingers through her short curls. "I don't have an answer. My life is what it is. We all want things, but we don't all get what we want. I'm happy."

"Would you consider coming away with me for a weekend?"

On either side of the car, pines rose, dark and dense. Madge frowned. She wasn't a child. And neither was he. These days, what he was suggesting wasn't scandalous.

"Too fast for you?" he said. "I'm sorry. We could have separate rooms. There's a lodge on a lake just out of Pointe Judah. It's not far to go, but pretty and quiet. I thought it might give us a chance to get to know each other better."

"I don't know what to say." And she would not lash out and sound like a prude. "With what's happened around the parish, I feel I should be available, if…if I'm needed."

"Cyrus is lucky to have someone as devoted as you," he said. "He's a good man, though."

"Yes, he is." Her vision blurred.

"Will you look at that?" Sig said. "Those are raindrops on the windshield. It's coming down again. We are having one wet time of it."

"I like the weather here. But I grew up with it, so it seems right." Making conversation with him wasn't comfortable for her.

Another ten minutes, and they'd reach the rectory. She could hold on that long, but she didn't see how she could go out with him again.

Not his fault.

Sig took his foot off the gas. "Okay if we stop for a few minutes and talk?"

Talk and what else? She laced her fingers in her lap. "That would be nice. Maybe there's a view somewhere around."

"You're all the view I need."

Her heart gave a giant thud.

Taking it easy and smooth, he steered from the road to the shoulder, then beneath the trees.

She glanced over her shoulder. They hadn't seen any other vehicles for ages.

Sig turned off the engine.

They both stared ahead.

"I'm not so practiced at this," he said. "At least, not anymore. I've been so busy establishing myself with my work, I've become pretty solitary."

"Where did you live before you came here?" she asked.

"On the East Coast. I met the Savage twins back there. Last year, Roche asked if I wanted to come here and work with him, and I thought, what the hell, something completely different."

She couldn't just tell him to drive on. He was nice, really nice. "And you like it here?"

He looked at her. "Better and better. Look, Madge, I don't think you've led a very…I don't know…social life? You're quiet, at least on a personal level. We've got nothing but time, and we can take it. I guess I'm asking you to give me a chance."

This was more than she could handle. "We'll have coffee soon," she said and felt ridiculous. "Vivian Devol—she's the sheriff's wife and runs Rosebank with her momma—she'd be happy for me to have you over one Saturday or Sunday."

"Nice," he said in a voice flat enough to let her know "nice" wasn't what he had in mind. "How come you agreed to go out with me that first time?"

She was grateful it was too dark for him to see her much. "Why, I believe you underestimate your charm," she said. Sometimes you had to try to be what you weren't—for the other person. "You are a nice man. Why wouldn't I agree? And I agreed a second time, remember?"

"I think I'm making you uncomfortable."

"No! Oh, don't be silly. How could you make anyone uncomfortable, Sig? You're a pussy cat."

He didn't laugh.

He did undo his seat belt.

Madge sat, straight-backed, in her seat.

"You're wasting yourself," he said. "I think you know what I mean."

She shook her head. The thought of getting back to the rectory, climbing into her little car and locking the door beckoned like a valuable prize.

"Cyrus takes advantage of you."

"He doesn't, Sig. No, absolutely not. You've seen how he encourages me to go out and have a good time."

Sig settled his hand on the back of her neck. "Of course," he said, stroking lightly. "I think I'm already getting jealous of Cyrus because he spends so much time with you. Will you think about the weekend?"

"I will. I'll let you know." Sometimes you had to say whatever it took.

"There are cabins around the lake. I've only driven past, but I did stop to see what reservations were like. Just in case you decide to let me take you, I've got one on hold."

He thought that after two dates she'd be ready to stay in a lake cabin with him? Was that normal for these times? It wasn't for her.

"There are some trails out from there. We could take a picnic and go hiking."

"I've never been hikin'."

Sig took a moment to say, "You're kidding. Madge, Madge, your education needs taking in hand. There's fun to be had out there. Doesn't have to be wild, but you can't miss everything there is to enjoy."

He was probably right about that.

"We'll see," she said.

"May I kiss you?"

Madge looked up at him. Her throat had closed, and she breathed through her nose. When he'd taken her out before, he'd kissed her cheek quickly when he took her home, nothing more. That evening had been difficult for her, too.

"You are beautiful," he said. "I don't know how far I'd have to go to find someone as beautiful but unspoiled as you. You should see your eyes." He laughed a little. "I don't want to do anything to change you."

Madge couldn't speak .

Gradually, he brought his face closer. He touched his mouth to hers, softly, without demand.

He smelled nice, fresh, like soap and clean laundry. Appealing. *Close your eyes and give him a chance.*

She didn't want to be here. Or with Sig.

His arm slid around her and he pulled them together. Again he kissed her. He had a nice mouth, even if it did feel foreign and she couldn't relax enough to respond.

"Loosen up," he murmured, pressing his lips along her cheek to her ear. "I'll take care of you."

Jumpy, fighting down dread, she put a hand on his shoulder.

His breathing speeded and grew heavier. "That's right," he said. "I won't do more than you're ready for."

She wasn't ready for anything.

Sig kissed her again. He found her belt buckle and released it so he could take her all the way into his arms. This time he put his tongue inside her mouth. She heard the sound the moisture made, couldn't keep her nose out of the way of his.

He drew his head back and she saw him smile, and the feverish light in his eyes.

This wasn't what she was about. Or perhaps it was, just not with him.

If she was to hope for a full life, she had to get past her inhibitions. Sig wouldn't force her to do something against her will. He was a good man. He'd be a good partner…a good father.

You can't make yourself desire a man just because you want children.

Sig adjusted his weight, leaned over and pinned her. That's not what he meant to do, she told herself, but her mind screamed that if it was, then it was her fault. If she didn't stop him, how could he know what she didn't want?

His mouth was wide open on hers, his tongue reaching. He slid a warm hand up her thigh and rubbed his fingertips in her groin. She gasped, and he kissed her more deeply; he must have thought the sounds she made were of passion.

She didn't have the strength to force up against him. Every move she made increased his excitement. From her groin to her belly, his fingers slid and spread, not hard or painful, but inexorable.

Madge caught at his shoulders and her arms shot forward. There was nothing to grip. Sig made groaning sounds and moved her head hard, from side to side.

He didn't know she wasn't responding.

Panic caught at Madge's throat.

Sig slid a hand between them and inside the bodice of her dress. He held her breast, moved his thumb back and forth over the nipple. It grew hard, and through the panic came horror. Madge screwed up her eyes, hardly able to make out anything of him at close proximity and with almost no light.

Moving shadows, the gleam of skin.

Driving the heels of her shoes into the carpet, using both hands to push as hard as she could, she fought to shove him off. And the instant a hand was free, she slapped him hard across the face.

He leaped away from her.

Madge threw open her door and stumbled from the car.

"Madge! Get back here, now. For God's sake, get in."

She wouldn't listen to him. The rain grew heavier, warm and thick, and a strong breeze pushed it toward her. Running into the squall, she turned an ankle and cried out. A second's pause and she tossed the shoes away.

This was country she knew—all of it. Without a second thought, she took off between the trees. Rocks, pieces of wood, debris of who knew how many years, tore at her feet. Branches and fallen snags scraped her legs. With her arms thrown out for balance, she kept her face turned ahead and rushed deeper into the vegetation.

Where she needed to go was maybe a mile away, a mile of rough, undergrowth-clogged ground.

"Madge! Please let me take you home." She heard crashing as Sig plunged between the trees.

The sound of his voice, and his big body coming for her, only made her strides longer. Pain stabbed at her ankle. She heard her cotton skirts rip. Things plucked at her face.

A yell soared out. For all she knew, he'd run into a tree. This was all her fault. She couldn't change a thing now, but she could have back there—if she'd been less of a coward.

"Madge!"

Farther away now. But he must still be coming after her. Of course he was. She could stop, face him, tell him she couldn't be what he wanted her to be.

But what if he wouldn't accept her answer? What if he pressed her again? He might think she would change her mind if he tried hard enough. Men could be like that. She wasn't a complete neophyte.

By instinct, she made a turn to the right. Beneath her feet, she felt a downward slope and half slid, half toppled between fallen trees. Mushiness pushed between her toes. Mud. And probably blood. She didn't care. Instead of running and crashing about, she stepped cautiously until she found a thicket heavy enough to crouch behind and hide.

She listened hard, as hard as possible with the wind picking up and the warm rain falling harder. When it was like this, there were a hundred sounds vying for attention.

For as long as she could hold still, she waited, scarcely breathing.

If Sig called her name again, she didn't hear him.

She had made it work. By taking a different direction, heading for the bayou and falling silent, she had thrown him off. What she'd done to him was horrible. He would be terrified for her, but she couldn't face him now. Once she got where she was going, and it wouldn't take too long unless she was unlucky enough to hurt herself again, but once she got there she'd call to let him know she was okay.

All she had needed to do was let him know she wasn't ready to get physical with him. Easier to admit than pull off.

Sig was a psychologist. That didn't mean he wasn't also a man.

Madge huddled. She had run away to be alone, but she didn't want to stay here. Scrambling, she stood and carried on, hunched over, until she was close to the bayou.

Her purse was in Sig's car. She paused for breath and felt sick at the thought of having to see him again, to talk to him and apologize— to try to explain that he'd been right to think she wasn't very worldly.

Clinging to the track at the edge of the bayou, she mostly walked, afraid to run in case she tripped in the dark and couldn't carry on. Every cut and bruise stung. She kept thinking about a hot shower and washing her hair—and putting a locked door between her and the world.

After that, she'd call Sig to tell him to forget all about her.

When she saw a distant, flickering light, she knew safety was close. The light would be inside St. Cecil's where sconces burned at all times.

She would rinse her feet and legs under the faucet at the back of the rectory, go inside quietly and make a call from her office. Then she'd slip out again and get back to Rosebank.

No reception committee awaited Madge inside the rectory. She'd been half afraid Sig might have called Cyrus. If that had happened, every light in the place would have been blazing and Cyrus would have called for help to find her.

Sig hadn't called.

Perhaps he thought something would almost definitely happen to her and he didn't want to be blamed.

In her office, she used the phone as quietly as she could, not that Cyrus was likely to hear anything way up in his aerie under the roof.

Sig answered with a quiet, "Yes."

"I'm sorry," she said.

"Damn you," he said and hung up.

All of the tension left her body, and she trembled wildly. It was over.

The phone rang and she snatched it up. "Yes."

"You little idiot," Sig said. "Did you think you'd call me and I'd be glad… Christ, I *am* glad to hear from you. I feel like my kid just ran across a freeway in rush hour and made it to the other side. Shaking you hard would feel so good—for about ten seconds. Good night."

"Good night," she said and hung up.

Back in the hall, barefoot, she looked up the dark stairs leading to the floor where the big room was, the one where Cyrus met with small groups of parishioners, or even with just one if they need comfort or simply to talk. Also on that floor were a number of mostly small bedrooms where those in need were given a place to stay for as long as needed.

Madge started to climb.

She needed peace.

Tonight she wanted to curl up in cool, white sheets and forget that she was a woman who belonged in no world. Rosebank was just a place to keep her things. She had no home, no committed companion on her journey. And the choice had been hers.

She started toward the little bedrooms at the end of the house nearest the church, but couldn't keep going. Back she walked, all the way to the opposite end of the corridor where a door stood open. On the other side of the door, more stairs, these very narrow, led upward.

This was the last, the highest flight. At the top, in the big, bare room, Cyrus would be sleeping on his single bed.

Madge sat on the bottom step and rested her forehead on top of folded arms.

Chapter
26

Later the same night

Roche needed a shower.

Cold.

Damn the bigmouths in this town. And damn Lil Dupre for the sneaking, dirty-minded prude she was.

He had hoped the story of what Lil saw and embellished that night had gone away. Enough time should have passed. But why did he think so, really? Once the mud hit you, it never completely came off.

This wasn't the first time he had taken refuge in his offices on Cotton Street. He came here to think, to find the quiet he must have, regularly, or to deal with any inner demons on patrol. After the scene with Bleu, all the demons were out. He'd driven roads to nowhere for hours before coming here.

Once inside the building, via the waiting room, he entered his consulting rooms through a door behind his receptionist, Crystal's mosaic desk.

Crystal was beautiful—an asset to him—around thirty and married. And Roche had never looked at her and wanted to have sex. Sure, he thought she was sexy, but that was different.

His "little" addiction took a very different form from that of most sex addicts.

Roche tore off his shirt.

Air-conditioning didn't cool the kind of heat he felt.

He balled up the shirt and shied it across the room. What was happening to him, with Bleu, hadn't come up before. He had never felt what he felt now.

Just lust?

Could be. He was the doctor, the shrink, but he didn't have all the answers.

Love?

He loved his twin. In a way, he loved his father. But the kind of love a man could supposedly feel for a woman? He didn't know, but he did care about Bleu, he did dream about her, waking and sleeping. He could still feel her skin on his, her hair slipping across his face.

He could still smell her perfume.

And he could still feel her encasing him.

Torn apart. His body and mind betrayed him. Sweat ran down the sides of his face. An erection sprang hard.

Hard, but not only-wanting-sex hard. He wanted Bleu. Now. And he couldn't have her. She thought he could be a rapist.

From the office, he could go into a bathroom, and a bedroom containing a single bed and a closet where he kept spare clothes. And there was a galley kitchen for those times when he really felt like holing up here.

He kept wine in the refrigerator and the other booze in a cabinet in the office.

She danced nude in his mind.

Roche kicked off his shoes and walked into the bathroom. The bedroom stood open to his left and he went in there, unbuttoning and unzipping his pants as he went. When he got them off, hopping from foot to foot, he was grateful for the freedom.

Inside the dark walk-in closet he saw a shape reflected in a mirror on the far wall. A man. Tall and straight, his face indistinct, the man looked back at Roche. He started to turn away, but let his gaze pass over the rest of the man in the mirror.

Ready for sex. Wanting sex.

Roche averted his eyes, but an image exploded in his mind. Another room, another mirror, the same man, but with a woman. God, she felt like heaven, looked like heaven.

Cool-looking, covered with a white cotton spread, the bed invited him and he closed his eyes. Shudders convulsed him. He shook with the effort it took to hang on and deal with the power of his arousal.

But his need was for her and no one but her.

He hit off the lights and fell onto the bed. Stretched out on his back with his fingers shoved into his hair.

Light in the bathroom sliced a glaring wedge through the door. The gleaming blade cut over the bottom of the bed, over his feet, his lower legs. Every sense shivered and opened like a wound.

At first, Bleu had been frightened of him. She argued otherwise, but he had known what he felt emanating from her. He wanted to tell her the truth about himself, but couldn't blurt it out. He didn't know how.

How would he explain? "I'm sexually addicted, not to any and every woman I see, but when I am with one, alone, and she's willing, then I want to take her and not just take her, but own her."

Even that was too simple, too general.

I become someone obsessed, insatiable. Sex can be a work of art. Two people can satisfy one another, or they can come together with mind-blowing perfection.

And that was so damned esoteric, he made himself sick.

It could be he didn't have to put anything into words, ever. By that morning, she hadn't only started to melt—she showed him how much she wanted passion. She had reveled in herself and the way she felt, the way she felt with him.

Bleu, I don't just want you to want me—I need you to need me.

Chapter 27

Later yet, the same night

Fuck it.

He'd backed into something rough and hard.

Justice grabbed his ankle and rubbed. He had hauled the pirogue away from the bayou, between trees and stumps, over snarled undergrowth, rocks, earth that went from shallow mud to deep mud, depending on the spot you were in. This was as far as he had to go...tonight.

It had taken too long to get back here. Finding the right boat had been hard enough. Getting way back into the swamps in the dark, among the boxy houses that looked and smelled as if they were made of sheet rust, corrugated, had about made him crazy. And locating a boat no one was watching too closely had taken hours of crouching and running in ankle-deep water. He'd had to go to a settlement far enough away that they wouldn't come right on down to this part of the Teche after him and looking for their property.

Theft like that might make those swamp people, quiet though they might be, turn really ugly.

Ugly enough to punish someone so they could never do the same thing again.

Now he had to finish his practice run and retrace his path. This time it could be even harder.

Someone had to pay for the trouble that had come his way. If they'd left well enough alone, he'd still be on his way to getting exactly what he wanted, and no one ever the wiser about what they didn't see or know.

But they couldn't leave things alone. No, their sights had been set on change.

This next death had to be different. The sheriff and his boys would be looking for patterns. Well, he wouldn't be giving them any. A man and his imagination, just the two of them was all it took.

What they said about killing was true. Once you did it, the next one got easier, and the next. He'd been hasty with the first one, but he'd learned his lesson: never start anything without having a complete exit plan. Afterward, he had panicked.

But that was history. He'd worked hard and covered his tracks well enough to make sure they never caught him—ever.

This murder was going to be brilliant—as pretty as a picture. Well, damn, he might try his hand at painting that pretty picture one of these days. He had a long life ahead of him to do what he fucking-well pleased.

This one would be pretty and so goddamn painful, he'd have to make sure no one heard anything.

Pain. Pain in the darkness, and confusion. *Why are you doing this to me? What have I done to you?* The questions would come first, then the begging and the promises. He curled his lip and whispered, "You were born, sucker, that's what *you* did to *me*."

The sacks of dirt were right where he'd left them, carefully weighed, tied shut. He hefted them, one by one, into the bottom of the pirogue.

They needed to be arranged so they'd be distributed like a person's weight. A particular person.

Satisfied he had it as right as it was going to be, he retrieved a canvas duffel with a drawstring at the top.

"What are you doin' to me?" he said in a falsetto.

He would pack the fool's mouth then and say, "Why, there's nothing for you to worry about. I'm going to make a nice hole in your brain so it won't overheat anymore."

From the duffel, he took an old-fashioned manual drill he'd found in a sale at a hardware store going out of business in New Orleans. They had stuff there he bet most folks didn't know ever existed. The drill didn't have a lot of choices when it came to the size of holes it made. There was nice-and-small, nice-and-big, and really big. He had finesse. Justice already knew he'd go for nice-and-small. Not such a mess that way; he didn't want to get anything on him.

He didn't need to, but he rested the point of the drill bit on the single bag of dirt at one end of the boat. A knob on top let him hold the tool in place with as much or as little pressure as he wanted. A handle in the middle of the shaft rotated under his free hand. Around and around it went, and the nice-and-small bit broke through the stretched sacking— just like it would through skin. It hit the rocky dirt he'd shoveled inside the sacks, and ground slower, kind of like going through gristle and bone.

That was good enough.

The job would be done.

He put the drill away.

Justice heaved and shoved. On the downhill path back to the bayou, the load moved faster than he'd expected. One of the benefits of soft mud and an incline. And the extra weight actually worked for him.

At the water's edge, he looped a fat coil of rope over his head and around one shoulder. He knew just how many feet of line he had, because he knew how far it had to stretch.

The only thing that could mess with him now would be if the water's current didn't do what it was supposed to do here.

Once launched, the pirogue wobbled a bit then settled low in the water. Justice took the oar and gave the stern a mighty shove, playing out the line at the same time.

He almost whooped.

Gently, smoothly, the dark shape slid forward and kept on going.

Justice shrugged off the coil and tied one end of the rope to a piece of metal pipe conveniently abandoned in the same place he'd found the boat.

He ran along the bank, using the rope to stop his toy from floating away.

There were the lights of St. Cecil's!

Hot shit—it would work.

Chapter
28

The next day begins

Cyrus woke up facing the wall.

A subtle lightening in the reflected shape of the uncurtained window became a smudgy wash of silver. The moon had almost emerged from mottled clouds.

The moon gave up, the light show faded and the wall receded again.

He closed his eyes and frowned, moved one foot carefully under the sheet, searching for Millie. The dog never left his bed during the night.

"Millie?" he said, and cleared his throat.

Not even a squeak.

He switched on the bedside lamp and sat up, pushed his fingers through his hair while he squinted around the big room. There she was, a barely noticeable bump propped against the bottom of the door to the rest of the house.

It took a moment to remember that Madge was out with Sig. The clock showed almost one in the morning.

He ran his hands over his face.

When she went out from the rectory, she didn't come in for Millie before returning to Rosebank. Not that it had happened often.

Sig and Madge would still be out. One in the morning wasn't late. Not in the world of men.

The sensation was there again, the disquiet, the clenching low in his gut.

A small sound reminded him that the dog was by the door.

"You want to go out," he told her. "Of course you do. You need to make more noise than that."

If he'd been sleeping deeply, he might be annoyed, but walking outside sounded better than tossing between being conscious and unconscious.

He retrieved his jeans from the closet floor where he must have missed getting them on a hanger last time. He did that a lot. Wearing a shirt didn't sound good. The air in the room felt as if he could grab sticky handfuls.

With his jeans on, and an old pair of boat shoes, he picked up Millie and opened the door. "We've got to get your leash first," he said. Madge never let the dog out without one. "Hold on, kid. Cross your legs. We're on our way."

He looked down and almost missed the next step.

Huddled over her knees, Madge sat at the bottom of the stairs. Even in the mostly darkness, Cyrus knew it was her. He braced his free hand against the wall. Millie didn't want to go out; she had sensed her boss nearby was all.

His heart beat uncomfortably. Not fast, but hard against his breast-bone. "Madge?" he said softly.

She didn't answer or move.

Cyrus leaped down the rest of the stairs. He reached Madge who raised her face. He flipped on a light and she flinched, held up a hand. She'd been sleeping?

Millie wriggled from his arm, landed in a flailing mass on top of Madge and licked her frantically.

"Madge," Cyrus said. He vaulted over her and knelt on the floor at her feet. "Just tell me. All of it."

She shook her head and looked away.

Her dress was torn. The top gaped and this time he turned his eyes from her. "I'll get Sig on the phone," he said, not wanting to believe what he was beginning to think. "He'll tell me what's gone wrong. One way or the other, he'll tell me."

"No!" She clutched at his arm. "It's not Sig's fault. It's mine. Leave it. I'm going to drive home now. I should have gone as soon as I got back here."

Cyrus looked her over more closely. "You're scratched. And your feet, Madge." Fury pounded at his temples. "Your feet are torn apart."

He bent to pick her up, but she punched his shoulders till he backed off. "No," she said. "I needed to rest. I've done that now. I'm going back to Rosebank."

He stood up, his hands on his hips, his breathing ragged. "Where are your shoes?"

"Forget it." She raised her voice but it was filled with tears. "You can't help me. It's not fair for me to be here."

"Where else should you go when you're in trouble, if not to me?"

"Not to you, Cyrus." The puzzlement in her eyes let him know that her own reactions bemused her. "No. Never to you anymore."

Ignoring her pushing hands and the knots in his own stomach, he picked her up and carried her to the nearest bathroom, where he sat her on the counter and ran water into a sink. "Don't you move," he said, pointing a finger in her face. "Understand? Try to leave that spot and I'll catch you. You'll wish you'd stayed put."

He switched on the lights over the mirror. The dress she wore was one of his favorites, red, soft cotton, the neckline square. A row of small buttons closed the bodice—except where there were buttons missing. Scratches had bled on her back, her arms. Twigs snarled her hair. Devoid of makeup, her white face turned his stomach. She stared back at him, and evidence of tears, mixed with dirt, streaked her cheeks.

He lifted one of her feet. Skin had stripped from the sole and she had too many contusions to count.

Moving past his own reservations, he threw a bath mat on the floor, turned the shower on full and pulled several towels from a cupboard. "Get in there," he said, pointing once more. "Not one word of argument from you. Just get in and make sure you get yourself as clean as you can. Here." He found a new nailbrush, still in its package, in a drawer. "It'll hurt, but scrub the dirt out of all those cuts. When's the last time you had a tetanus shot?"

Madge wouldn't look at him. "It's up to date," she said. "I'll be fine. Thanks."

"Good—about the shot. But you won't be fine. You aren't fine now. There are bathrobes and night things in the spare bedrooms. I'll get you something—and a first-aid kit. I'll knock on the door and put them on the counter. Holler if you need me sooner."

He held her face firmly and moved it toward the light. At first she lowered her lashes, then she raised them. "You might as well tell me about it," he said, furious at the marks on her. "This happened to you since you left with Sig. I'm going to call him now. Get in the shower."

"No, please." She caught his wrists. "You mustn't bother Sig. I was wrong."

He didn't understand. "Of course you weren't wrong. You're never wrong."

"Yes, I am," she said softly. "And I was this time."

She resembled a curly-headed waif, womanly, but pathetic and small. Whatever had happened, it hadn't been her fault. It wouldn't happen again.

One more moment and she'd be in his arms.

"In the shower," he said, and left, closing the door hard behind him.

The hot water stung Madge's skin. She could barely stand, and shifted from foot to foot, relieving the pressure on her wounds.

If she had told Sig to stop and take her back to her car, he would have. Wouldn't he?

She'd never know, because instead she'd panicked and rushed away from him. Only luck must have saved her from a real injury—or an encounter with some critter that would have done her potentially serious harm.

A thin wafer of soap broke apart when she peeled it off the edge of the tub. She made the best of it, and used what was left of a sample-sized bottle of shampoo.

Standing under the streaming water until the pain faded, Madge turned to the wall and rested her forehead. Of course, she had come back here to find Cyrus. As he'd said, where else would she go when she was in trouble?

Hopeless. Everything was hopeless. She pressed her fists into the tile. There was nothing about her that was too soft to cope. For years, she'd dealt with a love so strong, it was with her always. And she'd known loving Cyrus was pointless, a perpetual homage to a man who wasn't free to accept anything from her. But she hadn't folded. She hadn't run away.

She was not soft.

She wouldn't fold.

After tonight, there would be no more attempts at enjoying another man because it would never work. Good. That's the way she wanted it. Being around Cyrus was enough, and she should be grateful.

It *wasn't* enough.

To make sure her sobbing couldn't be heard, Madge turned the water on harder. The stream began to cool, and she turned it even colder until her skin smarted and tightened.

Her whole life was a joke.

She sluiced her face and turned off the shower. Standing on the bath mat, she toweled herself dry, rubbing too hard because pain closed out the deeper hurt.

The shampoo had a eucalyptus scent. Its clean softness soothed a little.

A loud rap at the door and Cyrus said, "I'm going to put a robe inside." He opened the door just enough. "There's a nightgown here, too. When you come out, I'll fix up those feet. Cotton socks would be a good idea, wouldn't they?"

Her throat clogged. It took seconds to respond, "Probably. Thank you very much for putting up with me."

He didn't answer.

Madge put on a pink cotton nightie and wrapped a white terry-cloth robe about her. No drawer gave up a comb, so she ruffled her black curls with her fingers. This wasn't a beauty pageant.

A very gentle tap sounded at the door. "Madge? You okay in there?"

To love and be loved. Hell on earth when the one you longed for was kept from you by invisible bonds.

"I'm good now," she said, and opened the door.

She looked him squarely in the chest—his broad, very human

chest. His shoulders and arms, often exposed to the sun when he worked outside, remained tanned.

Madge stared at him. He was a priest, but now, this moment, he looked nothing more than a man—a man in need. Longing tightened the muscles in his face. But she didn't fool herself. There was anger there. She must make sure he didn't continue to blame Sig for anything.

"I'm going to pick you up," he said. "Once we get some dressings and socks on you, I'll let you hobble."

"I can hobble now." She tried to pass him.

Without ceremony, Cyrus swept her up again and walked with her to the first of the rectory's small visitors' rooms. He threw back the plain white coverlet and sheet on the bed and propped pillows against the wall.

That's where he settled her.

"This stuff probably stings, but you need it," he said, brandishing a bottle and cotton swabs. He smiled slightly. "The only socks I can find are mine. We could save the laundry and put both of your feet in one of them."

She reached for the bottle. "Give me everything. I want you to get back to bed. Mass comes early."

Cyrus sat on the edge of the bed and pulled her feet onto his lap. "I've had plenty of sleep. If Millie hadn't known you were sitting there, I'd still be asleep. I get too much sleep."

She couldn't argue anymore. "My dog is a traitor."

"Why?" He started swabbing her cuts. They stung.

She sucked in air. "I don't see her hanging out in here. She'd rather be up in your room. It's probably more comfortable."

"It's just familiar," he said.

His thighs were hard beneath her calves.

Cyrus glanced at her. He looked a second time and frowned.

She didn't want to talk about how awful she looked. "I've got clothes in the closet next door—I'll use some of them when I leave. I've got to get fresh things to work in."

"Later. Much later. Madge, where are your shoes?"

"I lost them."

He stopped in the middle of applying a dressing. "Have I ever really pushed you? About anything?"

"Don't do this, Cyrus."

"Do what?"

"Blackmail me."

"I've made it too easy, haven't I?" he said, gripping her ankle with both of his hands. "I've never... What am I saying? I don't have the right to expect anything from you. You owe me nothing, including explanations."

There was steel in his hold. The tips of his fingers dug into her.

Madge blinked, her eyes filling with tears. Anger, frustration, deep, deep hurt and helplessness—she struggled to separate the forces crashing over her.

"We owe each other *everything*," she cried. "If there's fault, we share it. We could have stepped back the very first time we knew we liked being together. We didn't.

"I jumped out of Sig's car and ran away. That's how I did all this. I found the Teche and followed it here."

"Why?" Darkness gave him a stranger's face.

"He kissed me." She took Cyrus's clenched hand to her mouth and held it there. "That's all. He did what people do, what a man who thinks a woman's interested in him does."

"Did you tear your dress when you were running?"

"Yes." He must have seen the broken buttons, but he didn't have to know any more.

"He shouldn't have let you go."

"He tried not to. I hid. It was dark, and he doesn't know this place like I do."

He folded her hand in both of his. "Why didn't he call me?"

"Because..." She swallowed. "Sig knew I wasn't lost. I let him know I was safe."

"He couldn't know you were safe when you were out there alone."

Madge struggled to her knees beside him. She kissed his knuckles, rested her cheek where her lips had been. "This isn't about Sig. Please, we have to let it all go."

He stroked her hair and raised her chin.

His breath slipped across her face. The pupils of his eyes were huge.

"Time changes everything," she whispered. "It will for us. We'll be all right."

"I look up to you," Cyrus said. He looked at her mouth. "You don't do anything wrong. You're perfect."

Her tears fell, and she didn't try to stop them. "That's the Madge you've tried to make of me, not the Madge I am. Forgive me for this."

She touched her mouth to his.

His fingers convulsed around hers and she leaned against him.

Madge smoothed his face, his hair. She kissed him again, and he kissed her back. He squeezed his eyes shut, and his lashes flickered.

Harder she kissed him, and she slid her free arm around his neck. Cyrus kept his shaking grasp on her other hand.

Madge slid to sit on his lap and, finally, his arms went around her.

When they paused, he rested his forehead on hers.

She framed his face and made him look at her.

And beneath his tan, Cyrus grew so pale she could only stare at him. His eyes opened, widened. The sound he made was like none other she had heard.

"My, God," he said, his voice broken, and set her back on the bed. "Forgive me."

"Cyrus?"

He shook his head, doubled over and moaned. He convulsed, his face turned from her.

Then he left, stumbling away, not pausing to shut the door.

She stood up, stared into the shadowy corridor. It hadn't been *her* forgiveness he'd asked for.

"Oh, Cyrus. My poor Cyrus." She knew what had happened to him. How could she have forgotten the inevitable result of arousal in a man who denied himself any release. "I didn't mean to do that to you."

Chapter
29

A little later the same morning

"Me, I'm not putting one more foot down in this mud without some light," Wazoo said.

She was tired, irritable, and tramping around the Cashman property at three in the morning with Mary Pinney made her crazy.

When Mary called to be picked up, Wazoo had almost said what she really thought about that idea. Curiosity had put the wrong words in her mouth and here she was, her shoes squelching in the dark.

"Mary," she said. "I'm turnin' on the flashlight."

"Don't do that."

She hasn't lost her tongue after all. "Can you see in the dark, Mary Pinney?"

"No."

On the phone earlier, Mary had sounded excited and sure of herself. Not now. Wobbly, that was the way to describe her now.

"I can't see in the dark, either. And there's no one out here in the middle of nothin' to know if there's a light on anyways, girl."

"There could be."

Mary had at least a foot in height on Wazoo and she had the kind of presence folks remembered, but this morning the woman could have been an oversized child.

"We-ll," Wazoo said. "With the racket we been making, fallin' around and yellin', if there *is* someone else here, they know we are, too."

Wazoo snapped on her flashlight and Mary yelped.

They had come onto the property from the southern end, the one farthest away from St. Cecil's. Around them, old-growth trees blocked even a hint of sky. Wazoo didn't know how many acres of land there were, but figured plenty.

"What's your problem?" she asked Mary. "You're jumpin' around like a frog on crack."

"If you were scared, you'd be jumping, too. You're the one who said there was a cabin here. I've told you it's got to be the one George was talking to Kate about last night."

"He wasn't talkin' to you," Wazoo said. "You admitted you couldn't hear properly, and nothin' good comes of sneakin' around eavesdropping."

"You are my friend, aren't you, Wazoo?" Mary said.

Wazoo wasn't comfortable with feeling pressured, but she said, "Yes."

"I've been worrying about George and Kate," Mary said. "They spend all kinds of time together, and he gets mad if I say anything about it."

"It's gotta be 'cause Jim just died," Wazoo said. "George is tryin' to be helpful."

"George isn't the helpful kind. They're real close, if you know what I mean."

Now that was a conversation stopper. "Mm." Patience never came easily to Wazoo. "It's time to leave," she said.

"Don't you say another word till I'm finished," Mary said. "George said, 'Your old Eugene Cashman's sleeping with it at that cabin.' Then he and Kate laughed. They reckoned no one would find it, because they wouldn't dare go there. People around here are afraid to come in here. I would be, too, without you. You said there was a cabin for real. We've got to find it."

"I don't have to do anything," Wazoo said. "You're just dancin' around the details. Why did we have to come now, in the dark?"

"Because I told George we're going to paint the storeroom at the café early this morning. We want the smell to die down before customers come."

Wazoo scrunched up her brow. "Paint the storeroom?"

"We're not really going to. I needed an excuse in case he woke up after I left—not that he would. Nothing wakes him up until he's ready."

"I don't think we're gonna find that cabin," Wazoo said. "Maybe in daylight, but not like this."

"But you said it was here." Mary sounded close to tears.

"It is. So I've been told. But I don't know just where. You said there was somethin' interesting you wanted to show me there. But I don't think there's anything at all. You don't really know what you're lookin' for, do you?"

"Yes I do. There's a clue to who killed Jim Zachary. That's what's in that cabin. I know it is."

The light caught a defiant, "what do you think of that?" glitter in Mary's light eyes.

"Hoo mama," Wazoo said. "We gonna have to start at the beginnin' here. First, this Eugene Cashman does own this land we're trespassin' on, doesn't he?"

"He did. He's dead."

"It belongs to someone, girl."

Mary smiled, so quickly Wazoo almost missed it. "Of course it belongs to someone," Mary said. "I can't say any more about it, though. Loyalty is loyalty even when you know you don't owe any."

"Uh-uh," Wazoo said. "You won't say anythin' to convince me I ought to be here with you, so I'll be goin'. If *I* don't owe no loyalty, ain't no loyalty bein' wasted by this woman. I don't owe you no loyalty, Mary, excepting at the shop."

"Please do this with me," Mary said.

Her thick black hair hung around her muscular upper arms as far as the elbows. If Wazoo weren't a hard woman to scare, she'd be running from the vision in front of her. Mary looked wild.

Wazoo said, "I want you to come along with me, and I'll make sure you get rested up before opening time."

"No, and I'm not leaving till I've got what I came for."

"Good luck, then," Wazoo said.

"You drove me here."

"And if you want me to drive you back, the bus is leavin'." She turned away, keeping the flashlight beam trained on the ground.

"I can't be alone in the dark." Mary as good as screamed. She took Wazoo's arm in a painful grip.

That does it. "Get your hand off me," she said and shook Mary away. "Look where we're at. Do you expect me to believe you're afraid of the dark?"

"I am. I always have been. But there could be a clue here. Spike isn't getting anywhere. It's up to you and me to unmask Jim's killer and make sure no one else gets hurt."

"Hurt?" Wazoo said. "That's what you think happened to Jim Zachary? He got *hurt*? Hoo mama, if you ever decide an injury is serious, I don't want to know about it."

"Can I trust you, Wazoo, really trust you?"

"I've never liked committing myself." She tapped a fingernail against her teeth. What if there was something worth knowing about Cashman's cabin? "But you can trust me, girl."

"I think George is planning something awful." Mary turned her back.

Wazoo waited quietly.

"Let's try this way," Mary said, and began picking a path away from Wazoo. She didn't go far before she looked back. "Come on."

"Not till you finish sayin' what you started."

Wazoo kept a small gun in a canvas belt just above her waist, under her blouse—just for insurance. This could turn into a night when she would be glad she was cautious.

"I don't know why you're making this even more difficult for me," Mary said. "It could be that my life's in danger."

Wazoo had expected something like this. "Go on."

"If someone... Oh, I might as well say it. There's only you and me here."

"Glad you agree," Wazoo said.

"I don't know if I do, but I'm out of choices. If George wants this property, I'm in his way." Mary's voice broke and she coughed.

Wazoo absorbed the information. "I don't see how getting rid of you would give him this. Unless you're going to tell me it's yours and you've left it to him." She almost laughed.

"No. And I don't have any proof of this, but it's probably Kate Harper's."

That hadn't even been a start of an idea for Wazoo.

"I think it rightfully belonged to Jim Zachary," Mary said. "He inherited it. If he did, it makes sense Kate expected it to go to her."

If she'd done some investigating, Wazoo might have found out more about the land, only she hadn't known it could be important. "So what difference does it make to you? Or to George? You aren't in anyone's way."

Mary let out a long, shaky breath. "I could be. If George and Kate are planning to get together."

Wazoo laughed. "Kate Harper's a bit long in the tooth for him."

"She's fifty-something. Look at her. She's not old and she plays up to George. And he eats it up. I may not have made out everything they said, but they were talking about their future."

Holding up a hand, Wazoo said, "Hold it! We're gonna slow down. You think George and Kate—" she made an airy gesture with one hand "—you think they didn't want Jim around?"

"Maybe."

"I've got the picture," Wazoo said. "Now, what's it goin' to help for us to go to that cabin?"

"I told you. George put something there for safekeeping. I'm not sure what, but maybe if we can find it and take it to Spike, we'll save my life."

This woman should be on the stage, Wazoo decided. Or in horror movies. "Yeah, well, what would this thing be?"

Mary threw out her arms. "We've got to get this done."

"*What?*"

"I don't know," Mary said. "But it's something."

"You're tellin' me you heard Kate and George talk about hiding something without saying what it was?"

"You know how it is when two people are talking about something without really talking about it. It's like they're using code. Well, Kate said George was her hero for making sure Jim didn't throw everything away at the parish meeting. Now, how would George stop Jim from going to that meeting, that's what I want to know."

Wazoo didn't fill in the obvious blank.

"I'm probably wrong, but it could be that George…you know. And Kate was thanking him for it. Then she wanted to know if he had everything ready for what he had to do next. When George said he did, she asked what he did with 'it.' That's when he told her it was here."

Patience never came easily to Wazoo. "It's time to leave," she said.

Mary crossed her arms and glared. "I think Jim changed his mind about leaving this land to Kate. Maybe he was going to give it to St. Cecil's and he had the deed with him the night he died. George killed him to get the deed, then hid it out here. That could be it. It's George's insurance now. All he's got to do is get rid of me."

"You don't know any of this." Wazoo shone the flashlight on her watch. "What you heard didn't have to mean a thing like you're sayin'. We gotta go. Let's talk some more, and if we both think it's worth it, we'll come back."

"That could be too late for me," Mary said.

She had a point—if anything she said was true. "Then we better get help, because we're not cutting it on our own."

Mary backed away, and fell. She landed with her long legs straight up in the air.

"You stay still!" Wazoo called.

Watching the jumble underfoot, she picked her way toward Mary.

The hull of an upturned pirogue stopped her, just as it had stopped Mary who sprang up again before Wazoo reached her.

"Darn boat," Mary said. "I didn't see it there. I could have broken something."

"Did you?"

"I don't think so."

"Good." Wazoo trained her light behind Mary. "We've found the cabin."

The cabin, its walls and roof still intact, its open door sagging but stout enough, could easily have been missed. Long ago, vegetation had filled the clearing where the owner had built his tiny fortress.

Windowless, moss-laden and squat beneath old, old cypress trees—
if Mary hadn't fallen over the wooden boat, she and Wazoo might
have passed by without noticing anything.

Scraped up and bleeding in places, once she got inside the log
walls, Mary didn't have much to say. She produced her own flashlight, a thin, laser affair, and made methodical passes over the interior.

Wazoo assessed the one-room structure. A trestle table and a bench
rested at angles with the bottom of the legs buried in inches of dirt.

"There's about as much moss inside as outside," Wazoo said,
sniffing. "Smells like things been rotting here a long time."

"Where would he hide something in here?" Mary said dispiritedly.

"Nowhere," Wazoo told her.

The moss on the walls and ceilings glistened with moisture. The
air felt warm and heavy enough to pour into molds.

"Give it up, girl!" she said, and folded her arms. "There's no place
for hiding anythin'."

Mary didn't answer. She shone her tiny light along each joint in
the log walls.

After half an hour, Mary straightened and said, "I could have misunderstood what I heard. You're right."

"About what?"

"There's nothing hidden here."

Wazoo followed her outside.

"I'm sorry," Mary said, and sounded as if she was. "I read too
much into what they were talking about. But I'm not wrong about
the two of them being cozy."

"You could be," Wazoo said. "Give it more time, and see if George
is just being nice to Kate."

"You don't know him," Mary said. "He's not like that. But that
woman's not getting my husband."

"Sounds like you'd be better off if she did," Wazoo said.

"We'd better get on," Mary said, moving past the pirogue with great purpose. "Try to keep up."

So now it's my fault we're hangin' around here? The toe of one shoe dug into something firm enough to bring Wazoo to a stop. "Well, hell," she said. She'd hit a bag filled with dirt. The contents broke loose and filled both of her shoes.

Chapter
30

Same morning: Toussaint's waking up

Riding a bike was supposed to be something you never forgot. Bleu hadn't forgotten, but searing complaints from every muscle in her legs reminded her that it had been a long time.

She didn't know more about Roche's history this morning than she had last night. But she had been unfair to him, that was for sure.

She rode the ancient bike from the townhouse carport into the court-yard behind his single-story office building on Cotton Street. The only car in sight belonged to him. Not surprising, so early in the morning.

When he had left her place, she asked him where he was going, and he said, after looking as if he wouldn't answer, "To my office."

She couldn't be certain he either meant it then or that he would still be there, but Bleu had set off with the first pink streaks of dawn, as soon as the bike's lack of lights didn't matter so much.

Her cell phone, ringing in her pocket, sent her feet slamming to the ground. The brakes on the bike were almost gone, and she scuffed rapidly along until it came to a wobbly stop.

With her eyes on lights in one of Roche's windows, she answered the phone softly, "Yes." The number showed as "private."

"I probably shouldn't be doing this," a male voice said. "I couldn't wait any longer to check on you."

She recognized Sam Bush. "I'm doing well, thanks," she told him. "Thanks for caring."

"I do care," he said. "A lot. Have you got all your doors locked?"

"Yes, and my windows." He didn't have to know she wasn't where locks made a difference.

"Are you up?" Sam asked.

Bleu took an instant to respond. "Yes."

"Can I tempt you with some fresh pastries and coffee I just bought? We only see each other for work. It might be nice to get to know each other better. If you're okay having me at your place, that is."

He wanted more than she could give him. Bleu felt terrible, but she couldn't pretend something she didn't feel. "I'm leaving shortly." She glanced around, hoping a car wouldn't drive in and give her lie away.

"I could pick you up," Sam said. "You didn't get a loaner car, did you?"

Privacy was a myth around here. Everyone knew your business. Of course, Sam had been there after the fire yesterday. She forced a laugh. "No loaner. They didn't have one. But I'm looking forward to getting back into cycling. A bike someone left in the garage works just fine."

"Bleu—"

"Look." She interrupted him. "I don't want those pastries wasted. Will you be at the rectory later?"

"Yes." His voice went flat.

"Great. If you haven't eaten everything by then, I'll look forward to heating one up and giving myself a coffee break. I hope you'll join me."

"Sounds good."

From his tone, her suggestion barely beat out a prison sentence in popularity.

He rang off before she could respond again.

Bleu returned her attention to the building. She owed Roche, if not an apology then a chance to fully speak his mind. Last night, he'd left rapidly, his expression closed, and she had decided to wait until this morning to approach him again.

A cruiser pulled slowly into the courtyard. Bleu panicked. She considered riding off, but stopped herself. Goose bumps shot out on her arms and legs and her face felt tight. She didn't want to be seen coming here at this hour, but she didn't have a choice anymore.

It was Spike who pulled up beside her. He got out of the car, his hat tilted over his eyes at the usual angle, and stood with his thumbs in his belt. "I told the deputy who called me he had to be mistaken," he said. "Bleu Laveau wouldn't be fool enough to go ridin' around on her own on some old heap of a bike early in the mornin'. Not when she knows the kind of problem we've got on our hands. Shows what I know about human nature. Have you lost your mind?"

She heard a door open in the building behind her and took a deep breath. Roche had heard the commotion, too.

"Mornin', Roche," Spike hollered. "You got an early visitor."

Bleu's spine turned creepy. "How did you know where I was and what I was doing?" she asked, keeping her voice down.

"Told you. Deputy called me."

"Can't a person move around this town without being followed and reported on?"

"You can't," Roche said, arriving beside them. His eyes were tired, but he still looked way too appealing. "What's the matter with you, Bleu? Are you going to tell me that after what happened yesterday, you rode all the way here on that heap of junk? On your own? With no one around?"

"Nope," she said. "I'm not going to tell you that. You can come to your own conclusions."

The noise Spike made could only be a snigger.

Bleu met Roche's stare directly. He wasn't laughing. He did take the bike from her and looked it over with a disgusted expression.

"Thanks for keeping an eye on Bleu," he said. "Apparently she does need twenty-four-hour surveillance."

She bit back a retort. Arguing with these two, especially when she *hadn't* been smart riding around on her own the way she had, wouldn't win her any points.

Spike crossed his arms on top of his open cruiser door. "I would have come lookin' for you two shortly anyhow," he said.

Bleu felt suddenly very cold. "What's happened?"

"Don't go jumpin' to conclusions," Spike said. He glanced at Roche.

"Why don't we go inside?" Roche said. "I've even got coffee."

Spike took off his hat and revolved it by its brim. His dishwater-blond hair needed a cut. His long crewcut was tipping over at the ends, and the piece that tended to stand up in front parted in the middle. "I never thought we'd go even a couple of days without a real solid person of interest," he said, as if he hadn't heard Roche's invitation.

"Has someone else been killed?" Bleu asked quietly. "They have— I can see it in your face."

He shook his head.

"Spike," Roche said, "is there something you're not saying? Are you sure there isn't someone you're *interested* in?"

A sniff and an expressionless stare was all Spike offered.

"There is someone?" Roche said. "You don't have to say anything concrete."

Spike shrugged upright, and Bleu didn't miss the way he raised his brows, very slightly, at Roche. All these signals were wearing her down.

"Like I said, I wanted to have a word with you, Bleu," Spike said. "The reports came right back on the fire at your place. Like we thought, it was set in that barrel. There were oily rags in there, and you saw the firelighter."

She nodded.

"But you don't have any idea who might have done it?" Roche said. There was an edge on his voice.

"Nope. Except he's an amateur."

Bleu looked at him sideways. "What does that mean?"

"He wasn't organized. He could have got there with one thing in mind, then changed it. Maybe a couple of times. The theory is, he probably intended to break in, but he knows Roche's car and saw it at the bottom of the cul-de-sac so he had to wait."

"So you do know something about him," Roche said. "Whoever this is knows about me, too, including what my car looks like. And he knows Bleu and I are acquainted."

Acquainted. Bleu pinched her hands hard. Funny how a word could make a person feel almost dismissed.

"You're right," Spike said. "But that could be a lot of people. Our guy wanted to make sure you didn't go anywhere, Bleu. He got bored waiting, so he set the fire, but before that, we think he rigged your car. Like I said, he's an amateur. What he did could fizzle to nothing— or blow a car to pieces. We got something in the middle, thank God."

"He rigged her car," Roche said grimly. "Explain that."

"Arson people reckon he wired a bottle of gasoline to the ignition. He fixed it so when the key was turned, an igniter touched off the gas." Spike looked directly at Bleu. "Fortunately, we don't have a dead firefighter. But we could have had one—or a dead Bleu Laveau."

Chapter
31

Roche liked seeing Bleu inside his offices.

He liked seeing Bleu anywhere—more than might be good for his health.

She knew he was watching every tiny move she made, but that didn't seem to bother her. Like him, she was still wrestling with Spike's announcement.

"Before you suggest I'm hanging out here because there's nothing to do and I'm lazy," Roche said, "I've been getting through paper-work." *And trying to figure out where we go from here.*

"You don't have to explain yourself to me," she said.

No, he didn't. But she sounded defensive, and the set of her chin could mean she was thinking more than she was saying.

Once Spike left, Roche had insisted on putting the rusted bike into his waiting room, then locking all the doors in the building with the two of them inside. By the time he'd finished, she was eyeing him as if he could be the rapist she'd more or less accused him of being.

He'd dealt with plenty of anger, and he felt some brewing in Bleu. "You haven't said much since we left Spike," he said.

"Neither have you."

"Bleu? Tell me what's on your mind."

She moistened her lips. "I guess I'm still thinking about what Spike said. It's a horrible feeling, knowing someone tried to kill you."

Roche thought about it. "I don't think he tried that hard."

"But what he did could have been enough." She shook her head. "Spike said I got lucky. How can you say... What do you mean, you don't think the guy tried *that* hard? He booby-trapped my car, then tried to make sure I ran out and got in it by torching the house."

She had come to that conclusion all on her own, Roche thought. "That's a new slant."

"Who knows?" She flopped into one of the gray corduroy chairs in the waiting room. A single forefinger jabbed in his direction. "You asked me once if I was a quitter. I'm not, damn it. And I am sick of feeling pushed around. I didn't come to Toussaint to find another way to be frightened."

A wise man knew when to keep his mouth shut. But he admired her flash of anger and the courage she showed.

Bleu got up. "I'm getting a handle on my feelings. No one has to do anything they don't want to do, just because of me."

What, he wondered, *was the "anything" she had in mind?*

"From now on, I'll deal with my own problems. So you can stop wasting time trying to help me. I know I'm a charity case for you, and that's admirable. But I don't need your charity."

This wasn't an argument he could either win or lose without feeling like a jerk.

"You heard what Spike told us," she said. "He was playing it down, but I'm sure they've got an idea who the killer is. They're going to get him, and they don't want any civilians poking around in their turf before they do. I'm sure they're watching him so closely, they have to cover their eyes when he goes to the lavatory."

She paused and turned pink. "Why didn't Spike tell us who it is?" Her voice quivered. "Then we'd know who to watch out for."

"I don't think Spike does know. That's why he's so edgy," he said. "You're overwrought."

"I am *not* overwrought."

But she was more than agitated. "I'd like you to lie down now."

"I just bet you would." Pink cheeks turned scarlet. "I mean, that's the last condescending thing I'd better ever hear from you. You lie down if you need to."

"I will, if you will."

"This is serious." She spread her arms and her eyes glittered. "I'm never like this. I'm a quiet woman. And it's all your fault. Before I met you I don't think I'd raised my voice to a man. And I had plenty of reason..."

Her arms fell to her sides and she lowered her eyelashes. "Good grief. Don't take any notice of me. I'm a bit—I'm not myself. I had to push myself to come looking for you this morning." She looked up at him. "I felt sick about the way I treated you last night. I shouldn't have talked to you like that, when I've only got rumors to go on. I don't know if you're a rapist or not."

The next change in her color was even more interesting. Bleu became so white she almost matched her blouse.

"Forget it," he said hurriedly. "We're all strung out. I understood."

"No, you didn't. You stormed away in a rage. I could feel the electricity crackling around you."

"You're wrong. I was frustrated because I don't have a way to prove my side of the story, but I wasn't in a rage."

Bleu paced away from him. "The woman you...the woman you

were with, wouldn't she speak for you? Not that it's necessary to prove anything to me. I'm a good judge of character. But would she speak for you?"

"No." Damn, he detested this subject. "She's dead."

Bleu faced him again, frowning. "That's awful. Was she ill?"

"She died suddenly."

"And you don't like talking about it. Of course you don't."

"No."

"So all you've got to back up your story is your reputation and your character." Her sudden smile transformed her. "I'd say that's good enough."

He wanted to thank her, but waited for her to add a clunker, like it was good enough for other people but not for her.

"Why did you bring the bike in here?" she asked.

"What?"

"You brought my bike in and locked all the doors," Bleu said.

"We don't want it stolen." If he were the blushing type, he'd blush now.

"That heap of junk?" Bleu said. She wrinkled her nose. "I hope I get the insurance settlement fast. I need to go used-car shopping."

Coming clean had worked for him before. "I want you here with me for as long as we've got this morning. No one would be likely to connect you to the bike, but just in case..."

"You're hiding me away," she said, flipping up the corners of her mouth. "I've been kidnapped. Should I be worried?"

"That'll depend."

She gave him a questioning stare.

It'll depend on you and on me. "I thought we'd see what happens. Be open to anything."

She swallowed, swallowed again.

"You're not in any danger from me," he said. At least that was the truth. When the chips were down, he had iron control. He took her by the hand and led the way into his consulting room. Once more he shut—and locked—the door.

"What's with locking the doors?" she asked in a small voice. "All I have to do to get out is turn the handle."

"Uh-huh," he said. "Glad you noticed that. What I don't want is for someone to walk in on us."

"Your car's parked outside," she said.

"That doesn't have to mean I'm here. I always park out there when I come into town but I don't always stay in the office."

Bleu gave him a long look, then studied the room. "No wonder the townhouse looks tacky to you," she said. "Fifties funk isn't your style."

"I told you I'm into jukeboxes."

"You'd have a special room for them, like a museum."

"Wait till I get my own place here, and you'll see where I put them."

She felt her hair, as if she expected it to be mussed. It wasn't. "You're not going to stay at Rosebank?"

"Not forever." In the past couple of days, the question of a home had started to interest him again. "I want to do it right if I build. I've spoken to Marc Girard about architectural plans. We haven't gotten far yet, but we will. I'm wondering about the Cashman lot. I'd like being close to the bayou, and it's moody there. Moody appeals to me."

Her silence caught his attention. "What?" he said. "You don't think it would be good to build there? You don't like atmosphere?"

"I do. I was thinking about the school."

He grinned at her. "So am I. And I haven't forgotten that's the perfect spot for the school. Do you know how big that parcel of land is? Huge. It could be divided and the house wouldn't be within sight of whatever else goes up."

"You do a lot of planning, don't you?" she said. "In your own world everything works out your way. You don't even know who owns that lot now."

"No, but I will." He let the other slide past.

Bleu nodded. "What if someone calls you here this morning?"

Fortunately, he switched gears easily. "Someone like?"

She shrugged. "A patient."

"It wouldn't matter who it was. The phones are switched over to my service."

Why, Bleu wondered, didn't she try opening the door? If he stopped her, she'd know she had something to worry about.

She crossed the beautiful blue carpet and turned the door handle. The lock popped undone.

She looked at Roche over her shoulder. He hadn't moved. Propped against his desk, he watched her speculatively.

"Hmm." She engaged the lock again and faced him. "I'm a bit ob-sessive-compulsive—I have to check things out. But now I know, I promise I won't keep on doing that."

"It's okay if you do."

Bleu went to stand in front of him. Only inches separated them, and she inclined her face while she studied his eyes, filled with dark blue shadow. He matched her scrutiny, feature for feature.

"We're not a fit, y'know," she told him. "We're really different."

That brought a one-sided smile. "I'm glad."

"You know what I mean?"

"Of course I do, and I don't agree with you. What you call a 'fit' doesn't have much to do with experience." He touched the side of her face, pushed her hair back.

Bleu kissed his palm, rested her cheek there.

Light in the room was soft, but clear. "I like looking at you," she said.

"Ditto," he said softly, and shifted just enough to lean forward and part her lips with his. He put a breath's distance between their mouths and said, "Looking at you in that mirror was... I'd better shut up."

They kissed a long time, with Roche using only his hand on the side of her head to hold her. They breathed from each other, their eyes squeezed shut. Bleu's breasts tingled. The flutters in her belly concentrated and pooled into a low burn.

His other hand settled on her neck, slid beneath her blouse to fold over her shoulder, but only for a moment before he tugged her closer, landed her against him.

Never taking his eyes from hers, he reached between them to unbutton her blouse, his fingers shaking but still moving rapidly. Spreading the front open, he smoothed his hands over the tops of her breasts and inside her bra. He scooped her up and bent to lick the tender flesh, his tongue trailing closer and closer to her nipples, but never quite touching.

Unexpected sunlight through the window struck Bleu's eyelids and she flinched. She opened them and his head rested against her chest, his hair black against her pale skin.

Roche slid the edges of his thumbnails over her nipples. Bleu gritted her teeth. She stood there, passive, while he touched her. And he made her want him to do it, and do it.

The sunshine washed over them, over the office.

"No!" She was strong and she shoved at his shoulders, pushed his head away from her.

She wrapped her blouse over wet, reddened nipples and turned her back to Roche. She shook, not outwardly, but inside, and her teeth wouldn't stay together.

"I'm sorry," she said.

He didn't answer.

"It's not your fault. I let you think I wanted it. I came to you." *Never in daylight.* "It won't work. Darn, it won't work. I can't change everything about me quickly enough."

"Quickly enough for what?" He sounded gruff.

"You aren't going to wait for me to deal with my hangups. I've got them, Roche, and I'm fighting as hard as I can, but it's going to take time. I still can't believe.... When I think about us, together at my place, I wonder if that was me, or someone who took my place."

"That was you," he said. "I'll sign an affidavit if I need to."

She began buttoning her blouse.

"Start talking about the hangups."

"No." Bleu shook her head. There was nothing familiar for her anymore. She had promised herself a fresh start far away from things she knew—and detested—but she felt adrift, without foundations.

"We can take as much time as you need. You don't have to worry about anything happening *quickly enough.* What set you off just now?"

"The sun," she said, before she could decide not to tell him. "The sun in my eyes."

"Go on."

She didn't want to. "I'm not comfortable doing some things in the daylight."

He settled an arm across her shoulder. "Talk to me, Bleu."

"I'm not your patient."

He sighed. "No, you're not. You're far more than that. Look at me." Gently, he turned her toward him. "I do know you've had a hard time. Not why or how or most of what's going on now. But you have issues."

"Doesn't everyone?"

"Yes. But we're talking about you. You cover yourself up."

She opened her mouth but couldn't respond.

"Is that it? You aren't comfortable being undressed around me?"

Forgetting that he was trained in these things would be a mistake. "I want to drop this now."

"Nothing doing, Bleu."

"Okay, then!" She flung away from him. "I'm not comfortable with it. Not in the—daytime." She sounded crazy. "I'm not ashamed of my body, just—awkward."

"C'mere."

He couldn't make everything better by holding her.

"Come here," he repeated, but didn't wait for a reaction. "If you'll let me share this, we'll work through it. If you want to." He guided her to a chair.

She sat down and crossed her arms.

Roche turned on a lamp beside his desk and went to the wall spanned by a row of high windows. There were louvers and he tapped switches to close out the light electronically. "More comfortable?"

He didn't understand. But how could he? "I'm fine. I need to get to the rectory."

"When you go, I want you to take my car."

"Thanks, but no."

He smiled. "Are you afraid people will talk?"

"You know exactly how to pull my chain. No, I'm not afraid of that. I don't accept charity, that's all."

"For God's sake." He bore down on her. "Borrowing a friend's car isn't charity, but have it your way."

"Thanks anyway."

"Did you enjoy sleeping with me?"

"Don't." She blew out a gust of air. The office was filled with shadows; even Roche seemed a shadow. "I told you, I don't understand what happened. But yes, I did enjoy sleeping with you. I loved sleeping with you."

"And before it got light, you put on your pajamas."

"I expected you to bring that up."

"I have to, Bleu," he said. "But then I undressed you—"

"Please—"

"Just listen to me. Try to stop closing down. You were shy when I undressed you, but you let yourself go. You loved it, sweetheart. I know what I felt with you."

"I did love it," she whispered. "I want to feel that way again. All the time, when I'm with you. But I can't control when the other thing comes over me."

"Take off your clothes."

"What?" She gripped the arms of the chair.

"It's called immersion therapy. If you're afraid of snakes, get to know a boa, intimately."

She glanced behind her at the door, and freedom.

"I didn't say I was going to grab you and rip off your clothes," Roche said. "I just want you to do it."

"*Just?* I've never had a conversation like this."

"Will you let me make love to you again?"

"I don't know."

"Okay," Roche said. "We'll take things really slowly. But please kiss me again before you leave."

"I want to make love." And she did. She couldn't leave at all without loving him.

And there was the sex—she wanted that, too. Not just holding and joining, but learning more about that wildness he'd mentioned when he wasn't watching his words closely.

She stood up, unbuttoned her blouse again and took it off. The lacy demi-bra she wore didn't cover a lot, but she must be in the same shadows as he was.

Keeping her eyes on him, she slipped out of her shoes—and her arms fell to her sides. She couldn't go on.

"You're lovely, Bleu," he said, standing so close she could feel him. "Don't be uncomfortable in your own skin."

Again she crossed her arms, knowing she was closing him out.

"I'm going to give you a hug and go take a shower," he said. "I wish you'd use my car. I'll ride the bike—I like them."

"So do I," she said, and tried to laugh. "I've never...I never learned there could be different ways to make love until you. Can we try something else?" If she did much more shaking, she might never stop.

"Soon," he told her.

"Now."

Roche rested a forearm on either side of her neck. "No. Please give yourself more time."

"Now." If not now, then maybe never.

Muscles flicked beside his mouth.

"Do what I'm asking, Roche. Do it any way you want to."

She heard his breathing grow heavier.

Catching her by the waist, he lifted her from her feet, unzipped her pants and peeled them off. He set her down, still in her bra and panties, against the front of his desk and trapped her there with his spread legs.

His shirt had buttons, too, but he shucked it over his head, undid his belt and slid it from the loops. Looking steadily into her face, he unzipped his slacks and pushed them down. His shorts went with them.

Bleu looked at him and her skin tightened. She was wet and aching—and disoriented.

Roche's features were hard, the skin and flesh tight to the bones, his eyes feverish. With a forefinger, he drew a line from the center of her forehead to her chin, down her neck, between her breasts, to her navel and on to the moist place beneath the scrap of nylon barely covering the center of her.

"You're still sure?" he murmured. His chest rose and fell, and his body shone a little in the lamplight.

Bleu nodded.

"Here, or in bed? There's a bedroom—we can go there. Whatever you want." He barely parted his teeth when he spoke.

"Here."

"Your choice or mine?"

She didn't understand and shook her head.

"You choose the position or I will?"

"You." Her legs were weak but excitement mounted. She copied him, drawing a line down the center of him, stopping in the black hair where her finger met the root of his stiff penis.

He drove his teeth into his bottom lip, took her by the waist and spun her around. With one hand he bent her across the desk, with the other hand he parted her legs.

Bleu prepared herself as best she could.

He held her down by the neck and stimulated her, stroking, sliding over her clitoris. She bobbed at every touch, clutched the far side of the desk's top and jerked.

She shouldn't like it. She shouldn't feel that she would die if he stopped.

A climax split her, arched upward and outward. She pushed up on her hands, tried to face him, but he was relentless. He would not let her look at him.

Before the searing ripples faded, she felt him against the opening to her body, pushing slowly just inside. Very slowly into her vagina. He had swelled so much, yet they had been a perfect match the previous night.

But he was huge. He bent his knees, smoothed himself back and forth and tucked just inside her again.

He wouldn't fit.

He would be angry. Then he'd leave her. Hit her and leave her. Call her names and leave her.

Bleu screamed. She heard the sound bloom from her without deciding to make any sound at all. Again, she cried out and kicked at his shins, beat him with her elbows.

Then she struck at nothing but air.

He was gone.

Collapsed on the desk, her tears scalding, she curled her fingers over the far edge again. The echoes of throbbing hadn't left the folds between her legs.

She had disappointed Roche. Disgusted him. And he had left her alone.

Chapter
32

Many more showers and he might shed a skin.

Roche stood under a hard stream of lukewarm water. He was pretty damn sure he'd have a heart attack if he hit his skin with anything ice cold.

He'd had no choice but to walk away, stagger away, and come in here. Bleu Laveau was wounded, far more so than even he had guessed. But her courage humbled him. She was scared stiff, but forced herself to try—because she wanted to please him.

He turned up his face and the spray felt like needles jabbing his skin.

No. Not to please him, or not only. There had been two of them who wanted to test her capacity for sex.

And she'd almost made it there—past the inhibitions, or the shame or whatever it was that tore a scream from her. That scream had knocked him away from her as her feet and elbows never could have.

Roche faced a wall and braced his weight on his arms.

He heard the shower door open behind him and waited, his gut contracted hard.

At first she didn't touch him, but when she did it was tentatively, as if she expected him to reject her. A slow caress from shoulder to shoulder. The fingers of both hands pushed into his hair, kneading his scalp.

She reached past him for the soap and began to wash him.

He shuddered, ecstasy hadn't taken a holiday after all. His back, his chest, she rubbed circles over him, while he remained facing the wall. His butt, his hips and around to his belly. Circles on circles. She used her knuckles sometimes, pressing harder. She scrubbed the hair on his chest with her fingertips and kept on scrubbing, following the diminishing line of hair until it flared again over his pelvis. Then her hands closed around his scrotum. Little movements, weighting beneath his penis, feeling and shifting him around, the warm soapy massage destroying any chance of his holding back, or of denial. Not that he could have seriously considered denial.

She stroked him, firmly, smoothly, and brought him to the brink of letting go.

"Stop," he told her and when she didn't, took her hands from him and turned around.

For the first time he saw her naked in the light.

Had he known from the moment he saw her that she was perfection? Yes.

They kissed beneath the water, drank from each other's mouths, swallowed the spray. And he passed his palms over all of her.

"Roche?" she said, and he scrubbed at his eyes to look at her. Her eyes were dark, but she smiled and reached her arms around his neck, pressed herself against him.

He kissed her again, taking as much time as he was able, and lifted her. "Put your legs around my waist," he told her.

With her back on the tile, they made love.

She would be sore later, but he didn't think she'd care.

For moments she slumped against him, then she looked up. "We don't have a chandelier," she said. She wasn't smiling.

"Maybe next time," he told her.

"I'm not through. Think of something else."

The thrill he felt could be dangerous. It mounted and the blood pumped to a beat in his veins. He was stiff again.

Giving her no time to get the breath for a scream, Roche pushed Bleu's head to her knees, gripped her by the waist and shot her upside down. He lifted her until a very interesting part of her was on a level with his face.

"Roche!" She shrieked now, and grabbed for him with slippery hands.

"Yes, love. I'm here." He licked her thighs.

"The blood's going to my head."

"That's good for you occasionally. Hook your knees over the top of the shower."

"*What?* You're mad."

"Me? You wanted more excitement. Do it, and be quiet."

Fumbling, banging the door with her feet, she accomplished the task and he made sure she was safe in his arms.

Ignoring her protests, he buried his face between her legs and started a leisurely tongue massage where she was least likely to forget the event.

"Roche! Stop the slow motion. I'm dying here."

"No, you're not." But he tongued her harder, faster, nipped her clitoris and sweated over the unbearable clamoring in his own body.

Sounds he couldn't control jolted from his throat. Her arms were around his hips.

A great shudder racked her and her hips met his face in a greedy demand. Then Bleu's muscles softened. He rested the side of his face against her thighs and loved it.

Her mouth, sucking him in, came without any warning. For an instant, he tried to stop her, but her teeth let him know that would be at a cost to him.

"I'll drop you," he yelled.

She didn't take the bait. Didn't answer.

He didn't want her to.

The climax bowed him. With his eyes shut, panting, he turned Bleu in a sideways cartwheel motion until her knees rested on the shower floor. Still she held his penis in her mouth. She drank him in.

"Don't ever leave me," he said, when she was done, sinking down slowly to kneel with her gathered into his embrace.

Bleu looked drunk, like a happy drunk. "We're not finished," she said.

He laughed and managed to turn off the shower. "We are, until I get you into bed."

Chapter
33

That evening

"Could be the Knights of Columbus weren't our best choice for the decorating committee," Madge said. "This is—different."

She stood with Bleu, Roche and his twin, Max Savage, at the edge of the dance floor at Pappy's Dance Hall and Eats. Few guests had arrived yet, but the Swamp Doggies, with Vince Fox curled over his fiddle and stomping a foot, got the toes tapping.

"It's eclectic," Bleu said. "It's got a kind of disorganized charm." She glanced at Roche.

Felt banners hung from the ceiling, each trailing lengths of tasseled gold rope. Backed by Pappy's stuffed, nine-foot-long lacquered alligator and dressed in their tuxedos, some wearing their feathered cocked hats, the Knights hovered in a line at the front of the restaurant. They welcomed each arrival.

The place vibrated with activity. Max's wife, Annie, who managed Pappy's, ordered people in different directions with quiet authority.

It felt to Roche as if he and Bleu had been together for hours. She had gone to work at the rectory during the afternoon, and he had been at Green Veil, working with clinic patients. But she hadn't been out of his mind.

Bleu wasn't smiling, but she was staying close and watching his face.

Looking for his reactions, trying to read what he was thinking— he didn't need help figuring that out.

Anyone with a little perception would only have to look at them to see how they couldn't keep their eyes off each other.

Annie, small, blond and confident, came over and propped her hands on her hips. "Me, I'm grateful Pappy said no way to any potluck," she said. She looked only at Max. "The parish ladies still keep making excuses to get into the kitchens."

Max laughed and put an arm around her shoulders.

"They've decided they're going to have lunch in the parish hall after noon mass on Sunday," Bleu said. "They say they've got the food and they're going to use it."

"I'm not plannin' to stay very long," Madge said abruptly.

"But I need you," Bleu said, frowning at her cousin. "You can't duck out on me."

Madge said, "Excuse me," and walked away so fast she banged into the closest table, knocking over a candle in a knobby red glass chimney.

"Something's up," Bleu said, watching Madge right the candle before rushing on. "Tonight of all nights."

"Shit happens every night," Roche said.

When Bleu chuckled, he was glad he hadn't put it more elegantly.

Max said, "Madge isn't herself. She looks as if she's expecting a disaster." He looked so much like Roche that Bleu couldn't help searching for differences. They were small, but there nevertheless. Roche's eyes were an even brighter blue and he had a thin, white scar above his left eyebrow. Max laughed more than Roche and didn't examine things around him with such care, or appear to withdraw into himself as Roche did.

"Hey, you three. How's it going?"

Roche turned to see Cyrus. "Good, I think. I didn't see you come in. You just get here?" The priest looked windswept.

"Uh-huh." Distracted, Cyrus checked around. "We're missing a lot of the usual suspects."

"They'll be here," Roche said. He had already caught Bleu doing an anxious head count.

"I hope so," she said. "But I won't be surprised if they stay away. Most people have been questioned more than once. I can't blame folks for thinking we should take some steps backward on any church building projects after what's happened."

"Excuse me," Cyrus said. Bleu doubted if he had heard a word anyone said before he left the group.

"I'd better get back." Annie bobbed to kiss Max's cheek and took off.

"The mystery's getting solved, bro," Max said to Roche, nodding across the room.

"What mystery? Ah."

Bleu followed the brothers' glances to where Madge stood looking out into almost total darkness with Cyrus at her shoulder. Her arms were crossed. His hands were in his pockets.

"Are they talking?" Bleu said. She blew out a breath. "None of my business."

"Those two deserve some peace," Roche said.

Max swung up onto the balls of his feet. "Yeah. And to answer you, Bleu, no, I don't think they're saying a word to each other."

"We can't help them," Roche said. "Cyrus loves two mistresses. Or... That wasn't put very well, but you know what I mean."

He was, Bleu thought, a deep man. He regarded Cyrus and Madge with a hint of sadness.

Tables draped with red-and-white check cloths surrounded the dance floor and extended into an area dedicated to dining at one side of the building. There, windows covered walls that edged the downhill-sloping forest. A skylight, surrounded by so many business cards tacked to the ceiling that they must add a useful layer of insulation, was mirror-black tonight. Not a hint of a moon showed.

"Girards and the Gautreauxs," Max said. "It'll fill in fast now."

Reb and Marc, Jilly and Guy arrived together and immediately got into conversation with the people in the lobby.

Spike's dark-haired wife, Vivian, arrived next with her mother, Charlotte, and Spike's dad, Homer. Charlotte, a smart, youthful woman, and crusty Homer had been engaged for years, and there were running bets on when or if they'd ever marry.

Bleu felt ungrateful about being negative, but said, "I want to see some of the ones I didn't know would come for sure."

"I know," Roche said. He smoothed her back from neck to waist and played his fingertips over her ribs. "Give 'em time."

A steady trickle of people started to come through the door. Roche wished some of them didn't look as if they were making perp walks.

He kept glancing at Cyrus and Madge, who didn't appear to have moved a muscle.

"Have you got a knock-'em-dead speech prepared?" Max asked Bleu.

"You sure that's what she needs?" Roche said, grinning.

"He's got an evil sense of humor," Max said, pointing at his brother. "You know what I mean."

Bleu liked watching the brothers banter. "Let's get serious," she said. "I want to convince them this school is good for the kids and good for the town. The kids will get a balanced education and a good grounding in basic principles. Any town benefits from young people growing up on a solid footing."

"Our kids will be there," Max said. "I bet Roche's will, too. Once he has some."

Roche met his brother's eye. Max wasn't being funny. That had been a challenge.

Fortunately, Bleu's attention wasn't leaving the new arrivals as they came.

She said, "Most of all, I want them to donate," in a low voice.

He couldn't see the future, Roche knew, but he had only just begun with this woman and he was prepared to see just how far they could make a great thing go. She learned fast. Already, the cracks in her reserve were widening. He stopped himself from smiling. Bleu Laveau was all dichotomies: scared and determined, shy and wild, serious and funny. She kept showing more sides of herself, and he wasn't getting bored watching. Earlier today had been pure, wonderful madness.

"I've got a surprise," Bleu said.

Roche moved to where he could look directly at her face, and Max leaned closer.

"It's a secret, though."

"You can't lead us on like that," Max said.

She smiled.

"C'mon," Roche said. "Is it a good thing?"

Bleu nodded. "It's great."

"Congratulations," Max said. "Bro, is she ticklish?"

"How would I know?"

"You might. If she is, you could make her talk."

"It may not happen," Bleu said. She felt troubled at the thought, but so far she didn't see the man who had promised to give St. Cecil's campaign a boost. "I shouldn't have mentioned it."

She shouldn't. And she only had because she was trying to reassure herself the whole evening wouldn't be a bust.

Gator and Doll Hibbs walked in with Ozaire and Lil. Doll had her usual pinched mouth on, and Gator wore denim overalls—he always wore denim overalls—but he'd left his baseball cap behind and his gray hair lay greased across his scalp.

Lil had given her hair a fresh dye job and managed to turn it almost black. Bleu saw how the woman craned her neck to look around the filling rooms before she saw whatever she was looking for and shot away from Ozaire's side.

Bleu braced herself. Lil made a beeline in their direction. She halted in front of Roche and said, "I need to talk to you. Private."

He came close to refusing, but figured that would make more of a show than if he walked with her somewhere and heard what she had to say. She turned on her heel and threaded her way toward a corner where the jukebox lights flashed.

"I'll be back," he said to Bleu and Max, then followed Lil.

The Swamp Doggies struck up with even more fervor. Couples danced now.

"Me, I shoulda said this a long time back," Lil said the instant Roche joined her. She motioned him deeper into the corner shadows. "Sometimes you say things because you're excited, and the story gets bigger. I was upset. I could've died after that crash I had."

She was talking about an accident she'd had in her car a couple of years previous. "You came through fine," Roche said. "We were all glad."

"I shouldn't have said what I did about you. Or not the way I said it."

Wariness prickled in the hairs on the back of his neck. He decided to let her talk her way through whatever she had in mind. The incident she supposedly witnessed between him and Lee at the clinic was on that same night.

"What would a nice woman like me know about rape?"

He closed his eyes and bowed his head.

"I've decided it could be I wasn't fair." Lil plowed on. "Just because a body has a certain way of doing things, doesn't have to mean everyone else does 'em the same way."

"Mmm."

"Some people are more energetic than others. Isn't that right? You being a psychiatrist, you'd know about things like that. Who knows—" she patted fat black curls "—it could be we would all have enjoyed more *physical* things if we were worldly like you. That Lee certainly looked like she was having a good time."

This wasn't a subject Roche wanted to revisit. "Is that what you wanted to say to me?" he asked.

"Well, yes, but Ozaire's got something to say to you, too."

He managed not to groan.

"He had to go outside," Lil said. "But when he gets back, I'll tell him you're lookin' forward to a chat."

Roche stared at her, then remembered to say, "Yeah. Do that."

"He'll be pleased," Lil said.

"Good."

"He's wanted me to set things straight about the rape. Doesn't think it's fair for a man to be blamed for gettin' a bit frisky now and then."

"Thanks," Roche said. "Good of you to let me know. Now, if you'll excuse me."

"Bleu's a quiet one," Lil said, walking back beside him. "Still waters run deep, isn't that what they say?"

"Is it?"

"Oh, it surely is." She gripped his forearm. "It's the quiet ones who turn out the wildest. The teacher's pet gets lots of petting from the teacher. When I was in school, there was a gym teacher who tried to get me behind the javelin rack with him. I wouldn't go, I can tell you that. But...well, there were others quick enough to line up for a bit of slap and tickle, I can tell you."

"People will be people," Roche said. This woman was a real case.

"So if you and Bleu enjoy the rough stuff—" Lil let the words hang, but gave him a broad wink.

Chapter
34

"Wouldn't you like to be a fly on the wall over there?" Max Savage said, indicating the far side of the restaurant where Roche and Lil had started to move slowly back toward the group.

"I'm curious," Bleu admitted cautiously. She didn't know Max well enough to be at ease with him.

He pushed his hands into the pockets of his jeans. "My brother is a good man. Some people don't know just *how* good."

Bleu wondered if she should be flattered that Max wanted to sell Roche to her. "I'm sure he is," she said.

"I don't remember hearing where it is you call home," Max said. "Madge grew up in Rayne, didn't she?"

"Yes. I got to visit some summers. We were a horrible influence on each other." Bleu had loved those summers in Rayne when she had been free to be a little girl as she never was at home with her single father.

Max continued to look expectant.

"I lived in Wyoming. Cullen. My dad taught math and coached the high-school football team."

He raised a brow, just as Roche often did. "That wasn't what I expected. I guess I don't know what I did expect."

"I hate football," she said, surprising herself. She shrugged and crossed her arms. "Not hate it, really. At our house we lived the game all the time—there wasn't a choice. My dad's a good man, just a bit narrow in his interests." She smiled.

"You taught, too?" Max said. "Isn't that what I heard? Before you got into fund-raising."

"Yes." She usually avoided thinking about her few teaching years too deeply. Michael had dealt her a bad hand there, too. The thought caused some guilt—but if he hadn't died, she doubted she would ever have had another chance to do what she was trained for. While he lived his jealousy, the scenes he made got between Bleu and anyone she worked for.

Tables laden with food spanned the length of the restaurant and heaping plates appeared, emptied and were replaced constantly.

Gator Hibbs and Doll sat with several of the men from the ice plant and their wives, demolishing boiled crawfish, oysters and shrimp remoulade. They clutched napkins in their palms and swiped at grease-shiny mouths every few bites. The aromas would make an anorexic drool.

Bleu glanced toward Roche again. Ozaire Dupre had taken his wife's place and leaned so close to speak that Roche bowed his head and listed to one side to avoid having Ozaire's face in his own.

"This is a big crowd," Max said. "I'm feeling positive, aren't you?"

She smiled at him. "Yes. At least, I'm cheering up fast." The stream of people into Pappy's brought a rush of warmth. "They can't all be against the building program."

"Some will be, but most won't."

Max was a nice man. If you didn't know he had an international reputation as a reconstructive plastic surgeon, he could fit in just fine as the guy next door.

"Ozaire looks like a man with something to sell," Max said. "If I didn't think Roche ought to suffer sometimes, I'd rescue him."

Bleu laughed.

A tap on her shoulder turned her around. Madge stood there and her smile didn't fool Bleu. Her cousin was unhappy.

"Looks like a full house," Madge said. "I'm feelin' better all the time."

Without knowing what was making Madge unhappy, Bleu longed to hug her, to reassure her. "Good," was the best she could do.

"There's Wazoo. You've got to wonder why she cares about a Catholic school or a senior center."

Max chuckled. "She'll have an angle. Give her time."

"I don't believe my eyes," Madge said and sucked in air through her teeth.

Bleu said, "What?" but it was Roche who held her attention. Ozaire had moved on, and Lil, but people stopped him repeatedly. She watched him talk and smile, and the way others touched him, lightly, usually on the arm, but they wanted to connect with him.

He was charismatic.

She was ordinary.

He'll get bored with you.

Bleu felt cold inside. Removed from the noise and movement. A psychiatrist could find someone like her interesting. At least for a while, he could study her, interact with her, even try to help her.

She didn't want his help.

Her teeth snapped together and her back stiffened. Michael Laveau had messed her up, but she'd found her way a lot of the way back. She would do the rest of the healing on her own.

A lump in her throat belied the flash of anger and the brave thoughts. Roche was an exciting, virile, powerful man who had caused her to feel and want things that made her burn. She wanted him. He made it seem as if she had him, and it was up to her to make sure that didn't change.

If it was in her power to keep him in her life, she'd do it. She would not give him up without a fight.

"Bleu," Madge whispered urgently. "Did you hear what I said?"

Bleu shook her head, continuing to watch Roche.

"It's Kate Harper," Madge said, elbowing Bleu. "She doesn't come to anything like this, but she's over there."

Sure enough, dressed in black from her shiny, wide-brimmed straw hat to the shoes that just showed beneath a long-skirted dress, Kate Harper moved through the reception area, apparently accepting sympathy on all sides.

"Funny," Bleu said. "She was in white the last time we saw her. Now she's the wife in mourning."

"Kate and Jim weren't married," Madge reminded her.

"Why would she come to this?"

"I don't know." Madge stood on tiptoe for an instant, then just as quickly, dropped back to stand flat again. "Sam Bush is with her. That seems strange."

Bleu moved until she could see Sam. "He doesn't think it's right— the way there's been talk about Kate having something to do with Jim's death. He's one of those people who roots for the underdog." And she admired him for his in-your-face attitude.

"This group will always jump on an opportunity to talk," Madge said. "I don't think she drives, so she'd need someone to bring her. It was nice of Sam to do it—if she really felt she had to come."

"Exactly," Bleu agreed. "I'll have to get started with announcements shortly. I'm keeping things as informal as possible, although there are pledge cards."

Madge had stopped listening. She had half turned away and exchanged steady looks with Cyrus. He stood a few feet away, glass in hand.

There had been many occasions when Bleu had felt tension between Madge and Cyrus, but not like this.

"Can you tell me what's wrong?" Bleu said. "It's bad, isn't it?"

"Yes," Madge said simply. "Really bad and all my fault."

"Don't. Don't take on all the blame for anything. There's always more than one side."

"I'm glad you're here," Madge said. "I need you. But I made a sickening mistake and I don't think there's a way out. Not for Cyrus or me. And we're both going to be sad about it for the rest of our lives."

Nothing Bleu considered seemed the right thing to say.

Sig Smith wandered up to Cyrus and they fell into conversation. Bleu was grateful, until she looked at Madge who had lost all color.

"What is it?" Bleu asked.

Madge moved in close. "I think I'm going away from Toussaint. I don't know how long I'll be gone, but I'll keep in touch with you so you can say I'm okay. If anyone wants to know."

"Don't," Bleu said. "Let me help you. Nothing can be so bad it can't be worked through."

"The way you and Michael could work it through?" Madge said. She bowed her head. "I'm sorry. It wasn't the same."

"It's okay. But you aren't dealing with a Michael Laveau. Are you interested in Sig?"

"He's a nice man."

Bleu didn't need an interpretation of what that meant. "Okay. He likes you a lot, doesn't he?"

"I don't know."

"Madge?" Bleu said.

"Okay. Yes, he does, but he deserves someone much better than me. I could never be any good for him."

"Because you're in love with Cyrus?" Bleu watched her cousin's face.

"Yes," Madge whispered.

"Do you want him to leave the Church?"

"No." Madge was adamant.

"Is he thinking about it?"

Dark eyes filled with tears, and Bleu wished she hadn't pushed so far.

"I don't know," Madge said. "Please drop it. I know I can talk to you if I have to."

"Promise me you won't leave Toussaint without letting me know first."

Madge wouldn't look at her. "I can't promise that."

Chapter
35

Roche laughed with the rest at a joke Bleu made and felt absurdly proud of her. As if he had some part in her accomplishment! This was the second time he'd seen her give a presentation. She knew her stuff.

"What if your school is cursed?" someone shouted from near the kitchens. "Last time you talked, Jim died."

The room became silent.

"There's been no connection made—" Bleu stopped. She looked toward the darkness outside, then at the faces all around her. "I was going to say no connection's been made. But we don't know there isn't one, either. I can't give you any details about what Spike's found out."

"They've asked enough questions," the same man said loudly. "What do we pay these people for? That's what we'd like to know."

Roche glanced around and realized Spike wasn't there.

"These things take time." It was Marc Girard who spoke up. He stood, and Roche figured this was a man the community listened to. "Let's stick with the school. If what we can do fits in with what the parish decides it wants, Girard will donate all architectural services.

Just let us know when you're ready, and we'll present renderings. Max and Annie Savage will cover surveys."

The look on Bleu's face made Roche grin.

Applause broke out. He felt the mood change. And he silently committed himself to doing whatever he could to flush out Jim's killer. It didn't make sense that anyone would kill because they didn't want a school built. He was more sure than ever that the building projects were being used as a diversion from the real motive.

"What a community!" Bleu said. She all but bounced behind the microphone. "This is…" She raised her hands and let them drop. "Well, it is."

Laughter rippled forth.

"Hey, folks." A man Roche didn't recall seeing before made his way from the reception area. "I thought I'd miss this whole shindig. Me, I was late when my mother pushed me out and I ain't improved."

More laughed erupted amid cries of, "Hey, Doug. Join the party," among other comments.

"Some of us gotta work," Doug said. He faced Bleu and raised a hand. "Miz Bleu, like I said on the phone, we're gonna clear the land where the old school was. We can get started on that right away. And we'll do the gradin' once you know what goes where."

Cheers went up.

Doug bowed and kept on grinning. "We got kids to send to that school," he hollered.

Roche shook his head. It had taken a move from New York to a tiny Louisiana town to teach him that, once you accepted the little quirks, such as addiction to speculation, people could be unselfish enough to shock you.

He caught Ozaire Dupre's eye and almost returned the man's obvious wink. Instead, he nodded his head. Ozaire, so he said, was the go-to guy when someone wanted a dog. He'd heard Bleu was planning to get one when she could, and wondered if Roche would like to make her a present of a fine specimen.

Roche had two choices—leave the picking to Ozaire or put in an order for something special. No deals had been struck, but Roche was considering the idea. He'd get ten dogs, if he thought they'd make Bleu happy.

"You've got it bad, haven't you, bro?" Max said, tilting his body sideways in his chair to get close.

Roche jumped and gave him an evil eye. They sat at a table close to where Bleu was speaking. "I don't know what you're talking about."

Also at the table was Father Cyrus, whose expression hadn't changed in minutes, as if he'd zoned out. Madge, Roche had noted, was at a table with a group of people he didn't know. Miserable didn't come close to describing her aura.

He could feel Max staring at him. "What?"

"Are you doing okay?" Max said.

"With what?"

"Everything," Max said. "Loving a woman—being in love with a woman and everything else that goes with that."

"You're getting *way* ahead of yourself." But his brother knew him too well, so there had to be more explanation. "She's interesting. She interests me."

"What do you know about her past?"

"What the... Drink your wine."

"I suppose you know she comes from Cullen, Wyoming. I drove that way once. Nice-enough country."

He had never asked her where she came from, Roche realized. She was Madge's cousin, and he hadn't thought about her living in a completely different part of the country. He should have. She didn't have a local accent and she'd spoken of coming to stay with Madge when they were children.

"If it was me," Max said. "I'd be checking to see what I could find out. Just out of interest."

"You're not me. In my world, we let people fill in their own blanks," Roche said.

"From what I can tell, she's got a lot of blanks. Married to a felon. Widowed—"

"How do you know that?" Roche asked. He turned toward his brother. "Damn it, Max. Keep out of my business."

"You bet," Max said. "I like her, by the way. I did what comes naturally—I looked out for you."

The damnable part of it was that Max really thought that's what he'd done. There wouldn't have been any malice there anyway.

"I'm too old to need a keeper," Roche said. "But thanks for the concern."

"Is the sex working?"

"Goddamn it!" He checked out Cyrus. The priest was only listening to his own thoughts, but Roche took his voice way down. "Would I have said anything like that about you and Annie?"

"You did." Max swallowed some red wine. "What's the big deal?"

Their eyes met. They both knew how big a deal sex had been—and continued to be—for Roche. He didn't want to conduct his own therapy session with his brother. "Leave it be," he said.

"Sure," Max said.

Today, Bleu had amazed him. He wondered how much she had amazed herself and figured she ought to be in shock. Doing what came naturally would have a specific meaning for him from now on.

"I asked questions, because I understand you," Max said. "Worldly wouldn't be a word I'd use to describe Bleu. It might be a good idea if you stuck with women—"

"Leave it." Blood pounded at Roche's temples. "You are so far off base."

"I probably am," Max said. "Forget I shoved my foot in my mouth."

They looked at each other, and the old slow grins spread.

Cyrus pushed back his chair. He got up and joined Bleu at the microphone.

More applause—and cheers.

"I think you all know Bleu is Madge's cousin," Cyrus said. "Which helps explain why she's so good at what she does. Inspiration runs in their family. I promised I'd do my bit, too.

"That means I get to tell you the pledge cards are being passed out. The popular duties are my job."

This time the laughter was more polite than enthusiastic.

"Also," Cyrus said. "We have confirmation of something amazing. Pappy, who doesn't need an introduction, wants to match every monetary pledge made tonight."

"No pressure," Roche murmured, then took a drink.

"But awesome," Max said. "We could be talking big bucks for Pappy." He elbowed Roche. "You written any checks yet?"

"I keep quiet about my charitable works," Roche said, smirking. "I hope to have an announcement one of these days. But don't worry, tonight I'll come up with something to put a little hole in Pappy's nest egg."

"Tell me," Max demanded, like a boy who had to know where the alligator eggs were.

"Nope. Might not work." But he wanted the Cashman parcel almost more than he'd ever wanted anything. A look at Bleu shook him. His life could be changing and why wouldn't he be crazy about the idea?

Because if it didn't work with her, he wouldn't be unscathed.

"You really want her."

His chest tightened. Without turning to Max, he said, "You bet I do. You know what I'm thinking around the same time I do, so I won't deny it."

"You're right," Max said. "Pointless. But this time I saw what you were thinking. Anyone watching your face would."

Roche pulled even closer to Max. "You and I choose wounded women. Know that? I could have great resources for writing a paper."

Max didn't look amused.

"Just joking." Roche shook his head. "I want to buy Cashman's, the land next—"

"I know where it is. Is it for sale?"

"I don't know. Don't even know who owns it, but I'm doing a search."

"I was right," Max said. "You do have a case on that woman. An expensive case."

"Max—"

"Uh-uh, I didn't say that was a bad thing. I made an observation is all."

Roche tipped onto the back two legs of his chair. There was so much noise in the place, it didn't matter if he and Max had a private conversation. "I may build a house on part of the land."

That got Max's absolute attention. "You sure?"

"No. I said I *may* do it."

"Why don't you announce your idea?" Max said. "Folks would love it."

Roche thought about it. "I'd rather get closer to knowing if it's possible."

"Just the idea that you want to do it would help Bleu," Max said, too mildly for Roche not to stare at him. "Another sign of her success."

He had something there. Roche had already started looking for alternate sites if Cashman's fell through. He flattened his hands on the table and pushed upright.

"Go, bro," Max said.

"Could I have a word?" Roche said loudly.

Cyrus, answering questions with Bleu, held out the mike at once. "All yours."

"Thanks." Roche faced the crowd. Bleu was frowning at him, and he shot her a smile. "You all know the property next to St. Cecil's they call Cashman's. I'm looking into making a purchase there, partly for a place of my own, but mostly to add to the options for the improvement projects at the church."

For seconds, everything fell silent.

He felt Bleu's fingers on his arm and couldn't keep satisfaction off his face.

"Whoa!" Ozaire stood and nodded his shiny head. "If that isn't the darnedest thing. It's the best thing I heard in a long time. Great place for the school."

Roars of agreement greeted Ozaire.

"Great," someone said, his voice loaded with sarcasm. Roche didn't know the man who spoke, but he sat with Kate Harper. Sam had moved off. This guy held one of Kate's hands in both of his.

"That's George Pinney," Cyrus told him quietly. "Mary's husband."

Roche didn't recall seeing the man, but put him together with what Bleu had told him about her visit to Kate Harper.

"The school needs to be where the old school was," Cyrus said, still very softly. "That's what the archdiocese agreed to."

Roche held the mike away. "How about a senior center? A multipurpose center?"

"Great," Cyrus said. "I don't know how to thank you."

"Don't try." Roche clapped the other man's arm. "The school's going to be built on the site of the old one," he told everyone. "But wait till you see the senior center and multipurpose facility we can have at Cashman's place." He grinned and the place went wild.

He turned to Bleu and she threw her arms around his neck. She'd regret it later, he knew, but for now he hugged her back, breathed her in and started thinking about when this party was over.

"I've got somethin' to say," a woman's voice said clearly.

Kate Harper, with George Pinney solicitously holding her elbow, stood and very slowly let her gaze wander over the dance hall. "My Jim died because you people's ideas are bigger than your pocket-books. They build this school, then what? How many of you got the money for tuition? There won't be a day when your children don't come home askin' for something for the school. You all let yourselves get carried away."

"Kate," Cyrus said. "These are terrible times for you. For all of us. We'll get to the bottom of what's happened."

"And will that bring Jim back?" Her voice had a whiplash quality, all Southern softness wiped out. "No. Well, there's one thing I can do, right now. Cashman's, as you call it, belonged to Jim and now it belongs to me." She pushed back her chair. "I think the killer expected Jim to make a big gift to the wretched school the night of your last meeting, Bleu Laveau. So he stopped him. Now my Jim's given enough.

"You don't have the space for a school and some sort of center on the property you've already got. If you build one thing without the other you'll have war on your hands. You need what I've got and I'm not sellin' that land."

Chapter
36

Nobody made a whimper for a long time.

Bleu stepped closer to Roche—for his comfort, and her own. Cyrus stood at her opposite side.

"That's spiteful." Madge's voice rang out, and it shocked Bleu to her toes. She looked at her cousin, standing with her chair pushed back, and wondered what else she didn't know about her. Fury changed her face, filled it with passionate loathing.

Bleu wanted to turn toward Cyrus, to see his reaction. She stayed right where she was. And she dreaded how devastated Madge would be if he tried to soften her outburst.

"I'm goin' to have my way," Kate said in ringing tones. "That land's valuable. It'll be sold when I decide. That won't be anytime soon. If you want some place for meetings, put it where the old school was. We don't need another one. That school's done enough killin' already."

"I'm sorry for your loss," Madge said.

Bleu held her breath.

"We're sufferin' right with you over Jim," Madge continued.

"We're never goin' to be the same. He wanted the school replaced. Each of us will have to decide what we think is the right thing to do."

Bleu let the breath out.

"Let's get to those pledge cards," Ozaire boomed.

The trance snapped, and talk broke out. Bleu dared to check out Cyrus's face. He was staring straight at Madge, who continued to stand. She looked back at him. Bleu had to turn away. It hurt too much to see the yearning in her cousin's eyes.

"Madge has some spirit," Roche said in her ear. "It runs in the family."

She didn't know how to respond, but she smiled at him. He was working a miracle for her, changing just about everything about her, or helping her to change it.

And she was scared, Bleu realized, afraid to accept that the wonder of it wouldn't all go away. People had affairs all the time, but that didn't make them commitments.

"Don't worry about the land issue," Roche said. "Kate's grieving. She's raw. She'll come around. If she doesn't—we'll figure out something else."

We. He talked about them as a couple, a pair. She wanted to relax and believe it. She wanted to giggle all the time and go nuts with amazement that he was here and he wanted to spend time with her.

She was afraid.

Roche pulled her away from center-stage and into a spot where they had privacy. "I'm a tough guy," he said.

Bleu blinked. "Of course you are."

"I am. I've got more bad habits than you can imagine, but I'm trainable, Bleu."

"What does that mean?" she said.

"It means I hope you'll give us a chance to see what we can be together." He smirked, there was no other description for his expression. "I'll expand on that. I already know what we can be together. Exhausted and silly-happy. But you know what I mean. 'Can I be what you need?' is the question. And whether or not you're even interested."

"I'm the one who needs the work," she told him.

Cyrus interrupted. "We don't have enough pledge cards," he said. "I never thought I'd have a reason to say that, about anything."

"I don't suppose it would be cool if I yelled, 'whee!'" Bleu said. She and Roche exchanged a long look. Later there would be a lot more to say. "I was trying to be optimistic, so I brought a big bundle of cards. I'll run and get them."

"Kate's left," Cyrus said. "I'll have to go and see her again."

Telling him to save his breath wouldn't go over so well, Bleu decided. There was something incredibly selfish about Kate Harper. Or maybe she really wasn't herself at a time such as this.

"Be right back," Bleu said.

She hurried to get the cards from Annie Savage's office. Bleu had left all her things there when she arrived. Annie and Max were very different, too. Could Annie help with all the questions Bleu had about being with Roche?

Terrible idea.

She didn't know Annie well enough for that.

"You're a wizard," a woman said as Bleu passed.

"No," she responded. "This is a very special parish."

On her way across the deserted lobby, she paused to check out the guest book the Knights of Columbus had left there. She couldn't take the time to read all the names, but the number of them made her do a little jig.

A thump behind her was followed by a sharp current of air.

Bleu shot around and let out a squeal. The outside garbage can had fallen over and wedged the door open.

She hurried, grabbed the door open wider and bent over to right the can. A length of cloth, jammed into her open mouth, made sure she didn't get a coherent sound out.

She and the garbage can were dragged hastily outside. The creep who had her dropped the can, but half carried Bleu straight across the upper parking lot and into the trees.

Bleu retched. The explosive bumps in her chest sapped her strength. All she could make were gurgling noises. The trees seemed to suck her in and close her off from safety.

The steel-armed person punched the middle of her back.

She threw up around the gag. Her head, shoved forward while the cloth was loosened, stopped her from choking to death.

The instant she took a clear breath, he gagged her again.

Her arms wouldn't work. They had no strength. She couldn't stand.

He jerked her upright and cuffed her across the side of the head.

She heard voices. People coming out of Pappy's. Were they looking for her?

"No one out here," someone yelled.

The voices went away.

Bleu shook, couldn't stop shaking. She didn't try to see who was behind her. He wouldn't let her anyway but if she *could* identify him she would have no hope of getting out of this alive.

The pressure of the arm around her chest slackened.

Before she could try to move, a dark, rough bag shot down over her head and upper body. Wrapped tight, she heard the distinctive sound of tape ripping from a roll, and felt that tape whipping around the outside of the bag to trap her inside.

She was going to die.

Chapter
37

A short time later the same night

"Those folks out there pretty much take care of their own problems." Spike couldn't remember the last time one of the bayou settlements had come to him for help.

"Bill Pelieu, it was who phoned," Rose said. He stood, straight-backed in the doorway to Spike's office. Rose was still sorting out just how close he wanted to get to his boss.

"Good guy," Spike said. "Did he say exactly when it happened?"

"He's not sure. Reckons they don't use that boat often. It's old and they keep it for emergencies. But it's his and he doesn't like it that someone else decided to clean things up for him. That's the way he put it."

A pirogue had gone missing from behind Pelieu's house. He and his friends had searched for it but had come up empty-handed.

"Damn." Weary, Spike shoved back his chair and stood up. "This has to be seen to. I won't have those good people being picked on when someone decides I'm too busy with other things to do anything."

He *was* too busy with other things, but he'd deal with the problem just the same. "Do you know how to get out there and take a complaint?"

The horrified expression on Rose's young face said it all. Rose was new to the area. He came from Texas.

"Of course you don't," Spike said, rubbing his eyes. "I'll go myself. It's time I showed myself out there again."

Rose coughed. "If I could be spared to come with you, I'd know how to get there next time."

"You've got it." Spike grinned and made for the coffee pot. "Call Pelieu back and tell him I'll be out in the mornin', first thing."

"Will do."

The phone rang as the door closed behind Rose.

"Devol," Spike said into the receiver.

"Roche here. I'm out at Pappy's for the fund-raiser. Bleu's gone."

"What d'you mean, *gone?*" He didn't need the coffee anymore.

"Disappeared. As far as any of us can tell, she's not on the premises. We haven't found any sign of her in the parking lots, and we're going through the surrounding areas. Spike, I think someone's got her."

The desperation in Roche's words matched the way Spike felt. "I'll put out a call for help, and we'll be right there." Dear God, don't let Bleu turn up dead.

"Someone already tried to get at her, remember?" Roche said. "They think if they can get rid of her, everything will stop with the school. We've got to talk about that—once we get Bleu back."

"Sure. Do you think what I think? It doesn't ring true that someone's so obsessed about the school, they'll kill to stop the project."

"I can't talk about killing now. But yeah, that's what I think."

Spike tried to measure his response. "They intend to take down as many as they have to." He'd never been much of a diplomat.

Chapter
38

A little later the same night

"Will I be all right?" she said. "No one will know I did anything wrong?"

Justice snatched up her panties and bunched them over her mouth. "I told you not to talk. I hate a woman to talk when I'm busy. Say another word and you'll be swallowing these."

Little wonder that no one had a clue what was happening. He, Justice, ran them around, confusing them more with every move he made.

He kept his hand where it was and held her against a wall in the closet. "You're going to like this," he said. More important, he was going to get what he needed: she would do what he wanted, when he wanted. Everything must come together quickly now.

She'd happily taken off her own underwear when he'd told her to. "You follow orders really well." He considered how he wanted this to happen. He didn't have much time, so it had to be fast.

But he also had to be satisfied.

He grabbed first one, then the other of her wrists and trapped them in manacles hanging by chains from the low ceiling.

She started to shriek.

"Shut your fucking mouth," he said, pushing his face into hers.

Everything but her underpants was still on her body. He hauled her skirt above her waist. Too bad he had to do so much of this by feel.

She felt just fine. But he couldn't locate what he wanted to use quickly enough.

He laughed aloud. He was slipping. From its sheath against his side, he removed the Italian knife. He gave himself a second to think, to make a decision. Then he reconsidered.

Still laughing, he plunged the handle of the knife between her thighs and inside her.

The chains rattled, she threw herself back and forth, her knees hitting at him as if she were a dancing marionette. Gasps of breath jolted from her. Why didn't she try to scream and shout again? Why didn't she beg?

If she thought he'd stop because she didn't beg him to, she was wrong.

Three more times he sunk the knife handle into her.

She jigged and puffing sounds came from her throat.

Time to use the part of his knife he loved the most. He withdrew it and felt her sag.

He flicked out the blade, pulled the neck of her top away from her body and positioned the knife inside. Swiftly, expertly, in one swift slash, he slit her clothes open until they fell away. He sheathed the knife and felt her.

Big breasts. That's the way he liked them. Her destroyed bra still hung from her shoulders. That was a picture he could see and like in his mind.

He had a pole stiff enough to do pull-ups with.

Pinching, squeezing, he pushed her breasts together.

She was panting again.

Women were so predictable; this kind played the game of "nice" when they were as raunchy as they came.

Pursing his mouth, he drew hard on one breast, sucked, knowing how he would mark her. She swung, shoving herself harder into his face.

If he had fifteen more minutes, he was lucky.

The zipper on his pants opened loudly, and he pulled himself out. Once he started, he gave her a little piece of news with each thrust.

"You made a big mistake."

Using only his penis, he lifted her from the floor.

"You tried to make deals with me."

He didn't give her feet a chance to settle on the floor again.

"You're sorry now."

This time the chains jumped.

"Listen closely."

He was getting too close, and he hadn't finished talking. Pulling out didn't make him happy.

"I'm getting everything I want. No one will get in my way. Don't try. Give me what I want, when I want it."

One more slam and he came. He clutched at handfuls of her torn clothing for balance, but he wasn't like other men. He recovered almost instantly.

"It's too bad there's another potential problem to get rid of. Someone was careless. Was it you?" He shoved his face into hers. "We both know it was. You didn't think I'd find out we've got a crazy lady who knows too much, did you? You should know me better."

"No one would believe her—"

"Shut up. She won't be left around to tell inconvenient tales—you'll help take care of that for us."

When she was out of the manacles, he said, "Don't do anything stupid. And be ready when I come for you."

Chapter
39

After midnight

Streams of light shot behind Bleu's eyelids. If she opened them, the bag sent more scratchy dust into her eyes.

She smelled wet earth, mold, rotting leaves. What felt like pipes dug into her back.

When she drew in air, crazy little sounds bounced from her throat. She shook so violently, she bit into the sodden gag. Only forcing her mind to be still, empty, let her breathe through her nose until the retching stopped again, and she calmed down.

It didn't last. The shaking started all over, and the biting, the carving pain from the base of her skull to her eyebrows.

Her ankles were bound together.

The man, he drove her here—never speaking, not touching her again until the vehicle bumped over rough ground. They had stopped, and he dragged her outside. He pulled her in one arm, then threw her down.

She didn't know how long ago he'd left her there.

Struggling only scraped the bag over her skin. She struggled anyway. Several times, she had fallen sideways onto the ground. Now she was sitting again, her back against the pipes, sweating, scraping her heels back and forth, trying to find a way to free her feet.

"*My God.*" She heard her desperation inside her brain. If she couldn't get away, that man might come back.

He *would* come back.

An idea niggled its way into her thoughts. She tried to force it back. Her trembling became spasms of shaking that burned her muscles.

What if Michael had asked someone to come after her? What if that person waited until she made the move to Toussaint, then came after her? Michael warned her she'd never be free of him.

An engine, its noise getting louder, didn't register at first. When it did, she tried to scream and felt tears pour down her cheeks. Closer and closer, a vehicle came. And then the engine shut off.

Bleu knew what vehicle it was and who drove it.

A door slammed.

She strained, but heard no footsteps.

Another door opened.

A jangle and a thud. Metal things hitting the ground.

The second door slammed shut.

Cold shot up Bleu's legs. The skin stretched tight and it ached. Slowly, she inched herself sideways along the pipes.

Too much noise. All she could do was pretend to be dead—or unconscious. Deliberately, she let herself slide until she lay on the ground again. She slumped there—her face and body twisted downward, her legs pulled up—and waited.

He was close. The metal clanged again. Another thud, this one louder, sounded.

Grunts shocked her. Sounds of something heavy shifting, a great slap against the ground.

Soon, he'd come for her. He was getting something ready first.

She mustn't make any noise, but mucus clogged the back of her nose and her throat. Bleu needed to cough. The hot tears mixed with grit in her eyes.

Something slid and the man grunted again, and he dropped whatever he was carrying.

She thought he laughed under his breath before the clatter of hard things sounded once more.

And he laughed out loud.

Grinding. A rough sound like cogs falling into place.

I can't, please, I can't do this.

Bleu remembered hearing something like that before. A drill, a very old-fashioned one, crushing its bit through wood. Only the sound was different.

A subtle pop and a cracking. He hadn't made the hole true, and whatever was around it had burst open.

Something to use on her? A box to bury her in?

Sliding, sliding. Sliding away from her. A heavy thing was dragged, while the man strained. He banged into things, but didn't curse.

And, finally, silence fell again.

Could it have been someone else who came back? Had the person failed to see her? She'd been very still. Bleu panicked. What if help had been feet away but, in the darkness, the other person didn't see her?

She moaned.

Listening so intently her ears hurt, Bleu squeezed her eyes shut and fought to hear any small sound.

Nothing.

How could she know if the person who had been there was good or bad? If he'd gone away, surely someone else would come eventually. Roche wouldn't let her stay lost. Neither would Madge or Cyrus or any of the others.

An abrupt thunder of blows on hard surfaces came from all around her. Louder and louder. She was like the inside of a drum absorbing wild beating on her shell.

Around and around it went. Starting at one side and moving in a circle.

Bleu got out a scream, and another. She screamed over and over and rocked her face on the hard ground. Gathering herself onto her knees, she curled over and fought as best she could inside the bag. She remembered her watch and managed to wrench it off. With the catch, she picked away at the cloth under a band of tape.

It wouldn't work. Or it would take forever. Or he'd hear and stop her.

He would stop her anyway.

Not for several seconds did she realize the hammering had ceased.

A door on the vehicle opened. The tools, or whatever they were, landed somewhere, probably inside.

For a long, long time, a sound like wind moving leaves grated at her. To remain quiet was her choice.

Once more, a door closed hard.

The engine turned over, and the rumbling receded slowly until Bleu was left in the dark inside the bag again, with the smells and the occasional skittering of a critter.

Don't let him come back again.

Chapter
40

Daybreak

Too weary to raise their faces, the men emerged in a straggling line from woods along the back way from Pappy's to St. Cecil's.

Roche kept his eyes down, still searching, even though he'd stumbled onto the broken blacktop on what was an extension of Parish Lane. The lane ran from the center of town all the way to join with Bonanza Alley between the rectory and the church.

"We've got to regroup," Max told him, arriving to throw an arm around his shoulders. "We don't know if Bleu's been found elsewhere. A report could have been called in."

Hardly able to hope, Roche used his cell phone to reach Spike. While he waited for an answer, Marc Girard joined them, then Guy Gautreaux with his black dog.

The sheriff answered his phone. "Spike here," he snapped out.

"Heard anything?" Roche said, driving a finger and thumb into the corners of his eyes.

It took a long time before Spike said, "Nothing. Goddamn it, it's like she evaporated."

Roche didn't want to consider that image. "We need to know where to start next." More searchers emerged from the trees and walked heavily toward him.

"Come on in," Spike said. "We've got more pairs of boots from the state. We need to make sure we're using everything we've got as best we can. We've already started sending for locals to help and we'll get more people from the surrounding areas. Ozaire knows someone with dogs—"

"Stop!"

"I'm sorry, Roche. We're all wearing thin."

Max move to stand in front of him, his frown deep. He looked into Roche's face.

"Into the station?" Roche said, gathering himself. A small crowd grew around him.

The sight of Madge, limping along the lane, shocked Roche, but before he could go to her aid, Cyrus came from behind her and put an arm around her waist. He half carried her. Sam Bush ran to hold her from the other side and the threesome carried on.

"Spike, you want us at the station?" Roche repeated.

Spike came back on the phone. "Can you wait right where you are?"

"In the middle of Parish Lane?" Roche said. "No. I've got to keep going. I can't waste any time."

"Wait a minute," Spike said. Then, "I want you to send as many as are able to go through the town alerting people. We probably need them now."

"Probably?" Roche heard negatives in every word spoken to him. "You don't think we'll find her, do you?"

"I didn't say that. Send them now. Then they need rest and so do you."

"I'll go with the others." He couldn't do anything else.

"Roche," Spike said. "I've asked the FBI for help. They're already in Toussaint."

"For God's sake—"

"I had to," Spike said. "I'd be negligent if I didn't. I'm telling you, so you don't get shocked when you fall over one of the agents."

"Thanks." He closed his eyes and muttered, "FBI," knowing everyone else would feel as desperate as he did, but he couldn't keep them in the dark.

"Wazoo called to say she thinks she knows something useful," Spike said. "I told her I'd see her at the rectory. She's on her way there now. It's up to you, but if you want to, you could wait and hear what she has to say."

Roche didn't think he could deal with Wazoo. He told Max what Spike had said.

"Roche," Spike shouted at him. "Say somethin', will ya? I can't hang on this line any longer."

"We're on it," Roche said and hung up.

He looked into his twin's face and Max nodded slightly.

"You think I should hear what Wazoo has to say?" Roche asked.

"Yeah. I'll get the rest going into the town. We've got to have re-inforcements. Calling in the feds was the right thing for Spike to do."

Max slapped Roche's shoulder and walked off.

Wordlessly, Roche continued on toward the rectory. Cyrus, Madge and Sam were ahead of him, and he hated to see Madge hobble. He figured she must have resisted being carried and knew Cyrus wouldn't push that. Or, given her frame of mind, she wouldn't let him push it.

He caught up with them. "Madge, have you hurt yourself?" he asked.

"A couple of days ago," Sam said promptly. "Turned her ankle."

"You should stay off that," Roche said.

Cyrus gave him a bleak look. "Yes, she should, but she won't listen. You know how hardheaded these women can be."

Madge didn't respond or look amused. She did visibly cringe when Sam lifted her into his arms before she could protest.

"I didn't know how bad it was," Sam said. "Don't start fussing. I'm carrying you to the rectory."

A movement caught Roche's attention: Cyrus lifting his hands and looking at them as if he didn't know who they belonged to. He glanced up and met Madge's eyes over Sam's shoulder. She seemed close to tears.

"What is it?" Roche said, falling in with Cyrus. "With you two? There's something horribly wrong."

"Yes," Cyrus said simply. "God will have to solve it, because I can't."

There was nothing Roche could think of to say.

They trudged along through the grayish light beneath a sky streaked with pink and purple. The clouds were brushed into ribbons, and the air still carried a little of the night's cooler temperatures.

"Spike says Wazoo's coming to the rectory with something to tell us," Roche said. "I don't know how I feel about that. I want to be out there looking for Bleu."

"I know you do."

Roche stopped walking. He ran both hands through his hair and searched around. A wild, desperate urgency overwhelmed him. "She never did anyone any harm. Your God wouldn't let someone do awful things to her, would he?"

"My God is your God," Cyrus said. He sighed. "For better or worse, He can be a hard master."

That left Roche with his mouth open. He had no way to answer what he didn't even understand coming from Cyrus.

When they all approached the rectory, the first person they saw was Lil. She rushed to wrench open the gate and trotted toward them, her hair on end and an apron flapping around her.

"Lil," Cyrus said, hurrying. "It's all right. Whatever it is will be all right. Be calm, please."

"Calm?" She panted. "Calm, you say? You better come now and hurry. There's men here from the FBI. Me, I never been so frightened. They're trompin' all over the house and all around the garden. Now they said we all gotta stay inside. Well, I ran right out, I can tell you. They're not makin' me no prisoner."

"Hush." Cyrus held her arm and started her back the way she'd come. "Did Wazoo get here yet?"

"Wazoo?" she cried. "Why, Wazoo? *There's a hex!* I knew it, there's a hex on us because we upset someone we shouldn't have. Wazoo's comin' to do for the hex? I don't know if that girl's got the strength. She talks a lot, but I don't know."

The pastor of St. Cecil's deserved medals for not lecturing his housekeeper on the dangers of believing in the occult. Roche admired the other man's control as he plodded toward the side of the house.

They arrived at the back door in a bunch.

Arrived in front of a dark-suited man with a crew cut, old scars from bad skin when he was younger, and a solid body. He held his hands together and dark glasses made him seem impassive. Roche wondered how difficult it was to see in dark glasses at that time of the morning.

The man stood aside and opened the door. "There'll be questions," he said, pleasantly enough. "Give your names to the agent inside."

Roche turned to glance at the garden. Lil had said they were searching that, too. Why would they look at either place, the garden or the rectory? They wouldn't find Bleu there.

He pinched his mouth shut.

Only two men stood in the garden, at the bottom. One faced the bayou, the other the rectory.

A white van, and then another, larger one, rolled down Bonanza Alley and Roche's gut squeezed. He knew crime-scene vehicles when he saw them.

He sprinted, went from nothing to an all-out run in seconds.

"Sir," the agent by the door shouted. "Sir?"

Roche ran on. He figured they wouldn't shoot him in the back. Both men at the bottom of the garden converged on him when he arrived.

"This is off-limits," one of them said. "An investigation is under way."

"Investigation of what?" Roche gauged whether he could get past these two. Neither of them had the brawn of their third man back at the house, but he had no doubt they could stop him.

"We can't talk about this yet, sir," he was told. "We've got a brand-new development here."

He noticed activity beside the bayou. Several more uniformed people, male and female, some in white overalls, faced the water, while two of their number hauled on the bow of an abandoned pirogue, pulling it to shore. A rope trailed behind it and had become tangled around a cypress stump.

Unless it had been tied up there.

Inside the shallow boat, he saw what seemed to be a body covered with a tarp.

He absorbed the leap of his heart into his throat and said the first thing he thought of. "I'm a doctor. Perhaps I can help."

"We've already got doctors," he was told.

"Do you know who's in the boat?" His mouth had dried out.

"No, sir."

"It's likely to be someone local. I could help with the identification."

Both men's expressions became uncertain.

"It might not be a body," he said, voicing aloud a vain hope.

"We're pretty sure it is. Why don't you wait right here. We'll let you know if they want you down there."

"Sure," Roche said, opening and closing his hands into fists. He shoved them in his pockets. No point showing these guys he was too personally involved.

"Roche!"

Wazoo, all but overbalancing in her haste to reach him, bounded headlong downhill. Hair and skirts whipped out behind her, and he saw how wild her eyes were, well before she reached him.

He caught her before she would have fallen.

She looked around him toward the pirogue and let out a cry. "I'm too late." She clutched Roche's sleeve. "Me, I should have done something sooner. I called Spike this mornin'. He wouldn't say one thing to me. I know someone's missing. Who is it?"

He kept a hand on her arm. "Bleu's gone. She disappeared after you left last night. You didn't stay long."

She crammed a hand over her heart. "I couldn't stay there. I feel this thing coming. Somethin' happenin'. I went home to... I had to think."

He dropped his hand. "Just wait," he said. How could *he* just wait? Inside, he was freezing up. An ice man with a throbbing heart and pain in his rigid throat.

Instructions were shouted from below. The boat glided to bump against the bank, and people hurriedly guided it alongside.

Roche broke away. He dashed around the agents and vaulted the low hedge between the garden and the path beside the bayou. Shouts from behind him got the attention of those on the bank.

"I'm a doctor," he said, fighting to compose himself. "Roche Savage. I know most people around here. I might be useful."

A balding man with fair coloring said, "Hi. Stick around just in case." He was being polite—but so what? Roche was where he had to be.

Warnings shot through the air. Watch where they trod, watch what they touched, follow protocol to the letter.

As soon as the fair man turned back to his fellows, Roche edged closer, waited, then made a few more inches of progress. He could see as well as anyone who wasn't actually at the edge of the pirogue.

The shape inside didn't have to be a body. Bunched up, the tarp could have been discarded there.

A technician reached out a gloved hand, took hold of the edge of the canvas and eased it first up, then, after glancing back at the other agents, pulled it back.

Roche saw a woman lying there, but one of the men obscured her face.

All attention was on the contents of the pirogue.

"Hoo mama," Wazoo whispered. "This is one time I wanted to be wrong."

Carefully, Roche got closer. A shudder crawled his spine.

He cleared the man closest to the woman's head.

"Sick, sonsabitches," the same man announced. "Why would anyone do that?"

Roche's knees locked and he made himself look down on a corpse, the body of what had been a woman. Congealed blood from a hole in her forehead covered her face and neck.

A look at the hair punched all the air from his body. He staggered, but caught himself. Long, very dark hair. Not Bleu's blond curls.

"No," Wazoo cried. "It's Mary Pinney."

Chapter
41

Birds.

Gabbling, scuffling birds looking at her, getting closer. A ring of them. Screeching.

They were planning to come, planning the way they would attack. Louder and louder. Ready to peck her through the sack, at her ankles, into her stomach to reach the softer insides of her.

Bleu jerked, kicked out her feet and opened her eyes.

Very pale, fuzzy light reached through the sack. She cringed at the thought of those birds. Big and black, buzzards, crows.

Imagining things.

There were birds, but they sang their morning songs, the ones she loved to hear when she was first up. The air felt warm, and dank scents had faded. Someone would find her; she knew it.

Why had the man done this to her? He knew she was here. Once more, her stomach clenched.

Why would someone try so hard to stop the new school from being built?

Bleu tried to blink grit from her eyes.

She hadn't wanted to visit Kate Harper with Cyrus and Madge. Her mind had been on Roche and what Madge had told her about him.

That day, Kate complained about the prospect of a new school. She'd talked about the fire and the children being killed.

No one in town had ever mentioned those children, but the older people must remember. The memory was too painful. It had to have touched so many families.

Bleu's exclamation made her retch again.

Building over the place where children had died was the reason. For many, the site must be a place of remembrance. The families— who were they? Where were they? Those poor people had to be talked to, because that's where the answer to Jim Zachary's murder would probably be found.

Someone should have brought their pain and horror at the idea of the forgotten children to Cyrus. All of the plans could have been changed.

For someone, anger had turned to a crazed quest for revenge.

Now, she saw it all.

Too late. Jim already died. The grieving relative of a long-ago-lost child had no chance to turn back.

"Bleu!"

She held very still.

"Bleu!" The second voice was different from the first.

They were looking for her, of course they were. She turned her head from side to side, ground her teeth into the gag. Since she'd been left there, she had tried to bite through the cloth and free her mouth. The stuff only sopped in more saliva that ran back into her throat.

"Bleu Laveau. Can you hear me?"

Yes, yes. I'm here.

More distantly, other voices cried out, but she couldn't make out what they said.

She tried, but no scream came from her.

Her arms were free inside the bag. She should be able to tear it apart. It wouldn't give, not even a little, because of the tape wound around and around.

They could trace some tapes and find criminals that way.

"Bleu, where are you?"

Here. I'm here. I'm here. Her own shouts got quieter in her mind. They were so tiny they were coming from miles away.

Slashing sounds started. Beating. A whole bunch of people were out there thrashing at whatever was around her, determined to find her. They would.

On her knees, she worked to crawl, but she fell. Her bound ankles didn't budge, one from the other.

She felt her tears. She felt intense pain where her flesh hadn't turned numb.

Bleu stayed where she was, facedown and crumpled.

The shouts went on and on.

Then they stopped.

Chapter
42

Later that morning

The body remained in the pirogue.

In the rectory kitchen, Madge, Doll and Lil kept iced tea and sandwiches flowing out to the volunteers who delivered them to gathering points for the searchers.

Roche heard the clatter and voices behind him, but he alternated his attention between looking out the window at the activity by the bayou and poring over lists of areas covered so far.

Cyrus came through the door. "They're questioning George Pinney, poor man. His wife's out there like that, and they're calling him a person of interest."

"They always look at the husband first," Roche said absently. He ought to be thinking about Mary more than he was. But as long as Bleu wasn't found, he didn't think he'd ever concentrate on anything else.

Exhaustion weighed him down. He pulled out a chair and sat at the table. Heat built steadily, outside and in. The steady production of boiling coffee made the kitchen almost unbearable.

"You've got to sleep," Cyrus told him.

"You haven't," Roche said.

Cyrus didn't answer.

"There's Spike," Roche said. The sheriff walked down Bonanza Alley with another man at his side. Roche didn't know the second person.

"There's a face I haven't seen in a long time," Cyrus said. "Lil, take a look at the man with Spike. Outside. Isn't that Bill Pelieu from the camp near Homer Devol's gas station?"

Lil stood on tiptoe to look through the window over the sink. "Uh-huh. It surely is. What would Spike want with him?"

"That's one of those questions," Doll said, although she wasn't smiling. "The ones you don't expect anyone to answer."

Roche noted that Madge continued to work without a word. She and Lil came and went regularly, ferrying urns of tea and coffee through the back door to waiting trucks and returning with empties.

"Spike's out there with Bill Pelieu," Wazoo said, straggling into the kitchen, her eyes still heavy with sleep. She'd been resting in one of the bedrooms. "What would he want with him? D'you think Bill is—was—someone Mary knew?" Wazoo said.

"Who knows?" Madge said.

Just looking at her made Roche uncomfortable. Whatever was going on between her and Cyrus had better be fixed fast, or both of them would have breakdowns.

"They're coming back," Cyrus said. "I'm goin' to ask. All Spike can do is tell me to get lost."

He went to meet Spike and Bill. Roche followed.

The breathless heat outside felt balmy in comparison to the kitchen.

The door slammed behind him, and he turned to see Wazoo, a slow-moving version of her usual self, on her way to do what came naturally to her—to see what she could find out.

Spike didn't look any better than Roche felt. His skin had a gray tinge.

"Hey there, Bill," Cyrus said to the skinny, dark-haired man with Spike.

"Mornin', Father," Bill Pelieu said. He hooked a thumb in the direction of the bayou. "Poor woman. That's my pirogue back there. Someone took it right outside of my house. Didn't think I'd ever see it again. Wish I hadn't now."

"Thanks, Bill," Spike said. "The boat's likely to be kept a long time for evidence."

"When you don't need it, burn it," Bill said, then walked away uphill.

"I should have told someone," Wazoo said.

When Roche looked over his shoulder, her eyes were fixed and filled with horror.

"I didn't want to go to Cashman's with her," she continued. "We didn't find anything, so I forgot about it. She said we should forget it."

"What is it, Wazoo?" Cyrus asked quietly.

The grind of machinery, loud, full-throttle, blasted out.

"What's that?" Roche yelled at Cyrus.

Cyrus covered his ears. "I forgot. Doug decided to start leveling the walls of the old school. I tried to talk him out of it, but he said he was going to do it for Bleu, so she'd see things were happening when she got back."

"I let Mary die," Wazoo cried, her words barely audible. "It was me—I killed her."

She flung away and burst from a standstill into a violent dash across the lawn.

Roche heard her sobbing. Wazoo was not a woman to cry, but she wailed. She ran so wildly, she had to stop herself from overbalancing every few strides.

And she skidded from sight at the far corner of the house.

"Cashman's is that way," Spike said. "That's where she's headed."

Roche glanced at Cyrus.

"Let her go," he said. "She needs to run. Sometimes, we need to run."

"Yes," Roche agreed. "But she'll stop when she's ready. Someone should be there then. Come on."

He took off after Wazoo. The other men joined him.

Minutes later, Spike said, "That woman, she can move. She's gonna hurt herself in there."

The heat alone should have slowed her down. In the tangle of fallen trees with their mantles of slick moss, the brush, sticks, rocks and debris from who knew how many years, Wazoo might have given up, defeated. No, she kept going, jumping, sliding, tearing her skirts away from grabbing twigs, her hair a tossing, black swarm about her head.

Cyrus said, "She'll do herself a terrible harm."

"Stop," Spike cried, gasping for breath. "Wazoo, stand still now. Y'hear me?"

"She doesn't," Roche said. The heel of a shoe hit tree slime and he slid. He did windmills and managed to save himself. "Should have let myself fall," he muttered. Keeping his feet would cost him some painful muscles.

Wazoo struck off to the left, away from the bayou. Both of her hands slapped obstacles away from her face.

She stopped, bent over to hold her knees and let her head hang down. Her hair trailed to the ground.

"Wait," Roche said, mostly under his breath. "Give her some space."

"Why would she say she killed Mary?" Cyrus asked. "She couldn't have meant that."

"Not unless she's capable of making a hole in someone's head with a drill," Spike said.

Roche studied the man's face. Spike had seen too many unspeakable things. His features were set in stark lines, his eyes flat and hard.

Cyrus crossed himself slowly.

"Stop your whisperin'," Wazoo said. "It's up ahead." She raised her head and nodded.

Roche saw dense trees, their trunks green and Spanish moss trailing from their branches.

"You stay behind me," Wazoo said. "I'll know if I'm right. But I should have come to someone for help. Me, I just didn't believe a word she said. It was all silliness to me."

"We're behind you," Cyrus said. His expression suggested he took Wazoo seriously. "What are we looking for?"

She climbed over rotting logs and led them between trees. "There," she said. "Old Eugene Cashman built that."

A log cabin, rough-hewn and completely covered with moss and ferns, almost blended in with its surroundings.

Wazoo gulped. Tears streaked her face. "Mary told me she could be in danger. I didn't believe her."

Cyrus put an arm around Wazoo. "Lean on me. Slow down and give yourself time to explain."

"It was there," she said, pointing to the right of the cabin. "An old pirogue, upside down. It had bags of dirt on it. I got the dirt in my shoes."

Spike tromped to the spot indicated. "No sign of any pirogue here," he said. "And no bags of dirt."

Wazoo tore away from Cyrus and examined the ground. "You don't know it *wasn't* here and I'm tellin' you it was. What d'you think you see there, lawman?" She pointed at the area.

Bending over, Spike looked closely, and Roche did the same. "I think someone used branches to brush away tracks or marks—and piled junk on top."

Too easily, Roche remembered Mary's grotesque corpse in the boat. "There was dirt under the body," he said.

"Mary, she fell over that pirogue," Wazoo said. "She didn't know she was going to die in it. You gotta go get..." She clamped her mouth shut.

"Go get what?" Spike asked her. He pushed his Stetson to the back of his head. "Go get what?" he repeated.

Wazoo shook her head.

"Don't hold anything back," Cyrus said. "If you really know something, you've got to speak up."

"I've got to be sure, first," she said. "It didn't have to be him who did it."

Roche looked from Cyrus to Spike. None of them spoke.

"I will tell you Mary was afraid someone would try to kill her. She asked me to come here with her at night and search for somethin'. She could only make guesses about what it was. We didn't find anything, so we gave it up. We never thought anything about the pirogue." More tears welled and ran over. "Why would we?"

"You looked inside the cabin?" Roche said. He walked through the doorway into a one-room space with a table and benches. "If anyone slept here, it would have to be on the table—or the floor. What do you think Mary was looking for?"

Wazoo shook her head. "A deed, I think. A letter, maybe. Something thin so it might be between the logs. There's nothing like that here, though."

"From what I understand, Cashman must have died forty years ago or so," Cyrus said. "Anything he left in here would be pretty messed up."

Windowless, the place was dark. Roche went to the closest wall and flattened a hand on a log. "It's probably infested in here," he said. "I can hear things crawling around."

Wazoo turned around. "Bugs don't bother me none." She walked behind the table and faced them again. She pointed behind her, and down. Her lips parted, but she only mouthed silently.

Alarmed, Roche pushed forward to peer over the table.

"Oh, my God," he muttered, looking at what was obviously someone taped inside a filthy sack. He knew who owned the feet he could see. "Bleu!"

"Wait," Spike snapped, seeing what Roche had seen. "And stop movin' around. We gotta preserve evidence."

"Bleu, Bleu," Roche said, falling to his knees beside her. He reached for her and saw movement. "I'm here, sweetheart. It's Roche."

Spike shoved his arms beneath Roche's and hauled him to his feet. "I said, 'Wait.' We've got to be careful if we don't want to lose—"

Forcing himself around, Roche pulled back a clenched fist and landed it on Spike's jaw. The sound of bone on bone made Wazoo gasp.

Spike hit the ground.

"Good Lord," Cyrus said.

Chapter

43

Afternoon, the same day

Madge pulled Roche aside. "Bleu's settling down. I don't know how I'd cope if that happened to me." She frowned, watching his face very closely.

They stood in the upstairs hallway at the rectory. Bleu, bathed with Madge's help, her wounds dressed by Dr. Reb Girard, was in one of the bedrooms. Next door to her, Wazoo slept again, helped by a sedative Reb insisted on.

"Bleu's incredible," he said. "I never met a woman like her before and I know I'll never get so lucky again."

Madge nodded, without meeting his eyes.

"You've got your reservations about me," he said. "I know what the rumors were. Something did happen, but it was never the way it sounded."

He got a faint smile that suggested a thaw. Madge Pollard was a lovely woman. She and Cyrus were polite to each other, but the long looks that passed whenever one of them thought the other wasn't noticing didn't bode well for a peaceful future.

"Bleu had a really nasty marriage," Madge said. "Michael Laveau hid what he really was until after he got her to himself. I don't know all the details, but it was bad. Bleu's admitted that. I knew there were serious problems, when he stopped letting her see me. He cut her off from everyone."

"She should have left him," Roche said, aware that his suggestion might not go over well around here.

Madge surprised him. "I told her that. I was getting ready to take some action—not that I knew what it would be—when Michael was arrested. Cyrus would have helped me. He believes everyone deserves justice. He's very open-minded about…" She turned the corners of her mouth up quickly. "He would always help me."

"I know he would," Roche said, without taking his eyes from hers. "He's an incredible man. One of a kind."

Madge didn't look away either. "I know."

"You haven't seemed happy." He could afford to take a little risk. "Neither has Cyrus. You're his right hand here. It might be perfect for both of you, but it's not, is it?"

"I'll check on Bleu," Madge said and limped past him. She looked back and added, "If she got hurt again, really hurt, I don't think she'd ever let herself love someone else."

Madge carried on and went into the first bedroom on the left.

He'd been warned, Roche realized.

Madge and Cyrus's issues had better wait until a killer was in custody. Roche knew what he wanted for himself. At least, he was just about sure. He thought Bleu wanted the same thing. What he wasn't certain about was the timing.

He wished he didn't get scared of losing her every time he considered trying to slow things down between them. Not that he was sure he could.

It would be unlikely, if not impossible.

Dr. Reb came from the bedroom, her red hair piled up, haphazard but still managing to look lush and gorgeous. The mother of two kids, she was slim and fit. She and Marc made quite a couple.

She put a finger to her lips until she drew close. "Bleu's been through a nightmare," she said. "The good news is that he didn't sexually assault her. She's in good shape physically, apart from bruises and some lesions where she tried to free herself. But getting over the shock could be longer-term than we'd like. She needs to be watched for delayed reactions.... You know what she needs to be watched for, Roche. Is that something you could take on—if you think it's appropriate—or should I refer her to Sig Smith?"

"Let's see how it goes," he said. "I'll ask her what she wants to do."

"Don't let her suspect you think she's got a problem—or that you think she could develop one." Reb turned a bit pink. "Sorry—there I go telling you your business again. That's the thing with being a small-town practitioner—you end up dealing with everything, and you start to think you know more than you do."

"You're modest," he told her. "I know your reputation."

"Thanks. On to the other issue. Want to tell me what happened to Spike? If he walked into the doorjamb at that hut like he told me, he'd either need to be even taller than he is, or leaning sideways. Even then, catching himself under the jaw like that would have been some trick."

Roche leaned on the newel post at the top of the stairs. "Is that what he told you? He walked into something?"

"Uh-huh. Lucky he wasn't knocked out, but it shook him up."

"I hit him," Roche said, examining telltale contusions on the knuckles of his right hand. "I saw Bleu and lost it. Spike wanted me to stay back, to cut down tampering with any evidence. I had to get to her."

That got him a long, long look. "I'd like Spike to get some sleep, but he won't listen."

"Everything's breaking open," Roche said. "We can all feel it. There isn't time to lay around now. He can collapse later. We all can."

"Yeah," Reb said, but not immediately. "Bleu says she's got to talk to Spike and to Cyrus. She's agitated and very determined."

He didn't miss that Bleu apparently hadn't asked for him.

Reb smiled. "You should see your face. She wants you, too. She also wants to get right up, because supposedly there are things she has to do. I've persuaded her to stay put for an hour or so." The doctor slid off her rubber gloves as if it took great concentration. "You could go in and keep her company, if you like. But make sure she doesn't overdo. Keep out anyone who doesn't need to be there."

"Of course." Try as he might, he couldn't manage to feel chastised. "Where's Spike now?"

"In the sitting room." She nodded down the hallway. "With Cyrus. I'll tell Spike to hold off questioning Bleu until you give the all clear."

He smiled at her. "Thanks."

"Roche!" Bleu called out from the bedroom.

Reb raised her eyebrows. "Her voice is mending really fast."

He went into the simple room where a single bed stood against one wall. There was a chest, a bedside table and a chair. White curtains fluttered weakly at the window.

"Hey," he said. She still smelled of lavender soap. "I'm going to sit here with you while you get some rest. Reb says you need to sleep for a few hours."

"I can't sleep yet," she said. Bleu gripped the sheet with both hands. "That noise is Doug clearing over at the old school," she said. "We've got to stop it."

Her reaction puzzled him. He sat beside her on the bed. "No, we don't. Anything that gets things started is good. Doug wanted to do it, so you'd see it was happening when you got back."

She wore a plain, white cotton nightgown and looked as appealing as if she were wearing a frothy piece of almost nothing. She didn't look as appealing as when she wore nothing at all. "Can I kiss you?" he said.

Bleu frowned, clearly agitated. Then she smiled at him and sat up, reached for him.

Carefully, he stroked her shoulders, ran the backs of his fingers up and down the sides of her face and neck.

She raised her chin in an invitation, and he accepted it. They kissed softly at first, but he'd known that wouldn't last. He stopped himself after he'd thrown back the bed covers and slid a hand up her leg.

"Sorry," he said, resting his forehead on hers. "It's all your fault for being so sexy."

Bleu caressed his face, pressed small, hard kisses on his lips and ran her tongue over his bottom lip. She teased out his tongue and his urgency began all over again.

Panting, she pushed on his chest. "We wouldn't like it if Cyrus walked through that door."

"He wouldn't. Not without knocking." He kissed her again, and held her. "You nearly killed me last night—I was afraid I'd lost you."

She lowered her eyelashes. "I didn't think I'd see you again."

Bleu played her fingertips over his mouth, but pulled the covers back up to her neck. "I've got to talk to Spike and Cyrus. I've figured it all out. Or I've made a good start."

"The deaths? Tell me what you think."

"It's what I know now. I don't want to say it all more than once. I'll get dressed."

"Stay here," he said and went in search of the other men.

They lounged on Cyrus's old, green leather couch in the sitting room, but shifted gears fast when he told them Bleu thought she had a revelation.

"I shouldn't be here anyway," Spike said. "I've got to get going."

Roche took him by the arm. "I didn't have an excuse for hitting you."

"Yes, you did," Spike said. "You wanted to get to the woman you love."

The bluntness startled Roche. "I shouldn't have done it. I apologize."

"Accepted." Spike narrowed his eyes. "If you try it again, you'd better be sure it's another sucker punch. If I see you coming, I'll enjoy evening up the score."

Roche believed him.

He knocked on Bleu's door and she called them in at once.

Bleu looked first at Roche. She loved looking at him. Even more, she loved feeling him.

Just the thought started her skin stinging.

"Hey," Cyrus said. "You're looking good, Bleu."

"Thank you," she said, glancing at the dark bruise on Spike's jaw. She'd been told about Roche swinging at the sheriff and was almost ashamed of her reaction. She liked it that he'd punch another man out to get to her.

Shameful!

Her exhilaration fled as fast at it had arrived. "We've got to stop Doug," she said, indicating the window. It sounded as if more pieces of equipment than before had joined in the job of excavating and leveling.

"We're not stopping," Cyrus said. "We're taking very close precautions. The town is swarming with uniforms. But we're not letting anyone scare us off."

"You and I didn't die," Bleu said seriously. "Yet."

Backing up each point as she went, she told them her theory about a deeply disturbed relative of one of the children who burned in the fire years ago.

Spike pulled the chair forward and sat down. "That must have been way before my time. Kate Harper went to the school, though?"

"Yes," Bleu said. "She told us about it, and it was horrible."

"I hadn't known the story before," Cyrus said. "Probably no one wants to talk about it."

They became quiet.

The sound of the machinery on the other side of the church roared on. Bleu rubbed at her arms and set her teeth. She wanted decisions, quickly. "What could it hurt if we said it had been decided that spot is just too small to be built on? You could tell everyone it's being leveled to turn into a garden now and you're going to the archdiocese to ask permission to find another piece of land."

Spike's radio crackled. He got up and left the room quietly.

"Cyrus?" Bleu said.

He looked bemused. "I haven't got any plans to go to the archdiocese about other land."

Bleu rubbed her temples, but didn't miss the grin Roche sent her way. "No, no," she said. "You haven't. I was thinking ahead. But it would be all right to say the area's only being leveled for now, wouldn't it? We don't know exactly what's going to happen after that, do we?"

Slowly, Cyrus shook his head, no.

"There. That's what we'll do then. If I'm wrong about what I think, and I don't believe I am, we can decide what to do then."

Cyrus didn't look as certain as she would like him to, but he was wavering in her direction.

A lot of noise came from elsewhere in the house. Banging. Laughter. Other sounds Bleu couldn't identify. "Why would anyone be laughing?" she said.

"Why not?" Cyrus asked. "Laughter's good. We're in the middle of a nightmare, I'll take any laughing I can get."

After a scuffle, there was a loud knock at the door.

"You don't need to knock, Spike," Bleu said, sitting straighter in the bed.

It was Ozaire Dupre who entered the room. Two leashed dogs trotted in ahead of him. "Spike had to go back to the station," he said. "Hope you're feelin' better. Seems like a good time to get this dog thing sorted out. Dr. Savage and me spoke about it last night— before you was kidnapped. He wants you to have a good watchdog, ma'am, so I've brought a couple for you to look at."

Cyrus looked benevolent. But Roche stared from Ozaire, to the dogs, to Bleu and back again. He didn't seem happy.

"This girl's mostly Australian sheepdog," Ozaire said, pointing to a large, shaggy black-and-white animal with a pointed nose, brown eyes surrounded by dark lines like kohl on an Egyptian queen, and a wiggling bottom with no tail. "I reckon she's got a pretty good mess of somethin' long in the mix, too. Look at her body."

The body was, indeed, long. Bleu held out a hand and the dog licked it all the way to her elbow. Resting her head on the mattress, she raised alternating brows while she watched Bleu.

Jumping up and down like Shrek's donkey, the other dog, a two-tone brown, as good as shouted, "Choose me." It had not been bred for beauty. Bleu pointed at it. "Dachshund. Schnauzer. What else?"

"These are both dogs that won't be available long," Ozaire said, as if Bleu hadn't asked him a question. "You don't often see specimens like these."

"Nope," Roche said. He crouched to ruffle the dachshund mix. "Ridgeback, too, I think. Look at his fur."

A line of short fur stood up along his spine.

The first dog climbed on the bed.

Bleu looked at Ozaire who behaved as if nothing was out of the ordinary.

The other animal left Roche and followed his buddy. Bleu got a face-licking from both sides before the pair settled down, each with a head in her lap.

"They're great dogs," Roche said. "But they aren't what I had in mind. We need a well-trained thoroughbred. Something with a reputation for making a great guard dog." He reached to lift the smaller one off the bed.

"Don't," Bleu said. "He's fine there."

Ozaire pointed to his offerings. "You won't find more loyal, protective dogs than those right there. If I were you, Bleu, I'd take my pick of 'em and have done. You won't be sorry."

"Look at them," Cyrus said. "Instant attachment."

"How old are they?" Bleu asked.

"Toady's nine months," he said, pointing to the dachshund mix. "Killer's almost a year."

"Someone called this pretty girl *Killer?*"

"Probably just for effect," Ozaire said. "Toady's a real suck-up."

"Who gets them—I mean, who's next in line after you show them to me?"

Ozaire puffed out his cheeks. He let the air out and looked at the floor, winding the leashes around his fingers. "They got left behind when some drifters moved on," he said, all but kicking a toe into the carpet.

"You mean they're like—brother and sister? They've been together?"

Ozaire nodded sadly. "I made up what I said about folks waiting for 'em. Reckon they'll go to the pound now. But don't you worry about it. You can't get all tied up in knots over every critter that needs a home."

Bleu blinked very fast. "So you don't even know how old they are?"

"About what I said," Ozaire said, still with his eyes lowered. "I know about dogs. You gotta look at their teeth and bones and stuff. Age I said is about right."

"Someone'll take 'em from the pound," Roche said gruffly.

"Probably," Ozaire agreed. "Could be. I'd better get on. Here. C'mon." He pulled on the leashes.

Bleu looked at Roche and shook her head. His half grimace, half smile made her grin. "I want them both," she said.

Ozaire straightened. "You got good taste. These two are winners. I'll give 'em another bath and get 'em all dolled up for you."

"They *are* dolled up," Bleu said. "And they're tired out, too." Killer and Toady appeared to be asleep.

"Yes." Ozaire did something close to a bob. "It's been a bad day, that's for sure, but you're doin' a good thing, Bleu. These two will take care of you. I'll help you train 'em."

"Thanks," Roche said.

"I told you I'd find the right one," Ozaire said.

"You found two," Roche reminded him.

"Will you listen to that?" Ozaire said of the pounding from outside. "Music to the ears. We gotta get on with that school—make this place live again. Doug's boys are tearin' things up out there."

Bleu wished she could get out of bed, and would once she was alone. "We're going to wait a bit on doing anything about the school," she said.

"Why would you do that?" Ozaire said. "The sooner we get on with it, the sooner that crazy out there knows he's beat."

"Can you keep a secret?" Bleu said.

Cyrus shifted and started to get up.

"We think the reason Jim died, and now Mary, is because of the children who died in the fire," Bleu said. She got a lump in her throat thinking about it.

Handing the leashes off to Roche, Ozaire shook his head. "What fire was that, then?" he said.

"Wake up, Ozaire," Cyrus said sharply. "The fire that burned the school down. The school people are dyin' over. Your family's lived here forever. You must know about it."

"Oh," Ozaire said. "I never saw it. Me, I was a little'un. I heard it was a terrible blaze. Went too far before anyone knew, so they couldn't do a thing about it. That would be with it happenin' in the middle of the night."

"It happened when all the children were there," Cyrus said, sounding angry now. "They burned to death."

Ozaire shifted from foot to foot, his face crumpled into puzzled folds. "Nope. It went up in the middle of the night. No one died."

Chapter
44

Midafternoon, two days later

Bleu sat at a table in the window at Hungry Eyes. Glaring like polished gold under a spotlight, sunlight bounced off the glass. She squinted and pulled sunglasses from her bag.

A bee buzzed just under the fan above her head, caught in a pocket of calm but surrounded by waiting currents of air.

Outside, the street glittered with fragments of mica. The sunglasses didn't lessen the painful brilliance much. Bleu raised her shoulders and shivered. Like the bee, she was becalmed in stillness but the storm waited. The sky should be green-black, heavy on the rooftops, filled with thunder and lightning; rain ready to fall in sheets that would sweep every surface with demonic, sparkling strokes.

Roche would meet her at the café as soon as he finished with his last patient. He had become her binding heat and her liberating storm. Whether he knew it or not, he controlled her future now.

"Bleu?"

Startled, she looked up at Wazoo and almost touched the woman's hand. Instead, Bleu spread her fingers at the base of her own throat. "Sit down," she said, more sharply than she intended. "What's the matter with you?"

Wazoo hovered, stared through the windows, looked over her shoulder. The only other customers, a woman and a toddler boy, talked at the back of the book stacks. The woman read to the boy in a low voice. He repeated words in bursts, laughing each time.

"You're tryin' to make decisions," Wazoo said. "Me, I got decisions to make, too. One decision."

Bleu kept quiet. Wazoo wasn't asking for input yet.

"You come here to be close to your man?" Wazoo said, nodding in the direction of Roche's office on Cotton Street. "You still frightened because you want him? He's a powerful man. Powerful sexy. You afraid he's gonna be too much for you?"

Little that Wazoo said shocked Bleu anymore, but she had caught her by surprise again this time. "What am I supposed to say to that?"

Wazoo went to the counter, reached over and picked up a jug of iced tea and a glass. She returned to pour for herself and give Bleu a refill. "Too hot to eat," she said.

"Uh-huh."

"We're in limbo," Wazoo said. "Whole damn town is holdin' its breath."

"We're feeling the same things," Bleu said. "Nothing's happened for so long."

"Only a day or so," Wazoo said. "Just seems longer. It can't stay quiet much longer."

Bleu looked at her and set down the glass. "Have you heard anything?"

The woman and her son came from the back of the store with a book in hand. Wazoo looked more relieved than she should to jump up and make a sale.

After the door closed behind the customers and the bell stopped jingling, Wazoo said, "Where you got the dogs?" She rejoined Bleu at the table.

"They're at the rectory. I would have brought them, but it's too hot."

"I thought you come to your senses and sent 'em back to Ozaire." Wazoo laughed. "You're the same kind of fool for animals as me."

"They're something. They've settled right in. You'd think I had them from birth."

"Roche wouldn't like you leavin' them behind," Wazoo said. "They supposed to be guardin' you."

"I'm fine," Bleu told her, wishing she felt fine rather than jumpy. She picked up a spoon, but dropped it without stirring her tea. "The handle's hot from the sun," she said, giving her fingers a shake.

"I heard you got the big story about Roche."

"Where did you hear that?" How many people knew about it?

"Doesn't matter. And I *mean* it doesn't matter. That woman, she went lookin' for him. She wanted to use him. They used each other. Slippery bodies, they always good to make the movin' easier, sexier. Why wouldn't a hot mudroom be real good? Hoo mama, I want me some hot mud one of these days."

"I don't want to talk about it."

"Roche, he didn't do anythin' wrong. He's just a man with an imagination and a real good way to work with it."

"I love Roche," she said, and sat quite still, frowning.

Wazoo smiled. "You surprised yourself." She chuckled. "You told him that?"

Bleu put her face in her hands. Loving him could be dangerous to her health. She didn't know why she'd admitted it aloud.

"Movin' on," Wazoo said. "They stopped workin' on that school place?"

"Yes." Bleu's voice sounded muffled in her own ears. "The old walls are gone."

"But you're not carrying on."

"Not immediately," Bleu said.

"I heard all about what Kate Harper said. Why would she lie about little ones dyin'? Could be, she's crazy."

"I don't think she's crazy," Bleu said. "In shock, that's what Cyrus thinks."

Smoothing the tablecloth, Wazoo frowned. "You know George Pinney?"

"No, not really."

"That's a beautiful-lookin' man. They reckon Spike doesn't think he's done anythin' wrong." She glanced around the shop. "Poor Mary, dyin' like that. Me, I keep thinkin' she's still here."

Bleu hunched her shoulders. She believed there had been a pirogue beside Eugene Cashman's cabin. And she was certain she had heard the murderer putting Mary in that pirogue and dragging her to the bayou. The other sound had been the drill, killing her. Knowing she'd been there, but couldn't do anything to help, sickened Bleu.

"Will you look at that?" Wazoo said.

The sheriff's cruiser shot to a stop at the curb. Instead of parallel parking, Spike nosed in and just left the car there. He slid out and came toward the shop at a rapid lope.

"I'm lookin' for you," he said to Bleu the moment he was inside. "Madge said you were meetin' Roche here. Good thing you're makin' sure folks know where you are."

"Why? Did something happen?"

Spike glanced at Wazoo who started to get up. "Sit down," he told her. "You'll find out what I say, even if I don't say it."

"Why, thank you," Wazoo said. "You were always smooth with the compliments."

Spike shook his head. "I'm looking for Sam Bush," he said. "Madge said you've been doing some work with him at his place. She hasn't seen him for a day or so that she can remember."

Bleu frowned. "Madge is muddled up. It's been days since I was at his office." She thought back. "He was at Pappy's with everyone. I haven't seen him since then."

"Excuse me!" Wazoo leaped up. "I forgot something. Be back."

Spike turned to watch Wazoo hurry behind the counter and through a door that led to a storeroom and a flight of stairs to the flat above. He met Bleu's eyes and raised his brows. "It's not like Wazoo to duck out on fresh information."

Bleu agreed, but didn't say as much. "Sam's probably busy working."

"He lives at Rosebank, remember," he said as if she would finish the rest of the thought.

She did. "You haven't seen him out there?"

"Nope. If he contacts you, I want you to listen, agree with whatever he says, then get to me. Get to me right then. If I'm not the one who picks up, you tell whoever does that I told you to talk to me."

"Yes." Bleu swallowed. "Do you think something's happened to him?"

"I can't talk about that."

"Then I can't call you if Sam calls me," she said in a spurt of anger, and then felt foolish. "I've been through everything that's going on from the beginning. Why can't you tell me why you're worried about Sam?"

Spike ran a finger around the inside of his collar and turned his head from side to side. They were all accustomed to stifling weather, but today was a scorcher.

"Spike?" she prompted him.

He tipped his face down and crossed his arms. Then he looked up at her. "It's not Sam I'm worried about."

Chapter
45

Wazoo didn't reappear until Spike drove his cruiser away. After that, she just about fell back into the shop and began cleaning up behind the counter.

"Everything okay?" Bleu asked.

"Why wouldn't it be?" Wazoo sounded edgy.

She lined up the big jars of candy on a shelf, clacking the glass together. In the middle of washing what few dirty dishes remained, she looked at the door, almost wild-eyed. And she muttered while she hurried to turn the sign there to read Closed from outside.

By Bleu's watch, it wasn't yet five. The shop stayed open till six.

Dishwashing resumed. And a conspicuous absence of conversation.

"Would you like me to leave?" Bleu asked. "You're getting ready to close up."

"I already closed," Wazoo said. She paused and wiped her hands. "I do have to get away early. You stay as long as you want. Just lock up when you and Roche leave."

"Okay. If you're sure."

Wazoo didn't answer her.

Something definitely was not okay. "Wazoo." Bleu got up and went behind the counter to take the woman by the shoulders. "Stop rushing around."

"I told you—"

"And I don't believe it's as simple as that. You've been acting strangely since Spike came in...before that even. Don't try to put me off, because I won't let you."

"You're imagining things."

Bleu kept a hold on Wazoo's shoulders until she lifted her chin and took a calming breath.

"I'm scared," she said.

Bleu's heart gave a big thump. "Share it with me. I'll help you."

"I've got to do it alone."

"No, you don't. Not something that scares you. Talk to me."

Wazoo held up shaking hands. "Me, I said I wouldn't tell anyone. I'll go like I was asked and I'll say someone's waiting for me. I'll come back to you. If I don't get here in a couple of hours... No, I'm gonna be okay."

"No!" Panicked, Bleu shook her. "No one should ask you to do something and not to tell anyone, unless it's wrong. You know that."

"He said his life depends on it."

"Who?" Bleu insisted.

"Folks don't think a lot about me, but I'm loyal and I like it that way. If I can help someone, I will. I didn't mean to, but I let Mary down. I won't let that happen again. He ask me to help him, and I said I would because I like him. He's in a jam."

"It's Sam," Bleu said, dropping her hands from Wazoo's shoulders. "Of course it is. Spike said something about him, and you took off. You don't know what you should do, but I'll tell you. You should go right to Spike. Now."

"And if Sam dies because I didn't help him?" Wazoo said. "Or because I brought the sheriff where he wasn't wanted—then what? I can't stop you from talkin' to Spike, but I can do what I'm goin' to do anyway. I'm leavin'."

Chapter
46

Fifteen minutes later

Roche was not to be disturbed during a session. He glanced at the flashing light on his desk phone.

Quietly, smiling reassurance at his patient, he depressed the button without picking up.

The flashing stopped.

Chapter 47

"Come in," Madge said, looking up when someone knocked on her office door.

It was probably Cyrus, who had started knocking every time he approached her in there.

She didn't know if she should keep on working here or not. "Come in," she called louder. So far, she hadn't been able to stay away.

Sig Smith put his head around the door. He smiled, but his eyes showed he was uncomfortable. "Hi," he said. "I hoped I'd catch you before you left."

"Hi," she said. This was the meeting she had dreaded. They had not been alone together since the night she ran from him.

Carrying mixed-colored roses, already in a vase, he slipped into the room. "For you," he said, and put the vase on her desk. "A peace offering."

A subdued rumble came from her striped chair where Bleu's Killer had settled. The dog overflowed the seat, but evidently keeping Millie from her favorite spot was worth the discomfort.

"You've got a new watchdog," Sig said. "Dogs." He saw Toadie curled on the rug.

Millie sat on Madge's lap. "They're Bleu's," she said.

"You're probably going to say no," Sig said, "but I'd like to take you out for a meal."

Madge tilted her head. She smiled at him.

"That's a *no?*" Sig said.

"The way I behaved the other night was ridiculous. I apologize."

He took a long breath through his nose. "I was the ridiculous one. You shouldn't have to fight a man off after a couple of dates."

"I'm not ready to go out again," she told him.

"I didn't think you would be." With one finger, he touched the card among his roses. "I mean this," he said and left her again.

This side of the house was cooler than the rest. All the trees screened the building. Madge figured that was why Bleu's new buddies had followed her there. That and an opportunity to irritate the small dog they looked at with disgust.

What should she do?

The door opened once more, without a knock. "Okay if I come in?" Cyrus said. Despite the heat, he wore a cassock. His collar was a stark strip of white against solid black and to Madge he looked untouchable.

He did come in, even though she hadn't responded to him. "Beautiful roses," he said. "I saw Sig on his way out."

"Yes."

"I'm worried about you."

"Don't be."

Cyrus bent to smell the roses. He glanced at the card and quickly away again. Madge picked it up, read, and handed it to him.

"You don't have to show me this," he said.

The card said: Please call me, and Sig had written his phone number under his name. Madge took it back from Cyrus, tore it in half and threw it away.

"Are you going to leave me?" Cyrus asked. "I feel you moving away."

She tried to swallow and almost choked.

"You need water," Cyrus said.

"No, I'm okay." She wasn't and doubted she ever would be.

He walked around to stand beside her, stroked her hair, rested his hand on the back of her neck. "If you go, I'll keep wishing I'd done something to stop you. I mustn't. It wouldn't be right."

"No." She closed her eyes. Her lashes were wet.

"But...I'll miss you forever. And I'll always feel guilty that I couldn't have made sure we didn't get to the point where you don't want to go, but you can't bear to stay anymore."

His hand settled on her shoulder and she put one of her own on top. "Cyrus..." Talking was too hard.

"I know. I understand, but you'll take part of me—the best part."

"I can't go, unless you make me," she said, broken. "You'll have to tell me you don't want me here anymore." Madge leaned her forehead on her desk. "I'm not being fair, but I can't help it."

Softly, he kissed the nape of her neck. "Stay, Madge," he said. "I don't have anything to offer but what we have, but don't leave me."

Madge reached back to spread a hand over the side of his face. She ran her fingertips into his hair and turned her face toward him. When he looked at her, she kissed his cheek, crossed her arms around his neck and held so tightly her muscles hurt.

"Madge—"

She touched his mouth and shook her head. "Who knows if we aren't the lucky ones?" she said. "We understand what we have."

"I understand what you mean to me," he said. He smiled slightly. "If you go, I'll have to pipe zydeco into the rectory. Think how that would look when the archbishop visits."

Madge smoothed her hands over his chest. "We can't have that.

I'll have to stay, so you can blame me for the music. I'll have to stay, because I don't want to be anywhere you're not."

"Ever?" he said, and his voice caught.

"Ever."

Chapter
48

Roche's patient left and he pressed his message button.

"Hi, it's Bleu. Your cell phone's off so I tried your office number. You must be busy. Wazoo got a call from Sam Bush asking for help. I can't let her go alone. We're not going far—just south of town. Talk to you later. And don't worry."

"And don't you go tellin' anyone," Wazoo shouted in the background.

He heard the sound of a rough-running engine.

Chapter
49

At the same time

"Slow down," Bleu said. "We don't want to miss the turn."

"If we get to New Iberia, we've gone too far," Wazoo told her, bobbing up to see. The sun fell lower in the sky and hit the windshield exactly where Wazoo normally looked—an inch or so above the steering wheel.

"Second turn on the left after the crossroads," Bleu said. Wazoo had written down directions.

They had passed the crossroads in the middle of cane fields. The crop rose way above head-height on all sides.

On this road, the intersecting turns were a long way apart.

"That's the first one," Bleu said, taking a quick look down a track between two fields.

Bleu's phone rang.

"It's gonna be that man of yours tellin' you we got to turn around." Wazoo said. "I'm not doin' it."

Bleu looked at the phone and saw Roche's number. She answered, "Hello, Roche."

"Where are you, damn it?"

"Not far," she said. "Sam's a good man. He wouldn't ask for help if he didn't need it."

"He didn't ask for your help, Bleu."

"No, he asked Wazoo because he knows she'll stand by a friend no matter what. Unlike some of us."

"What does that mean?"

"She doesn't worry about herself before she answers a call for help." Bleu couldn't seem to stop talking. "I don't mean you wouldn't help a friend," she added quickly.

"I know you don't." Roche paused. *"Bleu, we've got to think straight. Why would Sam call on Wazoo?"*

Roche was concerned for her. Bleu knew that otherwise he would never suggest she leave Wazoo on her own out here.

"Relax," she said. "We're about there."

"Where?"

"Not even to Iberville. Just off 347 in the cane fields toward Loreauville—"

"No," Wazoo cried loudly. "Don't tell him anything else, Bleu. Roche Savage, I got a gun, hear me? I always got a gun. Your lady is safe with me, not that I want her here. Now cool your heels a bit and she'll get back at you. Hang up," she told Bleu.

"Stay on the line," Roche said. *"Did you call Spike?"*

Bleu didn't answer him. He'd know what that meant.

"There!" Wazoo said. She made an abrupt left onto a cane-strewn dirt road. A few moments later, she pointed toward a white panel truck. "That'll be Sam. He said to look for a truck like that one. Hang up the phone."

"I don't see him," Bleu said. Her skin prickled. "Sure I see the truck, but where's Sam?" He should have come out when he heard them.

"*Bleu,*" Roche said, but he sounded calmer. "*Don't hang up.*"

She glanced at Wazoo, who concentrated on driving. The phone slid easily into the pocket of Bleu's jeans. What could it hurt for Roche to hear what they were doing? And she wanted a connection to him while she was out here.

The van stopped and the engine clanked before it fell silent.

"Where is he?" Bleu said. She searched in every direction.

"He's makin' sure it's me," Wazoo said.

"With this van? Who else would it be?"

"He can see there's someone with me," Wazoo said. "We'd better show ourselves, fast."

Grimacing, Wazoo pushed open her creaky door and got out. Bleu didn't want to, but she followed, and they approached the truck together.

All around them, the cane rustled.

Yellow dust hung in the air, and Bleu sneezed.

Wazoo raised an arm overhead and waved. "We've come, Sam. Where are you?"

"Oh, thank God." From the other side of the truck, disheveled, her face streaked with dirt, came Kate Harper. "He left me here. I can't drive this thing."

Wazoo closed her fingers on Bleu's nearest wrist and they both stopped walking.

"Sam left you here?" Bleu said, confused.

"How did you know where I was?" Kate said. "Who sent you?"

Bleu and Wazoo looked at each other and Wazoo said, "We didn't know you were here. Sam called me askin' for help."

"Sam called me, too," Kate said. "He said he needed me. He was always kind to me, and he was Jim's accountant. I just came. He laughed at me and took my car."

"Why didn't you call someone?" Wazoo asked.

Kate stared. "Oh, you mean with one of those phones. I don't like things like that."

Abruptly, she broke down. Sobs shook her body and she hunched over. "I was goin' to start walkin', but I knew it was too far."

"It's okay now," Bleu said. She started to reach for her own phone.

"Sam killed them," Kate said. "I thought he'd kill me. He kept sayin' he would, if I didn't do what he said."

Wazoo's grip on Bleu's arm tightened.

"Killed who?" Bleu said, her heart thumping. "You don't mean Jim? And Mary?"

Kate backed away. "I'm goin' to be in dreadful trouble, aren't I?" she said. "I should have told someone, but I was so afraid. I think he's waitin' for us somewhere. He wouldn't leave us here. Two—three more murders don't make any difference to him now."

What was Sam's real reason for calling Wazoo?

This track headed straight on. Bleu cleared her throat. "Sam must have gone back the way we just came," she said. "How long ago, do you think?"

"He did go that way," Kate said, looking around. "I don't know how long...not so long, though. He must have hidden himself and my car."

You don't drive, Kate. You didn't get here on your own. Bleu made fists. She had no idea whether or not Wazoo knew Kate didn't drive.

Wazoo rubbed her middle rhythmically and swayed.

Kate was a really bad liar. Sam hadn't driven out of here recently.

Bleu dropped her voice and asked her, "Where is he? Is he watching us now?"

Kate shook her head. "He's gone, but he's goin' to come back. I know I'm right about that."

She talked, gabbled, poured out a jumbled tale of Sam killing Jim for his money. Sam wanted her to marry him, she said. He threatened her so she told him she would. "But I never would have," she said. "You can be sure of that. He tried to make it look like it was George who was in the wrong. He pretended to be George when he talked to me about Cashman's place one night. Sam made sure Mary was listening and had me call him George. He pretended he had somethin' hidden in some old cabin. Reckoned whatever it was would prove what he'd—or what George had done to Jim."

"Why would he do that?" Bleu asked, then wished she hadn't.

"He said if Mary went to the cabin to look, he could be sure she thought it was George she'd heard and he really was going to kill her. Sam would have killed her anyway. He said he'd give her enough time to tell someone what she thought George had in mind, then murder her." Kate glanced all around and lowered her voice. "Mary let on she'd gone to Cashman's with Wazoo. So he said he couldn't leave either of them around."

Wazoo just stood there and didn't enter the conversation.

"Sam said again how he would marry me after Mary was dead and we'd share everything Jim left," Kate said. "It was all about the money. That's all it ever was. He went on about the school because Jim almost gave the Cashman land to the building fund."

They had to get out of there. "Listen to me," Bleu said. "We're wasting valuable time. Get in the van, both of you. We're leaving."

In a flurry of pale pink skirts, Kate twisted away and half ran, half staggered toward the van. Almost there, she stopped, fell to her knees. She waved her fists in the air and screamed.

"She doesn't drive," Bleu said quickly while she had the chance. "She's putting on an act—all of it's an act."

"I caused this," Wazoo muttered. "Mary told me she overheard that talk Kate says she had with Sam. Mary did think it was George. But we didn't find anything at the cabin. The pirogue didn't mean anything to either of us, so we figured she'd misunderstood what she heard and there was nothin' to worry about. I should have gone to Spike just the same. I kept thinkin' about it. Me, I shouldn't have cared if he laughed at me.

"They wanted me to come out here alone so they could get rid of me. I'm a witness and I'd have figured it out soon enough. They couldn't risk that. I'm sorry, Bleu."

The wailing continued.

"Don't be sorry," Bleu said. "I think Kate is a victim. Sam's done more to her than try to get money. She's not right in the head."

The sugar canes rattled together. To Bleu, they sounded like pebbles on glass. This was the first time she had stood in the middle of cane fields. They dwarfed her, closed her in.

"Kate!" Wazoo went to her. "Stop it. Get up and help us. We all got to help each other." She caught her by the arms and pulled.

"Sam found out Jim was going to give Cashman's to St. Cecile's," Kate cried. "The night Sam killed Jim, he would have told everyone about the gift right there at Bleu's parish hall meetin'."

Without warning, Wazoo released Kate and spun toward the truck. She put a forefinger to her mouth and Kate took big gulps, trying not to make any noise. She scrambled shakily to her feet.

Then Bleu heard it—banging from inside the truck.

Kate edged away. "There's someone in there," she said.

Wazoo was already on her way to the back of the white vehicle and Bleu dashed to catch up. "Someone's in trouble," she panted. "They're trying to get help."

Briefly, Wazoo looked at her. She hesitated. "I feel... We gotta leave."

"We can't," Bleu told her. "A person could suffocate in there."

"Stand still." George Pinney walked from the hidden side of the truck. He pointed a gun at them, kept pointing it while he swung open back doors. "Get in."

"George," Kate said in a quavering, tearful voice.

"Shut up," George said without looking in her direction. "Keep your mouth shut and you'll be okay. Get in, all of you."

"Me, I'm not gettin' in anywhere you say, George Pinney," Wazoo told him. Her face looked damp in the sun's glare.

With one hand, George pulled down steps. "You first, Kate."

Another wail issued from Kate. She rocked from side to side.

"Get in!" George flicked the muzzle of his gun.

Kate stumbled forward and did as she was told, disappearing into the gloom inside the truck.

"You two," George snapped. "In, or I'll shoot her right now."

Her meant Kate.

With Wazoo beside her, Bleu shuffled toward George. When she got close enough, he hustled her up the steps.

"You shouldn't be here," George said. "Wazoo's the one I want."

"Let her go, then," Wazoo said. "She doesn't—"

"Shut up," George said. "Don't lie to me. By now she knows what Mary told you."

By the time she saw Sam Bush, bound and curled up on his side, Wazoo had crowded in behind her and the first door slammed.

"It's Sam," Bleu said past a dry throat. "George is using him, not the other way around."

"Clever girl," George said with a snigger. "If I'd been the one to call Wazoo, she'd have gone straight to the sheriff, and I'd be on the run."

The second door shut and locked—loudly.

"Sam," Bleu said, bending over him. He appeared unconscious.

Wazoo joined her. "Is he dead?"

"He's breathing," Bleu said. "But he doesn't look good."

Continuous sniffles and moans from Kate disgusted her.

"You lied to us," Bleu told her.

"I never did like that George Pinney," Wazoo said. She felt Sam's pulse and opened first one then the other of his eyes to check the pupils. "But he made a bad mistake when he took us on. We gonna make his life hell, then laugh when they take him in."

The engine of the truck rumbled to life and the vehicle moved.

Bleu and Wazoo clung to one another for balance.

"Sit down," Kate said. "Right there by Sam."

Sharp and completely unlike Kate, that was an order.

Bleu looked at the woman, then at Wazoo who had already seen what Bleu saw now. Straight-backed against the panel behind her and very alert, Kate sat holding a gun. And this was no ordinary gun. Bleu had no idea what it was except that it was some sort of compact assault weapon. When Kate sat down in the truck, she must have known the gun was behind her.

"Come on," Bleu said, smiling at her. "You could no more use that on us than fly without a plane. You wouldn't even know how."

"Could be you don't want to test me on that," Kate said. "You two are a nuisance. You've made things hard, when they would have been simple."

Wazoo and Bleu sank to the dirty metal floor. "If we'd just stayed away and let the killin' happen, you mean?" Wazoo said. "Maybe you should have warned us off."

"Don't you go screamin' at me," Kate said. "Keep your mouth shut."

"What did Sam do to you except be kind?" Bleu asked.

"George said Sam was poking around too much. He knew too much about Jim's affairs. George wanted him out of the way." Kate shrugged. "Everything's goin' to be all right now. Spike and the rest of them will never figure out we know what happened to any of you."

Wazoo made a disgusted sound.

"And if you really want to know," Kate said, "George didn't like all the attention Sam paid me, either." She looked smug.

George drove fast. In the back, they were repeatedly thrown about and had to keep righting themselves. Bleu watched Kate closely, looking for a chance to overpower her, and she believed she could, particularly with Wazoo's help.

Sam worried her. He still hadn't stirred and she had seen blood matted in his hair.

"What if the cops come after us?" Bleu asked. It was risky to talk that way, but anything that caught Kate by surprise was a good thing.

"Dreamer," Kate said. "They'll never see us out here."

"Where you takin' us?" Wazoo asked.

Bleu wondered where Wazoo's gun was, if she could get to it, and how dangerous it would be for her to try.

"You don't need to know where we're going," Kate said and her smile sickened Bleu. This was a cold, self-centered woman.

They seemed to keep going for a long time. Bleu hated it when the tall compartment swayed and she felt sick.

The engine droned, obviously well-maintained. But George would have thought of that.

A different noise filtered in. Different and distinctive.

Kate turned an even paler shade than usual.

Chopper blades thumping the air with their rhythmic, whump, whump, whump and the staccato pummeling of the engine.

"Don't you move," Kate screamed. "George knows what he's doin'. They are never goin' to save you."

Rushing Kate would be too dangerous.

They all sat as still as they could while the truck careened from side to side. Not one of them spoke.

After a while, the sounds of the chopper grew more distant and faded altogether.

Wazoo held Bleu's hand and squeezed. They didn't look at each other but Bleu had never felt so abandoned or disillusioned, ever, and she'd had reasons.

The silly smile on Kate's mouth didn't help. She actually raised her weapon and aimed it back and forth over Wazoo and Bleu. "That was just coincidence. Probably crop dustin'."

Bleu didn't point out that helicopters weren't typically used for dusting.

She closed her eyes. Very far away, so far she could have imagined it, she thought she heard the chopper returning. What she didn't know was how it could help even if it did sight them and he knew George was a fugitive.

She hadn't imagined it; the chopper came back and she heard a bullhorn but not what the man was yelling.

Roche had gotten her cell phone location traced, Bleu was sure of it.

The next turn George took landed them all on their backs. Kate managed to keep her gun trained on them. For an "arthiritic" woman she was agile.

Faster and faster George drove, and then he stopped.

Seconds later he threw open the doors again. "Get out," he screamed. "Get out, now. Fast. And pull him with you."

Somehow they managed to drag Sam between them, without help

from Kate. Daylight turned the world shiny-white, until Bleu's eyes settled down again.

They were in a copse of trees and another, smaller truck waited there. A skinny little man shambled from the cab and stood by a back door that slid upward. It was open.

"They gonna be trouble?" he asked. "Man, you ain't paid me enough for trouble."

George tossed him lengths of twine. He came at Bleu and lashed her wrists behind her himself. The way he felt to her was familiar.

"You've had practice at this," she said. "You're the one that grabbed me at Pappy's."

"You should have been warned then, and stayed out of other people's business afterwards," George said.

In minutes, Sam and Wazoo were with Bleu in the second truck and the door slid down with a thud.

They were on the move again.

"They're taking us over the border," Wazoo said. "I saw the license plates. With us gone, George and Kate can slide into the background, right there in Toussaint, and no one will be wiser."

Bleu gave a thin smile. "They're not getting away with anything," she said. "We may not live to see it, but they'll get theirs. My phone's still on in my pocket. I can't believe they never checked for that. Even if the line I had open to Roche had been closed off, they do that ping stuff."

"My God," Wazoo said. "Sounds like a war out there."

Gunshots blasted in rapid succession.

"Sheesh," Bleu cried. "They've blown a tire here. More than one tire."

"What if that man—the one driving—comes for us?" Wazoo asked.

"If he tries, you'll use your gun and he'll be dead meat."

"You startin' to sound like a gangster, Miz Prissy. Must be that worldly man you hang out with. He's influencin' you."

Silence came but lasted only briefly before voices started yelling. A single shot sounded, followed by a lot of pained screaming.

"We better hope the right people are winning," Wazoo said.

"We'll be all right," Bleu said. "I wish Sam would wake up."

Wazoo shouted, suddenly, and the shout turned to a scream. The sound of automatic gunfire had started.

A line of bullet holes opened the side of the little truck like popping the lid off a can.

That line hit toward the top.

Voices yelled. The bullhorn blasted. Engines sprang to life.

And another row of holes split the side of the van, this one lower.

"Lie flat," Bleu shouted. "Help me get Sam as flat as we can."

"That's Kate's gun doin' that," Wazoo said. "Can't they pick her off?"

They struggled to stay down and get Sam stretched on his face at the same time—not easy with their hands tied.

The rapid fire blasted out again. Both Bleu and Wazoo screamed. This time the bullets entered their space no more than a foot above them.

"Why wouldn't we know Kate could shoot like that?" Bleu said.

"It's gotta be George," Wazoo responded, but a fresh bombardment of bullets drowned her out.

This one was almost low enough to fill them all with lead.

Bleu trembled. Spasms of shaking turned her body weak.

The chopper had never left the area. Bleu supposed it couldn't be of help in such confusion, other than to keep people informed of their whereabouts.

A single shot rang out. Then there was a moment of absolute stillness before the voices started up and, within a few seconds, the back door of the truck shot open.

First in was Roche. He pulled them upright, except for Sam who still hadn't stirred. "He's alive," Bleu said. She wanted Roche to hug her, but he didn't look at her as if that was going to happen.

"You can get rid of that mealy-mouth, disapproving face, Dr. Savage," Wazoo said. "Without us comin', Sam there would be dead by now." She frowned. "Most likely."

Two cops hopped in and set to work untying Wazoo and Bleu. Medics wanted to get at Sam, so everyone else got out of the truck. Bleu struggled with legs that didn't want to move. Once outside, she felt furious, then faint, then mad all over again. She held Roche's sleeve, and he finally put his arms around her.

"Stupid girl," he murmured, holding her crushingly tight. "Don't you know I can't lose you now?"

She was too light-headed to respond.

"Darn it all, you thick-headed, gun-happy fools," Wazoo shouted. "You killed George Pinney. You let that rat's ass get some peace before he could pay back for what he's done to good people and to a good town. I ought to punch you out."

Bleu felt instantly stronger. She turned to see Wazoo pointing at George's prone figure. "Wazoo," she said. "Cool it. We just got our lives saved."

"I wanted his life saved," Wazoo insisted, pointing at George. "Me, I wanted him lynched proper."

Nobody argued with her over that idea. "He's not dead, ma'am," a cop said. "Just wounded. But we reckon his back's broke."

"Broke?" Wazoo said. "Is that a fact?" A slow smile spread on her face.

"He's not getting away with anything," Roche said. "Neither is Kate. She's already spilling it to the police that she was an innocent victim. We've all got it figured out she was George's accomplice. You should see the stuff they found at her house."

Bleu frowned. "More guns."

"I was thinking of the whips and chains. Kate Harper likes—"

"Rough sex?" Bleu asked, all innocence. "That's a disgrace."

Chapter 50

Early the following morning

"Where to, now?" Roche said.

Bleu crouched between Killer and Toadie, put an arm around each of them. "I guess I don't know," she said.

The quiet, the last breath of night on the early-morning air, not a building or a human in sight on this part of Parish Lane, just the two of them, she would settle for standing still in the moment—forever.

"We can keep hanging out here, looking at each other, I guess," Roche said. He offered her a hand and, when she took it, pulled her up. "If that's what you want to do."

"Sounds good to me."

Roche took the dogs' leashes from her. "Two good ones I picked," he said of the animals. "I know my dog flesh."

She smiled. "Ozaire does, you mean. We got lucky."

He pulled her in front of him, held her upper arms. "We are lucky, Bleu."

Some would think his timing was weird, but it wouldn't get any better and it could become worse if he allowed them to fall into any pattern but the one he wanted.

"I don't feel muddled up anymore," Bleu said. "Not at all."

He smiled. She looked so serious, as serious as he felt. "That's good, isn't it?" he said.

"I don't know. Maybe." She sighed. "I'm so grateful Sam came around. He'll be okay, won't he?"

Sam had rocky days ahead, but he'd been flown where he'd get the best of care and Roche had been assured the other man would make a full recovery.

"Yes," he told her. "The swelling around his brain is more his body's way of protecting him than anything else. He came around and he recognizes people. That's what counts."

"Thank God," Bleu said. She and Wazoo had promised themselves they would be Sam's slaves if only he got better. Now he was recovering, even if slightly, and Wazoo had already mentioned they might want to rethink the slave bit.

"Do you know what you want? Is that why you're not muddled up?" Roche said.

Bleu looked away, toward Bayou Teche. If the trees weren't so thick, they'd see it from here. "I know what I want," she said.

"I talked to Cyrus already," Roche said. The priest, and Madge, were waiting in the kitchen when Roche and Bleu got back from an FBI questioning session earlier. "He says—"

Bleu cut him off. "That they'll want to carry on with the building projects, but not until after a decent interval. I heard him. I never did like that term too much. Who decides what's decent?"

"I don't know. I guess you just know when the time's right." He could almost feel the questions circling in Bleu's head. She didn't know if she had ongoing work here, at least for the moment, and she wasn't sure what that meant for her.

"Cyrus and Madge have made peace," she said. "I didn't imagine that, did I?"

"I saw it, too." Roche wanted peace, too, and he hoped he'd get it.

"You'll need to get back and see if you can catnap before you start work," Bleu said. Her eyes were suspiciously bright.

He tried a laugh. Not a good attempt. "Ever since we met, you've been telling me I need to go get some rest. Do I seem that infirm to you?"

She bowed her head. "I say it when I feel awkward, I guess. When I don't know what else to say."

The dogs had curled up together on the rough lane. They looked peaceful. "Look at that," Roche said. "They've fitted right in and they don't have a doubt in the world that they're safe now."

Bleu bit her lip hard. She couldn't bear talking in circles.

"I had a chance to talk to Cyrus on his own," Roche said. He wished he could calm his jumping nerves. "He's a decent man."

"The best," Bleu said. "What did you talk about?"

"Getting married in the church."

She felt blood leave her face. Not a word that came to mind suggested she should open her mouth.

Roche would not panic, even if she did look stricken. He dropped his hands to his sides. "Was that okay?"

Her voice came out in a squeak that embarrassed her. "Was what okay?"

"You know what I'm saying."

"I know what you're not saying," she told him. But warmth swelled within her. Her skin tingled. And now, if she couldn't control herself, she would cry.

"Madge thinks it's a good idea," Roche said. That had to be the lamest comment he'd ever made.

"I'm happy for her," Bleu said.

"I think I'm making a mess of this," he told her. "Cyrus says there's some preparation, but he would see to that himself, so it didn't have to be spread out over weeks."

"That's nice of him."

"Madge was excited. She says she's never been a bridesmaid. You would like a bridesmaid, wouldn't you? Or more than one, if that's what you want."

Bleu, stamping a foot, stunned him.

"What?" he said. "What is it?"

She covered her mouth, horrified. "I never did that before. I'm sorry."

"You're frustrated. It's okay." He paused. "I'm frustrated, too. I never did this before."

"You wouldn't like it if I shook you, would you?" Bleu said.

He grinned. "I might." She didn't look too amused. "When do you think we should do it?"

Bleu raised her chin and closed her eyes. Why not be reasonable and let him do this his way—which was to not really do it at all?

"Oh!" He bent over and kissed her, hunching her shoulders with the power of his grasp.

Once wasn't enough. When he pulled back a little, her eyes were still shut, but her lips were parted and shiny. Again, he kissed her, pushed his fingers through her hair and used his thumbs to keep her face turned up to his.

"I don't want to be here anymore," he told her between kisses. "Let's go back to your place."

"For sex?" she said.

He grimaced. "Do you have to be that blunt?"

"Someone around here needs to be blunt. Remind me to tell you about my whipped cream experiment."

Roche blinked and held her away. "I'm reminding you."

"Good. I'll keep it under consideration. But I'm not taking you home with me."

He looked aghast and overheated. "Why?"

"You're disappointing me."

Now he looked devastated. "Bleu?"

"I'm glad you, Cyrus and Madge are all on the same page," she said.

Roche frowned at her. Then he coughed and shook his head. "You women are so old-fashioned." He got down on his knees. "Better?"

"You're getting there."

"I've got to spell it out, right?"

She kissed his forehead and jumped out of his way before he could grab her.

"I'm an idiot," he said. "I thought I had said it right. I can't be without you, Bleu. Stay with me. Forever."

"That's what I want, too." With a hand either side of his face, she kissed his nose.

"Then say you'll marry me."

Dancing in place, landing pretend punches on the air, she said, "Of course I will. All you had to do was ask me. Get up and kiss me again, you fool."

Half an hour later, Bleu leaned her head on Roche's shoulder and they wandered slowly toward St. Cecil's where Roche had parked his car.

"Will you tell me about the experiment now?" he asked. Once, he couldn't have imagined being this happy, just because he was with a woman. That was before he'd met Bleu.

She looked up into his face. "If you fill a bathtub with whipped cream—from those aerosol cans—it melts after a bit. I thought I'd give it a dry—a wet run to see if I could surprise you with my daring ingenuity." She giggled. "I got in and it just got less and less when the air started going out of it. In the end I was cold and covered with slippery white stuff. It didn't cover me anywhere and I couldn't get a handhold on anything."

"I thought that was the point," Roche told her. "Except you'll need me for the handholds next time."